By the same author –


The Twelve Days of Christmas

The Release

For What Is Lost

The Deserter

Snake

We go blindly into the darkness

A Flat Country, with Hills


Visit www.edwardarrunsmulhorn.com to find details of other
publications, or contact eam@edwardarrunsmulhorn.com

# To every thing there is a season

## Book 1

Edward Arruns Mulhorn

First published in Great Britain in 2017
(Drafted 2007)

Paperback ISBN 978-0-9956341-4-5

ebook ISBN 978-0-9956341-5-2

Available in paperback and ebook format

www.edwardarrunsmulhorn.com

I thought the dead had peace, but it is not so;
To have no peace in the grave, is that not sad?
But up and down and to and fro,
Ever about me the dead men go;
And then to hear a dead man chatter
Is enough to drive one mad.


*Maud*, Alfred Lord Tennyson

So this is it. This is how it begins. This is where it begins. Somewhere along the A12. It started in London. Now it is happening. I am making it happen. I am making it happen as it has to happen. Each minute, each mile, inevitable. This is my now. This is me.

Did I want it to happen like this? Did I plan it, did I dream it this way? How strange. This bit, this actual moment, this turning my back, this driving away: this I never saw. I think, perhaps, I conjured an image, or stole it from a black and white movie: a romanticised version of me, stood in high heels in a smoky station, clutching a suitcase in my hand. But not this. Not the rain, not the night, not the car.

I think I blocked it out, this transition between two states, this gap between two paragraphs. If I had planned it, I would have filled it with substance. With something striving for meaning. With an action, a gesture, a speech. With a songlist of feminist anthems to blast in the car as I drive through the heartland of Essex. With something elaborate and ultimately absurd. I guess some parts of my life can't be planned. How can you plan for something like this without questioning what it has led from?

So how has it come to the point where it is? Such an innocent question with such an impossibly long answer. And I cannot answer it, because there is no complete answer. At the core, there is only a feeling. A feeling which at times seems absolute. Which at others is subject to the vagaries of doubt. And then, if you were to look at me then, could I say I know I am right? At the core there is you and me. We could go round and round forever, caught in the stranglehold of changeable feelings and moods. For years, that is precisely what we have done. For years, guided by our instincts, our emotions, our fears. The determination to make it work; the certainty it can't. Round and round in an endless mind-game.

And have we moved anything on? Sure, we are still alive; but being alive isn't the same as living. Not being vital, alert, engaged. We haven't progressed our lives through the relationship that ties us together. We have reached an imperfect stasis, an indefinite pause, where there is no advance nor decline. A lull which might never have been broken if we chose to stay where we were. Something needed to be done. Something; anything. Then we could let the planning take over; then we could lose ourselves in the detail and be distracted by it. And now, Dan, now we have made that decision, I find myself passing Hatfield Peverel, wherever Hatfield Peverel is. The planning phase has kicked in at last, breaking this whole desperate cycle.

Something had to give. The decision could have gone either way. So easily. I could have lain down; I could have buried desire; I could have filled my world so full of routine – of work, home, friends, and mundane pursuits – that the hollowness would suffocate beneath its weight, reducing to a tiny voice which cried to me in the depth of night, which whispered in my half-conscious ear. I could live with that; I could endure. For months, for years. Perhaps forever. I could take it, and in taking it I could retain all the comforts it entails. Our house, our savings, our friends, and Matty. All that is certain and known. Perhaps I could have endured. But the decision didn't go that way.

We know each other so well. We will never know another person quite as we know ourselves. Ours is total familiarity. Every pore, every habit; each action, each thought – almost before it arrives. That's good, surely, isn't it? But then, I would question how we use that knowledge. We are able to wind each other up. We know exactly each little thing that infuriates and annoys. Each twist, and what it will do: the inevitable pain it will cause. We have hurt each other on purpose sometimes, as though we relish witnessing pain, as though that pain can compensate for the shame of being together. Have you used your knowledge differently? Have you used it any more wisely than me? Have you used it to build on our love, and to nourish? Have you used it to keep us together?

Together. There are times when together we are both marooned. So isolated, so estranged. When we find we are living around each other, not through and with and because of the other. That is not togetherness; that is convenience. You know that. You know you cannot fabricate closeness, you cannot pretend it exists. When did we last share a laugh together? When did we last make love? Christ, Dan! Can't you see? What is the point of having so much if at the core there's a void? There is something not there. Something so absent it makes all else seem utterly futile. There are times when I've never been so alone as when we are together. You feel it, too. You know you do. I see it in your eyes sometimes. You know it. And you know that what's missing can't just be bought and plugged in to allow us to reconnect. What's missing is inside ourselves. This is a cliché – this whole thing is a big fucking cliché – but I'm going to look for what's missing now. And you would too, if you weren't the coward, if you cared about what you might find more than feared about what you will lose. For that is all you have now. Look into your heart, and you'll see. You have lost me already. And I you. We are both lost.

Kelvedon. Silver End. Coggeshall. Feering. Where am I? What are these places? How can I never have heard of them? I'm an hour out of London, and already I'm lost. I'm stuck in some parallel world. It was foolish to leave at night. Why did I do it? I could go back. I could start off again tomorrow. Then at least I could see. Sod it, Dan, we could just start over again ourselves. I could climb back in bed beside you. I could smell the freshness of the sheets. I could fall asleep in the warmth of your shadow. And then, tomorrow. The day. Not worse – not better, nor worse – than today. Continuing the existence we know so well, the life we have lived for so long. Bound to each other. Apart.

But that's just it, isn't it? We're not together at all. Not really together. We might appear to be; we might be told so by the system we live in, reinforced by the people we know. But what do they actually know? They see us living in the same house, and guess at the life within. It is only us who know what is shared behind the secrecy of those walls. And, in truth, what we share is so meagre. The boundaries of our worlds themselves are like walls. They are rigid and high, closed off from the other. With no intersection, no overlap. Our interests and passions are different. Our pleasure is always apart. Whether music, politics, friends, holidays, food – we are poles apart. We come together for the mundane, out of sheer necessity. Only then, and even then, resenting it when we do. When one of us moves a million miles to look in upon an alien place, and the other shudders their horror in seeing us there.

Was being together unbearable? No, it was tolerable. I could endure. But living to tolerances and degrees of endurance is like giving up on life itself. A resignation of selfhood, ambition, desire. How can a person do that?

Thinking and knowing that this is the limit, that this is all that there is. More mediocrity, more of the same, with nothing exciting beyond. With nothing more. An entirely predictable course until death; fused together forever in a cocoon of ostensible ease. Wouldn't it drive us both mad? If not now, then at some point in the future, when we looked back at what we did – at what we could have done – when this, the moment, came.

And it has come. This is a chance for us to seize. We both know the truth, and we still have time. Let's use it to find life, to breathe. Not squander our lives away in a palace of superficial comfort where we stick pins into each other to cure our bitterness. What we have falls short; it lacks fulfilment. This cannot be all that there is. Opportunity cannot be over. Not over already. There has to be more. If it won't come to us, then we have to go looking for it. We have to break through our numbing mundane and create some purpose to life.

Dedham. What's in a name? We have been dying, not living, for years. Existing with our hearts closed off to each other; both of us closed to the world. We have not dared to look for fear of seeing, for fear of finding the truth. Fear. That is no reason for staying together; that is no mantra for life. Let me give you another, Dan. Passion. Do you remember that? Where has that gone? When did that go? There was a time – surely there once was a time – when you looked at me, when I looked at you, and we both felt that something was there. There once was a time of holding and loving; a time of being in love. A time that we had, that we shared together. An innocence, a happiness, a hope.

Surely, once.

What made it go? Was something said or done that led it to die? No, it drifted. Day by day, month by month, year by year. A gradual erosion; a decay so slow that we didn't see. A rot we hid from our eyes, as we hid from ourselves. Not thinking to look till it came to this. So now, when all I need is the warmth of a hug to squeeze out all this pain in my heart, I cannot turn towards you. Or if I did, it would be to see you as the cause, not the cure, of my grief. For that is what you've become. There's no disguising it. There's no more need for lies.

No lies. Not now. Not to each other. Not to ourselves. This is the truth. I am here with Matty; I am driving past Copdock; I am driving away from you. The truth. I wish I knew what that was. In truth, is what I am doing here – right now – an act of strength, an affirmation, or is it just running away? Am I forging my own salvation tonight; or am I a teenager, sneaking out, unable to confront her own fears, too confused to know what is right?

Who can point to the truth with certainty – with even an ounce of conviction? We have one chance at life, and we have to do something; we have to believe that we can. Life in denial is no form of living. That would be running away. What I'm doing now is my own private truth. Whatever that turns out to be. Here, surrounded by infinite darkness, at night. I wish Matty was awake. I wish the rain would stop. I wish I could see. I wish I saw ten years ago the little that I can see now. I wish then I knew where I was. Then there could have been a whole second chance, erasing the past and beginning again. Then I could have found love, I could have been loved, I could have made love.

Do you love me, Dan? Did you ever love me? All I feel is that you have deprived us completely. You have strangled my love, you have restricted your own, you have denied me another man's love. I should have cheated on you when I felt myself to have been cheated by you. Then at least I would have known love, however fleeting, painful, destructive it was. These last few years I have ached to love. I have come to realise that love is all that there is, it is all we are given; it is the most elusive and exhilarating of gifts. Isn't it ironic, then, that love is the one thing I feel you have never been able to give. I have sat in our home surrounded by objects, and all I could do was ache. How could you not have seen that? How could you not have felt it yourself? Perhaps, in your heart, you are as barren as me, only you're better at hiding it. Perhaps you think that all our possessions can compensate for this emptiness. Perhaps Matty alone was enough.

Then you're a fool. You are losing him as surely as you have lost me. Now, truly, you have so little to love or be loved by. How will you survive on your own?

You must have thought this through. You can't still be in denial. I cannot care for you now. You must look after yourself. Now you are in London, and I am on the A14 heading for Needham Market. You must have known what was happening long before this. You could have stopped us from drifting as much as I could. If you had tried to do something to turn it around, I would have seen. I would have reassessed. As it was, you did nothing. We did nothing. We looked at life like casual observers; we tamely watched as the canker spread, we tamely allowed the rot to set in. Not even today did we try to prevent it.

Maybe we just don't care enough. Maybe we never have. If so, how can it be a surprise to you now, finding yourself on your own? That is the saddest thing of all – I don't think you are surprised. How could you be – you who know everything – you who disguise it so well. How strange. I know every inch of you, every fraction of being; yet some things I don't know at all. Some things resist the power to decipher. Maybe, behind that weight of knowledge, behind that burden of shared existence, we have always been strangers, Dan. Maybe there never was anything there. I would like to think there must have been something – some reason to talk, to date, to move in. But it was all so long ago. I think sometimes that what held us together was illusion, delusion, falsehood. No more.

Whatever the past, it is locked in the past. It is over. You are dead; you are buried; you are gone. What we had is truly and utterly finished. Now Matty and I are here, in the car. You are in London, alone. We are where we are, and we cannot resist it. This is the way it has come to be. It is inevitable; a natural cycle. Something greater than ourselves. We have moved apart as surely, as firmly, as if we had never been joined at all.

Whatever we once might have had is ended. You have gone from me and I from you. That is it. I hope London treats you well, and you found some food in the fridge. That is your life now, and yours alone. It is up to you what you do. You may spare a thought for me – you may think of me – turning off onto the A140 to Diss, but I don't care whether or not you do. And I would caution you not to think too much, not to regret, for it's all too late. I am moving on; I'm not coming back. I don't hate you; I don't feel hate. I just feel hollow to the core. I feel my life is over already.

And in some way, I feel it is all your fault. So, I am fixing the problem. Sitting here in the car, driving past Thornham Parva in the dark and the drizzle, I am mending my life, I am giving it back to myself. Do the same for yourself. Move on.

Move on.

And now, here is Marshfield. Find your own way, Dan. This path is mine. Mine and Matty's. These small quaint buildings squeezed shoulder to shoulder, like doll's houses crouched on the narrow pavement, all painted vibrantly pink. This is my world. These strange shops, each with their blinded windows, with bones of beams stuck through their skin. This is my future. These gutters rushing rain away; these bell-jar streetlamps slicing light; these broad hunched doors; these passageways; this brick clock-tower before me. This is where I begin. And now we are here in the heart of the town. It's ten at night, and there's no one in sight. No lights from the windows. No cars. No noise. No sense of life. Nothing but the sound of my windscreen-wipers; nothing but the sound of these wheels through the water. Nothing but the sound of Matty's breathing, regular and slow. Here is our chance to start again, to find new things to fill our world, to populate as we please.

Which is the way to Nettlesden? Here, to the left, to the side of the school – to the school that I think will be his. And now we are out of the town. Sparse hedges scratch scrawny fingers into the sightless void, then fade to swathes of nothingness that must be barren fields. Devoid of any substance. There are no lights but our own. No lines on the road. No horizon. No shape to what is ahead. No moon.

We will fashion a world from this emptiness, Matty. We will make this breathe and become our own.

We are moving on; we're beginning again. We will find new things in this land. Look, a white sign boasting a single word. Nettlesden. We have moved enough for the while. We need to know when it's time to stop. Here, on the left, is Mill House Cottages. There's a split in the hedge, and a grassy track that ends with the ice-white limbs of trees, spectral and cold in the headlights. The car exhales on the rain-wet turf, its underside prickled by the whispering grass.

Stop.

Matty is fast asleep. He doesn't flinch as I open the door and the light comes on in the back. There's a chill, but the rain has melted away. The air is thin; it cuts at my face. There is no welcoming light. Through the immense, clear blackness shrouding the car all I can see is the shadow of hedges, shivering slightly in a false breeze, protruding from the fathomless pitch and blending within it seamlessly. I sense a path, running diagonally to my right. The sheer frame of an ancient building rears before me: so tall it threatens to fall. With the engine cut, the single sound is the shallow breath of the empty wind in the hedge. If the stars were in motion, I feel sure I would hear them. But there are no stars in the sky. There is only this universal darkness – this endless, shapeless, stunning mass – retreating and crowding all around me, deafening in its silence.

The door is broad and squat. Here is a hole for the key. Inside, there is a deeper darkness, hunched and breathless as it awaits. To the right, high up, I search for the fuse box. I should have brought a torch. The silk of a cobweb brushes my fingers. Now light – huge, bald, angry light – floods the room as I flick the switch.

The room is low. Beams run from a spine across the ceiling, scarcely a hand's width over my head. They are curiously hewn, part-covered with bark, as though still living and growing. The floor is an undulating brick worn into hills and shallow valleys through generations of interminable shuffling. There's a long wooden table in front of me, washed clean with lime and contoured with age. In the corner there's a large easy chair, and to its side there's a dresser. On the far wall is a brickwork chimney, a small iron grate, a black metal door of what must be an old oven. To its right, a passage half hid by a curtain, leading towards the dark heart of the house. There's a stairwell here, winding into the night; the steps are wooden and crusted and old. I follow them upward. The sound of my shoes is unnaturally loud as they strike against its dull ribs. On the first floor I come to a sudden hallway, with rooms branching off to all sides. The door before me begs me to stoop. It leads to a room with a bed. The floorboards wince beneath my tread; they are bare but for a flat-weave rug. The drapes are a faded velvet red; they are thick and warm to the touch.

I should get Matty in.

The sound of my feet on the downward stairs pierces the dust-drenched, stale cottage air. Outside, light peers through the uncurtained window. Clumpy grass stands sodden and limp on the path. The glare of the cottage dissolves to nothing the closer I come to the car. I feel blindly across the wet metal surface, reaching out for the handle. I pull at Matty's arm; he stumbles half-conscious out of the warmth, bewildered and scratching his head.

Together, we stagger across the lawn. He is leaning against me, shielding his eyes from the brightness that shines from inside. I guide him upstairs, and into his bed. His brow is hot and moist with sweat. His body shudders as it meets the fiercesome cold of the sheet. I half-close the door; leaving just a sliver of light to break through the gloom, to wash its comfort into the room for when he stutters awake.

Now back downstairs. I should explore the house; I should unpack the car. A couple of bags, maybe. The garden seems almost familiar to me, though I have never yet seen it. The car boot opens thankfully. There's so much I brought here from London. Perhaps I ought to have left it behind – all these unwanted jolts from the past. But I'm not that strong. I pick out a bag of clothes for us both; I make one more trip for a box of food; then I close the doors and lock up the car.

In the corner of the kitchen there's a freestanding fridge. I tumble the food on its waiting shelves. At the bottom of my box is a bottle of Baileys. On the dresser I find an assortment of mugs. The thick liquid curls warmingly into the cup. It is smooth as it slips down my throat – entering my insides, working its fond caress through my body, into my sinews, up to my brain – soothing away the strain of the drive, thawing and melting my bones. A small refill. Here's to me. Here's to the now, and here's to the future. Here's to the world I will forge. I shiver.

There must be some heating somewhere. In a bite in the wall behind the chimney a boiler stands ready and idle. I turn the controls on full. I hear a surge, a satisfying throb, as it blasts into life, as it breaks the silence, its motor promising heat.

I lock the front door and turn off the lights, taking the two bags upstairs. From the grey of the landing, I look in on Matty. His brow is cooler now. The duvet and blankets are snug around him, though frigid to both of his sides. I would curl up beside him; I would steal his warmth; I would steal the peace in his mind. I stoop to place a kiss on his cheek, feeling the gentle down of his skin, the smell of his warmth. His body unconsciously yielding its love.

Across the landing, there's a wooden doorframe with a padded lintel to shield my head. It's so low I must partially bend my knees as I hunch through the unwelcome entrance. Inside is a bathroom, painted dull blue. There's an enamel bath; a basin, a loo; a wicker basket for dirty clothes. There is another doorway beyond, leading through to a richer blackness. So many doors and stairs. I brush my teeth; I wipe off my make-up. I run the tap in the hope of heat, but the water's too cold to wash my face. I cross the landing, past Matty's door, and enter another bedroom.

This can be mine, if only for tonight. I pull my nightdress from my bag and close the curtains. I undress in a limp pool of dismal greyness close to the side of the bed. The room is so cold; such an empty coldness. I hurry into bed.

The sheets are colder still, like ice. If you were here, I would huddle myself against your back and hug your heat away from you. You are always warm; you radiate heat; a balminess breathes from your body. I lock my hands between my thighs, shivering the cold from my skin. There must be a hot water bottle here in the house, but the thought of going in search appals me. In bed there's at least a promise of warmth: a tingling, a would-be warming sensation, which steals between me and the sheets.

I hug the duvet tighter. You had your uses, Dan. I could use you now. I could use your certainty, your calm. It was warm and safe beside you always. I could shrug off the strain of my day, I could slow the pace of my body and mind, when I snuggled down to your side. You were my peace, my solace, my comfort. And I've never been so in need of such comfort. Never more so than now.

How ironic that I want you now. In parting from you, in being without you, I feel the need that you're here. This is almost the first time in fifteen years that I have been in a bed on my own. Even now, I am lying here to one side: to the side that I know isn't yours. There's a crack in the duvet and air creeps in because of the space I have left for you. Are you lying in bed in London like me: a mirror image of myself? Are we lying in bed beside each other, over a hundred miles apart?

Perhaps you are not there at all. At last, some feeling has snuck inside you, breaking through to your shielded soul. You have borrowed a car to follow me here. Then perhaps I should leave the hall light on, so you can find your way through the house. I should leave the door open, too. So the first thing I hear is your soft-heavy tread on the stairs as you come up to find me. Then the creak of the door, and the shape of your body, silhouetted against the dim night. Mind you don't bump your head. Then you are beside me, here beside me, and all that warmth is wrapping around me. That warmth of being.

Come.

~

There is light round the fringe of the curtains – a thin slice of brightness where the velvet meets – casting a semblance of shape on the room. This bedroom is bigger than it seemed last night. The walls are dull yellow, half-grey in the shrouded eye of the reticent sun. Regimented beams break the long stretch of the ceiling. The bed is old and made of iron; its mattress high from the floor. Beyond it, close to the farther wall, there's an elliptical table, a chair. To the right is the door which I came through last night, flanked by a large chest of drawers. There's a smell to this room; it is fusty, unused. Unaccustomed to having people within it, though it shows all the markings of many lifetimes, of a long and memorable life.

I can hear the wind in patches outside; a low dull roar as it batters the cottage, buffeting into its thatch. There's a random scratching sound at the window, a rasping of claws on the outer walls. A searching branch, maybe. The sound is so clear, so close to my ear, as if nature has carved through the wattle and daub and is cleaving an entrance into the room. There's a hint of existence beyond. Of birdsong, of crowing, of barking dogs. There is such an absence of noises, too. No cars, no music, no horns, no sirens. Nothing beyond what nature can give.

It is cosy in bed. I have created my own warmth without you. I haven't slept this well for so long. I must be tired. I feel lazy. I feel I could lie in bed all day and listen to the sounds beyond – to the sounds from beyond, and to those inside – both full of mystery and intrigue. From outside my door, I can hear a gentle creaking, a bending, as though the cottage is gradually awakening. It is yawning, stretching, coming to being, brushing against the elements and slowly stirring to life.

The room is less stale than last night, but the clothes in my bag feel cold – almost damp with coldness. I shiver putting them on. Until this cottage has felt me within it, the bleakness, the indifference will remain. I need to claim it as mine. I need to make this space my home. Matty's door is ajar. He is still asleep. I wash; I put on some lipstick; I go downstairs. The stairs themselves are muted. Last night, my feet beat tumult on them, filling the empty air. Now it's the air itself that's alive, and this warped wooden treadway is hollow. I make a cup of tea; I unlock the door; I walk out into the garden.

Brightness. Not merely sunshine, but a clarity, a cleanness, carved in all that I see. Objects look crisper, their aspects sharper: the grass, the hedges, the car. The air smells different, too. It is cold but vital, stinging my cheeks, fresh as it enters my mouth. In front of the cottage is a patch of lawn bruised by the winter frost. In the bed to the right there's a spray of rosemary, a small bay bush, some sprigs of lavender. On the left, a low brick wall, projecting three feet from the cottage door. Two dozen paces in front of me there's a hedge obscuring the road beyond, matted with early spring growth. The hedge cuts back along both sides, marking the perimeter of the grounds. The lawn slips from sight through an unkempt rose-arch close to the side of the house. I follow it through, and now I am here at the back of the cottage, on a more extensive patch of grass, cushioned on either side by more hedge.

At the end of the garden, I come to a field. There's no fence, no gate, to mark its border. It's a single neat-sown stretch of land, unbroken by any hedge or road, extending into the infinite distance and spread out wide before me. It is perfectly flat. Not a rut, not a ditch, not an undulation.

Nothing to break its monotony. It is full of fragile fluttering seedlings running in measureless emerald lines beyond the scope of my sight. Against the horizon there's an occasional tree, a barn, a miniature telegraph pole to suggest where the field might end. Away to the right is an island of buildings, marooned in the midst of the crop. Beyond it, over the planted sea, a broader huddle of skeletal trees which mark the line of a wood.

Here, where the garden melds with the field, there is nothing to break the wearisome wind as it washes the flat-planted earth. Closing my eyes, I feel it surround me, blistering the skin on my face and my neck, tugging at strands of my hair. I feel it teasing my senses to life: stinging my nostrils, assaulting my ears, bruising me, coaxing me cry. Such openness here, and yet such oppression. I feel like standing with outstretched arms, drinking its majesty in. But with equal measure I could run inside, I could hide from its incomprehensible beauty, I could let those tears be my own.

I open my eyes once more. This land is so flat; the horizon so low; the pressing sky so immense. So big that I cannot capture it – not in a single gaze. It would seem there's not one sky but many, all crowding in upon each other, splayed in the vastness of space; subdividing and blending together, interlocked and overlapping; blurring and warring endlessly, shifting interminably, boundless. I find myself hunching, retreating to safety, towards the shelter of welcoming boughs.

I have entered another part of the garden. A long band of land that is planted with fruit trees, with a square weed-rich patch carved out of the grass.

I look back toward my new home. The cottage is fiercely, ugly pink with a dirty thatch like a mop of hair. It has lean-tos clinging to every side. Its walls are bloated and coarse. It's not built of brick, but is born of the earth, fashioned from clay that clothes it like skin, with wooden beams that are breathed into life. Three chimneys thrust stumpy thumbs through the thatch; windows peer out from their lintel brows; dormant roses weave round the walls, clinging onto the uneven frame.

I return inside. Still there's no sign of Matty. I have a refill of tea and some cereal, using the last of the milk. I want Matty to help me unpack the car, so he feels the transition between two worlds, so he acknowledges we have arrived. He needs to know there is no going back. I need to accept it, as well. I cannot question reality. Not now. Choices are over; decisions are made. I made my position quite clear. And in failing to make a choice of your own, you will have to live in the shadow of mine. You will have to live with its consequence. You will have to live on your own. All future decisions concerning yourself are yours alone. Not mine.

I make more trips from the car to the cottage, heaping all we have brought on the floor till the car boot sighs and is empty.

– Matty! Matty, I'm going to find the shop. We need more milk. I'll be back in twenty minutes.

I turn onto the road that leads from Marshfield. The leaves of the hedge have yet to bud, but it's thick with a dense weave of boughs. Behind its web of distorted growth, the cottage is merely a hint of pink. There's no pavement here, and the well-ploughed land extends right up to the road. To the left, is the single endless field that I saw before from my lawn. To the right are a series of smaller fields, divided by ditches and snatches of bush. Beyond them a large white house stares, unblinking, with two vast silos stood to its rear.

A hundred yards down the road I come to a house with a red-tiled roof. On its gate there's a painted sign. Six Bells. Not far beyond, a track cuts through the immeasurable field, leading to an island of trees sunk deep amidst a wave of seedlings. Part-hidden behind a naked willow I can see the outline of a farm, caught in a circle of barns. I march on. Beyond the track there's a white beamed house. It too has a sign. The Rectory.

Where the Rectory garden ends, the road bends right, skirting the sides of the clustering wood that I earlier saw from the cottage. The trees within it are bare of leaves; they are huddled close as if for protection, forming a wall at the wind-bitten side of the field. Some trunks have collapsed, or are propped like scaffolds, holding themselves at curious angles in the crook of adjacent trees. The wood seems to screen itself from the world, affording no pathways inside.

There's a church beyond the bend in the road, its square tower encrusted with flint. It stands on a rise with an irregular graveyard burgeoning out on all sides. The tombstones are old; their feet barren of flowers. The bare bones of trees, disfigured and tall, lisp and leer from its fringes. I can hear the hollow cries of rooks as they spiral high above nests. On the opposite side of the road, there's an ancient building with lettering stamped on its brow. The Serpent. A golden creature coils and writhes, caught in the painted frame of a pub sign. The door of the building beyond is open. It is Wayside House, the village shop.

– Hello.

– Good morning.

– My name's Sarah Margolis. I've just arrived at Mill House Cottages.

– Ah! Hello. Welcome! Come on in. My name's Bill. Bill Hawes. Margaret! Margaret, come down here for a minute. So, when did you arrive?

– Last night. Late.

– Terrible weather last night. Did you find the cottages ok?

– Yes, thank you.

– Margaret, look who it is. This is Sarah. Sarah Margolis. She's taken Mill House Cottages.

– Well, very nice to meet you! I'm so glad you've come down to say hello. We heard the cottages were being let. I think there are two of you?

– I've come with my son, Matty. Yes. He's still asleep, I'm afraid.

– That's boys for you. How old is he?

– Fourteen.

– That's nice. So, is it just the two of you?

– Yes.

– And are you down here for long?

– I'm not sure exactly. It depends.

– Of course. You're from London, aren't you? Have you been here before?

– Now, Margaret. Save your questions. Sarah, would you like a cup of coffee?

– I only really came down for a pint of milk. And to meet you, of course.

– Well, there we go. How do you take your coffee?

– That's really very kind, but…

– White or black?

– White, please.

— Not at all. Bill, I'll be back in a minute. Try not to bore our new friend.

— So, have you been here before, Sarah?

— Never. But a friend recommended Suffolk to me.

— Very good. It may not quite be London, but it has its advantages. What's made you decide to give up the city?

— Various things. I felt I needed a bit of space.

— Very wise. We've got a lot of space here. Lots of space and not many people. Have you met any of the village yet?

— No. I passed a few houses on the way though.

— That was the village. Mill House Cottages is at one end and we're at the other. I don't know what happened to the Mill House itself. It must have got lost on the way. Nearest to you is Six Bells. That used to be a pub. Peter Faraday lives there. He's a farmer. One of the new breed. Then, set back a way up a track, there's Rose House Farm where the Pooleys live. That's Uriah and Joyce Pooley. The other Pooleys — Uriah's parents — live at Burnt Tree Farm on the other side of the road. They're Jack and Martha. The Rectory belongs to people called the Merediths, who come up from London. Where in London do you — did you live?

— Bill! Stop nagging her! Sarah, dear, here's some coffee. Is that too milky for you?

— Thank you. That's fine.

— I hope instant's all right. We don't do posh coffee here.

— That's all there is in London, last time I went there. There are coffee bars everywhere. Doesn't anyone do any work anymore?

— Bill, stop being such a traditionalist. What do you do, Sarah?

— I'm a sub-editor. Freelance.

— How interesting. What sort of things do you do?

— Books mainly. Fiction. I work for a couple of houses.

– Does that mean you are going to be commuting down to London regularly?

– No. I'm planning on working virtually. I shouldn't have to go down very often at all.

– Virtual working! You'll be the first virtual person in Nettlesden. The rest of us are all a bit earthy and real.

– That's as may be. Now, Sarah, you've come at a super time of year. We've got Easter not far away, when the whole village comes together.

– And before that, you can meet most of them in the pub!

– Have you been to the Serpent yet, dear? That's the place to get to know people.

– Not yet. I arrived quite late last night.

– Everyone will know that you're here by now.

– Yes. They're certain to know. Our village has eyes. They'll have seen you already, for sure.

– Our community sticks together. It's close.

– We have to be close. That's how we survive. We all look out for each other.

– But it's so nice having somebody new, isn't it, Bill?

– Look, I'm terribly sorry. I don't mean to be rude, but I've gone and left Matty at the cottage alone, and I think I ought to be getting back. That coffee was lovely. Thank you.

– Yes, of course. How silly of us. Chatting away like that. You must have lots to do.

– Now you wanted some milk?

– Do you have semi-skimmed?

– Whole milk is all, I'm afraid.

– That's fine. Here we are.

– And here's your change. Come down and see us again soon.

– Whenever you like.

– Yes, I'm sure I will. Thank you. Goodbye.

I expect they have shuffled towards the window; they are standing there watching me walking away. They are talking about me; incessantly talking. They are sizing me up; they are figuring me out; they are guessing why I am here. Curious, unsatisfied, wanting more gossip. Making it up in their minds. For now, that's all they can have. For now, there's so much that isn't for sharing, so much that is still beyond all reason, so much that I need to work through. The truth remains so fragile. I cannot expose myself to these people, however hard they might pry. Perhaps I ought to conjure new truths to keep them away, to keep them distracted. To give me a welcome distraction too. An alternative past, a distorted present, like the ones that we used to craft for ourselves – pretending to be who we wanted to be, losing our truth in a lie. We were always so good at building a fiction, at hiding ourselves in pretence. I don't think we were ever caught out. Can you recall us talking to strangers, making up lifetimes where nothing was real? Fashioning such fantastical worlds that we almost believed them ourselves. I could do it again in this village. I could say that you're dead and have just been buried, but perhaps that's a little extreme. I could say you have gone abroad on assignment. You have entered a religious retreat. You are climbing a peak in the Himalayas. You are tracing the Euphrates back to its source. Any of those are credible stories. As real, as unreal, as the truth.

I turn the doorhandle and enter the cottage. Still no sign of Matty. No sound. It is dark and hunched inside. There's a smell of disuse, a skin of dust. An aging, a stain that can't be removed. The main room, cluttered with bags and boxes, shuts out the light beyond the windows, filtering life from the cottage.

– Matty?!

–

– Matty!

– Yea?

– Come down here!

– Why?

– Come down here now!

– Why?

– There are things here for you to take up.

– I've got them all.

– There's more of your stuff from the car.

– I'll come down in a while.


– Matty?!

–

– Matty!

– What?

– Have you had breakfast yet?

– Sort of.

– When you come down here, I want you to eat.

– Whatever.

– Don't 'whatever' me! Don't…

There's a knock at the door. Someone has heard me yelling at him. Someone's first impression of me has been formed from behind the front door. I thought in the country I'd be left to myself; I thought I was getting away. I thought I would find my freedom here. I thought I could bury my past. Again, a sound at the door. I open it. Outside there's a small and well-dressed woman, with sunken eyes, with skin pulled tight across her cheeks. She is waiting patiently on the step. Her hair is shoulder-length and grey; it is centre-parted and flecked with white. Her lips are dull and thin.

– Hello?

– Hello. I'm sorry to intrude. I'm sure you're busy and a visitor is the last thing you need, but I thought you might like a little local produce, so I've brought some round.

– O. How kind.

– Just a few things. From my garden. Here. There's not much to harvest at this time of year. And here, here's an apple pie to pop in the oven after lunch.

– Thank you.

– Now I should be off. I'll let you get on with it.

– Yes. No. Look, I'm so sorry. You must think me very rude. Do come in, please.

– Well, if you're sure. I don't want to be any bother.

– Please. Do. Come in. Sit. Can I get you a coffee?

– No, thank you. My name's Martha Pooley.

– And I'm Sarah Margolis. My son Matty's upstairs.

– How are you settling in?

– I haven't really started. I haven't even explored the house.

– They're over five hundred years old, these cottages. Just like warrens, aren't they?

– Why do you call them 'cottages'? Plural.

– It's a single building, but when it was built it was divided into three homes. Three separate families lived here. That's why the rooms are so small and low, and why there are so many stairways. They packed people in back then.

– But each home must have been tiny.

– A big room below and one above. They were large families then, too. Almost twenty people lived here.

– You seem to know a lot about it.

– I was born in Nettlesden and have always lived here. My family go back for generations. The history is something you can't avoid. It's in your blood. If you're interested, you should speak to my husband. He's an authority on the past.

31

– Where in the village do you live?

– Burnt Tree Farm. That's the white farmhouse over Cross Path Field. The one with silos behind it. We farm most of the fields to the south of the road. Jack's seventy-two now, but the fields are his home. They're a part of his body. He hasn't given up an inch of it. He won't do so till he dies.

– And who owns the huge field behind this cottage? Is that yours, too?

– Road Field? No, that belongs to Uriah, our son. He lives at Rose House Farm, which is built in a spinney in the middle of the field. He farms the fields that are north of the road. You could say that between the two lots of Pooleys, we farm the whole of the village. It may seem a bit of a monopoly, but that's the way it's turned out.

– I'm looking forward to exploring the fields and going for walks. The air's so clean here.

– It's good for you, yes. You should mind the farmers, though. They are very protective, and very traditional. There may be public right of way, but they think of themselves as the overlords. It's intensive arable land. Earning a living here can be hard. Every square yard of land is precious. They resent people walking on it. I shouldn't really say that of my own, but I think it's only fair to warn you. They are nice enough men besides.

– There are other walks too, presumably. I saw a wood beyond the field, just to the side of the church.

– No one goes there. No one save Uriah. He shoots and lays snares in that wood, so you shouldn't go there. Much better to keep from harm's way. You'll be fine if you walk round the edges of fields, if you come towards us and head south. There are good walks too at Oakham Green, and on the coast around Rackham.

– I'd like that. I think I ought to get to know the village first though.

– You'll meet the village fast enough. Nothing escapes them here. There's a fine line in gossip, and inquisitive eyes. If you want to meet folk you should join our church service. That's the place where you'll get to know them.

– I think I may.

– It's a curious world, this village. It's a different world. An alternative way of thinking and being. Things here don't happen like they do elsewhere, but that's not to say that it's dull. And it's coming to life now – now that it's spring.

– Yes, it's lovely.

– Good. It is nice. I'm sure you'll make your own way. But if ever you feel the need, if you want to escape, whatever the reason, there's a footpath over the road. It leads round the fields to Burnt Tree Farm. You'll always be welcome.

– Thank you, Martha. That's very kind.

– I'll leave you now to get on. You can return the dish when you're ready.

– Thanks. Nice meeting you. Goodbye.

– Goodbye.

A nice enough woman, if a little dour. She shakes my hand, but she doesn't smile. I walk her through to the gap in the hedge, watching as she crosses the road, as she takes an invisible path round the field, as she steers her steps towards home. She is thin, but sinewy, moving determinedly, striking a route through this washed-out land. She walks swiftly, with confidence, over stillborn grass, her hair disturbed by the random wind, its grey strands snatched in the air. Above her, the sky is a dirty white, an immense unbroken solitude. A soiled canvas awaiting a brush to bring its body to life.

I retrace my steps to the pink fleshy cottage. On the wall jutting out to the side of the door I can see a small bunch of flowers. They are held together by a bright blue ribbon, neatly tied in a bow. I recognise them at once. This is Christmas rose, like we used to buy in Columbia Road on a Sunday during the winter months, when nothing else was in bloom. I wouldn't have thought it would grow here.

I pick up the delicate bouquet. This is no thorny rose: its petals are frail and tipped with pink, its leaves almost leathery to touch. It is beautiful in its simplicity. This is the flower that was born of an angel, born of the tears of Madelon the shepherdess, for having no gift to give. And now I have also been given this gift, brought by an angel of my own.

I look around me. I guess these must have been brought by Martha. She must have put them down when she knocked. Her hands were full with the apple pie. And then she forgot to pick them up. Or perhaps she thought them a nice surprise for me to find once she'd gone.

I glance at my watch, failing to comprehend the dial. Time is a different concept here; it seems to serve no obvious purpose. There is wake and sleep; there is darkness and daylight; there is life and death. There are seasons.

Deep in the heart of the silent cottage, I can see a pile of bags and boxes still waiting for me to unpack them. There is no incentive to do so. I go to the sink in the kitchen, running the tap and filling a cup, splaying the Christmas rose round its rim. I feel hungry; I feel the need for fresh air. I take bread, cheese and ham from the fridge. I start cutting and slicing, picking up offcuts that lie on the breadboard, greedily stuffing them into my mouth.

– Matty!

–

– Matty!

– What?

– It's lunchtime.

– I'll be down in a minute.

– Come now.

– In a minute.

– We're going for a walk.

– I don't want to.

– You'll come for a walk.

– I'm busy.

– Come down! You can do whatever you're doing later.

– I can't.

– Now! I'll meet you round at the back of the cottage in three minutes. There are sandwiches in the kitchen. Wear your boots.

– I hate boots!

Martha suggested we walk near her farm. There are paths between her patchwork of fields, in grassy margins where the planting stops. Instead, I skirt the side of the cottage till I'm standing looking out over the field. There is something appalling, something enthralling, about a field so vast. About nature seen on such scale. The regular lines of fragile seedlings extend perfectly straight to a point beyond sight. There's an absence of weeds; there's an order exerted, as if the wild can be tamed. I think we can cut down the side of the field. We can visit the churchyard maybe.

Someone has come up beside me. It is Matty, his mouth full of sandwich. He looks at the sky, and shivers. I lead the way, turning along the edge of the field, steering up close to the road.

The band of earth is two feet wide, soft underfoot from last night's rain. Clods of mud cling to my boots. Stones have been dragged to the edge by the plough, and clumps of grass form sudden knolls, so we walk with our eyes to the ground. I can hear the suction of Matty's boots, the lisp as they brush through the still-wet grass. How alien the two of us must look, sludging along this line of earth, when there, on the farther side of the ditch, is the road.

We are approaching Six Bells and turn northwards again, skirting its bounds with the field. Rose House Farm is closer now, but obscured by a belt of shielding trees, distanced by the ranks of seedlings which ripple like silver-green waves in the wind. The shapeless farmhouse emerges and fades, masked by wisping sinews of willow, blown into sudden relief by the breeze. Across the chasm of fragile growth, I can make out a person who is looking towards us, stood in the forecourt, alone.

I wave.

The figure doesn't move. Perhaps it isn't a person at all. Now, as we carve our path to the church, a denser growth of determined trees erases the building entirely. The island becomes a copse, a corpse – an unwelcome protrusion which breaks the sheen of this ocean of fluttering leaf. Above it, the cold empty white of the sky, unbroken and sightless, crowds over the land and squeezes the air, suffocating us in its silence. I can hear the sting of the sharpening breeze, the squelch of Matty's boots in the mud, a metallic clanking from somewhere beyond.

We are traipsing alongside the road once again, then crossing the track to Rose House Farm, and now meeting the ditch dividing the field from the polished Rectory lawn.

The garden itself is large and proud, with heady bushes of white-bearded grass, a shrubbery hid by a curling wall, ornate black railings and heavy gates, a maze of box hedges inviting the gaze. Behind its gentle cultivation, the shadow of the encroaching wood rears against the solid sky. And to its right is the church.

We are coming close to the bend. We scramble through the scrub in the ditch, reaching the road and climbing an incline to the gate which leads to the church. There's a shrill rasp of metal as the handle turns. I follow the path up a further small rise, and now I am standing in the corner of the graveyard, gazing at the stern flint walls of the giddy tower above me. Laid out before it there are lines of tombstones, covered in lichen, thrust through the earth like a well-seasoned crop of the dead. Around its perimeter, there's a band of bald trees. I trace the boundary with my eyes, and, as I turn, I catch sight of Matty, walking away and into the distance, heading straight for the wood.

– Matty!

–

– Come back, Matty!

–

– Not that way!

My voice sounds shrill as it breaks through the silence and is absorbed in the body of cloud. I'm sure that he's heard me, but he pays no heed. He's walking on to the wood. He is close to it now. I see him stop as he reaches its skirt; I see him peering inside. I recall Martha's words about guns and snares. Matty isn't aware. I turn and walk swiftly out of the graveyard, along the track which leads to the wood.

I'm breathless when I catch up with Matty. I want to chastise, to impose my order. It is so important, here in this place, where rules have yet to be defined, where the only maker of rules is me. I need the wisdom of us both; an authority which needs no second opinion. Not just to enforce, but to steer and to guide. And I need to do it now.

My mind is alive to Martha's warnings; it speaks an instinctive distrust. I look at Matty, who is looking at me, who seems to be waiting for me to speak. But no words come. Instead, I gape at the trees. Matty follows my eyes; he stares at them too.

Somehow, I know he won't enter the wood. Not on his own, not now. There is something about it, or something within it. Something indefinite; something unseen. I can feel his intrigue, his longing, his doubt as he delves with his searching eyes through its depths.

We are standing where the field meets the trees, on a fringe of land which is torn by the wind – by the wind which is switching and dying around us, which is whistling into the whispering wood, which pounds and then in a heartbeat is gone. There's a belt of bramble and thorn round the trees, naturally fencing the wood from the land, the wilderness from the field. The trunks within are restless and tall, swaying and creaking, lisping their secrets, arching their dry sapless bones. Their canopies are bare, they are barren of leaf; their cracked limbs scratch at the vacuous sky, assaulting the lame wreathes of cloud.

Emboldened by each other's presence, we shuffle up to its edge. Matty thrusts his boot in the thorn, seeing it crackle beneath his weight, splintering to nothing, shrieking. He smudges out its broken face, brushing the bramble away.

We peer within. Within its body I sense a silence; a coolness, a closeness, a creeping unease. The bowels of the wood are dim and obscure despite the absence of leaves. There are many trees here; there are all types of tree. A natural wood, self-planted, self-tended, living and dying an endless cycle for years, perhaps for millennia.

In the early fringe, light penetrates still, allowing us fractures of sight. There are saplings straining and searching for being, stretching towards the would-be sun. There are trunks with roots that are wrenched from the soil, tangled with crude blocks of clay. There are twigs and branches strewn on the ground, twisted and broken by battling storms, torn from their trunks by the nearby trees. There's a mantle of dead and decaying leaves, an early weave of disintegration indistinguishable from the new growth. And all around there's a constant chatter – a groaning, a creaking, a weeping of trunks. A noise so unlike the shuffle of trees. An immense unhappiness, a loneliness. An endless solitude that has long blanked pain.

I sense Matty turning and looking towards me. He wants to know what this is. He hasn't seen this before. I would help him, but then this is new to me too. I cannot explain the sensation I feel; it cannot be captured in words. There is beauty here, a fearful beauty; a wildness that captures the mind. And there's ugliness, a wretchedness. Almost akin to an evil. Not that the wood itself is evil, but seemingly it's been washed by an evil, and it cannot expurgate the stain.

Matty and I meet eyes. He sees that I see. He knows my lack of comprehension. He knows if he runs that I'm sure to follow. We back away gradually, into the open, our eyes still firm on the trees.

We return to the fringe of the field, stumbling over its irregular contours. By the time we reach the graveyard's entrance, the wood has receded and with it the fear. I could almost summon the courage to enter, to read the inscriptions carved on the tombstones, to imagine those who are laid here to rest. But Matty has broken off from my side; already he heads up the road to the cottage. I follow him, keeping two paces behind him, till we reach the comfort of home.

Already the sky has grown dark. Time has lost meaning in a single day. I put on the kettle for tea. There are crumpets I have bought as a treat. I let great wads of melting butter steal into their hollow hearts. We sit in silence at the table, feeling the warmth from within. When the boiler fires we both react, starting at the sudden noise which fills the cavernous room. I get up and turn on the lights. Every light I can find in every room on this floor.

When I return to where we were sitting, Matty is no longer here.

From the well-lit room the day seems more distant; the hedge at the front is frosted in shadow; the rose on the wall curls thorny tendons, scraping its nails on the glass. Again and again, with an urgency that demands there is no denial.

I should begin the unwanted task of unpacking. I should dig out some music to drown out the world. From upstairs I can hear a muffled shuffling as Matty makes a home of his room. I would like to be close to him now. I would like to go up and hug him against me. That is what we both need. A big, broad-armed, squeeze-the-pain-away hug. One which warms to the soul. A cleansing, restorative, life-giving hug, just like the ones that you used to give me.

I walk down the corridor to the room at the end that I've never entered before. There are two armchairs here, and a sofa, a bookcase. And there, in an alcove set in the wall, is a large iron wood-burning stove. Back in the central room of the house, I empty a box maliciously, careless of contents which spill to the floor. I snatch up some paper and stamp on the box, breaking its back then tearing its limbs in the callous clutch of my hands. I drag my destruction through to the stove and cast it into the grate. I cover the cardboard with stumps of wood; I put a match to it all.

The paper flares up, the flames attracted to the wadding around it, licking the underbellies of logs, stealing along the sappy hollow between the bark and the trunk. It draws well, this stove. There's a richness of light, a feeling of warmth, melting my body and mind. This is my life, my world. I can make it work. Never so lonely, I will not be lonely. I will not succumb; I will not be consumed. Of all things to fear, it's loneliness that terrifies me the most, for it emphasises the sheer futility of all we do, of life itself. I refuse to let it intrude. I will not let it spread its cancer on either Matty or me. I will not be afraid. I will be strong, even when loneliness stands naked before me; even when love has slit its throat and clutches its hands about its neck as it chokes itself on its blood. I will be strong.

Outside, I can hear the rain begin. I can hear the uneven barrage of wind battering blind on these living walls. Cloudburst splatters like hail on the glass. I rise and close the velvet curtains against the dying eye of the day, though it does little to muffle the awakening storm.

~

I have unpacked all our possessions. All we have brought here is lain on the floor, stacked in disorderly piles. By the door are corpses of cardboard boxes that I have crushed with my feet. I have left them there for Matty to see, so he can see we've moved on. So he can witness there's no going back. Matty has already come down for breakfast. He has cast his eyes over all that is here. He is scraping his cereal bowl in the kitchen. He is sure to know what this means.

I have taken my computer upstairs. There's a small pink room beside the bathroom. I have decided to make it my study. There's a table there that will do for a desk. That is all I will need.

Now I stand amidst the islands of piles, wondering which should be next. I pick up an armful of paperbacks books, wandering through the ground floor rooms, searching for where they should go. There are windowsills, bookcases, the kitchen dresser; there's an alcove set beside the oven, a mantelpiece over the stove. Any of these would do well.

I put the books outside my new study and return downstairs to the piles. The pictures are harder. I want to avoid displaying my photos: these depictions of what we have left behind, which are still so raw in the mind. But even hanging my paintings feels wrong. Each is a story of where it was bought, each is a memory of where it once was. Each is a portrait of you.

Leaving the pictures where they are lying, I take a boxful of pots and pans and crockery into the kitchen. Much of this is already here. If I mix them up, I might get confused if and when it's time to depart. Maybe I should use what is here, leaving this box on the floor for now. Here in the corner, out of the way, where I can dip in if I need.

Under the box I have just removed, I spot the Turkish kilim we bought. I can picture it still, on a rail outside that village shop in the hills. I fell in love with it at once, though it was weathered and speckled with mud. Can you recall going into the store and asking how much the shopkeeper wanted? Can you recall him refusing to sell? How long did we sit there, cross-legged on the floor, drinking a lifetime of sweetened tea, as we looked through stacks of similar kilims, though none of them were the same? It was that one I wanted, or none at all. And I couldn't leave empty-handed. So, we didn't drive onwards as we had planned. We remained there for the rest of our stay, bouldering by day in the dry riverbed, picnicking in the shade of tall trees, dreaming of where we would hang the kilim if we ever brought it back home. We were so determined back then. Every evening we returned to the shop; we tried to cajole him to sell. Then, on our last day, early that morning, you came in and laid the rug on our bed. You just put it there; you said it was ours. But you never told me what you did to persuade him, or how much it cost you to buy it. Why did I never find that out? I guess I may never have asked you.

I pick up the kilim and inspect it once more. It is ragged and frayed and bleached by sunlight. It's like a friend to me still. Trusted, dependable, always beside me. Though I'd quite forgotten how we had got it till I saw it folded here on the floor – folded just as you had done when you laid it out on our bed. Where should I put it now? On the brick floor, here, in the middle of the room? In my little study upstairs? Maybe in the room where I sleep on my own. It would make any one of those homely. Brighter and lighter, and fuller with life. A reminder of happier times in the past; a reminder of what could have been.

I shudder involuntarily; these rooms are so cold. I glance at the window to check for a presence. It is almost as though I sense myself watched – as if a pair of eyes are upon me, staring into this room. In turn I look at each of the doors, ensuring that no one is here. Matty, I know, is upstairs. I can hear the familiar creak of the boards as he moves around on the floor above me. He's sorting a space of his own. For him it is easy, it seems. He has no past, and so little baggage. It's so simple for him to move on.

I pick up the bunch of cottage keys and go outside to the garden. I unlock and explore each lean-to in turn. There is one lined with shelves which house ancient tools: rusted shapes of curious design, whose purpose is mostly unclear. Another is bare save for scrapings of sawdust, with an opposite door leading into the house. I guess that this is the log store. The third I come to is empty and dry. It is well-enclosed and the lock is big. I prop the door wide with a brick. Then I bring all the clutter I've just unpacked – the rug, the pictures, the crockery, the ornaments – even the books that I took upstairs – all that I own except for my clothes – and pile it up in the lean-to. I work swiftly, furtively, wanting it done before Matty knows where it is. Then I kick back the brick and close the door, locking it all from my world.

Returning inside, I look around me. There is nothing to show but broken boxes; nothing of substance remains. The time will come – the time may come – to bring those objects back to life. Little by little, one by one. When a new existence has been created in which they can have a rightful place. When the memory they conjure is not so raw. For now, what Matty will see is these boxes – destroyed and useless, and ready for burning. That is all I want him to see.

Back in the kitchen I make our lunch. Then I call Matty down and we eat together, staring at each other across the table without exchanging a word. I wonder if he knows what I've done; I wonder what he thinks of me now. He squeezes a large slice of bread in his hand, sandwiching layers of ham and cheese, and stuffs it into his mouth. I envy him his innocence. So careless, so quite without care.

We have finished. Still we are staring at one another; still not daring to speak. We know what both of us want to do now; we have known it and felt it all day. We have known it ever since yesterday. I can almost believe he has been in his room, patiently waiting and listening out, knowing this moment would come. All that neither of us can know is the other's courage, or how far we will go. We will find that out, we will test our resolve, but not until we are there.

We get up and tip our plates in the sink. If I were in London, I would insist we washed up before I allowed us to leave. You know that's what I would do. I would hand you a dishcloth to do the drying, and Matty would put things away. Order makes more sense than confusion; chores can't be left when they need to be done. Why couldn't you understand that logic; why did you question my truth? And why can't I now, when faced with that truth, apply it to Matty and me? The truth is that nothing seems to matter now we are here on our own. The dishes don't matter; time doesn't matter; what we do is beyond our control. This earth, this land: this is all that there is. A natural order dictating the days, the seasons, the cycles which merge with each other – which emerge from the same, which live for a while, which die, and which then are reborn. We, the inheritors, move with its motion, and all we can do is submit.

We put on our jumpers, our coats and boots, and open the door to the garden. Outside it is bright; the sky is creased with luminous cloud which disguises the shape of the sun. The air is still, it caresses my cheek, its freshness fingers my skin. The grass feels crisp beneath my feet, the earth is firm to my tread.

We walk over the lawn and down the road, Matty taking the lead. At the track which points towards Rose House Farm I glance through the fabric of trees. Again, I see what I guess is a person, standing alone in the distant courtyard, like a shadow, the shade of a being. We pass the Rectory, abandoned amidst its manicured garden, the landscaped sweep of its beds. At the corner, shortly before the church, is the field-side track which leads to the wood.

We strike out around the fringe of Road Field. The tall trees rising as we approach, stretching their stiff limbs further upwards into the film of a transparent sky. We come to the place where last we stood, where the thorn that was felled by Matty's boot remains like a wound in its side. We rest on our haunches beside each other, peering in through the flesh of the wood with curious, cautious eyes. In the absence of wind I listen for silence, for a reassuring stillness to breathe from the carcases of the trees. Instead, from deep within their ranks, from a single tree and a thousand trees, there's a wince, a sappy whimper, a sigh.

Matty thrusts his boot at the bramble. The branches on the edge of the wood sway fractionally with idle interest. He raises his foot and brings it forcefully down on the thorn. The broken structure shivers and splinters beneath the weight of his tread; its fierce sound cracks on the sharpened air and carries into the trees. The wood is awakening; its eyes are opening. Matty withdraws his belligerent foot, kicking off ivy and wreathes of twine, the viscera clung to his heel. He smashes blindly once more at the thicket, and now there's the hint of an opening.

I steal a glance behind me, guiltily wondering if we've been seen. Again, I sense we are being watched, as if something is spying on us. Something besides these vigilant trees; something somewhere beyond. Across the fluttering lines of seedlings, the black-eyed panes of Rose House Farm, grey in the haze of the middle-distance, stare at us without seeing. I want Matty to know we need to hurry; there's an urgency that we hide. Even if that means trusting the wood to be our place of retreat. I catch his elbow and pinch his skin. I think he knows what I mean. He kicks and kicks at the undergrowth, carving an angry path within it. Now he creeps through the straggling boughs, and I follow closely behind.

Inside it is silent and cool. Matty stops within a few paces on an uneven floor of dead leaf. I straighten and look up above me. The trees are tall; sinewy silver-grey trunks stretch high; dense roofs of branch are thatched amidst dim patches of close mottled darkness. Smudges of sky break through the crowns, standing proudly like sores. Inside, it is equally bright and dark, the shadows shifting, defying sight. Clumps of undergrowth blur out of focus. Swathes of moss and twists of ivy stand sharp against the invisible backdrop. Splinters of light from beyond the wood split through the scatter of trees. The floor is obscured; it feels soft underfoot. It rolls in trenches and empty hollows, littered with fractures of broken tree caught in the throes of decay. There's a restlessness, a whispering, a constant yawning, an ancient aching, from every part of the wood.

– Matty…

My voice sounds hollow, absorbed in the air and hurried away. There is no echo, no resonance. We stand back-to-back, looking around us, searching for sense and for focus.

– Matty, there are traps in here. Careful where you tread.

Matty doesn't move. He seems absorbed in the act of watching, consumed by all that he sees. He is filtering life and colour and form from the clutch of shapeless substance and nothing that fidgets and blends all around us. There is a low persistent moan in the air. I would trace it back and find its source, but I sense it cannot be found. It isn't a single thing that moans. It's the wood itself – each tree, each trunk – enduring a perpetual pain that never worsens nor fades.

Matty steps further inside. He's more confident than ever I could be, and surer when faced with unknown. His feet invigorate the live bed beneath us, snapping the stale bones strewn on its floor. The wood about us shivers. He shuffles over the speckled earth, and I follow behind in his steps.

He stops by a trunk that has been upended. It is freshly fallen; it still seems alive. I look up. The bodies of trees rise dizzily high, splintering into fingers of branches, into sinews of twigs which snarl into tangles, twisting and scratching the blind canvas sky. The top of the canopy rises so tall that as it sways it seems to fall, reeling towards me with infinite slowness till I feel unsteady, unsure on my feet.

I realise Matty is no longer beside me. I look swiftly around me in all directions – looking without being able to see. He has gone. All that is left is a haze, a rush of shapeless colour and form. Erratic channels of light, and vistas of darkness.

There's no noise to signal where he has gone; only the throaty cry of the wood which seems to rise from the earth itself. Refusing to yield what it knows.

– Ha!

The sound appears close to my side. I turn. From somewhere – perhaps from the ground, perhaps from a trunk, perhaps from the fingertips of the trees – I can hear the sound of my son. He is near. Somewhere close, though I cannot see. My haste prohibits my sight. I feel the fear that washes round me whispering into my ear. I wait for him to appear. I'm unprepared to be alone, to be caught alone in this cruel jungle, trapped beneath this heartache of trees.

– Matty!
–
– Matty, come out. I can see you.

I hear a bending, a groaning of bones, a shuffle of flayed livid limbs. Uncertain seconds of aching stillness, of silence, of conscious watching and waiting. And now a wheezing, fierce in my ear. Matty appears from a torso of trunk, ten paces away, to my side. How could I not have seen him?

– Don't do that. Don't ever do that again.
– I'm just mucking around.
– Well, I don't like it.
– I didn't do anything.
– Martha says there are snares in the wood. She says that people come here to shoot. You have to be careful.
– I will. I like it here.
– I'm not sure it's safe. We don't know what's in here.
– There's dead stuff, that's all. Let's build a den.

– I don't think we should move things around.

– Why not? Everything in here is dead. It's not like it belongs to anyone. And we're not doing any harm.

– We don't know who it belongs to. It might not be safe.

– Of course it will. Do you want to help me?

– No. I don't like dens.

– Well, I'm going to do it.

Matty starts to forage around him, scraping his searching feet through the leaves, pulling at boughs with his hands. I watch him, not for wanting to watch, but for not wanting to be on my own. He needs a friend, a man, to help with construction. Someone at ease in this raw slice of nature; someone he knows that he can relate to; someone he knows he can trust. Someone like you. Someone exactly like you. But for now, his excitement dampens the need; he seems not to notice the absence of help. He works systematically, trawling the earth, testing the strength of the branches he finds, placing each limb into well-ordered piles, seeking out where he should build.

His gaze rests on a half-fallen tree, collapsed in the neck of a broken stump, like a long central beam, a natural backbone forced from the body of earth. He looks intent; I can hear his thoughts as he plans his basic design.

Now, of a sudden, he fires into movement, dragging at tusks of splintered branch, laying them over the back of the tree, anchoring them in the yielding soil by kicking their ends with his heel. He is building a body from broken bones; bringing that body alive. Now he is adjusting the branches, gauging the firmness of what he has made. Steadily, patiently, he fashions the ribcage; fuelled with desire, fixed in intent, seeming oblivious of all else.

I watch him as he works. This urgent creature, this dogged half-man, this wood-fiend I watch is my son. This thing which tugs at crippled branches, which snaps and cracks their shafts in his hands – this is the boy I brought from London, who I have let loose in the wild.

It's growing cold. In here we are torn from the light and the warmth, from the clarity pervading the sky. Here there are only shades of gloom. Above Matty's careful industry – the cracking of bones, the harshness of breath – I hear the interminable agony, the muffled screech of the wood.

– I think we should go back now. You can finish this later.
– I'm not done yet.
– You can't possibly finish it all today.
– I know. But I need to do more. I'm not ready to leave.
– I want to go. I'm cold.
– Go then. I'll follow you back.
– You can't stay here on your own.
– Why not?
– It's not safe.
– It is. You can see it is. To me it's safe.
– Do you promise you won't go further in? You won't touch anything that looks like a trap? You'll stay here, and come back soon?
– Yes, yes. I'm fine.

There's a sureness about him, a certainty. He seems to know that here he is safe, though he's never been here before. That knowledge instils him with strength. I know I would never come here alone, but I sense that he is secure. I would ask him to lead me out of the wood, but that would reveal the extent of my fear – such fear in the face of his strength. The edge of the wood is so close I can see it.

Through the trunks I can see fierce slices of light; I can see slim patches of field beyond. It doesn't seem to be far. I can get there without him if I steer towards it, if I focus before me, if I leave here now.

– I'm off then. I might go by way of the shop. There are a few things I need to pick up.
– Bye.
– Don't stay long now. Be back in the daylight.
– I will.

I set out, aiming for the slivers of daylight, for the spearing shafts of broken sun. Behind me Matty splinters branches – the sound interspersed with the groan of the wood, drawn together in a chaotic chorus, almost in haunting harmony. I step through the band of bramble and thorn, and now I am pacing the line of the field, striking out for the graveyard.

I walk through the gate, and onto the plain of bodies buried below me. Above, the edifice of the tower surveys the infinite flatness of fields, taller still than the trees. I would like to linger, to read the inscriptions of those who are here – who were loved – but the afternoon is dying around me, the day is sinking and cold. I cross the planted field of tombs and leave by a gate on the farther side which leads towards Wayside House. I enter the shop. Both Margaret and Bill are stood by the counter as though they are waiting for me.

– Sarah! Hello. How are you?
– Fine thanks.
– How's the unpacking coming on?
– It's getting there.
– If you need any help at all we'd be happy to help. Bill's quite good with his hands. Would you like a cup of tea?

– No, thank you. I just need to grab a few things before Matty gets back.

– O. Has he gone away?

– No, not really. We've been exploring.

– Where have you been?

– Here and there. To the wood.

– To the wood? Behind the church?

– Yes.

– What made you go to the wood?

– Well, we sort of ended up there. We walked along the side of the field and there it was.

– Nobody goes to the wood. I don't think I've ever seen anyone there.

– Except for Uriah, Bill.

– Well, of course Uriah. But nobody else.

– What did you do in the wood?

– Not much. We rooted around for a bit. But we're being very careful. We didn't cause harm.

– No, of course not, dear.

– I haven't worked out where it's best to go walking. Martha's told me about a few places, but I'd have to get there by car.

– So you've met Martha already? We thought you had.

– We saw her heading towards the cottage.

– Yes, she came to give me some of her produce. She seems very kind and pleasant.

– Martha, yes. Nice.

– You can walk round here if you like. There's a track in Thorn Field that leads to a copse. And behind Jennings' Land there's a pleasing stretch, too.

– I'm sure there are lots of places to go. I just need to get my bearings first. It's so flat here I can't really get a sense of what's where.

– Yes, it is flat. It's hard to gauge the lie of the land. You really need a bird's eye view.

– Bill, do you think…

– Yes, Margaret.

– Sarah, dear, Bill's one of the church wardens. He's got a key to the tower. Go with him and have a look. You can see everything from up there.

– That would be nice sometime, yes.

– Do it now. It's on your way home. It won't take any time.

– Well, I'd like to, but I need to get back for Matty.

– You'll be able to see him from the top of the tower. You can see the whole wood from there, plain as day.

– Well, I've got my shopping, and…

– Leave it at the bottom of the tower. Go on. Grab whatever food you want, then go with Bill.

I dutifully walk to the churchyard with Bill, leaving my bag of food by the door. Bill thrusts a large iron key in the lock. I shouldn't allow myself to be bullied, though I'm sure their insistence is born out of kindness. As well-intended as their ceaseless questions. Oblivious of how they irritate me; of how shallow they are for what they are; prying into my life. The key crackles as it turns in the lock; a metallic crunch as the bolt snaps through. Bill heaves the frame of the heavy door. I watch him enter, and follow him in.

We are standing in an airless vault, dimly lit by the narrow slit of a single window above. To one side, stone steps curl into a stairway, hugging the walls and leading to darkness. Bill motions to me; we begin our ascent. The steps are narrow, but a wooden railing shields the drop on the inner side. We take three turns round the sides of the tower then reach the thin slice of window. I glimpse at a snatch of the road and the fields, already lying some distance below me.

We turn again, moving steadily upward, losing direction and definition, being trapped and enfolded in night. Now it is pitch, and I can see nothing. I'm guided by only the sound of Bill's breath, by the steady beat of his tread. Even as I'm about to call out, to ask him to stop, there's a thin band of light from another window somewhere farther beyond. We move towards it gradually, clarity bringing confidence the more it grows as we angle upwards, one side of the tower at a time. Again, I slow to glance through the window, seeing a peep of stirring green stretching far below us. Bill is slackening, he paces himself, feeling his way with his hand on the wall. We climb through a patch of further blackness, revealing a dim light deep in its fabric – one which grows to an eery grey each time there's a turn in the stairs.

Now, of a sudden, there's a swathe of light, almost blinding in fury. The tower has opened onto a platform with windows cut on all sides, sheathed from the weather by wooden slats. Above us, a cluster of bells are hung beneath the mechanics of cogs and wheels. I look at Bill, and he grins. There's another staircase here to one side; fragile and narrower, built out of wood. We mount the steps till we meet a trapdoor. Bill reaches up to the bolt. And now there is open sky above us. A huge unbroken and unspoilt sky, spread out to greet us, to drench us with light.

Bill gives me his hand and helps me up. We are standing on the square of the roof, with a waist-high wall on all sides.

I follow Bill close to the edge. Approaching, I sense the dizzying height – the ground far below us which rolls into view, becoming more distant the closer I get. It is giddying surveying the ground. I find myself clutching the top of the wall and holding it tight, not daring quite to look down.

Instead, I look farther into the distance, an empty wind bothering my face. It takes a while to know where I am, to realise the house I'm looking towards is the same as that where I live. The cottage is tucked at the neck of the road, surrounded by sheltering hedge. Opposite, over the single street, a patchwork of fields in early growth are circling Burnt Tree Farm. I follow the fields with my eyes, from the farm to Wayside House and the Serpent, which lie a vertiginous distance down, close to the base of the tower.

Bill is pointing towards the fields, naming each one in turn. Steeple Field, Black Acre, Goddard's Piece, Bath Meadows. I feign an interest. It's the farther side that I want to see – the endless stretch of Road Field. I find myself surprised it has limits, that the whole vast swathe can be seen from up here. It is massive. Bigger by far than all the fields on the southern side combined. But even it has its bounds. At its heart sits the island of Rose House Farm, still partly obscured by the trees. No more than the hint of a roof, of a courtyard, of a cluster of stables and barns.

I follow the lines of Road Field round the tower, switching my gaze to the bend in the road, and then to the end of the planted earth, to the track that leads beyond the graveyard, that dissolves on meeting the wood. The trees seem less dense when viewed from above: their leafless tops like thinning hair, their canopies dormant and idle. I can see beneath their broken skin, almost into their heart. I can see beyond to the farther side. But within, I cannot see Matty. I was expecting I would hear their groans, I would feel their pain when stood above them. I listen through the crystal air, but I cannot hear any noise. From here the wood doesn't threaten or scare me. It doesn't even appear that big. I almost feel disappointed.

Bill interrupts me. He's eager to share his knowledge with me, to point out the country nearby. He rehearses each of the fields once more; he names each house and the people who live there; he tells me that on a clear summer's day you can see the faint band of the sea. But it isn't clear now, and nor is it summer.

The day is diminishing fast. The sheer white sky has grown ugly and dull; it stands an indefinite distance off, faceless and blind to what lies beneath. Behind the uniform banks of cloud, I sense the shapeless sun in decline. I take a final look at the wood, before suggesting we ought to descend while there is still daylight to guide us.

At the bottom of the tower Bill locks the door. He is talking still about the village; enthusing about the land and the houses, and those who dwell here, both living and dead. I pick up my bag and turn to thank him. He shakes my hand robustly. We walk to the gate and there we split ways – he to the shop and I up the road which lays a path to my home.

The day has expired in the shield of cloud by the time I come to the cottage. The pink of its walls glows duller and darker, almost tinged to a crimson. Unlit from inside it feels deserted; as lifeless and still as it felt in the graveyard. A sinking coldness clings to the air; it lies on my limbs and pierces my clothes, and I cannot shrug it away. Incongruously, I hear an ignition as the boiler fires and whirs into motion, fuelling invisible warmth through the rooms, bringing the cottage to life. I walk round the edge of the lower rooms until I'm stood at the side of Road Field. I look at the fading clump of trees that obscure the fortress of Rose House Farm, and beyond it I look to the wood.

I want to see Matty. I want to see a pinprick of life emerge from the trees before they are smothered in the all-encompassing blackness of night. When I stood at the top of the tower, this world seemed so distant, so meagre, so small. It was spread out before me, laid flat like a map; it was tame and absent of form. But here, when stood on this breathing earth, a heavy breeze pressing into my face, a coldness biting into my skin, this land is so visceral. I can smell it; I can even taste it. I can feel it feeling me, drawing me in, clutching me here in its claw. Both fiercesome and full of exuberance. I think you would like it, this savage beauty, this mystery, this solitude. I think, were we given another chance, we could find fulfilment and happiness here. We could be at peace in this place. Almost at peace with ourselves, with each other. In the knowledge that we weren't on our own.

Behind the deadening cloud, I sense twilight come. Huge, bleak, inevitable. The sky sinks closer onto the earth; it exhales and squeezes out all life; it suffocates the air. The tender planted lines of leaf evaporate into the ether; the field dilutes to shapeless shadow, colourless and cruel.

I hear the sound of a door behind me. Matty must have cut through the churchyard; he must have returned via the road. The natural skin of the walls is so thin I can hear him climbing the stairs. Then the sharp, irregular shape of light cast from his window across the lawn. Its singular beam both sheer and intense, deepening the shade of the twilight.

I know he is happy, now he has found a place for himself. Now he has carved out a purpose to be here, to help him move on from the past. As a child, he scarcely has to try. He arrives in a place and he makes it his own. He discovers it, accepts it, and swiftly becomes it. He reaches out and he wraps it around him. The past – that spiteful thing that once was – and the mental masochism that sat on its back, are set aside with no pain. He wasn't the one who decided to come here. He wasn't a part of the tortured process by which that decision was made. That repetitive churning of fact and emotion, that fear for knowing no answer was right. Without that he's free to do as he pleases, accepting this life as it is. He doesn't need to weigh it up, he doesn't need to judge. Not the decision, nor himself, nor the bitter process which led to the present. He just accepts and moves on. I should learn from him. I should learn to judge less and strive to live more, for I fear I will always fall short. I need to cut you out of my life, to amputate you from my mind. I need to be brutal, to sever you from me. Only then will I find something new, will I fill my world as Matty is doing. Only then am I likely to see things afresh. Not in relation to what has passed, but to see them truly for what they are. To pick them up and enjoy.

Here in the garden the imposing cloud has squeezed the life from the earth. A greyness fills the evening's pores; a shallow half-life rears around me, fused confused in a single mass, becoming a blinded entity. I creep between the cottage and hedge, feeling no motion, no up nor down, no balance nor being, no fulcrum, no core. I go in.

I walk through the rooms, drawing the curtains and turning on lights. I want the life-giving warmth of the stove, but I have exhausted the logs. I can hear the thud of dull noises above me. Matty's content to be on his own. I go upstairs to my study. I should set it up as I want it to be. I should write to my contacts, I should over-schedule, crowding my mind and my days with tasks which draw me out of myself.

I sit at the chair. I pick up my box of stationery and start arranging the pens on my desk, placing them into the coiled clay pots that we made when we stayed with your sister in Devon. I adjust the height of my angle-poise lamp, switching it on to make sure the glare doesn't interfere with my screen. I spill the remains of my stationery box into the jaws of a drawer. Then I pause and look at my handiwork.

This isn't moving on. This is building obsessive isolation. A self-indulgent sepulchre where I can bury myself from the world, where I can squander my life away. I have to move on. I must. I would love to snuggle up on the sofa with a blanket, a fire, and a decent book. Perhaps with a generous glass of Baileys. That is what I would like. If things were different. If you were here. But not now; not on my own. And besides, I've run out of logs. I've run out on you.

I leave my study and go downstairs. In the kitchen I scrub the skin of potatoes, skewering them, sprinkling them with some salt. There has to be more than this. There must be a purpose.

– Matty!
– What?
– Matty, I'm going out. I'm going to the pub for an hour. Is that ok?
– What about supper?
– There are baked potatoes in the oven. They'll be ready in an hour. I should be back by then. If you're hungry, help yourself to bread. Is everything all right up there?
– Yea.
– Did you have a nice day? Was it good in the wood?
– Yea.
– Ok, I'm off now. I'll see you in an hour.

Outside, the darkness is thick. There are no stars, and no hint of a moon. A coolness shivers through the hedge; it hangs in the sparce bald air of the street. I should have put on some make-up; I should have brushed my hair. This will be the first judgement I face. At least they will judge me for what I am, not having sight of the past. As I approach the bend in the road, the sheer side of the stern church tower stands tall, printing a deeper shade on the dark. The wood has been extinguished from sight, drowned by the solid weight of the night, as if it no longer exists. I can see light spin from the Serpent's windows. The pub looks peopled and welcoming. It emits an easy murmur of being. There is no escape for me now. No going back.

I stand in front of the blind wooden door, then lift the latch and go in.

I walk into a hallway which splits to both sides. To the right, the glass in the frame is unlit, suggesting an absence of life. To the left, the glazed glass flickers and glows with the pleasing glance of a fire. I push at the door, finding myself in a long low room with an uneven floor, and a fire set deep on the farther wall roasting a tree trunk to cinder. There are clutches of tables grouped together on either side of the fire. Opposite them, a bar is set to serve both this and the room beyond. Around the bar are a scatter of stools; at the end of the room there's a billiard table; beyond it some French doors closed on the night. There's a woman perched on the stool beside me. She's blonde, and she wears her make-up thick. Her red leather skirt is cut to the thigh. She is laughing with a younger man who is sat on the stool to her side. Behind the bar, I can see a man is bent over, busy at work. At the tables, there are two separate couples, hunched in warm conversation.

I absorb it swiftly, conscious the scene about me is ebbing in the time that it takes me to scan the room. Now a silence pervades the pub; all eyes have switched and are trained on me. I make my way to the bar.

Someone is already coming towards me from out of the blur by the fire. It is Bill. He's smiling at me with knowing, in welcome. He escorts me up to the bar, insisting he buys me a drink. The bent back beyond us has straightened and turned. An overweight man, with a harsh square fringe, with weary eyes and a pleasant smile, serves me a half pint of beer. Bill acts as my host, delighted to know me, keen to show he's my friend.

He brokers the introductions. This is Travis Jones, the landlord. Travis apologises. He tells me the pump is not drawing well; he is fixing it with a wrench. He waves the implement in the air, as if to validate the claim. From Travis we move to those on the stools. The woman I learn is his wife, Samantha. The man beside her is Robert Witton, a labourer who works on Jack's farm. The formalities over, a silence speaks as we search for something to say. Travis excuses himself once more and bends down under the bar. He toys with the pipes, which cough their defiance somewhere down by his knees. I mumble some meaningless words at Samantha, but I feel little interest in her response. I feel she wants me to leave. We stumble through pleasantries until they run dry, until Bill invites me back to his table, where Margaret is eagerly waiting.

She smiles. She pulls out the chair beside her, urging me into the seat. The two at the bar slip back into banter; Travis clanks at the pipes from the counter. The pub slides into an easy whisper. Tranquillity is being resumed.

Margaret leans against the table, reaching out for my hand. She wants to know what I thought of the tower, what I think of the village, and of those who I've met. She wants to know what has brought me here; she wants to know who I am. She is forcefully clutching my hand. Holding my fingers possessively, as though she can squeeze a purpose, a meaning, from the pressure applied to my palm.

I steer the talk back onto themselves. I ask how long they have had the shop, and if they were born in the village. My questions are answered in sullen staccato; they are brushed aside for her own. Again and again Margaret fixes on me, as though I must justify who I am, as though my existence has to make sense. I pretend to listen; I deflect where I can; and beyond them I take in the pub.

Samantha looks to be younger than Travis, probably in her late thirties. Her laugh is a cackle; she slaps Robert's shoulder; she leans over the bar when refilling his glass. She seems determined that she must be merry; her voice is unnaturally loud. I can see her laugh, but her eyes don't laugh. She seems to be willing herself to be happy, though that laugh is hollow and forced. I wonder if others can hear it too. I know nothing about her, and yet I feel sorry. Sorry she finds herself here, stuck in Suffolk, with a portly older man with a fringe who is scrabbling around on the floor.

As if on cue, her husband emerges. Travis has tinkered enough with the pipes. He tries the pump and seems satisfied that the beer is now drawing well. He starts polishing the taps with a tablecloth, wiping the counter, lifting the objects, putting them back in their place. He seems to be a nice enough man, content to watch his wife at the bar flirting and pouring out drinks.

Margaret draws my attention away. She demands to know what made me leave London. She wants me to tell her more about you; she wants to know where you are. She would like to be my confidante; for me to let her into my world. I look at Bill, who listens in silence. He appears to collude with his wife. There is something wretched about her enquiry. Something inevitable. But I cannot just get up and leave without danger of alienation. I offer to go and buy the next round for the slender reprieve it affords me.

I stand at the bar by Samantha's side, though she seems engrossed in her own private world and doesn't think to look round.

— Travis, hi. Could I get another half pint, and two glasses of red wine?
— Sure you can. This is Adnams, Suffolk's finest ale.
— It's very nice. How's your pump?
— Fixed. Sorry about that. Bit rude.
— I love your fire. It's so warming.
— It's good on a winter's day. Yes. A trunk can last a whole evening.
— Where do you get it from? The wood?
— That's right. I can't go there myself, of course. The wood sort of belongs to Uriah. It's not really his, but he's made it his. He cuts down trees and makes logs for the village. It's more of a pastime for him. I get him to cut mine big, so they stretch right across the whole grate.
— Can you lift them? They're huge.
— I sort of roll them, like barrels. Being a barman, you kind of get used to large objects. It's the only exercise I get. That's enough about logs, anyway. How are you getting on with the interrogation?
— The what?

– Bill and Margaret. Have they sucked you dry of your soul yet?

– Well, it's… I wasn't quite expecting it to be…

– It's supposed to be the barman's job. I come a very poor second to them. I won't even try it on you. It's nice to have new people in the village. A bit of new blood. We should be encouraging it, not scaring it away. It's nice having someone younger, too.

– Now you are trying it on!

– I'm not. Well maybe I am. I'm a Londoner too.

– Where from?

– Greenwich. Near Blackheath Royal Standard.

– Ha.

– Why do you laugh? Do you know it?

– Not at all. It's just it seems so far away, that's all. Even after a couple of days. Civilization. People. I don't mean…

– No, I know what you mean. I feel it too. Sometimes I wonder what I'm doing up here.

– What are you doing up here?

– I don't know. Maybe something like you. Trying another way.

The door opens. I know it more by the coldness which clings to my shoulder than by the sound of the hinge. A man in his forties walks in. He is large, with a thick neck, a bullet-like head; he has short-cropped hair, and narrow eyes. He places his elbows on the counter, and stares at space in front of him. There is mud beneath his fingernails; his hands are scratched and scarred by the soil. Travis breaks off and turns towards him; he fills an old pewter jug with beer without the need to be asked. The man takes a long slow draught. A trickle of beer steals down the pot; it drips from its side and onto his stubble.

– This is Uriah.

Uriah straightens and looks at me. His eyes are void of any expression, but I feel his gaze fixed firm upon me, working slowly down my body and back again to my face. I expect him to speak, but there aren't any words. I feel the uneasiness of the silence; I feel the need for it to be filled.

– Uriah. That's a curious name.
– Is it? It's familiar here.
– Yes, I'm sure.
– It's been in the family for generations. The same as the land.
– Really.
– There've been Uriah Pooleys in Nettlesden since the village was founded. We've owned and farmed the land round here since the mediaeval times.
– I've recently moved into Mill House Cottages. I've seen your farm across the field. I've seen someone standing there in the courtyard.
– I doubt it.
– What's it like living in the middle of a field?
– It's where I'm supposed to be. The only place I could ever be. The land's mine; it belongs to me. The land, the farm, the Pooleys. It's all the same thing.

Uriah turns away from me; his last sentence is said to the counter. He comes to a close, and stares at the bar. I can think of nothing more to say. There is nothing more to be said. I look at Travis in search of a clue. He raises his eyebrows fractionally, as if telling me that's all I will get.

– I should get back to the others with these drinks. It's nice to meet you, Uriah.

There is no response from Uriah, no turn of the head. Only a slight smile from Travis. I pick up the wine and what's left of my drink, then go back to Margaret and Bill.

Here by the fire it is warm; their faces are red with the heat. I can see from their eyes that they have been watching; I know they have heard every word. I feel they are urgent to speak to me more, to hunch in whisper before me.

– So, you've met Uriah.
– Yes.
– He lives at Rose House Farm.
– Yes, I know.
– He didn't always live there. He was born in Burnt Tree Farm, on the other side of the road.
–
– Did he say that Road Field belonged to him?
– Yes.
– Well, that's not quite right. It may be his now, but it wasn't always. Road Field didn't belong to the Pooleys. Uriah got it when he married Laura. The Sheldrakes used to farm that land.
– I thought his wife was called Joyce.
– That's his second wife. Laura Sheldrake was his first. She disappeared. That was a long time ago.

They look at me conspiratorially, their faces close, their voices low. They are savouring this to the full. They are stretching it out, this knowledge of theirs, this hold they have over me. Their words suggest a secrecy, a mystery that would draw me in, that would draw me away from myself.

– Goodness, I've just realised the time. I left Matty looking after the baked potatoes. I expect they'll be hollow by now. I really should leave.

I get up swiftly. They urge me to stay, but I've put on my coat; I've stepped back from the table and am shaking their hands. Samantha and Robert are still by the counter, though they don't look up as I pass. Uriah is staring through the bar into the darkened room beyond, his elbows seemingly part of the wood. I nod to Travis on reaching the door; he watches me into the cold. And now I'm outside, I am on my own, stood on the road by the church.

The change in temperature shocks me. The air cuts through my clothes to my skin despite the absence of wind. I walk up the slope beside Steeple Field, and round the bend in the road. There's something different about tonight. I look up to see what it is. Trails of cloud float swift and low beneath a clear arching sky. And in the nothingness beyond there's an endless scatter of stars. So keen, so bright. And there are so many. Here, in the absence of light from the ground, they illuminate the moonless night. They cast a shadow, the spectre of shadow, on the featureless fields below. Once more, the sky seems unwatchable. Now though, the trifling patterns of weather no longer bother our atmosphere. Instead, I see into the infinite distance, into the yawning soul of space. Limitless. Watchful. Serene. It is so, so beautiful; so vast. I feel the urge to cry. We are so small, so incidental. Why do we hurt so much when we are so small?

As I come up the incline of the road I am met by a cooling breeze. I feel it brushing my cheeks and cleansing my pores, bringing a freshness and a renewal. I have reached the cottage, and now the door. Inside, the lights are all on. I can feel its warmth. I can smell the crispness of baked potatoes. I go in.

~

Give me the strength to be reborn; give me the strength to start anew. Sow me deep in this plentiful soil and give me the space to grow. Let me put down my roots in this soil; here let me fashion my home. Protect me if I fall by the wayside. Don't make me prey to the creatures around me; don't let me wither away. Let me find a new life and live. Let me ripen and reach fulfilment. That is the reason I left. That is the hope I have come in search of: the promise I want to be mine. Let me prove I was right to leave you. Let me prove I can live without you. Let me prove it to you and to Matty. Let me prove it to me. That I am happier on my own. That I am better for being without you. That I don't need to depend on you. Now I have found myself in good ground, give me the strength to grow.

*And he spake many things unto them in parables, saying, Behold, a sower went forth to sow;*

*And when he sowed, some seeds fell by the wayside, and the fowls came and devoured them up:*

*Some fell upon stony places, where they had not much earth: and forthwith they sprung up, because they had no deepness of earth:*

*And when the sun was up, they were scorched; and because they had no root, they withered away.*

*And some fell among thorns; and the thorns sprung up, and choked them:*

*But other fell into good ground, and brought forth fruit, some an hundredfold, some sixtyfold, some thirtyfold.*

*Who hath ears to hear, let him hear.*

Jack's voice is deep and resonant. His manner assured. He comes to a close and stands at the lectern, looking out at the congregation. He picks up the paper and folds it in quarters, placing it back in his pocket. He's tall and thin, with silver-grey hair, cleanly parted one side. He wears a tweed jacket and a plain green tie. He walks with care, his head held high, towards the front pew where Martha is waiting. He stoops and sits beside her. Martha's eyes are fixed before her, but I see her stretch her hand to take his. A squeeze of approval; a faint, tight twitch of a smile.

The vicar returns from his quiet corner; he's wrestling the service from Jack. His voice is absorbed by this hollow chamber, this cavern lit by dim natural beams which emerge from the bodies of three distant saints trapped in the stained-glass over the cross. The walls of the church are sulky white, stretching far to a hammer-beam roof, its detail obscured, its struts like stalactites, high in the shadowy vault.

In front of me Jack and Martha are kneeling. Their devotion is impressed in their posture: in their rigid heads, in their sealed eyes. Their bodies express a penitence, a servitude for the whole of their lifetime. These people who live and die by the earth. Who toil and plough and sow without question, believing their harvest to be God's bounty, believing their grain His blessing to Man. As with generations of Pooleys before them, they are kneeling here in this very same pew, sternly humble, stung by a pride which hangs over them, stout as a shield.

In the front pew opposite sits Uriah, stone-faced and staring blindly before him, through the altar and the marble frieze stamped on the farther wall. His chest is squeezed in a fierce-pressed shirt, his thick neck thrust through its stubborn collar, muscular and raw. His body is frozen as though in denial. He mouths the words, but he doesn't pray. Throughout the service he doesn't kneel.

On his farther side, Joyce sits and twitches. A woman with awkward eyes and hands – always exploring, endlessly restless – her fingers caught in a constant motion: clasping her elbows, stroking the tweed of her shapeless, colourless skirt. I sense her wanting to turn towards me, to look at me, to meet my eyes.

Uriah places a hand on her wrist, gripping her firmly, letting his clasp sink its strict print in her skin. Her body quietens; her movement slows. She retreats back into herself, she calms, becoming as silent as stone.

Matty yawns; he fidgets beside me. He doesn't want to be in church; he can't feign devotion like me. He's not aware how important it is to show humility to the village by humbling himself to their God. All that he wants is to run to the wood, to feel the sharp air full in his face, to hear the creak of the trees. He wants to scratch beneath its skin, to tear at the scrub which clothes its body, to stare at the innards within. To explore the darkness locked in its depths, to dig through its deeps and to find.

It is dark here, too, in this church. But this is a different hue of darkness. A deadened darkness, unbroken by movement, breached by the faintest shiver of noise. There is nothing to find beneath its rafters; no more than demise, a dull suppression, a contrition for being alive. These people, this service, this place is so cold. As bitterly cold as their lives. This village, this country, these fields all around us – exposed to the wild, and so cold.

Martha retraces her steps to her pew, having received her Communion. For an instant, I see her glancing at me, breaking her deferential trance, projecting approval I've chosen to join them, that I am a part of their congregation. She sits on the bench in front of me, her body upright, her brown tweed jacket just inches away from my hand.

I rise, feeling self-conscious for knowing the worshippers have turned from their God and are focused instead upon me. They've paused their prayers and their private entreaties to undress my life with their eyes. They are wondering why I am here on my own. They are wondering why I have come. And, trapped in the very same pattern of thought, their speculation turns towards you: wondering who and where you are, and why it is you're not here. I might ask the same question myself. Where are you, now, at this very moment? What are you doing right now? You who were never at peace in a church. You who hated to pray.

I stand in the transept, here, on my own. This is no solace, no sanctuary. Matty has chosen not to join me. He will not come to the front with me. Not for a blessing, not for salvation, not to deflect this attention.

I blindly step towards the chancel. I kneel, I receive, I return. In returning, I see a spectre of faces swallowed up in the dusk of the daylight, trapped in these grey stone walls.

The service ends. Jack and Martha file after the vicar. Next, it's Uriah, still clutched onto Joyce, still quietening her with the hold of his hand, shielding her with the bulk of his frame. Then Bill and Margaret turn and walk out. Now it is Matty and me. We are the last to depart. To escape the church; to abandon it; leaving it like a broken vessel, destitute and forsaken.

Outside, we come together again. The day is bright and broad beneath a scintillating sky. A sleek breeze ripples the twisted grass sunk in the hollows between the graves. Matty pulls at my arm. He wants to go home and put on his boots, to cut round the field and enter the wood. That is what we agreed. Enviously, I watch as he runs away up the road, away from the church and all that is here, shedding its grasp as he goes.

– Sarah, I'd like you to meet my husband, Jack.
– Hello.
– I'm pleased to meet you. I'm pleased you are able to join us.
– Thank you.
– We're a small village. A small congregation. The church is at Nettlesden's heart. It's important we come together.
– Of course. It was a very nice service. I thought you read very well.
– Jack reads the lesson each week. He chooses the text, then Colin Inchmore builds his sermon around it.
– You must know the Bible terribly well.
– The Bible is our handbook. It teaches us how to live our lives. When to plant and when to harvest. When to work and when to rest. How to behave to our fellow men. How to give thanks to our Lord.
– Yes, I suppose it does. I'm not really that well-acquainted.
– Is your son confirmed?
– He's baptised.
– I'm not talking of baptism. I asked if he was confirmed. I expect Colin Inchmore can grant him a blessing until such time as he is confirmed. And then he can fully take part in the service. In due course, he'll be able to receive Communion. I shall speak to Colin about it.

– You really needn't.

– It's important we honour tradition and the faith of our fathers. I'm pleased to make your acquaintance. Excuse me.

– Goodbye.

– You shouldn't mind Jack. He's a bit old school, but he has a good heart.

– I'm sure.

– I'm glad you were able to come. It's sad there're so few of us here. They are threatening to amalgamate our service with St. Giles' in Marshfield. Then they would shut these doors for good. An active church is the heart of a village. Without it, it would lose its soul. Closing the church would destroy us. It would destroy Jack. That's why he's so keen, as a God-fearing man. I hope you will come every week.

– I will try, yes.

– If you're not a part of the church, you are not a part of the village. That's not a threat; that's just the way that it is. Now I should go. I should be with him now.

– Yes. O, Martha, thank you for the apple pie. And thanks for the Christmas rose too.

– The Christmas rose?

– The bunch of pretty Christmas rose you brought me. Was it from your garden?

– I'm afraid I don't follow you.

– I found some Christmas rose by my door.

– That wasn't from me. That must have come from Joyce.

– From Joyce? I haven't met Joyce. I doubt that she even knows me.

– Nevertheless, it sounds like Joyce. And I have no doubt that she knows you. Even if you haven't yet met. Believe me. Now I should go.

– Goodbye.

Martha moves towards her husband, who is stooped in sober conversation with Colin Inchmore, the vicar. She stands respectfully to one side, a hand on the lifeless strands of grey hair that are fretted and worried by wind.

I search out Joyce with my eyes. I would like to meet her, to thank her in person, to find out the sort of person she is when not in the clutch of Uriah. But she isn't here, and nor is he. Instead, there is only Bill and Margaret, grinning at me despite the cold, rubbing their hands and braving the wind in the hope of learning my secrets. I wish them good day. I explain that Matty has gone on ahead and I need to catch up with him.

I walk through the shivering uncut grass which creeps around the heads of the tombs till I reach the gate and am down on the lane. A hundred yards in front of me, Uriah is ushering Joyce up the road, then turning into the track that leads across the field to their farm. She arches her back, she raises her head, as though she is seeking me out. But before she is able to meet with my eyes, she is steered down the track; she is swallowed by the fringe of the hedge. By the time I reach the head of their track, the two grey shapes have blurred into one; they are melting into the indistinct island, dissolving into the distance.

I walk home and shove at the door. Matty's boots have gone from the hall; there are breadcrumbs scattered over the table; there's a dirty plate in the sink. I call his name expectantly, filling the cottage with sound if not presence, deluding myself that he's waiting for me.

Outside, I stand at the edge of the field, feeling the stern wind puncture my ear and scatter my hair in my face. Perhaps I will see him from here.

Beyond the thicket of Rose House Farm, the wood stands idle and still. There is no movement within the trees despite the spoil of the wind. No sound. No sign of Matty. The wood has engulfed him, absorbing him whole. And he within its living tissue, tearing at boughs with his hands.

I return inside; I go into the kitchen. It is windless here, but still cold. Colder still for being so still, so drained of life and so vacant. I crave a warmth to steal through my skin, to thaw my soul, to wrap me in its embrace.

I empty a can of soup in a pan; I cut slices of bread to make toast.

I need warmth. I walk to the room at the back of the house and stare at the wood-burning stove. If only I had an armful of logs. The coldness clasps its fingers around me, piercing me, turning my limbs to stone. I could petrify here, I could fuse to the floor, as nature conspires to erode my being. I hear the toast pop up in the kitchen. I tug my feet from atrophy and stumble back towards its promise, turning on lights on the way. I spread butter thick; I spill soup in a bowl. There's no need to worry about my weight, here where the living is good. My lungs feel clean; my skin is taut; my muscles hum with the sting of use.

I help myself to more soup, more toast. Then I mount the stairs and enter my room, pulling on some old clothes. I look at the face in the mirror. This is no place for vanity. Here I can be myself. I remove my nail varnish and trim my nails. I wipe the lipstick from my mouth. This is me. This is how you liked me best. As the person I am. With no artifice. With a skin that smells and feels like skin, in all its imperfection. This is what I didn't give you – not as often as you wanted – because I needed to be something else.

Something else that I wasn't. And that was more important then. Though now it has lost its importance. Now I can start again. I can be the image I see before me. The person I am. I haven't seen this for a long, long time. I have hidden from it; I have sought to disguise it. I have almost forgotten what it looked like. I have almost forgotten who it was.

Without make-up the day seems colder; the air yet closer about me. It feels inviting too. Wind flurries about my unspoilt face, prickling me with its sharp-soft breath. The vacant sky is bone-white and brittle; grey wisps of cloud blow over the field. The seedlings stretch at their fragile stems, flapping their leaves as if in flight, dancing green and silver-grey. A living carpet, a rippling sea, throbbing with urgent new life. I walk beside it, buoyed by the wind, kicking my feet through the clutching grass, till I come to the track that leads towards the ghost of Rose House Farm.

The track is a mixture of shingle and stone, of surly pools of concrete and brick. It is dented and pockmarked, with crusty holes cradling stubborn pockets of rain. It runs straight – straight from the road through the field – and is consumed in a conspiracy of trees.

As I round Six Bells the wind rushes at me, howling and scratching my cheek. Chips of stone are kicked out by my feet and clatter into the soil. I feel exposed on this endless plain, flanked by wings of whirring seed, having nowhere to hide. I feel almost nauseous too, for the furious motion of these frantic leaves, struggling as they are tasked by the wind, as if they would break from their delicate roots. Above their sound I can hear my own – each step, each breath – as it smacks on the air. And deeper still, I can feel the throb, the surly beat of my heart.

I look up, sensing someone is watching. Fragments of farm and barn peer out from behind a clutter of trees. In the courtyard, brushed by the movement of shadow, I see an outline, a body perhaps. I raise my hand, and wave.

The shadow shifts in shape; it unfolds. The island of farm is ever-changing, appearing a solid entity then splintering away from my sight. Neither real nor unreal, it's an earthy illusion, a sparkling spectre, squat in the heart of a field.

I am coming close to the farm. The trees are unclothed. They brush against the sky with low murmur, scratching their talons against the barns. The closing courtyard seems barren of life; the whispering shadows I thought were a person stand quivering against the side of the house. The crunch of my feet on the stones is loud above the slender slice of the wind.

Surely one of the people who live here has heard me. Someone will come out and greet me.

I stand in the middle of the yard, surrounded by barns and watchful trees, with the faceless house square before me. The sliver of track is dissolving behind me over an infinite chasm of field. I had thought there would be the telltale tendrils of climbing roses against the walls, their skeletal fingers gnarled and dormant, awaiting the season to bud. But there are none.

I walk towards the waiting porch. There's no knocker, no sign of a bell. I tentatively rap the door with my knuckles, hearing the hopelessness of my efforts mocked by the blank wooden frame. I curl my fingers into a fist and drum at the bald slab of wood. The door resists me, dulling the noise, scorching my firmly clenched hand.

I step back to look at the house. There seems to be nobody here, though I saw them return from the morning's service. I suppose they might be resting upstairs; they might have gone to lunch with Martha; or perhaps they have gone for a drive to the sea. Each image I know is a lie. They are here. I know it. I feel it inside me. This is where they must be.

I skirt a bay tree and peer through a window. There's no light from within; no sense of movement. Bones of furniture jut out at angles, and they are all I can see. I creep a fraction closer still, my feet in the flowerbed, my breath on the pane, the shivering glass on my forehead.

– What do you want?

It is Uriah. I stand up swiftly and turn, taking a pace away from the window, hoping he hasn't been watching me.

Uriah stands by the doors of a barn, with folded arms and a steady gaze, as if he has been there a while. He doesn't speak, he just stares. He waits for me to come to him across the void of his yard. My face is blistered by the wind, my steps uncertain the closer I come. I feel myself stripped by his gaze. If the track were nearer, I could walk away, I could make some excuse to depart. Instead, I find I am drawn towards him, till I'm standing here in the dusk of his shadow, the earth from his flowerbed fresh on my boots.

Uriah's cropped head is raw and red; he is wearing a shirt with the sleeves rolled high; he seems impervious to the cold. He looks at me impassively, his eyes surveying my face and my shoulders; lowering his gaze to my breasts and my belly; now back again to my face. I feel powerless. Powerless to speak, powerless to resist, powerless beneath the fix of those eyes.

– I'm sorry to bother you.

– What do you want?

– I was wondering… I've been told that you have wood… logs for the fire… you cut them for people…

– What of it?

– I've got a wood burning stove in my cottage, but I'm out of logs. I was hoping I could get some from you.

Once more his eyes drift down from my face, surveying my body casually, lazily. Though without any interest, without desire. Perhaps he didn't hear what I said; perhaps there's no need to reply. He doesn't move from where he stands, though he isn't waiting for me. He seems not to feel the monotonous wind slicing through this desolate farm, quarantined from the rest of the village, distanced as though it's infected.

– I would buy them from you, of course.

– It's Sunday.

– Yes.

– The seventh day. The Lord's Day.

– We could arrange for later in the week. Or if it's inconvenient, I can go to the wood myself.

– The wood is mine. I do all the logging for the village.

– Yes, they told me.

– To go there is trespass. Keep away from it.

– I don't need much. Enough to see me through to the summer. I live at Mill House Cottages. It's over there.

I am pointing absurdly towards the barn, drawing an imaginary line in the air, across the field to my home. Of course he knows where I live. He's looking through me, not thinking to speak. He's so close; his eyes as though dead.

There is nothing more to be said.

I look up and look at him, just for an instant, as I mumble a feeble goodbye. In return, his eyes bore into my body – through my skin and into my flesh – till I feel the shame of being ravaged; I feel defenceless, impotent.

I turn and walk towards the track which hurries away from the farm, feeling his eyes upon me still as he stands unmoved in the yard. To my side, a dormant willow tree clatters its branches, like long dry fingers, against the walls of a barn. Beyond it, the scrub on the verge of the field is shocked into life. As if it also has eyes.

I walk swiftly down the length of the track, wanting to build a sweat against the creeping cold which surrounds me. I feel the eyes upon my neck, as if distance is unable to shield me.

Back on the road I am tempted to run, to return to the cottage, to hide. This is absurd; it is foolishness. Instead, I turn down the slope of the road till I reach the bend where the graveyard waits for the weary. Then I take the path that leads to the wood.

He cannot do this to me; I mustn't allow it. I mustn't let him intimidate me. Yet the way he stares, and how he stares, this I am helpless against. It has been so long since a man has shown interest; so long since a man has looked at me; so long since I feel I've been seen. I think I was blind to the look of others. Or perhaps I only had eyes for you. Such things are irretrievably lost; so distant it seems they never existed. I know that Travis looks at me too, and when he looks, I feel the warmth of a man with whom I could share. I can imagine him being affectionate. Thinking of me and doing things with me. Wanting to make me feel special. What would you make of that? Would you be happy for me if I told you? Or would you be jealous, or full of regret?

Perhaps you don't give a damn. Though it's one thing to walk away from you; it's another to return with a different man. And, were I to do so, what then? I cannot picture your face in response. Do you think I don't dare to see your response; or don't dare for the pain it would cause you?

Close to the wood I come to a large pile of logs. I guess Uriah will take mine from here. Perhaps, at some time in the future. There again, he may not, for we agreed nothing. Nothing seems certain with him. He's a man made of stone in a lifeless house in an empty field with a distant wife.

Where was Joyce just now? Was she hiding?

There's a cry, an urgent flapping of wings. In front of me is a rusty cage, stamped in the earth at the fringe of the wood. Inside the cage there's a bird. It is grey, its wings flecked downy-brown, its russet head stretched urgently, its beak attacking the bars. I wonder who has laid this trap, and what would induce them to lay it. I wonder why they felt the need to trap such innocence in a snare. The creature squawks demented fear the closer I come to its gaol. It flutters its useless wings in distress, vainly attempting to fly.

I come up close. So close I can see the shocks of panic distorting its movement, blinding its eyes. It scrabbles in its rigid tomb, thrashing its wings, its neck, its head, against the unrelenting bars. It screams at me accusingly, an agony of short shrill shrieks. Bewailing its freedom with piercing cries that crease the wind, that stab at my brain.

I put out my hand and clutch at the bars. The frame is heavy; it's sunk in the earth. As I pull at its base, the fevered bird pecks at me with its beak. It nips the tip of my thumb.

I step back, thrusting the stub of my thumb in my arm in an effort to deaden the pain. Stupid bird. I retreat to the path, two paces away. It is quieter now I am not so close; its flapping is weaker, its cries less urgent. It seems it is willing to die.

I hurry on to Matty's entrance, and creep inside the shade of the wood, thankful to hear the bird's lament blocked out by the trees and filtered away until it is lost to my ear. Now there is only the sound of the boughs weeping on meeting the whispering wind, yawning and aching and coming alive. I stop on a patch of leaves by the fringe, listening out for the splinter of sticks, the cracking of timber that leads to my son.

No sound.

I wish I remembered which way we went when he started building his den. In every direction I see a track, but none is a path laid to guide me. I walk forward slowly, hearing a crusty shuffle of leaves, a crackle of twigs beneath my boot. Branches above me shiver to life, their buds like opening eyes. I hear the frightened wings of a pigeon, clapping a startled escape. Now I am stood on a damp bed of moss, softer and moister than sinking sand.

I should follow my footsteps back to the field. Matty will come when he's ready. I search for the path that I have just taken, but the tangling brush has woven around me; the track which I took only moments ago is lost in a forest of scrub. Yet over its head, on every side, is the hint of escape, the sliver of day, teasing between the dry grating trunks, enticing me to walk on. I wade towards a splinter of light, expecting the trees to fall away, expecting the silver-speckled earth of a planted field to appear.

I find myself in a partial clearing, snarled still deeper within the trees. All about me the wood is moaning, too overwhelmed by the pain to cry. It is closing about me, drawing me in. Now I am here at its heart. I look down at the ground. Scattered amongst the decay of the leaves are bright red plastic cartridges discharged from the barrels of a gun. This is the place where Uriah must stand as he blasts at birds in the branches above. Here, in this wood that winces its freedom, this is where he shoots and snares. Here, in this guarded and creaking wood, where Matty and I are both trapped. It is here he captures his prey.

I turn around repeatedly, looking for a way out. The trunks blur into a blinded confusion, the noise of the leaves beneath my feet like the constant breaking of waves. I see nothing before me; but, as I turn, I sense that someone is watching. If I turn and turn again, once more, perhaps they will vanish and wipe away. But I dare not; I am frightened to fall. I stop, giddy and panting for breath. The surrounding trees are slowed into focus, gliding back to motionless bodies stretching their brittle bones to the light.

It is Matty. He's standing a few paces farther off, a quizzical look on his face. I explain that I have been looking for him, I have come to find him, but I've lost my way. The more I justify my purpose the more helpless I know that I sound. But he wants no apology. He only wants to be my guide, to lead me through towards his den, to show me what he has made. I follow him gladly. He knows this wood; he feels his way through; to him its cries are a welcome sound.

Matty has stopped and is pointing before him. I follow his hand with my eyes. There, through a tumble of saplings and bush, I can make out a wall of broken branches stretching over a splintered trunk. He motions me closer, and now I can see there are several rooms to his den, each with a thatched roof bound up in ivy, with walls that are plastered with moss. He smiles, his face is a rush of excitement, flushed with exertion and speckled with soil. He is willing me on to inspect the inside, bidding me round to the front.

At the entrance the leaves have been scraped away to reveal the rich brown earth of the floor. It is dark within, almost pitch. He urges me in, but I am reluctant. I don't want to find myself trapped underground, having no means to escape. Instead, I tell him to go in himself, and he slithers into its depths.

I can hear him creeping from room to room, explaining the workings within. His voice is fierce with boyish pride for having built this living structure from the bones of the wood strung together with twine. He emerges into the open once more, wiping earth from his palms.

He stands beside me, fired with a passion, describing what will come next. He talks of tunnels and walkways and ramparts. Of towers that stretch to the sky. This is a world he can shape for himself, where he is master and king. I'm happy for him that he can be happy, busy with both his mind and his hands. But this is far from a paradise. This is a furtive growth of trees where Uriah comes to shoot and to snare. I suggest it's time that we leave.

Matty doesn't want to come home, but he has no grounds to resist, knowing that he can return when he wants. He leads me away from the stealth of the trees, sure-footed, straight, and with measured tread. We creep through the thorn and around the wood, marching in silence along the blank road till we're facing the cottage once more.

There's a mass of logs tumbled into a pile, blocking the car from the road. Uriah has chosen to work on a Sunday, dumping so many stumps of wood that he's formed a natural barricade, deliberately sealing us in.

I feel despair well up within me, but Matty construes it a challenge. He brushes past me, excited and eager, wanting to show his prowess. He runs through the arch to the back of the house; he seems to melt into the hedge. For precious seconds he's lost in its folds, then his head reappears – he is coming towards me – he is wheeling a barrow before him.

He tosses clutches of logs in its belly, feeding its bowels till it's full. Then he shunts the barrow towards the lean-to which has sawdust lining its floor.

I unfasten the padlock and pull the door wide. Matty raises the barrow's handles, scattering logs on the floor. We hear them land with a roar. Again and again, he journeys between Uriah's mound and that of his own – one steadily growing as the other depletes – until the driveway is clear. I help him, plucking up logs to his side, intrigued by his strength, his adroitness, his speed.

Matty tips the last load in the mouth of the lean-to, then he lets the barrow fall from his fists. Sweat and dirt and fragments of bark stick to his face and cling to his arms. I feel a sense of fulfilment in him. Like this he is still a part of the wood: though not within it, a part of it still.

We pause. The pile is so large that it blocks all access. Matty climbs up its broken back, but the logs give way beneath his feet, and his legs are buried up to his knees. He pulls himself free. We walk back round to the front of the house and enter the shed from the inner door.

In the partial light of the tired afternoon, Matty inspects the vacant floor, feeling the screed with his hands. He has fallen naturally into this role; he instinctively knows what to do. He, who has seldom been in the country, has become the woodsman, the forester. I stand and watch as he works. Who did he learn these strange skills from, not having been here before? Who was the person who taught him this? Was it you who tutored him in the art? It must have been. I wonder when you found the chance. Some time, perhaps, when my back was turned. When you were alone; when I wasn't watching. It was a conscious act of defiance by you, knowing that I was elsewhere. Though the shame of it now is here in the showing. I missed a stage of his growing up; I missed a moment of parenthood. I missed a chance of watching you both – watching you both as father and son – working together and forging a bond.

Matty crouches, signalling to me to pass him a first batch of logs. I do so, stripping the top of the pile. One by one he assesses their shape, laying their bodies flat on the floor. One by one he builds a base. Mechanically, I pass him more logs – watching the line becoming a platform, the platform becoming a wall. It's a thing of beauty, strong and secure. Each log is leaning in on the others, supporting them and forming a buttress, balanced and perfectly poised.

I leave the last of the logs to Matty and return to the house to lay the stove. I call him through, and he enters the room, cradling logs like a child in his arms. I light the fire and together we watch – watching the sleek flames eating the paper, watching them blacken the bark of the wood, watching the sap on the blistered logs as it bubbles and turns into vapour. As the tongues of flame lick the walls of the stove, as the fire breathes its heat through the room.

For a while, Matty watches, and then he walks off. I can hear him moving about upstairs. For him the pleasure has been in the task of working the wood with his hands, of sorting the logs and building a structure, of seeing that structure complete. Once in the stove the logs lose their interest; they are lifeless, they are here to be burned. He feels no warmth and no joy in this room. For him there is only the loss.

I return to the lean-to once more, flicking the switch to blind the room with the artificial beam of a light. I inspect the wall Matty's made. It's a perfect assembly of rough-cut logs; a tribute he's built to the trees.

Outside, beyond the lean-to wall, I can hear their kin as they catch in the wind, as they twist and shiver, as they ride out the dusk. Beyond this dull room a turmoil of life is beating against the cottage's walls. This house which is built from the bones of the earth, from the trees and the mud and the reeds. Strands of grass steal into the room, sneaking beneath the outer door; creepers push between bricks in the floor; ivy twists through a crack in the window; branches clatter against the walls. The living world is imposing upon us; it's demanding an entrance into our home.

~

Matty blows into his hands. He shuffles his feet while we wait. He is cold, but more than the creep of the cold, I can sense that he is uneasy. He doesn't like standing on the road with his mother: a fourteen-year-old boy who is almost her height. He wants to send me away. He would like to, but he doesn't complain. He knows in a few minutes he will be free.

I watch him from the crook of my eye. He is wearing a clean pair of trousers, a sweater, a brand-new blazer, a tie. He looks so unlike the woodsman now. He toys with the leather straps of his satchel, buckling and unbuckling them needlessly. We have come out early so as not to be missed, and now we stand by the kerb. A cold wind sweeps down the road from Marshfield, glancing against the bushes and grass, blowing irregular gusts at our backs. Over the fields in front of us, Burnt Tree Farm stands sheltered by trees, staring out from lidless eyes, dwarfed by the silos behind it.

Matty turns and faces the church, listening intently against the wind. And now I can hear it too. The strain of an engine approaching the slope, the swish of wet tyres on the glistening road.

As the bus approaches I put out an arm. I sense Matty wince with the shame. He would prefer it if I'd left him alone. He fears I will kiss him, or try to hug him, or reach out and tidy his hair.

The bus glides to a halt. Matty sprints off to open the door, relieved to escape from my charge. He glances towards me, and I wave goodbye. Then the door closes in, and Matty's entombed. With a metallic clunk of changing gears, the bus grinds forwards and lurches away, picking up speed as it heads towards Marshfield, leaving the hint of a straining engine dulling the grey morning air.

I stare after the bus, long after it's gone. Even kindergarten wasn't like this. Not even that very first day. Then, at least, I walked Matty there; I saw his teachers, his bright-coloured classroom; I knew he was there; he was safe. Now he's taken away by a bus; he has gone. Gone, like he's leaving for good. Like part of my body has been severed from me.

Like part of my life has been lifted away. You would be so proud if you saw him now. And you would feel so abandoned too. You would feel so alone. Like this.

In the kitchen I put on the kettle for tea. The element braces itself and breathes, hissing defiantly into the room. I look around me as it struggles to boil, at dormant objects exposed to the scorn of the cold uncoloured light of day. It is going to be like this every morning: a constant parting, a continual absence. A losing and a losing and a losing of my son, till he is torn from me. I want to follow his bus; I want to drive to his school; I want to see him, to watch through the windows. I want to know he is safe. I want to tell him I love him, I love him. That my love for him is all I have. There is nothing else besides. Would it be such tremendous weakness to do that? Knowing how much he would hate me for doing it. Knowing he wouldn't know why I'm there.

I'm so close to walking across the lawn and getting into the car. I feel an urge to be physically sick. An urge that grips me with loathing and fear. With something I cannot contain. We are not supposed to be alone. We are not built that way. I know you would understand what I feel. You, who are living a loneliness now as equal and dreadful as mine. A loneliness that is perhaps worse. With busy days and barren nights; a crowded office, a sepulchral home.

Our home. What do those walls feel like now? Does it seem a home to you still? That place where you know yourself alone – day after day after day alone – with nothing more but the same? With nothing to counter the realisation; with nothing to lessen the pain. I expect you are staying later at work. I can see you standing alone in the rain, awaiting a train with a jostle of strangers. I can see you walking along our street, glancing towards the shuttered windows as you put the key in the lock. Can't you see the decision to leave you was kindness? I can see you hanging your coat in the hall; I can see you picking up leaflets and letters; I can see your hand as it feels for the light; I can see you searching the fridge. Of course separation is not without pain. The hurt from such a sudden amputation, the horror for finding yourself on your own. And then, in the darkness, in the depths of one's being, it cannot be so grave an admission to say there are times when perhaps I might miss you – knowing you're no longer here as you were – a shelter, a companion, a friend. All of us hurt for being alone; trapped in our own different realms. We have to believe it was right.

I stand on the step by the door. The sky is drained; the air hangs limp; the slightest of breezes toys with the hedge. A coldness sucks at my cheek. Dew clings fast to thick clumps of grass standing shocked on the lawn.

I walk towards the gap in the hedge, to the place on the road where we stood for the bus. Where Matty and I stood waiting. There are no cars now, no signs of life. On the other side of the road, the ditches bury themselves in the earth. Burnt Tree Farm stares over them, sightless.

Instinctively, I cross.

Between two fields there's a drunken path scratched through the clutches of grass. I stumble down the uneven track, the wetness dampening my shoes. I hunch through a cluster of tight-knit trees, stepping over the roots which run like ribs, standing proud of the earth. On the farther side the path resumes, fringed with scuffs of bramble and bush. A raised wind teases the fresh-planted fields, it searches within my knitted sweater, sinking its icy breath on my skin.

The path twists and turns at the corners of fields. Now the beacons of siloes loom over the treeline, stretched into the sky and belittling the farm.

I walk round a hedge and the fields fade away. A gravel path leads to the door.

I knock.

I can hear a shuffling within. Through the frosted panels a wooden floor stretches down the length of the hall, with doors leading off to both sides. One opens. I take a step away from the porch, watching as Martha calmly approaches, almost as if she's expecting me. She opens the door and smiles her slight smile, which never quite reaches a smile.

– Hello.
– You should have worn a coat. And boots. You look cold. Come in. Take your shoes off and put them there.

She watches me as I pull at my shoes. They are hot and soft, and drip onto the mat. My socks are muddied and rain-wet too. I peel them off self-consciously. I sense that Martha's still watching me. She feels like my mother – sterner than my mother – scolding me with her silence.

I lay my shoes and socks on her mat, clumsily and ashamed. I wonder what sort of parent she thinks me, seeing how little I care for myself. Still she watches, not speaking. She leads me down to the end of the hall, and here we enter a flagstone kitchen. It stands at the head of a long sloping lawn, with a view of the fields beyond.

– Would you like some coffee?
– Yes, please. I hope this isn't an inconvenient time.
– No, it's not. Have you come to return my dish?

– No… I forgot it… how foolish of me. I'll nip back and get it…

– Another time. You're here now.

– The pie was delicious. Thank you. You're a very good cook.

– I'll give you the recipe.

– Thanks.

–

– I've just seen Matty off to school.

– In Marshfield?

– Yes. It's his first day. The bus came to pick him up from outside the cottage.

– It will get easier.

– What will?

– Living here will get easier. Living on your own.

– I'm fine. I've got lots to do. There's my work, and there's still a lot of unpacking. There's also more to discover. Matty enjoys exploring the wood…

– The wood?

– Yes, he's making a den. Generally, we're both doing fine.

– It's always hard at first. Living in the country is hard. On the mind, not just on the body. You have to have hard skin. But once you come to accept it, it's easier. Either that, or it breaks you. You need to have purpose in life. To find your niche; to find something to do.

– I'm expecting a lot of work to come in.

– You need to have something to do. If you never enter this world, you won't survive it. You can't stand on the sides and just watch. Either you are a part of this land, or you are entirely separate from it. Do you understand? Do you see what I am saying?

– I'm not sure.

– Nettlesden isn't for those who are faint-hearted. You can't expect it to give something back until you commit, you offer yourself up. You can spend years here and live at its edges, like that man who runs the pub with his wife, but unless you engage, you'll wither away. Gradually you will die. Your son has started to engage, but I fear you haven't yourself.

– I'm sorry… I don't know what you think… what you've been told…

– I suggest you join the Community Council.

– The what?

– It's a good way to engage. A good way in. The Council is made up of the people who live here. We decide what is best in the interests of the village. We determine its future. And in doing so, we preserve its traditions, its past.

– That sounds interesting.

– Next Sunday, after church. Bill Hawes, Peter Faraday, Travis Jones and myself. The village exists because of the people. When the people change, the whole village changes. Without people it doesn't survive. We need to protect the village's health in order to safeguard our own.

– From what? From whom?

– From everything. You are not that naïve, Sarah. But you don't know the ways of the country. I've warned you about gossip, and those who would gossip. I would warn you about those from the outside, too. About the threat, the danger they bring. At the moment, you appear an outsider. The village is watching you.

– Yes … yes, I feel that.

– What do you mean?

– It's almost as if the village has eyes.

– I wasn't speaking literally.

– I am. I've had this feeling – ever since we got here – of being watched. As if someone is watching me.

– Have you seen anyone watching you?

– No. Well, I might have. I've heard sounds; I've seen what I thought to be people, but what has turned out to be something else.

– Have you ever felt this before?

– No. Never. I'm not used to the country, I guess.

– Maybe. Here, have some soup.

– I had breakfast a moment ago.

– I'm giving you some soup. It will warm you up. It's fresh and hot. Eat.

– Thank you.

– This is a bag of food from my garden. A few more vegetables. I don't use chemicals on my patch.

Martha sits and watches me eat. She has finished speaking for now. I feel I ought to find something to say. But there's nothing trivial here. There's no need for pretence.

Heat emits from the rounded bowl; touching its rim with my hands feels good. The soup is thick; it's creamy in colour; a blend of potatoes and onions and leeks. A hint of spinach maybe. It caresses my throat and the walls of my stomach, smoothing the barbs of my fear. Soothing my loneliness. It's potent; it works like a drug. It makes me feel strong. It fuels my desire to engage with the village. Martha is right; she is full of goodness. We sit together in comfortable silence, content just to be, and at peace.

She sees I have finished; she takes my bowl. She doesn't offer me more. She rises and places my bowl in the sink. It's her way of telling me now I should go.

Martha leads me back down the hall, placing her hand on the latch. My socks have been laid on the radiator; they are hot but damp to the touch. They fit round my feet so snugly and warmingly. I tie my laces, and stand.

Martha holds open the door. She is smaller than me; her shoulders are narrow; her forearms are thin, almost frail. But I can feel the strength within her. The strength of her body, her mind. She nods at me; she almost smiles. I take my leave and walk down the path towards the hedge, beyond the hedge, and onto the track which skirts the field, knowing she follows me with her eyes.

I cross the road towards the cottage. I glance towards its ugly pink frame. Even from here, on the road by the car, over the distance of startled lawn, I can see the welcoming flowers. There, on the wall beside the door. A bunch of tender pure-white snowdrops, tied in a tiny but perfect bouquet, with a blue ribbon looped in a bow. The first true flowers of spring. So fragile, so tender. Again, Joyce has come and has reached out to me. Again, she has gone before we can speak.

In the house I fill a cup with cold water, untying the bow and watching the flowers arrange themselves in a natural cascade. Joyce is wanting to talk to me, she is speaking to me in her own timid fashion, using these flowers as her words.

I leave the cottage and walk down the road, neglecting to put on a coat or my boots. They are all, in their own way, inviting me in. All these people who live in this village. All of them wanting to be my friend. I'm so caught in myself I am missing the present, I'm missing the chance to fit in.

I turn up the track towards Rose House Farm. There's an easy whisper of breeze in the air, so slim, so slight it's like silk. Thin strips of washed blue sky emerge from the nebulous sheet of broken cloud and melt with reflected sun. There is life in the fields, there is life in the air. I feel their vitality strengthening me. Pigeons rise from skeletal trees, alarmed as I come near the farm. I see patches of house, the brickwork of barns, woven in pools of shifting shade. Near the ditch which runs by the foot of the field, someone is standing and looking at me. I wave.

Perhaps it is only the trunk of a tree, for it disappears without seeming to move, without acknowledging me. Yet I sense someone's presence; there is somebody there. I start forward, directly towards them.

– Get off the land!

The ferocious sound slaps into my ear, breaking on me like a wave. I search the flat landscape and look for a source. It is Uriah, large and fierce, though some distance away. He is shaking his fist in the air.

I look down at my feet. I am scarcely more than a yard from the concrete; I am stood on the earth in the field. So close to the track, but not on the track. Enough for him to have seen.

I back away onto the stone. I want to shout an apology at him, to say that I'm sorry, I made a mistake. But I fear that nothing placates him. He stands alone in the bleak sweep of crop, a solid shape of enmity. The broken backs of a half-dozen seedlings stare up at me from the earth. The stems are beyond my power to mend. The trees round the farm sway haughtily, sneering at me with their scorn.

I turn towards the road once more. I sense that he's still watching me, as are the shadows that stretch from the farm. Everyone, everything, watching me. Staring into my back. I try not to walk too fast, nor to stumble. I want to escape, but I will not run. All that I want is to build a friendship; to extend and engage, as Martha would have it; to become a part of this world.

I re-enter my garden, too angry and restless to hide myself in the house. I need to find an occupation, a distraction to shake out my shame. I walk around the perimeter, searching for something to do. I could knock down Matty's wall of logs and build it over again. I could trim the hedges. I could cut the grass. None of this needs to be done. In the garden almost nothing is growing; nature hesitates to give birth. Here are some snowdrops of my own; the promise of buds on the branch of a tree; some leaves sprouting out of the lawn that in time will yield me a daffodil. The rest is still dormant; it is waiting to feel the strengthening rays of the pale, pale sun which hides behind the low-hanging cloud.

I stand at the end of the lawn looking out at the field. Uriah has gone. Gone are the precious blue strands of sky, the light and the shadow which bothered the farm, which muddled its memory and played round its lips. If this were my field, then I would have purpose. I would plant it and tend it; I would nourish and grow. In time, I would watch it mature.

I turn from the field towards my own garden. Above the growth of the hedge nearby I spy the branches of well-clipped fruit trees poking into the sky. I walk round the hedge to inspect them. There are six trees in all — all leafless and idle — their tips sprouting tightly closed buds. Apple, cherry, plum, or pear. I will have to wait for another month until I know what they are. To their side is a line of stunted stalks, of fruit bushes heavily pruned. Currants perhaps, or gooseberries. There's a shed beyond them, and a patch in the earth tangled with straggling weed.

The shed door opens reluctantly, wheezing its hinges, scraping its base on the bald patch of concrete that beds it. It is dark inside; the smudge of the window is thick with cobwebs and dust. There are spades, rakes, forks and buckets in here. And the barrow that Matty used for the logs. I reach to a shelf for a pair of gloves. A spider tiptoes over the wood, resentful at being disturbed. I shake the gloves vigorously before putting them on. I pick up the fork and re-enter the day.

The patch is unevenly square: about twenty feet long on each side. Grass encroaches from neighbouring borders, though the sides are sliced into a trench. The earth is of a different texture entirely from that in the field. It's finer, darker, richer, more subtle. It is choked with the chaos of last year's weeds. But nothing is firmly established here; there's no bramble, no nettle, no thorn. The patch is mostly sheltered from wind, but open to sun and to rain.

I step out onto the soil. It is moist and forgiving beneath my feet. No one can shout me off here. I reach down to clutch the stem of a weed, jerking it up in my hand. The top-half breaks with a snap. I throw it onto the side of the plot and tug at the stalk that remains. I pull evenly, trying to gauge what will happen – if first it will break or come free from the soil. I feel its roots are easing beneath me; I feel a gradual rebalance of power; I feel the soft suction as it lifts through the earth and presents itself in the air.

There's a circle of soil where once was a root, revealing the crumbling earth. I grasp another weed by the neck, determined to pull it out cleanly. I plant the fork beside its stem, levering it up from its base. I shuffle randomly through the patch, removing all of the larger weeds, laying their shattered bodies out in a pile on the grass by the plot.

I step out of the patch, catching my breath. There are pools of torn earth where the weeds once stood. There are swathes of squashed earth and compacted growth that my boots have crushed in the soil.

I wheel the barrow out of the shed and back it over towards my pyre, filling its body with weeds. Then I empty it into the side of the hedge and stand back surveying the plot. I mark out a small square of soil in my mind, no more than the size of a stretching arm; I kneel down, beginning a methodical sweep, pulling and teasing up with the fork till the growth comes away in my hand.

Once most of the vegetation has gone, I pluck at rogue seedlings with finger and thumb, pinching them free from the patch. I straighten my back. I can feel the strain on my unused muscles; I can feel the sweat on my skin.

I feel drained. I should give up now; I should spare myself from enduring this thankless, needless pain. The day has hardened; the sky is firm; the breeze is cut with a clamping chill; the harsh air scorches my cheeks. I feel a coldness creeping inside me; I feel the glaze of tears in my eyes.

I mark out another square in my mind, adopting a rhythm, a pace. Each weed becomes a thing in itself; it's no longer a part of the whole. Each motion I make is my only thought, from the weed to the barrow to the soil.

I clear a second square of growth. Now the barrow is full. I empty it out on the pile by the hedge and unthinkingly mark the next square.

Here on my knees on the uncleared patch, one hand pressed into the compact soil, the other prising the weeds from its bed – my face only inches away from the ground – I can feel the give of the earth. I can smell it; I can almost taste it. I can sense the life that it gives. I no longer notice the pain in my limbs. I no longer notice the wider world – the sky, the field, the lightness of wind – its shape, its colour, its form. All I can see is this small square of earth, this stretch of intimate soil.

As I heap another full barrow of growth onto the mound I have built by the hedge, I steal a glimpse at the emptying patch, at the lengthening strip of rich brown soil laid out at the fringe of the grass. Then I start again. I don't know the names of these fragile seedlings, nor do I know what they will become. But, as I pluck at the infant growth, as I scratch at the soil and let it breathe, I develop a learning of my own.

I am coming towards the end of my line. There is only one more square till it's done. I feel an onus, an urgency, without knowing why that should be. I ache to look up and reward myself by seeing a line of tended earth, knowing the gardener is me. I have lost all sense, all measure of time. I scarcely feel I know where I am, or what it is I am doing. I am only aware of the soil around me, of the plants that spring from the ground. That is all I can think of now; that is all I can see. These weeds that scar the patch's skin, that pierce its flesh and suck its bone. There is nothing beyond, nor needs to be. All that I know, all meaning, is here.

It is done.

I wipe my nose with the back of my glove, wincing away the earth from my eyes. In front of me is a line. I stare at it, stupidly pleased. Standing upright I feel the strain in my shoulders, my knees, the base of my neck. My fingers are numb with pinching out weeds. Sweat feeds a stream in the small of my back, clinging my shirt to my spine.

I empty the barrow and bring it back round. I don't want to leave, to go into the cottage. I want to enjoy this feeling, this moment, knowing this work is all mine. Mine is this patch and everything in it. All that has yet to be placed in the soil, all that has yet to be nurtured.

The soil is barren, but light and rich. I can feel the life it will give. I see worms and centipedes working within it, a robin stood to one side. The hedges will shelter it and protect; the sky will lay a blanket upon it, enriching what grows here with sunshine and rain.

I replace the fork and gloves in the shed, then I walk back through the arch to the house. Inside it is almost oppressive with heat, with an absence of wind or of air. I prise my boots from my sweaty feet; I take off my trousers and socks. Leaving the muddied pile by the door, I climb the stairs to the bathroom.

My feet are swollen and sore; my hands are caked with earth despite gloves; my nails are thick with the dirt. I look at myself in the watching mirror. Leaves tangle my hair; earth smudges my cheeks. There are splatters of weeds on my face. My skin is blanched by the blistering wind, its blemishes standing out proud.

I run the bath and take off my clothes, self-consciously locking the door. My body breathes, damp and frigid with heat. My flesh feels heavy, ugly, and used. I feel a throbbing pain in my toes as sensation returns to my feet. I wash my hands as I wait for the bath, scrubbing my fingers to scratch off the earth. I dry my hands and feel through my hair, scraping out dirt that clings to my scalp, sprinkling leaves and soil on the floor.

I step into the waiting bath. The water glides around my body, suffocating me, stifling my breath. I sit up and scrub at my skin with a flannel, seeing it blotchy and raw as I scrape. I feel my sweat dissolve in the water; I feel a cleanness, a lightness of being; the plasticity of my flesh.

I get out and rub my back with a towel, my body too humid to dry. I feel almost shy as I unlock the door and tiptoe back to my room. My shirt smells clean; it is dry and fresh; it closes over my hot, damp flesh, hiding me from myself.

I return to the bathroom once dressed. The water in the bath is cloudy; twigs bob and float on its surface. I pull the plug. I bend over the basin and wet my hair, applying shampoo and then conditioner, picking at tangles and clumps. When I turn, the bath is lined with mud; the plughole darkened with earth.

It's still so hot when downstairs. I turn off the boiler and open the door, feeling the afternoon breeze in my face, feeling it creeping beneath my clothes: invigorating, pleasingly cold. In the kitchen I cut hunks of bread and cheese, filling the folded slices with chutney. I eat with a hunger – eating while slicing another thick slab of bread.

I am still eating ravenously when Matty appears at the door.

He looks at me, but he doesn't speak. His shirt and trousers are clean and pressed, his shoes have retained their shine. His face is smooth and pale. He looks as if he has come from London. He looks out of place in this room. He closes the door and inspects the boiler, reaching out for the dial. The engine whirrs and blasts into being, preparing to spread its unwanted heat into this bloated room. I come towards him, happy to see him, so happy to know he is here. I want to hold him, but he backs away. Instead, I offer him bread and tea. He sits and waits for the kettle to boil.

Matty speaks in monotone, relaying the day in pared down speech, prompted by questions alone. The bus takes a roundabout route to Marshfield, picking up pupils in every village, and so the journey is long. The school is tiny: a half-dozen rooms with a tarmac cage for a playground. There are eighteen students in his class, but it's shared with the year group above him. There are equal numbers of girls and boys, and most of them live in Marshfield. There are two other children who come from our village, but both are much younger than him. None of his class have lived in London, though most of them know it to visit. He likes the teachers, and they're not very strict. He thinks he's brighter than most in his class.

Matty gets up and stands by the window. The light has faded; it has washed from the clouds; the dusk is drawing in fast. Hedges appear as formless shadows; the shapes of trees in the edging darkness are swayed by a sunken breeze. His silence speaks what he cannot say. He wants to be out there in the wood. He wants to build and tunnel and dig, to bury himself and be gone. The thought of waiting until the weekend is continual torment to him. I understand now how he feels.

He tells me he's been given some homework. It's his excuse to depart. I listen as he mounts the stairs, as he opens the door and enters his room, as he takes off the trousers and shirt that constrict him, as he pulls on a sweater and jeans.

Each time he moves I can see a tremor chasing along the beams on the ceiling, pumping the arteries of the cottage, bringing its fleshy walls alive. I can hear the slightest movement he makes; I can see the motion of every sound. And, when he is still – when there's nothing to hear – I sense I can feel him breathing.

~

These hands like claws, having scratched at the earth, having pulled from the soil, having worked their bones deep into the ground till their tips have bled – ingrained with a dirt that will not wash – now clasped together in prayer. These knees that are swollen from scraping the tilth, being torn by stones and pierced by thorn, spreading their pain from my shins to my spine, now kneeling in prayer in this pew. I have dug all week. I have dug my patch. I have thrown my body onto the ground; I have prostrated myself on a bleeding earth; I have laid bare a hungry and generous soil. And now, at last, I have done.

O Lord, I have done. I have done myself in. And now I am tired of the doing.

But though I rest on this seventh day, I know my job has scarcely begun. For in kneeling on the fresh-cleared earth I have pressed it down, I have squeezed out the air, I have compacted it into a clay. Now that it's cleared of every weed I must dig it over again. I must let it breathe; I must work in manure; I must rake it even and fine.

105

Only then will the patch be ready – laid out as new, as a fresh clean carpet, free from the stains of the past. A soil where I can begin again, scratching my mark upon its bosom, planting where seeds have yet to be sown. I will lay it out as I want it to be, having no template to work from. And then I will tend it and bring it to life; I will nurture its offspring and harvest its store. Nature and I will work it together, enriching the soil and giving it breath, hugging it close to our warmth. We will work together to increase the yield. Enough so Matty and I will have plenty; so we can find a peace in this land, free from the fear of evil beasts. And nothing shall make us afraid.

*If ye walk in my statutes, and keep my commandments, and do them;*

*Then I will give you rain in due season, and the land shall yield her increase, and the trees of the field shall yield their fruit.*

*And your threshing shall reach unto the vintage, and the vintage shall reach unto the sowing time: and ye shall eat your bread to the full, and dwell in your land safely.*

*And I will give peace in the land, and ye shall lie down, and none shall make you afraid: and I will rid evil beasts out of the land, neither shall the sword go through your land.*

All week I have knelt in the patch. From the time when Matty leaves for school till the time when his bus returns. My face has been bruised and battered by wind; my skin has hardened and developed a sheen; my insides are pure, they feel crystal and clean. I have watched the clouded sky above me dragging its weight through the leaden day; I have felt it empty its tears upon me; I have seen it break and reveal a beauty – a radiance, a rush of pure light – casting the air, the trees and the grass in a restless brilliance. I have heard the muttering breeze in the hedge; I have felt the blast of the blinded gale. I have seen it drive the metallic scarers, and heard the laboured clank of their wheels, as their wings ground out a bleak warning. I have heard a sporadic blast, like a shot, and have seen the scattered confusion of crows crying their homelessness and alarm. I have raised my eyes from my patch to the field; I have seen its infinite stretch of seedlings swept by interminable wind. And at times I have heard no wind at all. Just a stillness, a dampness, an emptiness. A barrenness which signals no sound.

Martha knows that I lied to her. She knows the loneliness that I feel. How I watch each day as Matty departs; how I wait for him to come home. The watching and waiting, and then, when he is home, the wanting to show him my love.

It shouldn't have happened like this. I see his reserve as he comes through the door; I see his resentment when eating his supper; I see his relief as he goes to his room. Martha knows how that wears me away. She knows that the hollow cottage derides me, as I sit in the still of its sterile womb. She knows I have mailed all the agents I know and still there's no sight of new work. She knows that I spend my days in my patch, in the hope that the land will yield its increase, and that from it I carve some reason to be. In the absence of having another employment, in the knowledge that all the fields are denied me, this plot alone can be mine. I will tame it. I will make it my own. I will call on the wind that strikes from the field, on the skies that melt with the rain; I will ask them to nourish my humble patch, to tease life within it and nurture it. The promise it offers is what I will live for. It's my reason for being, my hope.

That is the comfort I need right now – a purpose to be that is free from the past. Here, in the love of my neighbours and Matty, I intend to lead a new life without you, finding a way on my own. A life which contains no regret or remorse; a life which is rich and fulfilling and good; a life where charity, faith and contentment fill the space that was left by you. Draw near, and give me my peace.

*Ye who do truly and earnestly repent you of your sins, and are in love and charity with your neighbours, and intend to lead a new life, following the commandments of God, and walking from henceforth in his holy ways; Draw near with faith, and take this holy Sacrament to your comfort; and make your humble confession to Almighty God, devoutly kneeling.*

I didn't leave London with the intent of finding myself on my own. Nor did I consciously come on my own. And I want to make these people my friends. I want to share this world with Matty; I want to live it with him. Yet all I have felt since we first arrived is the insistent slow rupture of growing divide. I fear a gradual erosion of being with both of us lost in our own separate ways. I have tried to bridge the space that divides us, to use the time that we have together. I have tried to cement the bond that we share.

Matty sits in the pew beside me, staring in front of him blindly. I know he wishes he wasn't here. He doesn't need the things that I offer; he's found a place of his own. That world is the wood, with its clawing branches which tug at his fancy and tempt him away. The wood – with its hollow cries and its deep-set eyes – with the secrets it hides in the ground. I know he would like me to go to the wood, to build his dens, to dig his pits, to forage within its dark lairs.

That is what he would share. And I would too, if I could. For the warmth of pleasure I know it would give him; for the pleasure I sense it is sure to give me – simply for being there with him.

Yet there's something there that appals me; something so stark it defies all description. A sensation that creeps down my spine. I cannot see it – I can't even name it – but I sense it so close, and so real. I feel the wood possesses a being; I feel the beat of its desolate heart; the throb of the blood in its veins. I feel it creeping into my soul and disclosing the secrets it hides. I cannot go where he wants me to go, nor will he stay here for me. How can my fear outweigh my love when I care for nothing but him?

Perhaps there is someone here who can help us; some kind heart which is full of compassion; someone who in true faith I can turn to, to help me heal the divide. Someone here to confirm and strengthen, someone here who is full of goodness. Someone to bring us closer together.

*... who of his great mercy hath promised forgiveness of sins to all those who with hearty repentance and true faith turn unto him; Have mercy upon you; pardon and deliver you from all your sins; confirm and strengthen you in all goodness; and bring you to everlasting life...*

Which of those here could I trust to support me? To help me to mend now I'm here on my own. In the far-side pew are Bill and Margaret. I can feel their eyes are boring within me, burning to know who I am. But not for my sake, nor for Matty's comfort. They would feast on our being; they would drain us dry; they would twist our truths and then spit us out once we were sapped of our juice.

Uriah and Joyce are sat before them. Joyce would be a comfort maybe, if I knew who she was, if ever she spoke, if he ever allowed me to see. She sits in a world a whisper away, a world so entirely removed. There is no knowing, no way of knowing. She is so much a figment, a shadow of being, that if ever I stretched out attempting to touch, she would fade in my hands and dissolve.

Jack and Martha are seated in front. Surely Martha is someone to guide me. She is a person who knows, who can see. She, who kneels in the pew before me – silent, noble, discreet. Of all who are here, surely she is the one who is able to steer and sustain me.

She would understand; she could lessen my pain. She could see the void that was left in my heart the instant I chose to leave you. She could fill the space with her love. She has the knowledge to bring me comfort. She has the power to give me peace. She has the strength to make me whole. Amen.

*The Peace of God, which passeth all understanding, keep your hearts and minds in the knowledge and love of God, and of his Son Jesus Christ our Lord: And the Blessing of God Almighty, the Father, the Son, and the Holy Ghost, be amongst you, and remain with you always. Amen.*

We rise. Colin Inchmore walks down the aisle, followed by Martha and Jack. Joyce is ushered away by Uriah. I place a hand on Matty's arm as we stand awaiting our turn. He turns towards me and smiles. He knows he is almost free.

Outside it is bright. The threads of silk clouds wash the globe of a smiling sun and shy from its brilliant rays. All about us is fierce with life. The grass, the trees, these people's faces, even the wind, is alive.

– Martha, might I have a word?

– We have the Community Council meeting to attend.

– Before that.

–

– I would appreciate your advice. You've got a son. You've got experience of bringing him up.

– That was a long time ago. Uriah is different.

– But he was a boy once. He was brought up here, in the country. You've experienced that.

– Uriah was always alone. He was happy being alone. He was always outside, in the fields and the wood, doing whatever he wanted.

– Yes, Matty's like that. He likes doing that. He likes the freedom it offers.

– Well?

– And I'm happy for him too. I really am. But it's so different from being in London. In the evenings, we used to sit on the sofa and watch TV. We would do his homework together. On the weekend we would go to the cinema, or round to some friends, or to a museum. We would sometimes take in a show. We were always together.

– And all of that's gone, now you find yourself here? You don't know what being together might look like, now that you're here in the country?

– He likes to go to the wood. But other than that, he hasn't settled. Not into the cottage, nor into school. And he can't spend his life in the wood. I want him to spend more time with me, to accept this new life that we have. I think that the wood is his escape. It's his denial. Of where we are and why we are here. And it's worse because I don't like the wood. I don't want to go there myself.

– Quite right. You should keep him away from the wood. Have you tried speaking to him about this?

– I've tried, but I don't want to be too hard on him. He's still coming to terms with this new way of life, and I want to give him some space. I don't want to deny him something he likes, but I fear it will pull us apart.

Martha looks into my face. I can see she is thinking of what to say. I think she knows the answer already, but she seems reluctant to share.

Over her shoulder I catch sight of Matty. He's still here; he is stood by the gate with Uriah. They are wrapped in talk, like two good friends, attentive to what the other is saying, seeming oblivious of all else. How does he even know Uriah? When were they introduced? They must have met in the village shop, or on the road, or in the field, or maybe even the wood. Of course, they must have met in the wood. They are bound by the wood; both of them, bound. To live it, to breathe it, to bring it to life. Even now, even here, in the deadening graveyard, they are bringing its essence to life. They are weaving its world in the air with their hands.

Martha has followed my eyes.

– I think you should come over for supper.
– I've got Matty.
– Yes, bring Matty. Come tonight.
– Are you sure?
– Yes. I think Jack can tease him from the wood. Jack can show him what else is here. He can help you to find things that the two of you can learn to share and enjoy.
– That would be lovely. Please.
– Around seven thirty then.
– Can I bring anything?
– Perhaps my dish. Now it's time for our meeting.
– I'll join you in a minute. I'm going to see Matty off.

Martha walks down the gravel path and over the road towards the church hall. In the graveyard there's nobody left except us. Uriah and Matty and me.

I start towards them, but they notice me. They stop talking, breaking apart. Uriah utters a few final words, then nods and departs through the opening gate without acknowledging me. Matty remains on his own.

– I didn't know you knew Uriah.
– Yes. We met in the wood.
– What were you talking about?
– Stuff.
– What sort of stuff?
– About things in the wood. That sort of stuff.
– Did he tell you about his traps?
– Yes.
– And?
– Stuff.
– What sort of stuff?
– Stuff! Things.
– I'm not sure his traps are safe. I'm not sure you ought to go anywhere near them. I'm not sure you ought to go to the wood.
– That's what he said.
– I think he's right.
– I don't. I'll go there anyway.
– We've been invited to supper tonight.
– Who with? I don't want to go.
– With Jack and Martha. They're both very nice. We'll do it this once. If you don't like it, you don't need to do it again.
– Once then?
– Yes, once. So don't stay out late. Have you got your sandwiches?

He holds up the bag for me to see. Then he turns and is off – straight through the graveyard, straight to the field, straight to the track that leads to the wood – walking so fast it is almost a run. He is gone.

I walk towards the church hall. In the shade of the porch, I strain to look through the windows into the rooms inside. In the first, I can see Colin Inchmore and Jack, bent over a Bible, exploring the text. In the next I can see a half circle of chairs, a table with cups and an urn of hot tea. The group is already seated and talking. I push open the door. As I enter, they falter and lurch to a stop; all of them turning to greet me.

– Sarah, come in. Have a seat. I think you know most of the people here. Bill Hawes. Travis Jones. Peter Faraday. Have you met?
– No. Hello. I'm Sarah.
– Peter. Nice to meet you.
– We've just started. Help yourself to some tea if you like. Now the principal item on the agenda today is the Summer Fair. The Fair will be held, as always, in Steeple Field. I know each of you has begun preparations, so let's start with a brief update. Bill, would you like to begin?
– Yes. I've got a permit from the Local Authority, and the police have been informed. They are planning to keep a small presence here throughout the afternoon. But after last year they are more concerned about what might happen later on in the evening.
– Why? What did happen last year?
– The Rectory was broken into, Sarah. The Merediths weren't here. Bill's alarm went off too.
– They've advised us to stay on our guard. To watch out for people who come but don't enter the Fair.

– Aren't the police taking any precautions themselves?

– They never caught the perpetrators. However, they do know there's a well-organised gang that operates over the county. They plan on doing some low-key surveillance in the hope of getting some positive IDs. There will be two gates into the Fair: Peter on one, myself on the other. We'll be selling tickets at a pound a person; children and concessions at fifty pence. As usual, we'll encourage people to pay, but we won't confront those who slip in the sides. I've got enough stewards to manage the car boot sale, though I'm short of people on the car park.

– I could do that.

– It's rather a thankless job, I'm afraid. You don't get to see much of the Fair.

– That's fine. You'll need to tell me what to do though.

– Thank you, Sarah. Bill can brief you separately. So, the security side of things seems well-planned. Travis, where are we on entertainment?

– We've got about fifteen stalls confirmed, and I anticipate doubling that number. About half of them are local traders, and most of those are from Marshfield. The others are journeymen. At the moment there's a lot to eat, but not a lot for people to do. We've got a roundabout and a shooting gallery, but that's about it at present. I've asked the organisers of the annual Eye Show to recommend a few other stalls. On top of that, there'll be some games for the kids, organised by the teachers at Marshfield school.

– Will there be any drink on site?

– Only soft drinks. The Serpent will be closed from two until five. At lunchtime, we'll serve in plastic mugs so people can take it onto the field.

– What happens if anyone brings their own drink?

– Our policy has been to turn a blind eye. But if someone seems drunk, or is being unruly, we'll notify the police. How are the displays coming on, Peter?

– The car boot is fine. It runs itself. It's sufficiently well-established in the yearbook, and the same people seem to turn up each year. I'm at eighty per cent of capacity already, without even having to advertise. The same goes for the vintage cars, and the steam engines. I've deputised this bit of the Fair, as they like to run it themselves. I've given them drawings of the field so they know how many members can show. To be honest, it's more a matter of keeping down numbers than of trying to drum up their interest. On that point, though, I do have a question.

– Yes?

– We've been doing more or less the same display for years. I think everyone enjoys the steam engines because they're fun and interactive. The children can pull of their whistles. But most of the display is usually cars. They're not particularly special, nor well-preserved. They're not vintage either; they're just old. They might mean something to the over-sixties, but they mean precious little to those who are younger, and they take up so much of the space. Over the past couple of years, I haven't noticed many people taking much interest in them other than the members themselves.

– What are you suggesting?

– I'm suggesting we do away with the lot. Keep the tractors, the steam-engines, the bicycles, and the vehicles from the war, but cut down on the number of cars. We'll create more space, and there'll be less pollution and noise. We could make way for more games and for more entertainment. For things that appeal to the children.

– I see. What do you think, Bill?

— I take Peter's point. Being part of that older generation myself, I confess I like wandering round the cars, for old time's sake, if you will. I've got used to them, as they've always been there. It wouldn't feel the same without them.

— No, it wouldn't feel the same. But then I would question why we are doing it. Is it simply for the sake that we've always done it, or because we know it's what people want?

— I'm afraid I agree with Peter. For ages I stuck with traditional beers, assuming that people liked draught beer, and it wasn't a pub without them. But now there's only one beer on tap. The rest is all in bottles.

— Thank you, Travis, for that insight. Sarah, what do you think?

— I haven't really got an opinion. I've never been to the Fair. I'm not much into cars myself, as anyone knows who's looked in my drive. In principle, I would agree with Peter, though tradition has its part to play, too.

— Well, it seems the Council is split on this issue. I propose we put it to the vote. Being an odd number, we should reach a position, so long as there are no abstentions.

In closing her sentence, Martha looks squarely at me. Her voice is strained, her body rigid. I look away and meet Travis' eyes. I can see a kindness in his face, much as when I first met him. He knows what I feel, he can sympathise, though there's little he can do to protect me. I think he and Peter are probably right, while Bill and Martha are swayed by tradition. The decision will come down to me.

There's a wrench of wood from behind us. The door is opening on the tense, bleak room, splitting its ugly silence. Jack's face and shoulders appear in the gap. He has done with Colin Inchmore now. He wants to know what progress we've made.

There's a pause. It is Martha, as his wife and the Chair, who feels it her duty to speak. She explains the reason behind the vote, then stops to await his reply. For Jack it appears there is no decision. The vintage cars are part of the Fair; they have always been there and they always will. He withdraws, having spoken as much as he needs. We accept his authority. The semi-circle adjusts and exhales; it shakes itself free from uncertainty; it resettles and starts off again.

– As you can see, Sarah, each of us has a specific task to make a success of the Fair. I was hoping you would take one on too.
– If you like. Of course.
– Good. We appear to have everything in place, but as yet no one knows when it is. We need publicity. Posters. That sort of thing. If we can agree what we want to say, perhaps you could promote us locally. It would be a good way for you to meet new people, and to get to know our treacherous roads.

It is decided. There are a few more exchanges and then we break off. The business of the Council is done. Martha is calm and composed once more, exchanging some parting words with Bill.

Travis comes up and takes my shoulder, walking with me to the door. I think he wants to sympathise, to excuse, to explain it away. His eyes speak where his words will not follow. Again, he lays his hand on my arm as he volunteers to give me his help. He did the same job when he first joined the Council; he knows where to go, and what Martha will want; he can accompany me round as my guide.

Travis smiles. It's a generous smile. A bit like yours, but more timid, less tender. I thank him for being considerate.

We are standing by the side of the road, the tinsel of trees in our hair. He squeezes my hand. I've survived my first meeting he tells me. He crosses the road and goes into the Serpent. I watch the door close, then I start back home.

As I come to the lawn which surrounds Mill House Cottages, I can see another dance of colour laid on the wall by my door. Another tribute of flowers. This time it's a bunch of wild daffodils, caught in a blue ribbon tied in a bow. Stolen with love from the hedgerow.

I've been wondering when I would find my next token. What bloom Joyce would pick out and give me. I imagine her led from the church by Uriah, scouring the ditches for colours and scent. I imagine her slipping her shackles at dawn – like a shadow, a spectre, a slight breath of wind – to pluck this bouquet and then bring it to me. I can see her gliding back to her home – like the breeze, like a shade, like a lone patch of light – over the track with scarcely a sound till safe in the clutch of the farm. Her errand discharged, unbeknown to Uriah. I imagine her pockets are full of blue ribbon, which she furtively cuts when alone. I imagine her laying this bunch on my wall, placing it there with her fidgety hands, knowing herself both unseen and unknown, lost in her secretive world. None but the hedgerow has witnessed her movement; none but the flowers will know. They know, but they will not confess. I wonder if Joyce can brighten my kitchen all through the spring and the summer.

I spread pâté on toast, I crunch through an apple, watching the flowers as if they would speak. I wonder what prompts her to bring them to me. I think it may be her form of a welcome, in the only language she knows. But perhaps it's a signal, a warning to me, a plea that I don't get too close.

The jug sits on the enchanted table, exuding a sunshine caress through the room, a modest scent of pure innocence. A message from Joyce, bestowed upon me. Bursting with life though destined to wilt – destined, in time, to be thrown on the compost, as dead as the others she brought.

I make myself a cup of coffee and sit at the table admiring the flowers. Such simplicity; such complexity. I pull on my boots and open the door, walking out into the day. The rays of the sun are fierce in my face; the air alight with a freshening glow, sleek and supple and buoyant.

I walk down the road towards the track that leads to Rose House Farm. I look across the unfolding field, keeping the island in sight. The trees round the farm are less severe now clothed in awakening leaf. The casual wind plays at their slender branches, teasing false shadows to dance in the courtyard, arousing the farmhouse to life. Living things are shaping to being, watching and waiting for me to arrive.

I will see Joyce now. I will speak to her now. I will know.

I stumble on to the farm. The track is cruel beneath my feet; lumps of brick and broken stone are scratched by my boots and spat from the path, scattered into the dense planted field. I feel the breeze to be stealthily strengthening the further I venture down the track, the more I'm exposed on this flattened terrain. The trees on the island appear to grow fainter the closer I come to its core.

I can see a figure blurred in the distance, stood in the heart of the yard. At first, it doesn't seem to move. Then it grows – growing faster than all around it, as it breaks the bounds of the farm. I know it approaches deliberately. I know that it won't let me pass.

It's Uriah.

He accosts me without a gesture, a word. We stand face to face in the stranded field, equidistant from the farm and the road, blocking the path we would take. I look up, expecting a challenge from him, but he offers nothing to me.

– I've come to see Joyce. Is she here?
– Yes.
– I haven't met her properly. I've come to say hello.
– She doesn't want to see anyone.
– O? Is she unwell?
– No.
– When might be a good time for me to come and see her?
– She doesn't want to see anybody.
– Never? I find that hard to believe.
– She doesn't like company.
– I got the impression she'd like to see me.
– What impression is that?
– I'd like to say hello. I'm her neighbour.
–
– I think she'd like to meet me, if you'd let her.
– I don't.
– This is really very awkward, Uriah. I've never been in this situation before. Are you denying me the right to see your wife?
– I'm telling you people should keep to themselves. This road is private property.
– Are you throwing me off?
– I'm saying it's private property. You shouldn't interfere.
– Then could you at least let Joyce know that I called. That I tried to call. That I would be delighted to see her some time – at any time – if she would like to come round. Could you tell her that?

His face is impassive and swollen by wind. He stands imposingly, here in my path, the bulk of his body solid before me, his gaze fixed upon me and stripping me bare. He's so unlike the man of this morning who was talking so freely and openly when standing next to my son. Behind him, his fortress marooned in the field looks out at me with stern eyes. I turn and walk away down the track, knowing he's watching me still. He is watching me till I reach the road, till I shuffle along its unbending slope, till I'm hidden behind the hedge at Six Bells.

Back home I walk round the side of the cottage and stare out over the field. Uriah is no longer there. The ground is unbroken and the track has vanished, as if he has rolled it away. The tide has come in; his world is unbridged; once more he's marooned from mankind. Yet, though it is cut from the rest of the village, I sense Rose House Farm is alert and alive. It is watching me, like a single grey eye stamped in a furious and fervid green face that is speckled with light, that glowers unblinking, tirelessly staring at me. Beyond the farm I can see the wood, I can see the trees that are closed to the light, closed to the warmth which spins from the day. Matty is somewhere inside.

I walk round the hedge towards my patch. It looks barren now I have let it breathe. In my mind I conjure it rich and fertile: the green of luminous lettuce and peas; the curled compact leaves of cabbage and sprout; the fragile tufts of carrot-heads which hide their peeping roots in the ground; the beetroot with its purple veins; the laughing, fat-bodied radishes; the umbrella fans of courgette plants which harbour fruit in their shade. Around it all a ring of sweet peas, filling the air with their scent.

I watch the afternoon uncurl and lie lazily on the land. This is my day of rest. The earth is dormant, breathing so slowly the rise and fall of its chest is unseen. I hear the sound of its shallow exhale, a random shiver across its skin, breaking the quiet of repose. Clouds weave through the stretching sky, painting a shifting shade on the earth. Birds cut through the air at angles, clapping their tasking wings. A hare sits proud in the middle of the field, its long thin ears erect. The body of earth is tarnished by time; its colour darkens, drained by the day; trees and hedges and the few scattered houses melt away to a molten grey, absorbed in the distance like smoke. The land hunkers down, preparing for slumber, pulling its mantle up to its chin.

Matty has returned from the wood. I can hear his footsteps taxing the stairs; his breath through the sheer breathing walls; the metallic squeeze of angry springs as he throws himself on his bed. Inside, the boiler is grinding out warmth which is gradually filling the rooms.

I go upstairs and take a bath. I call out to Matty, reminding him that we're going out, he needs to be smart. I stand in my towel in front of the mirror. I examine my face, the lines of my face, the contours and feel of my flesh. Reluctantly I put on some lipstick; I line my eyes with mascara. The person I see doesn't feel like me. She looks like the one that you used to know. The one you were disappointed by. I have dresses and skirts hung up in the cupboard, but I feel indifferent to trying them on. Instead, I pull on a pair of trousers, and a blouse which I hide beneath a fleece. I watch myself in the pool of the mirror: this strange woman brushing her hair.

We should leave.

In the twilight Matty and I cross the road, tracing the path which leads to the farm. He is wearing school shoes, a pair of jeans, a hooded jerkin, a hat. I follow, confident in his tread. The cool breeze bites at the tail of my coat; it searches into my skin. Colour evaporates from the grass; the fields are being washed away. I feel the comfort of the torch in my pocket.

We creep through the deeper shade of the thicket which arches its back across the track, then through to the broader margin of earth which awaits on the farther side. Before us a thin light spun from low windows winks out its welcome to us. We walk across the crisp gravel path and step up onto the porch.

Matty knocks.

A shaft of light from an opening door spills out across the corridor floor. It is broken by Martha's thin form. She pulls back the bolts and ushers us in, taking our coats and guiding us through to the room from which she just came.

The drawing room has a crimson carpet, aflame in the reddening glow of a fire. Jack is seated in an upright chair on the farther side of the grate. He rises stiffly and invites us to sit. He offers us both a drink. He carefully places more logs on the fire, and the fusty walls become alive, our faces bright in reflected flame.

Both Martha and Jack are wearing tweed. He is attired in a jacket and tie; she in a skirt with a plain white blouse on which she has clasped a fine brooch. It seems they have formally dressed for dinner. Martha slips away to the kitchen, refusing any offer of help, leaving us to be entertained by Jack, here, near the warmth of the fire.

Jack's company is impeccable; he engages us with no seeming effort; he pleases without trying to please. His voice is melodic and low; his words selected with care. In the first exchanges he searches us out, unlocking the people we are, divining the things we hold dear. He senses our interests and steers towards them – to the fields, the crops, the country, the wood – laying the village out before us and easing us into its heart.

We cross the hall to the dining room while Jack continues to talk. Martha appears in pockets of light thrown up by the fire and the flickering candles, then vanishes back into shadow. Now she has served us all, and she sits. Jack interrupts himself to say grace. We eat a game stew with large lumps of meat drowned in a thick, warming sauce.

Matty is asking about the fields, about what is hidden and buried within them, about what he might find if he scratches their surface. Jack responds, he digs through their layers, he searches deeper into their core. He lays them before us, for us to explore, beginning from when life began. He speaks of the humans who lived in Britain 700,000 years ago. He talks of the flints discovered at Pakefield, of the artefacts and the tools. He explains what the earth might have looked like then; of how its climate would have been home to mammoths and sabre-tooth cats. He speaks of the changing shape of the land, of Britain connected to the landmass of Europe by a bridge which stretched from Sussex to Suffolk, allowing mankind to migrate. On the table he traces the floodplains of Bytham, which sliced through the country and cut it in two. In giant strides he walks through millennia, showing the contours changing the land. He reveals the secrets of the soil, the ancient rocks of London Clay, the younger cloth of crag.

He stands with us at the top of a rockface, showing erosion shaping the coast as the boulder clay is washed away by the constant graft of the waves, as the crags collapse in a hungry sea. He points towards the longshore drift which pulls all matter down the coast. He leads us to the cliffs at Covehithe which retreat five yards every year. He explains how Man has countered nature, building bunds and shingle banks, erecting walls and concrete piles. He shows the workings of a groyne to break the motion of the waves, to trap the sediment and the sand. He tells the tale of a winter's night when the tide rose to uncharted heights, bursting defences, opening the land to the fury of the oncoming sea. He guides us over the flooded fields, showing the corpses of thousands of cows, of houses abandoned, of streets laid waste. He escorts us down to a mortuary where over three hundred bodies lie, including some of his kin. He prophesies more of the same.

We have finished the meal. Matty sits enthralled by the journey, his questions answered before they are spoken, his mind awash with Jack's words. I watch the boy and the man before me sharing an intimacy, a connection, feeling within me both joy and pain. This is the fuel to feed him now; this is the sustenance that he needs. A surrogate father to make amends for the one that I have denied him.

Martha has come and collected our plates; she stacks them on a waiting trolley which she wheels away down the hall. Through the open door I can hear muffled noise as she lifts them into the sink. I pick up two dishes and follow behind her, down the dusky corridor until I come to the light. The kitchen is stark and fiercely electric. It shows no shadow, only clinical whiteness. Martha is stood at the sink.

She turns abruptly on hearing me enter, spreading her arms in front of the sideboard as though she doesn't want me to see. I can sense her annoyance at having me here, but I want to leave the others alone, to let them establish a bond.

– Can I help you?
– No, thank you. Do please go back. I will join you all in a minute.
– I'd rather leave them on their own. This is so good for Matty. He's loving it.
–
– Jack knows so much. He's so good at bringing things alive.
– He likes to have the opportunity. He loves history, tradition, the land. This is everything for him. By passing it on he can let it live on. Without the past there is no present, and without that there's no hope for the future. The land is the only thing that is constant, though it's constantly changing itself. The land is cyclical, built around seasons. Only Man moves in a linear path. We learn from the past, but we cannot repeat it. Nothing for us happens twice.
– Jack knows exactly how to talk to a boy. He knows what a boy wants to hear. He must have been a wonderful father.
– Yes, there are similarities. Between Matty and Uriah. Uriah was taught these things too. But he interpreted them differently.
– What do you mean?
– Jack instructs through the ways of the past. He doesn't tell people what they should do. He's too traditional for that. He lets them derive their learning themselves, to take from the past a pattern for living, to apply it however they choose.
– How do you mean? How does Uriah apply it?

– Uriah is my son, and as such I love him. Family is all that there is in life. It's the single most important thing. It must be protected at all costs. Matty will learn the same lessons from Jack. But he will interpret them differently.

– I'm sorry. I don't mean…

– No, you didn't. Will you carry this tray, please? We will take our coffee in the drawing room.

I walk down the unlit corridor and return to the crimson room with the fire. The embers are dying, and the heat is shy. I place the tray on a nearby table; I pick up a poker and prod at the cinders, striving to summon a flame. Then I stoke the grate with more logs. Again, the room becomes alive, its depths awakening, shocked into being, as shadows of flame stud the walls. Matty and Jack have entered to join us; they stand either side of the busy hearth, leaning against the inglenook walls.

– Have you found anything in the earth?

– Many things, yes. But never a Hoxne Hoard.

– What's a Hoxne Hoard?

– Hoxne is a village on the county border only a few miles from Marshfield. There was a man called Eric Lawes who went to look for his hammer in a field, not very far from here. He never found the hammer he'd lost. Instead, he found an old silver coin. It was buried about four inches down. So he dug a bit deeper and found another. Then, twelve inches below the surface, he chanced upon the whole Hoard.

– What was it?

– There were fifteen thousand coins. Most were silver, though some were gold. There was jewellery too, and tableware. There were silver pepper pots, ladles and spoons. All buried in a box which had rotted away. A treasure trove.

– When was it from?

– The coins dated from the late fourth century. By then Roman Britain was in decay. It was severed from the might of Rome, and subject to attack from the north. The Anglo-Romans must have hidden the treasure, being unable to take it with them, intending to retrieve it when they returned. But they never came back. So their secret died through the passage of time. Their secret remained a perfect secret till Eric happened to unearth it.

– Did he get to keep the coins?

– No. The law demands if you find buried treasure you need to tell the police. It's all in the British Museum now. They declared it treasure trove.

– What's that?

– It applies to objects of value that have been hidden through time, for which the owner cannot be found. It leads to an inquest and reverts to the Crown, but is often purchased by a museum, and bought at full market rate. That sum is then passed on as reward.

– So he sold it?

– Effectively, yes. Peter Whatling, the tenant farmer, and Eric both received the reward.

– How much did they get?

– Slightly less than two million pounds. They have lived very well since then.

– That's amazing! Do you think there's more to be had?

– More in the ground? Of course. East Anglia was prosperous in the past. It was one of the most affluent regions in Britain. And it has an ancient history. You could find almost anything here in the fields. The earth is history; it contains the past. It will yield things up to you if you look. Valuable things that you least expect. There are many secrets buried here, and not all have yet been discovered.

– What about in the wood? Is there anything there?

– Who knows? Things may have been hidden there too.

– No, there's nothing to find in the wood. Jack is just teasing you, Matty. The wood is deserted. There's plenty to explore in the fields. That's where things grow, and where things can be found. That is where we have always dug. It's best to steer clear of the woods.

Martha's voice is unnaturally strained; her body is rigid and tense. I feel a sense of uneasiness, just as when the Council was voting, when Martha sought to sway my opinion. I see a tightening in her face, so great her desire to exert control, to shape our minds as she wants them to be. The change is so subtle it's lost on Matty; it even passes her husband by. It is only me who appears to feel it, and only then for an instant. It is softened and fades in the charcoal glow which steals from the grate and is gone. Martha's body relaxes once more; her lips almost shape her mouth in a smile. She invites us both to celebrate Easter, here in her garden with the rest of the village; to join them in hunting for eggs.

~

Rain drips like a mist from the faceless sky, silent, like the shadow of rain. So faint I scarcely feel its print on my hair, on my cheeks, on my splintered hands. Raindrops stand like dust in the sun, proud on the arms of my fleece. Crystalline; sparkling transparent wetness. Even here, in the wind-worn half-woken field – ecstatic, luminous on the tips of the leaves – shimmering, glittering in the wearying breeze. The rain teases the broken face of the soil with an effervescence, with bubbles of light caught in the furrows of blinded earth. It feeds my plants like bread and wine, like milk and honey, like blood.

Behind me lies my treasured plot. So raw, so bare; such a thing of beauty. For another full week, with spade and rake, with these two hands – these hands like claws – I have shaped and fashioned the earth. I have scooped manure from the Faradays' stable; I have spread it onto the sunken earth. I have thrust my spade at this dumb, blind body, splitting its skull and letting it breathe. Through the gaps of its flesh, I have plucked out stones; I have snatched deep roots from beneath its skin. I have watched the worms crease agony; I have watched the bloated robins feed. I have left its clods to the freezing frost and its frigid fingers, working invisibly to unpick the stubborn stitch of its seams. I have broken it down to a crumbled carpet, a fine flat weave, a soft smooth tilth. I have fed the body with lime and bone; I have nurtured it like a child.

Now I look at this thing I have brought into being. At its soft smooth flesh, at the curve of its belly, at its needy and unsullied face. So great is the love that I feel. Tomorrow, in the full of that love, I will furrow lines within its brow and sow its body with seed. Here I will plant the joyous roots: lines of carrots and parsnip and beetroot. They will be joined in the coming weeks by potato tubers, which stretch even now towards the sun in the stillborn shed, nestling in egg trays I was given by Bill. Beyond the roots I will plant the brassicas: seedlings of cabbage and broccoli and sprout, which struggle for life in trays in the kitchen, watching the world from the warmth of the sill. At the end of the patch will be rocket and lettuce. There, to their side, I will plant my onions; I will drill a channel for peas. Then, when the soil is ready to receive them, when the earth is as warm as our Sunday bed, I will fill the vacant space with tomatoes and a clump of tender courgettes.

On the farther side of my patch, I will weave sweet peas up the skeletal trellis which stands barebuned in the idle rain. I will plant out a row of stooping sunflowers to guard the patch with their thousand eyes, to bow their heads as the summer sweats, wearying them with its warmth. Tomorrow it will all be born. The cycle of life will begin.

I imagine Jack, the prophet of nature, the wizard who conjures this seasonal store, holding his arms aloft to the heavens. This land is not a thing, but a being. We, its servants, merely pass through. We touch upon it fleetingly, consumed by its beauty, its infinite bounty, and then we are torn from its breast. The land is the body to which we are born: our mother, our brother, our master, our home. The land is the body in which we are buried: to feed our children, our children's children, to start the cycle anew.

My boots sink into the sodden earth; they crush the clumps of knotted grass. The weight of the cloud is on my back, closing and pressing upon me. I am walking round the side of Six Bells, across the track which leads to the farm – which winks and shifts in the delicate breeze – beyond the tranquillity of the Rectory's lawns, to the edge of the churchyard, and then to the wood.

I pass the depleting stack of logs, swollen and stained by insistent rain, stung with the stale stench of mould. I march beside the fringe of Road Field, its lines of beet in frantic motion, seeming to meet at a point beyond sight.

I come to a belt of nettle and thorn, woven into an impenetrable thicket around the base of the wood. Beyond this rush of angry green – somewhere beyond it – is Matty.

The trees are clothed in uncurled leaf; they shuffle a song which is fickle and tuneless, which drowns the hollow creak of their trunks. Their shadow obscures the heart of the wood, it spills on the decomposing floor, till all but my first steps are hidden. I come to an entrance, a bite in the thicket, and coax myself into its breast.

Inside, the air is muffled and thick; the breeze is spent, and without its breath the harsh chatter of leaves dies away. The floor around me has sprung into being, with stunted growth that catches my feet as if it would drag me within it. The moan of the trunks is almost moist; the dry splintering sound of its barren bone has grown to a supple, sappy cry of pain from that which has come alive. I can feel it breathing – the beat of its heart – the life that is stirring within it.

– Matty!

The thick-fleshed trees and the creeping floor absorb the sound of my voice. I hear an unnatural flurry of wings as a bird retreats to blind skies. I enter further and call once more. The collapsing trunks, the broken branches – all that is strewn on the ground, or is buried – are being devoured by new life. Moss and fungi grow like a cancer. Armies of insects march on parade, hoarding their booty or seeking out prey. Every inch of this aching wood – the floor, the trees, the leaves, the vault – is shifting with motion, is stretching for life.

– I'm over here.
– Where?
– Here. Can't you see?
– Where?
– Here. Right in front of you.

It is Matty. He steps out, detaching himself from the trees. I can see him clearly before me. He is wearing jeans and an old red sweater; his unkempt hair is tangled with twigs. He isn't trying to hide from me, yet he blends with the wood, he seems to become it, as if they are one and the same. It is only by focusing on his sweater that I can distinguish him. He moves, he fades back into the trees, becoming a part of their broader movement: his sound their sound, his breathing as theirs.

I follow the thread-bare red of his sweater as he steers us both through the wood. I cannot keep apace with him, but he knows I am here and compensates; his path is gentler than were he alone. I sense we trace a familiar track, though I do not know where it leads. Around me the saplings are bursting with leaf. Brambles scratch at my naked arms, creepers wind themselves round my legs, pools of nettle snatch at my feet.

I follow Matty, trusting his judgement, trusting his knowledge and strength. In front of us the receding gloom shivers and creaks with anticipation. Above us, roof after roof of twisting leaves block out all semblance of sky. Beneath us, an undulating floor which cracks with my weight and snares my feet, which threatens to drag me into its depths.

We have arrived. Matty has turned; he is signalling to me; he wants me to come to his side. Here is the place where his den once stood. I recognise it by the fallen trunk that he used as a central beam. It rests in the crook of a nearby tree; it's absorbed in a hillock of green.

Matty grins. In a single movement he sinks to the ground; he slides down an incline and slips from my view.

I stare after him — at where he should be — seeking the red of his sweater.

I shuffle forward, approaching the mound. Now, though I cannot see, I can hear. I can hear his voice from within the ground. He is in there, buried within. Beneath a roof of living matter, of earthen walls entangled with fern. His den has seemingly come alive. It has woven into the wood.

Matty reappears. He stands before me, pointing around him, showing me tunnels and towers. I try to make sense; I follow his arm; but all I can see are trees and leaves, are patches of scrub, are ditches and furrows that trace the wood, carved by erosion and time.

He sees that I don't understand. He points again more vigorously, urging me to look through the trees and to see what is lying within. He leads me to a trunk and points upwards. There, above us, is a splay of branches, tangled with murmuring leaf. It's a tree, yet he would have it to be a staircase which spirals into a tower. He tries to show me the steps of the ladder, the railings, the ramparts, the impregnable walls, but I see no more than a clutter of branches couched in a chaos of nascent leaves.

Matty stands at the base of the trunk, looking at me with pride and hope. Then he throws out his arms and begins to scale the solid wall of its side. He climbs up the snarling bark with ease, and melts in a sheath of bright leaves. I can hear his feet on the clattering trunk, the sudden gasp of the startled leaves as the branches strain with his weight. His sound is the same as the sound of the wood; he mirrors its aching, its unnatural creaking, its abrupt and tortured surprise.

I search for the comforting red of his sweater through the arches of newly born leaf. I sense he is there, high up in the trees, his body suspended in pockets of nothing, his feet as if standing on air. The wood groans and sways with irregular motion, each tree as a part of a single body, sharing a singular pain.

Now, from somewhere close beside me, I can hear him calling my name. He appears for an instant, he falters and waves, then he fades back into the rustling leaf and is fused with the shadow once more. Again, far off to my right this time, I hear a call, I see shuddering leaves as he creeps invisibly through the trees. Now all is alive, it is creased in motion, sharing an agony brought to life by the terror and tremor he brings.

Silence. I have lost him again. I feel that eyes are focused upon me; I feel myself being watched. I turn around. I sense Matty is close. His eyes like the eyes of the wood, all-seeing; his supple body like that of the trees. And now he appears, he resumes his shape, he steps from the trunks and stands by my side. He beckons to me, and once more I follow, close behind him – each foot in his print – till we reach the far edge of the wood.

Matty thrusts out his arm, demanding I stop. He points to the base of one of the trees, tight on the fringe of the wood.

About two feet from its base is a switch – a flexible twig – that is tied to the trunk by a cord and bent back, that is held in the clutch of a post. At the end of the switch is a small wooden cross, with its arm sharpened into a spike. A thin stretch of wire leads from there to the tree, pulled taut and close to the ground.

I stare at it uncomprehendingly. Then, in my mind, I see. I see an animal tripping the wire, I see the cross detach from the post, I see it fly with the strength of the switch, I see the spike as it enters the flesh, as it pins the beast to the trunk. I see the creature skewered clean through, bleeding to death whilst nailed to the tree.

— Who did this?
— It's Uriah's.
— It's barbaric. It shouldn't be allowed.
— I don't think it is, but he doesn't care.
— Are there others like this?
— Others, yes.
— You can't come here. Not ever again. It's not safe to be here when there're things like this.
— It's perfectly safe if you know where they are. And I do. I know where all of them are.
— Has he shown you?
— Yes.
— What has he shown you?
— These snares.
— Has he shown you how they work? How to make them?
— Yes.
— And what do you think of them?
— I don't think I would like to be caught.
— Can you dismantle it?
— I could if I wanted. But it wouldn't matter. He would just put up more if I did.
— Have you seen anything caught in a snare?
— No. But I don't come to this part of the wood very often, and the snares are all on this side. Come, I want to show you something else.

Matty steers his way through the wood till it lightens, revealing the field beyond. I follow. I want to be his counsellor, but all I can do is feel a revulsion, a sense of foreboding which creeps through my flesh. I can see, but I can't understand. I can't begin to make sense. I wonder if it is Matty or me who is losing our reason, our sense of control. I think, were you here, you would reprimand Matty, you would help him to see right from wrong. But maybe instead you would turn towards me, you would say it is me who is losing her grasp, who has lost all sense of what's right.

Matty carves a trail through the living green wall till we come to the fringe of the field. The sky is dull, the day in decline; the earth has smudged to a colourless form, a single, amorphous entity. Matty stands on a belt of cropped grass between the wood and the field. He waits until I am watching him, till I'm looking at him as he stands upright, a half-dozen paces before me. Then he jumps to one side; he is gone. Here, before me, he's consumed by the land. He was here; and now he has gone.

I lurch through the grass to the place where he stood. Searching and wanting to find him out. Daring, not daring, to see. Now here, here's an opening – a small hole in the ground. And inside the hole here is Matty.

He climbs out, grinning a wide grin at me, pleased to see my confusion.

– There are lots of them. All along here. In a line.
– What are they?
– Tunnels, I think. They're all underground.
– What's in them?

– I don't know. But they're man-made. Look, they're made of concrete. They've got walls.

– Has Uriah explained what they are?

– No. He doesn't know I come this far. He's told me there's nothing to see here. He says I shouldn't come this side. Especially not to this place.

– He's right. I don't think you should go inside. You don't know what might be in them. You don't know where they might lead.

– There's nothing in them. I don't think. They haven't been used for years. They're all grown over. No one would ever think to come down here.

– Let's go back. It's getting late. We can ask Jack when we see him next. He'll know what they are and who built them.

The afternoon is ugly and thickening; the skies are growing denser and darker; slow rain is settling in. We trudge round the wood towards Road Field, seeing the island of Rose House Farm emerge through a grey wall of rain. We come to the stack of sodden logs, to the track which leads towards the church. I follow Matty, feeling a lightness, a lessening of fear, the further we walk from the wood. As we reach the corner of the graveyard, I steal a final look at the trees as they vanish into the dusk. There, at their foot, I can see the outline of a man who is standing motionless. He appears to be shouldering a gun.

I try to keep up, to match Matty's pace, as he stubbornly strides up the road. I feel the need to talk to him, but I'm uncertain how to begin. We bend our heads to the strengthening rain which is driven towards us on the breeze as we walk up the slope, as we pass Six Bells, as we come in sight of our lawn.

Matty has broken into a run; he's inside before I am close. He seems not to have noticed the latest offering, laid here on the wall by the door. Joyce has come and gone once more, leaving a present of flowers. This time it's a bunch of anemones. The wind flower, sprung from the blood of Adonis, stabbed by the tusk of a boar. She has left them, caught in a soft blue ribbon, like treasure to brighten my world.

I pick them up and go in. I lay my coat on the back of a chair and kick off my boots in the hall. In the kitchen I fill and turn on the kettle, hearing the reassuring whirr of the boiler blasting and breathing its heat. I cut slabs of bread for the hungry toaster. I open two cans of beans. Then I go to the bathroom to dry my hair. I lock the door once inside.

I stand at the mirror and look at my face. At the limp hair clung to my temples and forehead, at the pale cracked lips, at the flakes of dry skin on either side of my nose. I put out a hand towards the mirror, tracing my image in its reflection. I recognise neither the hand nor the face.

Where are you, Sarah? Where have you gone? You, who are buried and lost.

I run the bath. I sit hunched on the loo as the water flows, as steam curls into the room. I feel my body convulse with a motion beyond my power to control. I let go. I feel the burn of my useless tears as they break against my thighs. I feel the forced inhale of my breath, the rub of the air on the back of my throat, the shudder of my labouring chest. How could it ever have come to this? How has it happened this way? Turning so far and so fast from the known, that where we are now makes no sense.

Downstairs I light the wood-burning stove. I try to fill the cottage with warmth. I return to the kitchen to make beans on toast; I call to Matty when they're ready.

We eat greedily, noisily – eating not speaking – helping ourselves till the beans have all gone. Then we retreat to the heart of the cottage; we slump in the armchairs facing the stove, watching the fire as it burns.

It grows late. Through the uncurtained window I can see the garden being swallowed by dusk. The hedge, the trees, the sky have all faded; they have fallen away from my sight. Now all I can see are the quivering rose-stems, stood out against an unfathomable blackness, scratching the frame of the glass. Matty reclines, not asleep nor awake, his eyes transfixed on the flame.

– I'm going to the pub for a bit. I'll be back soon. You can put yourself to bed if you're tired.

In my bedroom I change into a clean pair of jeans. I pull a thick sweater over my head. I stare at the mirror once more. I watch as my hand applies some mascara, a smudge of lipstick, some moisturiser to freshen my face. I watch myself brush my hair.

It is cold outside, despite the cloud. It is dark in the absence of moon or stars. The rain has washed from the sky. I walk swiftly down the heart of the road, looking to neither side of the road till I reach the door of the pub.

It is bright and cosy inside. A huge log roasts on a pleasing fire; there's a gentle murmur of voices. The Faradays are sat in a corner, working through papers, engrossed. Travis is cleaning the glasses and shelves; he's holding a cloth in his hands.

– Hi there, Travis. Can I get a half of Adnams?

– Sure. So how are you? What have you been up to?

– This and that. Getting there.

– That's good. Is it beginning to feel like home?

– Sometimes it does, yes. Sometimes not. It's very different.

– I think I know what you mean. Even now I wake up sometimes and wonder where I am.

– How long have you been here?

– Over five years. Perhaps more. I've lost all sense of time. Days just happen. Months disappear. Sometimes slowly; sometimes – ha! – like that.

– And how's Samantha?

– I guess she's ok. She doesn't want to come down today.

– Isn't she feeling well?

– No, it's not that. It feels different when you live in a pub, that's all. When you're here every day and all of the time. And some days, you don't feel you can. I know I've got to, so I've learned to detach, but with her there's no obligation. Besides, I like being here. I like the company.

– Who are your regulars?

– Bill and Margaret pop in every night once they've shut up the shop. Robert Witton comes when he's flush. Uriah is usually here. Other than that, it's passing trade. And not many pass this way these days. How are you getting on?

– I think it's going all right. I'm trying. It's easier with some than with others, if you know what I mean.

– You'll always be an outsider to some, no matter how long you've been here. It took me years to break in. And there's still one or two that will never see me as a legitimate part of the village. I wasn't born here. Nor were my parents. I'm not a part of the land. Outsiders are naturally viewed with suspicion. The village feels threatened from the outside.

– I'm glad it's not only me who feels like that. But it's a bit of a shame all the same.

– You have to keep plugging away. In time you will wear more barriers down. Can I give you the other half?

Travis is reaching across for my glass when I hear the opening door. I can feel the coldness wash through the room; I can sense who it is without turning. I can hear the scrape of his boots.

Travis fills the old pewter jug as Uriah approaches the bar. He wears a thick coat that is moistened by rain; his scalp is shiny and wet. There is mud on his boots and his trouser legs; there are stains of mud on his hands. He places a shotgun beside the bar; its barrels aimed at the roof.

– Hello, Uriah.

–

– I think I saw you today, by the wood. Were you there this afternoon?

– Maybe.

– Have you been out there shooting?

–

– Did you catch anything in your snares?

He turns and looks at me directly. His eyes meet my own and don't sway. He looks at me, he looks through my skin, as if to find the reason I know, the reason I care where he's been. Moments pass, but I will not yield, I will not turn from his gaze. He seems to find the answer he needs. His eyes glaze over once more. They drop from my face to my chin to my neck, to my chest to my thighs, and back to my face. Then he twists away, raising his jug to his mouth.

– And how is Joyce? Is she well?

His eyes return and lock on my own, as if piercing into my skull. He seems to grow large, to come closer towards me, though he doesn't move from the bar. The room is sweating with stifling heat which spits from the ravenous fire. The air is blistered to cinder. Each breath I take is sucked through the walls and chased out into the night. I feel the pulse of blood through my temples. I put out a hand to steady myself. There is somebody close to my side. Travis has come to rescue me. But it isn't Travis, it's Peter.

– Same again please, Travis. Evening, Uriah. Well, hello you, how are things?
– Very good thanks.
– I've seen you from Six Bells. You've been out at the back. Have you dug in all that manure?
– Finally, yes. I didn't think it would be so tiring. I didn't think it would take so long. I'm exhausted, but it feels quite good now. I'm excited.
– There's something special about the land. It's almost magical how things grow. Look after it and it'll look after you. Have you treated the soil at all?
– I did a test like you showed me. And I've spread a bit of lime. That's all.
– Good. Then your plot's organic. You'll taste a difference.
– Bullshit.
– You will. That's why people buy what I grow. It's more than the principle. It's the taste.
– Bullshit.
– What's wrong with organic, Uriah?
– It's stunted and deformed. The yield is poor. The crop is snagged by weed. It's so much bullshit.
– It's what a lot of people will pay for, no matter what you might think.

144

– I was twelve when I started to work for my father. I was sent to Black Acre with only a hoe. It was planted with beet, and it wasn't clean. There was fat hen, charlock, winter weed, warlock, coltsfoot, twitch. Each thrust jarred into my wrists. I did less than a row that first day. It took two weeks to finish the field. I could do four rows a day by the end. My father thought horses were better than tractors. I'm never going back to that way of thinking. Never.

– Organic isn't going backwards, it's progress. It's learning from the past; it's applying all that we know. It's moving on. If anything, it's you who's standing still.

– Bullshit. I know the land. I live the land. It's in my blood. It's been through generations of Pooleys.

– I respect your tradition, Uriah. I respect your father. But you must see how things continually change. It's not only your heritage, but also your livelihood.

– Organic farming's a fad. Only my method will survive.

– As you like. Anyway, Sarah, what are you going to grow in your patch?

– Just the basics, I think. Some carrots, beetroot, onions, spinach, peas. I've got runner beans, tomatoes and courgettes in trays. And I'm chitting potatoes in the shed. That's what you call it, isn't it? 'Chitting'?

– You haven't got a fucking clue, have you?

– It's not nice to talk like that, and it's not fair. She's starting out. She's done her research. She'll learn through experience, like you and me. There's no short cut for that.

– It's a veg patch. It's a silly little strip of earth. Do what you want with it.

– Do. Plant it. Tend it. Enjoy it. I'm glad the patch is clean. Look, I've got to get back to Jemima now. Not too early, not too deep, not too thick, Sarah. Remember that when you sow.

Peter picks up his drinks and wanders away. Uriah turns to the unlit room, staring into its space. Travis pretends to be sorting the peanuts; their packets crinkle with sympathy. It is time I was going back home. I stand and turn towards the door, returning Peter's parting wave. Travis steps out from behind the bar; he follows me to the porch. A coldness slithers under the door. I can feel its chill on my feet.

– It's easier with some than with others, you know. You'll always be an outsider to some. No matter what you do.
– I guess.
– The important thing is that you make it with some. You've made it with Peter, with Bill and Margaret, with me. Remember that.
– I will. Thanks, Travis.
– Listen, I don't know much about farming. I can't help you with that. But I can help you with other things.
– Like what?
– Like with the Fair. I can help you with the leafleting. Would… would you like me to take you to Oakham Green? We could put up posters. It's pleasant there. After Easter sometime.
– You and me?
– Yes. Me and you. I could show you around. We could go for a walk. We could get some lunch maybe.

Travis opens the door on the night. The cooler air creeps into the porch, pinching my fire-warm skin. I pull my coat about me closer, bracing myself for the walk. I nod. We say goodnight. I step out into the empty blackness. The road is polished with recent rain; the air is hollow and clean. The sound of my feet on the heavy road reverberates through the trees. Travis watches me to the bend, peering through a crack of light, then he gently closes the door.

146

~

The body of the church is bright with daffodils placed in the crevice of every window, reflecting the rays of a searching sun. The pale walls creep with an early warmth. The crimson carpet flickers with heat like glowing coals in the grate. The dense wooden pews house adults and children. This building has been resurrected, revived; its skeleton has become flesh.

Colin Inchmore welcomes the village on this day of renewal and rebirth. He thanks Joyce and Martha for arranging the flowers, for filling the church with their scent. He says that the eggs the children have brought will be given to a hospice nearby. In the pew behind us are Rosie and Buster, the Meredith children, debating in whispers which egg is the best. In the opposite pew the Faraday girls sit upright with egg-baskets laid on their laps. We stand together; we sing Alleluias; the sound of our voices floats through the church and stretches up to the hammer-beam roof.

This feels like the very first day of my future – a chance to forge a fresh beginning, to start anew and to be at peace with myself and the world around me. Dormant winter has burst into life; it has shed its shackles, it has borne bright spring, and with the spring has come a rebirth. Seeds have pushed up through the earth, bringing colour and joy.

*The first day of the week cometh Mary Magdalene early, when it was yet dark, unto the sepulchre, and seeth the stone taken away from the sepulchre.*

*Then she runneth, and cometh to Simon Peter, and to the other disciple, whom Jesus loved, and saith unto them, They have taken away the Lord out of the*

The skies are clear, they are washed with sun, they ring with the voices of eager children. This is the long-awaited awakening. This is the hope I have held in my heart. This is where I begin. Deep in the past there was discord and pain; a hurt and a hate that punished us all; that dragged us into a sorrowful place which was steeped in death and decay. We have buried that now. That life is ended. Divorced by distance; distanced by time. Removed too far to return. Even were I to seek it out, to run to the tomb where I know it lies buried, to roll back the stone and to look within, I know I would find nothing there. For us there is no resurrection. Yet that does not mean we are dead. We have merely been dormant. And from that latency can spring life. A richer, a riper, a better life. We can rise and seize it if only we dare. We can live and be true to ourselves.

*sepulchre, and we know not where they have laid him.*

*Peter therefore went forth, and that other disciple, and came to the sepulchre.*

*So they ran both together: and the other disciple did outrun Peter, and came first to the sepulchre.*

*And he stooping down, and looking in, saw the linen clothes lying; yet went he not in.*

*Then cometh Simon Peter following him, and went into the sepulchre, and seeth the linen clothes lie,*

*And the napkin, that was about his head, not lying with the linen clothes, but wrapped together in a place by itself.*

*Then went in also that other disciple, which came first to the sepulchre, and he saw, and believed.*

*For as yet they knew not the scripture, that he must rise again from the dead.*

Jack comes to a close and raises his head; he looks out over the pews. He is pleased to see what is here. This is his village; this is his hope: a new generation to inherit the earth. Now is the time for renewal and rebirth. He walks from the lectern and sits in his pew. Martha squeezes his hand.

Colin Inchmore invites the children to come to the altar and offer their eggs. We witness a gentle commotion. Buster leaps forward to get there first; Rosie waits for her mother's hand; India and Nutmeg walk up the aisle parading their eggs with undisguised pride. Colin Inchmore receives them all, carefully placing the eggs round the cross. Then the children clatter back into their seats. There's a final hymn, a final prayer, and we walk out into the light.

At the entrance I shake Colin Inchmore's hand, thanking him for the service. He smiles wearily in reply; he's already late for Marshfield. The village assembles on the gravel outside, clustered in groups which spill onto the grass and around the heads of the gravestones. I would introduce Matty to some of the parents, but he's wandered off and avoids my eyes.

Children are running amongst the tombs, the sun and the dappled shade on their backs, the crisp breeze ruffling their hair. There's an easy murmur of idle chatter, a kinship, a unity. Martha is working the groups in turn; Jack waits by the gate shaking hands. Matty is striding down the road with Uriah, locked in eager debate. I search for Joyce, but I cannot see her; she's already glided away. One by one the groups disperse, stuttering, strolling up the street, heading for Burnt Tree Farm. Now only Bill and Margaret are here. They seem to be waiting for me.

– Well, dear, happy Easter. How are you?

– That was a lovely service. It's nice to see the church so full.

– Twice a year it's busy, yes. The whole village is rounded up. It's a condition of being invited to Martha's.

– And you've met the Merediths now?

– Yes.

– And all of the children?

– I think so, yes.

– So that makes everyone.

– Almost, yes.

– Who have we missed?

– I know everyone by sight, but I haven't met them all. I haven't met Joyce.

– You still haven't spoken to her?

– No.

– Well, that's not surprising.

– Why not?

– She isn't the sort to talk.

– I think she wants to. I think she'd like to, if Uriah would let her.

– But he won't. And even if he did, I doubt she'd remember how to talk, or what to talk about.

– I'm sure she's very friendly. She's a little shy, that's all. She's tried…

– Has she? How has she tried?

– What did she do?

– Nothing really. It doesn't matter.

– She may have tried, but she won't be able to.

– What do you mean? Is there something the matter with her?

– There's nothing wrong with her. It's who she is.

– Who is she?

– She's Uriah's wife. Joyce Pooley. But her maiden name's Joyce Bayles.

– She's the younger sister of Tom. Tom Bayles. Hasn't anyone told you about him?

– No.

– No, they wouldn't. Well, it was him. He's the one. The one that ran off with Laura Sheldrake. The one that ran off with Uriah's first wife.

– Uriah is married to the younger sister of the man who eloped with his wife. Don't you think that's a bit odd, Sarah?

– It's a coincidence, I expect. That's all. What her brother did has got nothing to do with her. I don't see why it stops her from talking to people. I expect she's just shy.

– It's no coincidence, Sarah.

– Don't you see? It's in the blood. She knows.

– She knows. And he knows that she knows.

– I'm not sure I understand. I'm not sure I want to.

The breeze toys with the knotted grass near the path; it shuffles the silver leaves on the trees, shivering their branches, enticing their shadows to dance on the graves and the stone church walls. Patches of people are walking ahead, up the road and along the track that leads through the fields to Burnt Tree Farm. I suggest that we ought to join them. I hurry them both away from the church, keen to catch up with the rest.

Martha has set out two trestle tables by the open French doors in her kitchen. There are teacups and glasses; there are plates with cakes; there are biscuits, flapjacks and scones. Through the open doors I can see the children are running around at the top of the slope. I excuse myself from Margaret and Bill, and search the garden for Matty.

He is here, he is still in discussion with Uriah, at the farther end of the lawn. In front of me are Samantha and Robert. I join them, pretending to listen. They are happy enough for me to be here so long as I don't interrupt.

Travis is talking to Crispin Meredith by a buddleia close to the house. He's reliving his life in London maybe. He glances up to look at Samantha. Or perhaps he's looking at me. I wonder what goes on in his head, seeing her arm on Robert's shoulder, seeing her lips so near to his ear. I wonder how he feels in the pub, watching her almost every night as she turns her attention elsewhere. Maybe that's why he has asked me out. To take his revenge; to flirt with me, being the only one here who is single. Though maybe he likes me for who I am; he might be attracted to me. What a curious concept. It's been so long since I felt attractive, since I felt I had the power to attract. You stifled that feeling with your indifference; you choked my belief, you let it die. It's been dead so long I have quite forgotten how I ought to respond. I don't even know if I want to respond. To harbour feelings for another man, for someone other than you. How strange the thought. Being together or being apart, there has never been anyone else.

Martha has come out onto the lawn and is gathering the children about her. She explains the rules of the egg hunt. Buster's are blue, Rosie's are red, India's are silver, and Nutmeg's are green. Matty, too, has hidden treasure, though I cannot hear what it is. I hope he will have the heart to join in, though he's standing aloof and unsure. At fourteen, he's neither a child nor a man. He is at the mercy of both. At times swayed by either, by circumstance, depending on what comes his way. Now he is locked in talk with Uriah. Now he is being a man.

India is tired of looking for eggs. She has seven already, but she can't find more. She thinks a fox may have had them. I offer to help, as a means of escape. We walk round the garden hand in hand. Her mind is that of a seven-year-old child; she talks about nothing but eggs.

I guide her over towards Uriah, hoping to hear what they say. He and Matty connect so well, talking as man to man. With no condescension, no artifice. You would be so proud of him now. I glance up as we amble towards them. Uriah isn't awkward with Matty; it seems to be only with me. I can hear his voice is fluent and smooth, though what he is saying escapes me. He would make a good father, I think. Fiercely protective, tough and yet fair, prepared to die for what he believes in: for his family, for the land. I wonder why he hasn't had children to pass on all that is his. Perhaps it's not his decision to make; it is nature having her way.

India has found another egg. A sparkle of silver in the cup of her hands. It's evident she is delighted. We have come to the farther side of the house, and out of her parents' sight. They have told her that she can't eat chocolate until she has had her lunch. But she cannot help scraping the egg on her teeth, scratching the skin of chocolate away, if only to see how it tastes. Perhaps she is not so innocent. Now the rest of the egg has been consumed, and with it has gone the ecstasy. There are two more silver eggs to find. She tells me I haven't been trying my best. I'm no longer useful to her. She's right – I'm not – I've been looking elsewhere. I've been wondering what has happened to Joyce. She may have marooned herself on her island; she may have been denied by Uriah; or she may be here though she cannot be seen – she's watching us from behind a bush, or from in the heart of a hedge.

Martha is marshalling us all up the slope; she is making us stand in a single long line. Even Uriah must comply. We are all presented with a hard-boiled egg. The rules are simple; they are fixed in stone. They haven't altered for over a century. Jack stands on a chair at the end of the line, holding a flag in his hand. His posture is noble, dignified, proud. He's enacting tradition, fulfilling his purpose, oblivious of how absurd it appears.

Far below us, at the base of the slope, Martha marks an imaginary line. She is the judge; her word is final. Any egg that is not properly rolled will forfeit the right to a prize. The first one over her line will win. We stand expectant, unexpectedly nervous. At Jack's command we all bend over, placing our eggs on the grass. Now we are crouching – all of us crouching – watching out for the flag. The inhabitants of Nettlesden, framed in spring sunshine, awaiting a signal from Jack.

The flag drops.

I push at my egg with tentative fingers, fearing the humiliation of disqualification, conscious of bodies bundling past me, of eggs racing out of control. I prod at my own with greater force, urging it on down the hill. I give it a heave and chase behind it, flipping it over again. I feel a surge of confidence now; I think I have got a technique.

I hear a cry from somewhere below me. I sit on my knees and look up. Across the slope are a litter of bodies, standing or crouching or flat on their backs. There are eggs, there are shells, there are fragments of yolk, strewn randomly over the grass. Two dogs have run free and are nuzzling the lawn, clearing detritus away.

Somewhere below me I catch sight of Matty. He stands euphoric, his arms in the air, an egg, triumphant, held in one hand. Martha declares him the winner. We crowd around him on the sun-spoilt slope, cheering him, shaking his hand. The village unites, it comes together – not as it does in the church or the pub, but here on the Pooley's lawn – as one.

And Matty and I are right at its heart.

~

# Summer

There was a time when I didn't think I had the strength to do this. A time when I didn't think that I could make it work. There was a time before I left when leaving was unthinkable. And a time of being here when I thought it unsustainable. There was a time when all I knew was breaking down; when everything I saw and heard reminded me of you. But now that time is past. Now it is time to plant and tend; now it is time to grow. The past has passed; the future beckons. I have done with killing; I have done with weeping; I have done with throwing stones at you. Now it is time to heal. For me and you, both separately. To begin anew, to embrace what we have, to rekindle love in our separate ways. To find what is lost and buried within us; to discover it can be good.

*To every thing there is a season, and a time to every purpose under the heaven:*

*A time to be born, and a time to die; a time to plant, and a time to pluck up that which is planted;*

*A time to kill, and a time to heal; a time to break down, and a time to build up;*

*A time to weep, and a time to laugh; a time to mourn, and a time to dance;*

*A time to cast away stones, and a time to gather stones together; a time to embrace, and a time to refrain from embracing;*

*A time to get, and a time to lose; a time to keep, and a time to cast away;*

*A time to rend, and a time to sew; a time to keep silence, and a time to speak;*

*A time to love, and a time to hate; a time of war, and a time of peace.*

Jack folds his paper into his pocket, looking out over the pews. This is our time; a time that is ours. A time of sowing and tending and growing, of feeling the sun on the broad of our backs as we labour over the soil. A time of building and cementing new friendships, of securing the village and keeping it close. A time for discovery, for raising the dead. A time to face up to the truth.

Jack walks solemnly back to his pew, upright and rigid with pride. His face is caught in shafts of light, which slice through the stained-glass panes. I can feel the heat of the sun on his skin, its insistence kissing his wincing eyes; I can feel the welcome cool of the shade on the flagstone floor and here in the pews, where the sun has yet to encroach. There's a smell of life, of hope, in the church. Flowers are strewn in every alcove, ecstatic with colour and scent; a vibrant breeze breathes through the door and wafts its charm down the aisle. Trees through the windows bustle and sway, the commotion of leaves like the roll of the sea, like resistless waves breaking onto the land.

This is a time of plenty. My work has come through. From a drought, I am drowned in new projects. I have found enough work to see through the summer, a schedule so full it will busy my days. In the garden my vegetables grow; long lines of leaf soothe the bald scalp of earth, moulding new shapes in the ground. A fusion of green, a living texture, sucking life from the soil with such greed I can almost watch as it grows. Already the lettuce is fit to eat; the bulbous bodies of radishes have burst into being and wink at me as they sit and wait to be plucked. Already the spinach has started to yield: it submits to my hand, it melts in my mouth – a sensation of taste, a softness like silk.

The days grow long, the evenings lengthen. I walk by the side of awakened fields; I walk between hedgerows thickened with life; I walk in the shade of a million leaves, shuffling shadow and light. Matty comes back from school on the bus, he eats then goes straight to the wood. I watch him run down the side of the field, the sun and the wind in his hair. He is free. He buries himself in the trees. Day after day, till the sun sinks low, till the fervour slips from its fiery eye and the waning sky steals to pink. Then he returns, exhausted, delighted – with mud on his palms, with leaves in his hair – hungry for food and for sleep. He is so unlike the Matty I knew – the Matty from London – the boy that once was a child. You wouldn't know him now if you saw him. I think you would pass by him on the street; you couldn't tell it is him. He has grown so much – as distant and tall as the trees that mature in the wood. He has grown so swiftly there was no transition; it is hard to think him my son. This man-boy, seated here in this pew; this stranger, this native I love. I see his contentment, I feel his strength, protecting him like a shield. That is all I could ever want; everything that I need. His happiness, my happiness. There's no need for more. Fed by earth's lifeblood, intrepid and eager, at ease with himself. This is a time of peace.

Colin Inchmore blesses his flock. He raises his hands as if he would pull the sunbeams into the heart of the church, piercing its soul with the light. He walks towards the sun-struck door, with Jack and Martha following behind. Then Uriah enters the aisle. Joyce is half-hidden in the crook of his shoulder, cast in a constant fringe of shadow, beyond the measure of sight. Now Margaret and Bill are waiting their turn. Then it is Matty and me. We spill out in pairs, we stroll past the graveyard, enveloped in life-giving warmth.

We shield our eyes from the wind-whipped brightness, merging as groups which dissolve in the sun only instants after they form. The exchanges are formal and swift. I search for Joyce, but she's no longer here; it's as if she's been consumed by the sun, unable to exist beyond shadow, beyond the stealthy edge of the day. Matty exchanges some words with Uriah, then he runs through the gate towards Steeple Field, transformed to the wood-sprite once more. I call him to me, and we walk up the road, away from the others, till we come to our home.

Matty changes into old clothes while I cut some sandwiches for his lunch. He comes down, snatching the bag from my hand, plucking two apples from out of the bowl, running out onto the grass. He turns and looks as I come to the door. He's so full of life, so full of living, so full of being alive. I would keep him here longer, I would capture this moment, I would hold it and treasure it, locked in my heart. But I feel the force of longing within him, his urge to be lost in amongst the tight trees, and it would be cruel to detain him. His happiness my happiness; his passion my pleasure. I wave; I watch him depart.

In the cool of the kitchen, I make myself coffee, then take it upstairs while I change. I need something smart, but nothing too formal. I run my hands through my clothes. Nothing I see seems right on me now – either it or my body don't fit. It has been so long since I tried. Deep in the distance of ancient past, I remember a time, a comment, a look. Something akin to a compliment. You liked the skirt I was wearing. You thought it fitted me well. What did you mean by that simple phrase? Why did you say it to me? You let down your guard for an instant then, or perhaps you just said what you felt. You designed it to get the better of me;

you designed it to injure me in some way. No. Because I looked at you and I stared. It was in your eyes; it was in your voice. So unexpected, so sure. And once you had said it, I knew that you meant it.

What did I say in reply?

Here, hidden behind my winter coat, I find the very same skirt. How long has it been since I wore this? I wonder what blouse I was wearing that day. I wonder what made it so different. It might have been a special occasion, though I cannot recall what it was. I can only remember that comment. If something was special, it no longer is. For now, I need nothing fancy.

I put on some make-up; I brush my hair. I am not Samantha, I will not pretend. I pick up the posters and go downstairs. I make more coffee as I wait for the car. I sip it nervously, cursing myself. Now I'll need to go to the loo all the time; he will think I have got a condition. I tip the rest of the cup in the sink.

I hear the slowing and stop of a car; the gentle sigh as it comes to rest on the wastrel grass of the verge. Travis steps out and smiles in welcome. I pick up the posters and walk towards him. Gallantly, he opens the passenger door, closing it once I am in. The windows are down, and through them I catch the smell of the fields, the whip of the breeze, as we ease out of the village, unseen.

Travis drives slowly, describing each road, explaining where each of them lead. He points out ponds and ditches and tracks; the roadside stalls where plants are for sale. I feel the strength of the sun on my arm; its gradual heat which steals through the car; the sheen of haze on the fields beyond.

Now we have come to a village. He glides the car to a halt as we enter; he stretches into the back. I get out, clutching the posters he gives me, watching the car as it slips down the road and vanishes over the brow. On a telegraph pole I spread out a poster, feeling within my pocket for tacks, easing them into the dry, dead wood. I look about me to see who is watching, stung by a feeling of guilt. I cross a small bridge and enter the village. Here on the left there's a pub. On the right there's an antiques shop and a store, with a post office sunk to its side. I slip furtive posters under each door. At the pub the barman asks for some leaflets. He comes every year, he assures me. He props up a poster beside the till. I continue walking along the street, stopping at telegraph poles.

In the distance, at the end of the village, I can see Travis busily pinning up posters on either side of the road. I work my way towards him slowly, my confidence growing, a warmth within me fuelled by the sweat of the sun. Together we climb a gentle rise which leads towards a squat church. I can hear thin voices, the sound of an organ, muffled and locked in its bowels. We swamp the parish board with our posters, then hasten away from the crime. Back in the car we pull away; we are swallowed into the blinding green of lush trees and strict-planted fields.

More villages, more people, more telegraph poles. A swirl of movement and light, of sunshine and shade – the land laid out on every side, gasping at the thickening air, in rapture at the stare of the sun. Travis' voice is a smooth deep hum, like the sound of the engine, rising and falling, soothing, content. His words losing sense as they snag on the hedges, as they blur with the fields which swim to our sides.

At Oakham Green Travis stops the car, letting me out on the verge. Again, we work from both ends of the village, meeting once more at its heart. This time there's a basket held in his hand. I follow his footsteps down a track until we come to a weir. Travis leads on through a clutch of trees; he opens a gate and enters a field. Warrens and burrows are scratched in the earth; an easy river curls through the grass, its fringes broken by reed. We walk to its side and gaze at its flow, at the burst of brilliant sun on its face, at the shadows which finger its depths.

Travis comes to a stop. We have reached a bend in the river. From here we are blind to the gate and the road. On the farther side, in the middle distance, a farmhouse nestles beneath a knoll. I can hear the sound of unseen geese, of a dog, of a straining tractor engine, faint in the hot, heavy air.

Travis spreads a rug by the river, caught in the shade of a tree. We sit. He takes bread, cheese, ham and baby tomatoes out of the basket he's brought. There are two plates, two knives, two bottles of beer. This is the county line, he tells me. On the opposite bank it is Norfolk.

– This is my favourite place. I come here often.
– With Samantha?
– No. On my own. Samantha doesn't like it here.
– Why not? It's gorgeous.
– I don't mean the river. I mean Suffolk. All of it. She doesn't like it here.
– I guess it's hard to fit in. You said that yourself. Others have told me the same.
– It's hard to fit in if you want to fit in. But it's harder if you don't even try. If you don't want to be here; if you've never wanted. Then it is almost impossible.

– I thought you both made the decision to come.

– Sure. We both made the decision. I think. But it's one thing to make a random decision, and another living with it. You can look at any place on a map; you can see pictures of it, of places like this. The river, the country, the sun. But until you're here you just don't know. You don't know the people, you don't know yourself. You don't know how it will feel. You don't know until it's too late.

– She doesn't like it, then?

– No. It's not a question of like. She hates it. If I were bitterly honest with you, I guess I don't really like it myself. But I've learnt to live with it and its drawbacks. I try. But she doesn't try – she resists it. She won't engage; she blocks it out; she pretends it doesn't exist. If she stays in the pub, if she watches TV, she can almost remove herself from the country, she can almost deny that she's here.

– That's not much of a life.

– No, but it is survival. It's her way of surviving. Until something else comes along.

– If you don't want to be here, then why don't you move?

– Move where? I've tried London. I've tried Essex. I tried a place in the Midlands, too. Each is different, but they're all the same. I don't mind the place; I don't mind the job. What matters most is the people. You can swap them out too, if you really want. But I can't swap Samantha or me.

– Where would she like to be most?

– In London, probably. But it's not the place anymore. It's the situation. It's us. I'll never be good commercially; I haven't got the nous. But that doesn't matter. I can live with my own limitations. I don't mind doing a mundane job so long it gives me enough to live on, so long as it keeps me engaged. I could run a pub anywhere in the world and I'd be happy enough so long as I knew that she liked it.

– What would make her happy?

– I don't know. Something else. Not this. We've forgotten how to make ourselves happy. We've forgotten what happiness is.

– What would make you happy?

– I haven't asked myself. I'm too much of a coward. I don't like change. I'm more tolerant than Samantha. I would be happy if there was someone here, someone I felt I could share with. Someone who I could go for a walk with. Someone I felt I could talk to. Someone who cared, someone I loved, someone who loved in return.

Travis is lying back on his elbows, surveying the river, the flats of Norfolk, seemingly calm and relaxed. But his voice is searching; it is asking questions. He feels uncomfortably close. I stand up, stepping into the sun, allowing the heat of its gaze to consume the awkwardness that I feel.

It has been so long. I've forgotten the pain of intimacy; the doubt, the foreboding it brings. The interchange of complex feelings; the gap between what is said and unspoken; the silences stronger than words. And I have only you to compare with. I have never known anyone else. It was so different then, and so far in the past. I had forgotten what it was like. You threw your love at me like a tempest. Yours was a flash of electricity, which shocked me to life and sparked my heart with delicious yearning and wanting to be. Wanting to be, for the hour, for the day, for the rest of my days, with you. With you, beside you, always, forever. There was such fury, such energy then. It was so much more intense than this: more forceful than this could ever become. How strange I remember so clearly now all that I thought I had lost. All that was buried and gone. And in surfacing, it seems not as raw as I thought or I feared it would be. This man I am with is so different to you. He is nothing like you; he will never be you. He hesitates closeness, he hides what he feels: his advance is so slight that he can retract if he senses it isn't returned. He can withdraw, he can shut it away, pretending it doesn't exist.

A film of cloud is obscuring the sun, stretching its shadow across the field. A soft wind ripples the river's surface, and all within it is lost.

I shiver slightly. I think it is time we should go. Travis is chivalrous, opening gates, holding my jacket, walking beside me ready to offer his hand.

The sun is broad in our faces once more by the time we arrive at the car. We make three more stops to put up our posters, Travis assuming the role of my guide.

It is mid-afternoon. Travis opens my door one last time, helping me out of the car. The sun is full in his face. He squints. He brushes the back of my hand with his own, almost as though it were meant. It has been an enjoyable day, and I thank him. I watch him step back into his car and drive away down the road to the church, towards the desolate pub.

I shuffle over the lawn. On the wall by the side of the door there's a posy. A clutch of wild iris caught in the sheath of their long thin leaves, tied with a ribbon in a matching bow. The flowers are soft, impeccably blue. Removed from the hedgerow and brought to my home. Plucked the wilderness; given to me.

I put the stems in a vase on the table. They stand erect and burstingly blue. The single source of light, of life, within the gloom of this room. Then I go upstairs to change.

It feels more natural to be wearing my trousers, with the smell and the stain of earth on their knees. I walk through the garden, around the cottage, till I come to the field of beet. The roots are beginning to swell in the earth; their bodies are pressing against the soil. The island of Rose House Farm is asleep in the haze of the long afternoon. Beyond it, the shimmering wood stands silent, holding within it my son. I walk round the hedge to the vegetable patch, inspecting it, pulling at weeds. If I watch it each day I remain in control: the slugs at my mercy, the weeds contained, the produce picked when just ripe.

To the side of the shed, Matty's built me a cold frame from glass and bricks he has found. Inside it are cucumber plants and tomatoes; the early shoots of tender courgettes push their green-yellow stalks through the compost, their closed heads wearing the shells of their seeds. I raise the glass to water the stems, watching the droplets cling to the leaves, watching them soak through the earth. As the afternoon cools and becomes more distinct I tie back the roses, I hack at the hedge, I weed round the bed surrounding the cottage, holding the new growth at bay.

The sky is fainting palest blue, bejewelled by the stroke of a sinking sun, when Matty returns from the wood. He is hungry and happy. I make him tea, cutting the loaf of bread in thick slabs which I spread with butter and jam. We sit on a bench at the back of the cottage, looking out on the field.

– We should have a barbecue.
– I don't think there is one.
– No. We should make one. We can cook on a fire.
– Where? Here?

– Yes, here. We can turf it again in the autumn. I can make a grate from some bricks. Have you got any sausages?

– Yes.

– Let me cut out a patch. It won't be large. I promise it won't hurt the lawn.

– What have we got to burn?

– Wood. We can go to the wood for some fallen branches. There's heaps of wood we can use. Please.

I watch as Matty stakes out his patch, slicing into the turf with a spade, cutting out small neat squares. He lays them in the shade by the hedge. He'll water them daily; he'll keep them alive. He brings an armful of bricks from the shed, and a metal grate we can use for a grill. I watch him as he builds his structure – expertly, deftly, precise – as though he's been doing this all his life. I look at the sweat on his temples, his neck; I look at his hair which sticks to his forehead; I look at his arms which are scratched yet soft, at the supple pads of his hands.

The car is furnace-hot, having been in the sun all day. We open the roof, we wind down the windows, sticking our faces out through the frames, feeling the breeze in our hair. I park on the track to the side of the church; I pick up a groundsheet and open the boot. We collapse the rear seat, creating more space, then saunter across to the wood.

The grass is thick at the fringe of Road Field, sweltering in the sweat of the sun. The land is so urgently green, so fresh, so plentiful and alive. The wood is alert as we approach, watching us through a lattice of nettle, a sharp profusion of thorn. I trace Matty's steps till we come to an entrance. We hunch beneath the dense-leafed trees which scrape their branches against our backs.

Inside, it is silent and cold. I look around blindly, standing quite still till my eyes adjust and I'm able to see. In the absence of sight, I can hear Matty moving. I can hear his feet on the fallen branches; I can hear the slight inhale of his breath; I can hear the rustle of opening canvas as he spreads the groundsheet out on the floor.

And now, gradually, my sight is restored. I see the glinting specks of sun through shifting gaps in the leaves; I see the shape of severed trunks stood proud from a sea of drab scrub; I see Matty swinging the weight of his body, hung by his arms from a single bough; I see the bough crack, its backbone shattered, the dead limb tearing itself from the trunk, stunned and shrieking with pain.

Branch and boy collapse to the earth like corpses, here at my feet. Then Matty stands up, panting with pleasure, placing the ends of the tortured limb between the two sides of a ditch. He steps back then launches himself at the branch; he lands on its spine and it splinters beneath him, flipping its ends up into the air, piercing the wood with its grief.

I lend him my hand to climb from the ditch, then I turn away to find wood of my own. Fingers of twig stick up from the ground. When I pull, whole branches appear through the leaves as the bodies unbury themselves. I break off some sticks we can use for our kindling, though much is so rotten it crumbles when touched; or I feel it so sapless, so brittle and dry, it will burn to cinder before it gives heat. There are branches here too, half-hid in the ground, that bend and tear and refuse to surrender. There are stubborn saplings, there are self-planted shoots, lying amidst the dead wreckage.

Once the groundsheet is full, we grasp onto its corners and wrestle it back to the fringe. The tall trees shake their disapprobation through the shapeless locks of their leaves, creaking an eery wretchedness at being so cruelly betrayed.

We skid the sheet on the slide of the grass till we come to the open car, then we lift it high and into the back in a single tangled confusion. The boot refuses to close, so I drive with branches scraping the road, shrieking their enmity. At home, we disembowel the car, dragging the sheet and its bones to the back. Matty takes charge of sorting the wood while I go to the kitchen for food.

When I return, I find Matty is ready. Two low brick walls line the sides of his trench, with the grate placed above like a metal-beam roof. Beneath the grate there's a roll of paper cocooned in a wigwam of twigs. To his side he has laid out three piles of wood, sorted by girth and sized for his hearth.

Matty awaits me with matches in hand. He has dragged the garden bench from the lawn so it faces the fire and looks over the field. He instructs me to sit while he works.

Crouching before me he strikes the match, placing it into the heart. The stealthy breeze inspires the flame to lick across the curling paper, then up through the frame of waiting twigs till they snap and roast at its touch. I watch the kindling twisting and writhing, crackling into a seething powder, as the flames search blindly up through the grill, hungry to snatch at the air. Matty places more twigs on the fire, maintaining the wigwam, building its core. The fire responds and consumes. He lays stouter branches beneath the grate, and the flame erupts and spirals to life. There's a noise like wind which comes from the fire, breaking and snatching at all that it's fed, melting the field in its haze.

Matty squats on a low flat log he has placed by the side of the fire. He refuses to sit on the bench. He stokes the rampant heart of the flame till it coils with heat and collapses the wigwam into the coals of its bed.

I look beyond him, up at the clouds, seeing them creeping to pink. The sun is ponderous and huge, dragged down by its weight towards the earth, shifting in brilliance the further it falls – from the unwatchable, through shades of gold, to a deepening red that stains the sky, dripping its blood on the land. The field darkens and loses its shape; the beet leaves ripple its soundless surface, as busy as waves on the sea. The wood behind them thickens and deepens. It turns to a single solid mass, hunched in haughty defiance. Swallows and martins are stretching their wings, feeling for food in the thin, blank air. The garden closes tightly around us; the fire brightens, easing its warmth and comfort into my wanting skin, casting my son as an amber statue shaped from the living flame.

In the dying embers of the day, I lay potatoes on Matty's walls, while the sausages scream and blister with heat. Now the flames are as tame as tongues which lap at the charcoaled grill. The fire is a bed of living colour breathing against the scorched bricks.

We eat in blindness, trapped in a closing pocket of light which radiates from the blaze. The food fuels and fills my eager insides, relaxing both body and mind. Matty and I sit close to the fire, sharing its flame, its singular heat, shielded from the shadowing dusk. This is my family, my sanctuary, my home. I need no more than what this can offer – this creeping contentment, this infinite moment – shared for a fraction of time, for a lifetime. Entire and complete in itself.

Through the dark which expands and encroaches around us, I sense the fields are gradually cooling, the beet leaves brittle against the breeze. Rose House Farm is sunk in oblivion; the wood beyond is petrified, outcast by the world that surrounds it.

~

I can see a queue of cars which stretches all the way down the road, past the church tower and round the bend, into the fields beyond. On the other side, too, a frozen line, fused to the road by insistent heat, extending beyond the shop and the pub, blurring into the trees.

By the time the cars have reached the gate, the children have sprinted towards the Fair, pursued by mothers and brothers and sisters. All who are left in the cars are the men, over-heated and angry.

Serpent Meadow is already half-full. I have marked out the grass with clear white lines, so the drivers know where to park. I point the direction, I show them the route, I check that they understand. They nod and drive off wherever they choose, ignoring my marshals, abandoning their cars in random spots of the meadow.

All afternoon there's a solid snake of cars creeping into the field. I stop for an urgent drink of water, swilling it round my thirsting mouth, sprinkling it over my face. I have taken off my luminous jacket; I have discarded all semblance of control. I stand, a mad woman with screaming hair, blocking the path of furious drivers, waving my hands to flag them down, demanding they park in my rows.

Bill is positioned beside the gate that leads into Steeple Field. He smiles at children as they skip straight past; he chats to locals whilst others stroll by. Almost everyone enters for free. Beyond him, over the car boot sale, Jack is standing on the stage with a microphone in his hand. He is welcoming all to the Summer Fair, as if welcoming them into his home. Steam is rising from behind the hedge; the air is alive with the sound of machines, of grating metal and muddled voices, of music pumped from the stalls.

My field is full; it is over-full. Cars double-park and block all access, whilst more attempt to come in. I look around for my trusty marshals, but they have both been drawn to the Fair – their teenage self-control found wanting – unable to resist the allure. I wave at Bill, who returns my wave; I beckon to him with my hand. All he does is salute me once more, ignoring my desperate entreaty.

I walk into the road and hold out my arms, raising them over my head. I can take no more, and nor can the field. I can almost hear the drivers' hate as the fury builds in their cars. A horn sounds, echoing down the line. Now there's a symphony of pure spite blasted from the waiting cars. All of it aimed at me. Some vehicles break from the ordered snake and bump onto the verge by the pub.

I close the gate on the choke of cars and make my way down the broken road, shrugging my unwelcome news. But before I get far, I am called back again: a woman stands on the bars of the gate, waving and shouting at me. She wants to get out; she has had enough. We go in search of her car. We find it sandwiched between two others, blocked in and unable to move. I make a note of their number plates, then walk over to Steeple Field.

The PA system has been entrusted to a boy about the same age as Matty. He flicks a switch with nonchalance and the microphone buzzes to life. I find I am talking in number plates, as I ask the owner to return to their car so the vehicle beside can get out. No one stops to look or turn round; no one seems to notice. The music blares above my voice, the rides clank rusty melody, the engines rumble their peace. The boy looks at me judgementally; he senses my powerlessness. He takes the microphone from my hand, dismissing me from the stage. I return to the car park and find, bizarrely, the offending car is being moved. The woman drives off without saying goodbye.

The afternoon is thick with noise, with the smell of candyfloss and beer. Jack is on the stage once more, announcing the start of the games. A roar of approval comes from the Serpent as fathers urge their children on. Travis seems to be using discretion when it comes to closing the pub. I shoulder my way through the crowd.

From within the fumble of faceless people, Matty blurs into sight. He has put himself down for the hundred metres; he has entered the sack race as well. He has come to find me, to ask me to watch. I tell him I will join in a while: first, I need to exert some control. I watch him run back into the mêlée, feeling an envy for knowing his freedom, wanting to be as careless as he, wanting to be there to watch him.

A jam has formed inside the car park as people are trying to leave. I wander through the steaming metal and guide them back to the road. Over my shoulder, beyond the hedge, I can hear the games have begun. I can hear the expectant lull as they ready, the static of suspense as a race is run, the fury of celebration.

Travis is sauntering between the cars; he is coming over towards me. The police have told him to close the bar, so he's offering to take my place for a while. I thank him warmly. I see the pleasure punched on his face.

Through the gap in the hedge, to the side of the stalls, a track is chalked in the grass. Children are seated on bales of straw, whilst parents are standing behind. An egg and spoon race is in full flow, led by a child who holds her egg so high it almost touches her nose. There's a surge of people and noise around me, urging participants on. The girl crosses the line and throws up her arms to a frenzy of raucous applause.

A teacherly woman sternly announces the start of the three-legged race; she commands all those who have put down their names to present themselves at the front. There's a commotion as pairings couple themselves; a tying of feet and inspecting of knots; a sneaked yard of practice and tumbling over. Now they are formed in a crooked line. The teacher barks them away. They lurch down the track with a shriek of pain, hopping and laughing, collapsing and crumbling, stumbling onto the grass. An improbable pairing has found a rhythm and has sprinted into the lead. They are already crossing the line. There's another explosion of sheer delight; an unknotting, a soothing of shins.

The contestants for the sack race are called. I search in the crowd for Matty. He is there, he's running towards the start line, he's selecting a sack with care. He climbs in and draws it up to his chest, holding the hessian fringe. He gives a tentative hop. Adults and children are lined up beside him, shuffling into a row. There's a curious hush as all wait.

They are off.

Matty springs forward, taking short frequent leaps, preserving his balance as he steers clear of bodies. It is he and two men who strike out in front. All the others have lost their control; they have tripped over their feet or lost hold of the sack; they've collapsed in a snarl on the ground.

The three in contention are equally matched. Both of the men have more powerful leaps; the ground seems to shudder beneath their weight. But Matty is agile, his hops are more frequent, the energy used is much less. He eases into the lead. They counter by taking still greater leaps, and after each leap there's a longer pause. One falls. And now, with a final bound, it is over as Matty crosses the line.

The children beside me turn to look as I scream celebration at him. I push through the crowd in an effort to reach him, but by the time I am there he has gone.

The wheelbarrow race is the next to be called; contestants are paddling in line. I stand on a bale so I can look out above the uneven ocean of heads, through the mass of colour around me. Matty appears to be shooting at ducks in a gallery at the end of the field. He is loading the gun, he is taking his aim, he is firing at targets inside. Now he's returning the gun to the stall. He's receiving the praise of someone beside him. I can see them patting his back. Uriah.

Behind me I hear the blaring of horns, a shouted voice on the afternoon air, splitting its warmth with pure rage. I need to go back to the car park now. I find Travis trapped by a small group of people, each of them pleading a cause. His apologies failing to please or placate them. I step up, eager to rescue him, instructing drivers and cars to move till the group disperses, the anger abates, the field gradually thins.

I glance back over to Steeple Field; the prizes are being awarded. A small crowd stand at the front of the stage, cheering each winner who climbs the steps for the honour of shaking Jack's hand. I watch through the slender gap in the hedge in the hope I see Matty taking his turn. In time, I hear his name being called. He mounts the steps and is greeted by Jack; they stand man to man for several moments, though I cannot hear what they say. Matty turns to receive the adulation, holding his medal high in the air, then he leaves and is lost in the anonymous field.

The car boot sale has come to a close; the engines are winding down. Jack is thanking all for coming, for being a part of this annual tradition. He hopes to see us next year. His speech tails off and ends in silence. The crowd is already dissolving away. The Fair is weary; it's frayed at its seams. The pace of exit is speeding up. I shepherd a stream of cars through the gate; the families flushed with the day.

Now my temporary car park is almost bare; the rest can depart on their own. I walk back into Steeple Field, watching the engines hoisted on trailers, the stage dismantled, the bales of straw being tractored into a stack. The stalls are being packed away, their sides are collapsing in on themselves, their platforms are hooked on the back of large trucks. The Faraday family are in the field picking up litter and filling black sacks.

Now Matty is here to my side. I want to tell him how proud I am, but before I can he is talking to me, and I know from his voice he is angry. He is angry I didn't watch him compete; angry I wasn't there at the end to see him collecting his prize. I tell him I did, but from the car park. I was tasked with completing a job.

He looks at me, but he isn't listening. He doesn't think that I care. Now all he wants is to go to the wood – now, before it gets dark. I want him to help with the clearing away, but I don't want to anger him more. I want to return to the cottage with him, to spend time together, to sit round a fire. I just want to be together with him. I want that; I want it so badly. Why does it have to be so hard?

Reluctantly, I let Matty go. I watch him down the field to the pub; I watch him to the bend in the road; I watch him onto the track by the church. I watch him vanish from sight.

I look in his wake towards the wood. Matty has found his place in this village. He had found it, there, in the wood. He fits. He has found a purpose with no seeming effort, no pain of having to search for something, no pressure upon him for making it work. I think I am thinking too much, I am trying too hard. I should try to be a bit more like him, living and trusting to luck. As I am, it will take so long to move on, to look at the past without feeling guilt, to look at myself and forgive. And I cannot forgive myself for what's done without forgiving you too. You, who never asked for this outcome. I think the time for forgiveness has come. I think now it's time for a final reckoning. After all these months since I stole away on that cold wet night; after all I've achieved, after coming so far. Now it is time to bury the past, to accept what it is, to put it to rest. With no resentment, with no ill-will. To acknowledge it wasn't all bad. There were times that we had when we knew it was good; when we were happy for being together; when we lived, when we loved, when we looked to the future, and the things that we saw made us glad. There was comfort, and peace, and security. The delight of sharing in Matty.

The joy seeing him grow through us both. It was just not enough, nor stable enough. It was just interspersed with such pain. That pain has disguised the good that was there. It has led to denial, and in that denial, I am caught in a vortex and cannot move on. So now is the chance to build a new platform based on the truth not the lie. To start again, but not with the pain. Not with a sense of regret. We should try that now, in our separate worlds, in our lives which are wholly apart. Or which should be. Except that they seem to resist separation; they seem reluctant to break. Do you feel that too? That despite the divorce of distance and time, you haven't faded away. You haven't melted from my thoughts, as sure as the rain in the eyes of the sun. Instead, you linger on, you persist. You stay with me, like my shadow, my conscience. It can't be me who is keeping you here, for I had seen you dead and buried. I gave you up when I left.

Travis is here; he is touching my elbow. He looks at me strangely as if he has heard the meandering drift of my mind. He tells me to stop; we have done enough. I wonder how long I have stood here in silence. I wonder how long he's been watching.

I look up. The heat has stolen from the day, though the sky is still bright; the sun is perched to the side of the wood. Most of the cars have departed. Two or three families play on the grass – children and parents tumbling together, laughing and cuddling and holding hands. Even with Matty I'm not complete. I think I'm content, but I am not whole. There's a need for another being beyond me, for another reason to be. A need for a man who is always here – a person in whom to trust and confide – to share in the shame of being alone, and in sharing to wash it away.

Bill is waiting impatiently when we reach the door of the pub. We sit at the bar while Travis draws beer; he insists the drinks will be on the house. We relive the events of the day. Travis is pleased; he has done more trade in a single day than he usually does in a month. Bill is also content. He has spoken to half of the neighbourhood, exchanging gossip and news. I relax back into their comfortable chatter, hearing their tales from the afternoon, feeling the tension wound from the car park gradually washing away.

Travis is pouring a second round when Uriah enters the pub. He stands alone at the end of the bar, staring into the blankness. I would like to go over and talk to him now, to find a way of being his friend. I am caught by the thought that no one is with him, no one is there he can share with. I would like to thank him for being with Matty; I would like to thank him for making him welcome, for sharing his knowledge with him. I would like to start off over again – to earn his friendship, to win his friendship; to find out how I might win it. Matty and he have much in common: they attract as fiercely as I repel. I have watched them: comfortable in themselves, comfortable when being together. I almost envy the friendship they have, the ease with which it was made. Uriah is passionate, protective, strong. He could be a surrogate father to Matty. In the absence of you he could stand in for you, till you are there again by his side.

I watch Uriah as he stands in the corner. There is nothing I know of the man. I wonder why he hasn't had children. I wonder what he did in the past to lose his first wife, to drive her away. I wonder what life he lives now with Joyce. I wonder what they do on their own, when they sit either side of their kitchen table, marooned in the heart of a field.

Travis is telling Bill of two people who came all the way from Cambridge. He thinks that is what the village cries out for: an influx of people, more trade. That would be good for the shop and the pub. The village is not enough in itself; it cannot survive on its own. He hopes that those people will come here again; he hopes they will talk to their friends. He wishes the village would hold more events, giving more people reason to come.

Without warning, without shifting from where he is standing, Uriah offers a view. The village needs to look after its own. Outsiders come to take, not to give. They're not safe. They intrude; they dig up things that are buried. They threaten the village's way of life. They are gipsies, travellers, nomads, vagrants. They have nothing to give; they have nothing to fear. Nothing they have is held dear.

We listen politely until the end; none of us care to dispute. When he's done, I stand, it is time to leave. Conveniently, I have an excuse: I am having supper with Martha.

Uriah raises his eyes for an instant to survey the person who is meeting his parents. Then he turns away from the room. Travis wants to escort me outside, but he doesn't dare in the face of Uriah. He says it instead with his eyes. Those eyes which watch wherever I go, which speak in a sea of uneasy silence the things he doesn't dare say. So different from you in every respect. But someone, someone who wants to share. Someone perhaps I could learn to love.

A thin band of cloud filters in from the west, closing over the sky. The breeze has risen; it is brushing away the touch of the sun and its heat. In Steeple Field the Faradays have made a pile of black plastic bags to protect them from blowing away. I wave and see them smile in return.

The late afternoon is bland and dull, sinking into a shapeless dusk as I come to the cottage door. Here, laid on the bricks of the wall to its side, there's another treasure from Joyce. This time, it's a bunch of forget-me-nots. Reminding me that Joyce is still here; reminding me not to forget. She has caught them neatly up in blue ribbon, the same as with all her fragrant offerings ever since I arrived.

I pick them up and enter the cottage, placing them in a jar filled with water that I place on the table before me.

I make a cup of tea; I collapse in a chair. I draw my jacket more tightly around me, hugging my heat and curling my legs up onto the base of the seat.

I recall the faces of those in the cars: the resentment, the anger, the frustration they felt, helplessly waiting to enter the car park, helplessly seeking retreat. Their voices, their postures, their gesticulations, betraying the feelings within.

I urge myself out of the chair. In the bathroom I run an ankle-deep bath and sit in its shallows while bunching my knees, feeling a coldness creep down my spine. I get out and wrap my body in towels; I go to my bedroom and crawl into bed. It is damp but forgiving between the sheets. A gradual heat steals across my wet skin, warming me, thawing my flesh.

I close my eyes.

When I look again the day has changed: it is neither light nor dark. The uncurtained window shows outside an unbroken, colourless sky. From below me I hear the boost of the boiler, the trickle of water which drains through the pipes, dispersing a fragile heat. I lie on my back, in the give of the bed, looking up at the crooked beams on the ceiling.

I aimlessly trace their uneven shadows, fading into drab grey. Downstairs, I hear the click of the door; I hear Matty kick off his boots in the hall; I hear the dull thump of his tread on the stairs, the grate of the metal latch to his room. It would be so easy to turn over now; to close my eyes and to blank my mind; to sleep then awake to another day.

I get up and put on my dressing gown to conserve my heat while I look for some clothes. I call to Matty; I remind him of supper. He mumbles some words in reply. I find a sober black skirt which I wear with tights and a velvet top. I clasp a string of pearls round my neck. I clip my nails; I brush my hair. I catch myself in the glance of the mirror, looking at someone like me. I moisturise my face and my hands. I feel myself shiny and raw. I powder my cheeks, I brush at my skin, wiping the wrinkles away.

Matty is waiting by the foot of the stairs. He wears school clothes, but without the tie. He has brushed his hair with his fingers. He is holding a canvas bag to his side, as if to hide it from me. In the stale twilight air, we trek between fields till we reach the comfort of Martha's door. She is standing expectantly in the hall. She loosens the bolts, and invites us in.

The fire in the living room blazes in welcome, shedding a generous heat. Jack rises and formally shakes our hands; he bids Matty sit to his side. He has noticed Matty is carrying a bag and asks to see what he's brought.

Matty dips his hands in the bag with the zeal of opening a Christmas stocking, handing the objects one by one for Jack to hold and inspect. There are flints, there are shards of pottery, there are twisted, rusted pieces of iron, there are square glass bottles, there are splinters of bone.

Jack examines them all with care, sharing in Matty's delight. He wants to know where each was found, how it was lying, and how deep it lay. In return, he explains their function: what each of them is, and how it works, and when he thinks it was made. He can even guess the person who owned it. Jack knows the land, and what lies within it. He and the land are as one.

I look at Matty, wide-eyed and attentive; I can see he is drinking this knowledge in as keenly as Jack is passing it down. Jack and Matty, the man and the boy, almost like father and son. They are sharing a natural inheritance; they are sharing the ways of the past.

— What else have you found?
— That's all I've got in my bag. But I know there's much more. The land is full of stuff buried within it.
— Yes. You're right. The whole of our history — the history of Man — lies buried under the ground.
— There are tunnels, too. I've found some tunnels.
— Where?
— On the farther side of the wood. On its fringe.
— Describe them.
— They're about four foot deep, but it's hard to tell because the earth has collapsed in around them. I think they're made out of concrete. The roofs are just below the soil. You wouldn't know the tunnels are there, except for where they've been smashed. Do you know what they are?
— Have they got any markings? Any distinctive features?
— No, they're just empty concrete tunnels.
— The concrete is thick, isn't it? Strong enough to support a great weight; strong enough to withstand a blast. That is why they were built. I know exactly when they're from. They're from the war. There was an American airbase here.

183

That whole field, Road Field, was an airstrip. That's why it's so flat and so big. I was still a boy when they built it. Everyone in the village – and there were lots of us then – grubbed out the hedges and levelled the earth; we filled the ditches with rubble and stone which we brought in convoys of horse-drawn carts. When it was done, the Americans came. They erected a fence around the field. The whole place became a military zone. They built runways and hangers and fuel dumps and arsenals. There was even a hospital, a theatre, a dentist. They had shops which sold biscuits and chocolate and nylons. Things shipped straight from the States. You needed a permit to get on the site; but at Thanksgiving, at Christmas, and sometimes in summer, they'd invite us over – all of the children – and they'd spoil us with attention and gifts.

– So, what are the tunnels?

– They could be many things. For storage, for protection, or merely foundations. But I know they built a network of tunnels to allow them to go between different buildings, even during an air raid. You'll have to show me where they are. Then I can tell you what they were for.

We relocate to the dining room while Jack continues to talk. He tells us about the war and his boyhood, about the village of Nettlesden when it grew to the size of a town. He remembers names, and the numbers of planes; he describes them in detail, as though they're still here.

I sit and listen, as absorbed as Matty; aware of the distance, the passing of time, yet feeling it relevant, brought back to life, by the immediacy of his recollection. For Jack it's even more real. These things he describes may no longer be here, but that doesn't mean they are dead. They were, they are, they continue to be, connected by the power of the land.

After the main course Martha rises, collecting the dishes and taking them out. I wait for a moment then follow behind her, carrying the casserole with me.

Martha is rinsing the plates in the kitchen; she's stacking the pans in the sink. All through the meal she has not said a word; she must know Jack's stories by heart. She may have been part of what he describes; she is a part of this history too.

Seeing her here, in the stark kitchen light, I am witnessing part of the past. It seems strange she chooses to be so silent when she knows so much, she has seen so much, she must have so much of her own to tell. But for now, she's content for Jack to relive it. She has no interest in sharing her memories. As though she prefers the past to be hidden, to be buried deep and left to decay.

I watch her as she stands by the sink. She doesn't like having me here. She's irritated we are asking him questions, we are prodding into the past. She's irritated about something yet deeper, something we haven't yet found.

She hears me behind her; she stands tall and turns. Her face is tight and severe.

– I am glad Matty is taking such an interest in the country.
– Yes, so am I. I was worried he would be so lonely here. I was worried he'd be at a loss.
– It's good. A child of his age is naturally curious. They like to explore and discover new things. I remember the same with Uriah. I see a similarity sometimes.
– Was Uriah like Matty when he was a boy?
– In some ways, yes. But very different in others. Anyway, I'm not talking about Uriah now, I'm talking about Matty.

– Yes, Matty.

– He should stay to the fields; he should look for things there. There's plenty for him to find in the fields. He shouldn't go into the wood. It's a dangerous place.

– Dangerous?

– Yes, there are all sorts of things that are hidden in there. There are snares and potholes. He could hurt himself. He could disturb things that should be left where they are. It's all right for Uriah – he knows what is there. But for Matty it's new, it's unknown. He could do much damage – to himself and to others – even if by mistake. I'm asking you, as a favour to me, to discourage him from the wood.

– I've tried to stop him from going. I feel that it's dangerous, too. I instinctively feel it, and he knows how I feel. But he likes it so much. It's a part of his life. I don't want to prevent him from being happy.

– You need to be strong. For his sake, and your own. You must tell him. I want you to do so. I wouldn't want to see him get hurt. I wouldn't want either of you to be hurt.

Martha is looking into my face; she is searching into my eyes. This is not a request; it is a demand. It's undisguised in intent. She warned me before, when I was here last, and I listened but failed to respond. Now she is telling me what she requires; what she wants me to do. I feel remorse and anger within me – both at her and myself. Ever since we first met, she has doubted me – my parenting skills, my authority. She has sought to impose her will on my own, whenever she has thought fit. If Jack is becoming like Matty's father, then Martha is morphing into my mother. I feel the same shame, the same indignation as when told off as a girl. Like my mother, Martha's convinced that she's right; she's not reticent to lay down her law.

Martha hands me a bowl of fruit, and we walk back into the dining room. Matty has moved from the fringe of the wood, and now he's deep in its heart. He's talking of snares he has found in the trees; describing how they are made. For him the snares are the same as the things he has brought in his bag to show Jack. They are part of his broader discovery; they are what he has found in the earth.

I can see Jack shuffle uneasily. For him, they are far from being the same. His interest stops at the edge of the field, at the point where the present meets with the past. He respects the natural world he's a part of; he doesn't seek to destroy it. In his excitement, in the glow of the room, Matty can't see Jack's response. I try to turn the conversation, but Matty demands to be heard. He's eager to share the depth of his knowledge, the intimate detail of all he has learnt; and in divulging the extent of that learning, he betrays his tutor to us. As Jack has taught him the ways of the field, so Uriah has shown him those of the wood. It is evident from the intricate detail, not only to me, but to Martha and Jack. And I sense Jack's shame in acknowledging it.

Over dessert, Jack harkens back to the village during the war. He fills the time till the meal is done, till the coffee is drunk and we say goodbye, with pleasing and amiable talk. He shakes Matty's hand, warmly, sincerely. He stands before him, man to man. But Matty isn't so much of the man that he can't be swayed, he can't be saved. And Jack would take upon himself the role of rescuing him.

It is dark outside. The air breathes a chill for lacking the cover of lumbering cushioning cloud. Stars are distant, and the moon is new. We stumble through the ghosted grass, along a twisting invisible track, until we come to the thicket.

To either side of the copse there are ditches. The crackled slice of the moon reflects from the watery face of the pools. I can hear the wind as it snags on the leaves; a shuffle of air from within the bush. This place has eyes; it is watching us. I hurry through. I whisper my apprehension to Matty when safe on the farther side.

To my surprise, Matty shares the same feeling. Not often, but sometimes when he is with me, he feels it. A sense of us being watched. From the fields, the hedgerows, but never the wood. The wood has never imposed. For him, it isn't a place to fear — to feel himself watched by the dead or the living, by those that he knows or hasn't yet found.

There's a pleasing warmth inside the cottage; a comforting pleasure in light. Matty is tired and goes to his room. I pour myself a glass of Baileys. I recall what Uriah said in the pub, that those from outside are a threat to the village. And now I can picture Martha's face; I can hear her words in my mind. It's dangerous for Matty to go to the wood; she wouldn't want to see him get hurt.

The door is all that separates me from that treacherous world that lies beyond. I can hear the breeze as it scratches the keyhole, fingering into the room. I plug the hole with the iron key, turning it, locking the door. Then I check all the other doors and the windows, ensuring that all are shut fast. I would have a man to live in this cottage, for the strength and security it affords. Someone for Matty, someone for me: to protect us both, and to shield. I know who he is, and I know where to find him. But I have no way to summon him here without destroying all I am building, without unpicking all I have done.

~

– The Merediths' was broken into again last night. The same as last year.

– O dear. How terrible for them.

– Crispin's on his way up now. It's ironic that they live in London, but it's safer there than here.

– Was anything taken? Do you know?

– Bill says that a window appeared to be broken. But the police were there so he wasn't able to get a look at the damage. It makes me feel nauseous thinking about it, thinking about who it was.

– Do you think it was someone who came to the Fair?

– Yes. It could have been any of them. A person with a vintage car; a person with some candyfloss; a person with a child. Someone who looked across the road and saw the Rectory. Without any cars in the drive. A nice posh house for the taking. I don't suppose you saw something, Sarah. Something or somebody strange last night.

– It did feel a bit like something was there. But I always feel like that when it's dark.

– Yes, dear. It's horrible. Ghastly. I think we should get some bars on these windows. And get some cameras too. I told Bill we should do it last year. Imagine if they came to this shop. They know we've got money because of the post office. They know there isn't a policeman for miles.

– You may be right, Margaret. But I'm more worried about Matty than burglars. He spends so much time in the wood on his own. What if someone was there? If someone was hiding. Do you think it's safe for him there?

– In the wood? No, dear. It's dangerous. Bill will tell you. He's been there. There are all sorts of traps in the wood.

– Snares. I know. They belong to Uriah.

– And other things besides snares.

– What other things?

– I don't know. But there are other things. He shouldn't go to the wood. He shouldn't be left on his own. None of us should. I do hope they catch whoever it was. It doesn't feel safe – not even by day. The village needs to be protected. At times like this it all feels too close. We're not cut off from the rest of the world. From time to time something comes and disturbs us, and it's never anything nice.

Margaret picks up the loaf of bread, the tomatoes and cucumber, the cheese and the coleslaw, the wafers of ham, the cans of beer, and puts them into a bag. She is clearly distressed by last night. She likes to gossip, but this is too close, this is too real and too frightening. I say goodbye and walk up the road, looking into the Rectory's drive for a sign that Crispin is here.

Back in the cottage I walk through the rooms, inspecting the windows and doors. The locks are old, but still sturdy and strong. There are bolts on all of the doors. Besides, this cottage is tired and dirty; it doesn't suggest there are valuables here. I shiver. I must remember to lock the door when I leave, regardless of how long I'm away. I must tell Matty to do that as well. Matty. I wonder how much I should say to him now. I wonder how he will take it.

There's a knock at the door. For an instant I think it will be the police, or a stranger who's chancing their arm. Then I remember. I swing back the bolt and open the door. Travis is standing outside. He's grinning; I think he wants to come in. I tell him to wait; I will just be a minute: I need to pick up my bag.

I lock the door and try it for strength, then we cross the lawn to his car. He goes round the bonnet to open my door, and we drive away up the road.

Travis has heard the news from last night, but he doesn't seem to be worried. He has lived in tough neighbourhoods in his time; he says he's accustomed to crime. I glance at the person beside me. His is a strange philosophy: prepared to take what comes his way; accepting his lot, whilst never quite happy; unwilling to change for fear of losing the little he has that he seems to enjoy. I am not sure whether I envy him, or if I pity him more.

We have turned down a track which leads past a stream to a patch of scrubland squeezed between fields. At the side of a thicket, we stop and get out. The sky is immense and intensely blue, scuffed by occasional drifting clouds which are swept slowly over the land. The air is full of the sound of birds from within the scrub, from on wing.

At the end of the track is an old brick windmill, its sails pinned to prevent it from catching the breeze. It is bigger and earthier than the fairy-tale object I saw from afar on the road. I imagine the solid creak of its sails, the rows of sacks that are laden with corn, the warm thick air, the choking dust, the smell of chaff and of sweat. The crowd of labourers, the horse-drawn carts, the miller's wife with her plump red arms, wearing a pinafore over her dress.

We stroll down the track alongside the stream, following it as it curls round the fields and threads its way through a spinney. We stand on two planks which are bolted together to form a ramshackle bridge. Travis kicks at a twig with his boot, and we watch as it sails down the bubbling water, casting a shade on the shallow bed. We climb up the incline, into the trees. The grass, the bushes, the leaves close round us, all exquisitely green. This belt of trees is not like our own – it is welcoming, light, and alive.

We shuffle through to the farther side; we re-join the stream at its base. Travis has thoughtlessly picked up a stick and drags it behind, like a boy. As the trees open out, we see fields before us, spread wide and bursting with barley. We cross the stream, retracing our route, the sails of the windmill looming larger, stealing the rays of the sun.

I return to the car to fetch the food. The air is unpleasantly humid and moist. Travis takes the cans of beer to the stream; he traps them close to the bank with a stone. He spreads a rug near the foot of the windmill, caught in the shady lattice of sails. He reclines on his elbows and watches me as I carve the bread, as I slice the tomatoes, as I cut thick wedges of cheese.

– It's times like this I'm pleased that I'm not in London.
– Yes, it is nice.
– Do you think you will stay here?
– I don't know. I haven't really got any plans. My plan was to escape from London. I think Matty likes to be here.
– And do you?
– I think so. Yes. Sometimes. It's different, that's all. In many ways, I'm still finding my feet. I like the sun, I like the sky, I like my vegetable patch. I never thought I would say something like that, but I do. I think the people are mostly kind. I think life is hard but more honest. I am getting to grips with being alone; I am coping with living alone.
– And Matty's dad?
– I don't know how he's doing. I've shut him away from my mind. I don't want to open old sores. In time, I hope it will be less painful.
– Time and distance do that. They allow all the pent-up feelings to wane. To show us how things really are.
– Perhaps. And you?

– I guess I will stay here. I have the pub, which scratches a living. I have freedom, fresh air, and good food. Like you, I cope with the loneliness. I try to cope. I survive.

– You can't be lonely. You've got Samantha. You're surrounded by people. Every day, every night, in the pub.

– I'm surrounded by people, it's true. But that makes the loneliness even more stark. The emotional isolation. At least you've got Matty.

– Matty's a child. You've got Samantha.

– Samantha is a… no, that's not fair. Samantha is a different person from me. I've known her for twenty years or more, but we've never really talked to each other. Not like this.

– Like what?

– Like how you and I are talking right now. Honestly, openly. Sharing.

– Anyone can talk like this.

– Anyone can. But not many do. They talk, but they may not connect. I think we see things the same way, Sarah. We understand one another. I was young when I met Samantha. She was pretty and chatty and full of life. That appealed to me then. I think I would look for a very different person if I were to do it again. That's what age and self-knowledge do. I didn't know what I wanted then.

– But you do now?

– Yes, I do.

I retrieve the cans of beer from the stream. I can feel that Travis is looking at me, even though he is trying to lounge on the rug like a man who hasn't a care in the world. I sense he is coiled and tense inside, uncertain of how I'll respond. As uncertain and wary as I am. We do connect; it is true. And it's nice, so nice to have someone here.

Someone I feel that I can relate to. Someone whose company I can enjoy. Someone aware of where I have come from, someone who knows how that feels. Travis is that in so many ways, for being an outsider too. And that should make it feel right. But that feeling is swamped by another feeling – the greater feeling of guilt. A huge wave of guilt. Guilt that I'm having a picnic with him when his wife is watching TV in the pub, quite unaware we are here. That on its own destroys the illusion that this is harmless behaviour. But the guilt runs yet deeper. I feel guilt we are making slight of the village; guilt we are shutting ourselves from its fear. I shouldn't be here, by a stream in the sun; I should be in the village, protecting Matty, protecting all it holds dear. And deeper still, within my subconscious, a guilt pervades the core of my being. Guilt this is Travis, not you.

I return to the rug and sit on its edge, handing Travis a beer. I start talking about my vegetable patch, about what grows in the fields. He senses the shift in my mood and withdraws into the easy mundane. We maintain connection, a shared way of seeing, though not at the level he seeks. Despite that, I sense no frustration. He can withdraw, for not having committed; he can continue to pry. He senses no rejection from me; only a slight uncertainty. He can live with that; he's not in a hurry; and I think I could live with it too. And then, in time, we might make it work; I might let it come round, as guilt subsides, as distance makes a stranger of you. Time and distance do that. They lessen the pain; they lessen the memory; they almost make us forget. I know that already. There are times I have woken up in my bed – still unfamiliar despite these months – and wondered why I am here on my own. I have woken and asked myself why we split, and I can't remember the reasons.

We clear away the rest of the food and follow the path of the stream. The fields around us are flat and planted, the track we walk is uneven. Travis forces his boots through the grass. Rambling doesn't come easy to him. I can hear him slipping and heavily breathing, struggling to keep to my side. I can't believe he likes rural life; he so obviously doesn't belong. In Epping Forest you would take Matty with you; you would teach him to see without being seen; you would zigzag the paths not walk along them; you would blend with the mantle of green. That is where he discovered his love – there, in the forest, with you.

I suggest to Travis that we turn around. I think it is time that we leave.

We drive back in silence. Travis draws up on the verge by the cottage. I step out of the car before he has time to unbuckle his seat belt and open my door. I am feeling guilty once more. Guilty for sitting here in his car; guilty for being with him. Burnt Tree Farm is staring at me from the silver dots of its eyes. From Six Bells, too, they could see me now.

I thank Travis before closing the door. I watch as he drives towards the church, as he rounds the corner and slips away. It has been an enjoyable day. Travis can be a pleasure to be with; his company is casual and easy; it is almost deceptively harmless. I like the time that I spend with him. But I know I would like it so much more if I felt it was truly innocent.

The front door is shut, but it's been unlocked. Matty must already got back from school. I wanted to be here when he returned – to talk to him, to lay down my law – so he wouldn't go to the wood. There may be a chance that he's still in his room; he's getting changed before leaving.

I call upstairs, hopeful, fearful of Matty's reply. There is nothing. No movement, no noise. My voice filters up the hollow stairs, it echoes through the empty hall, it bounces off the bare walls.

I'm prepared for what I should say. I must tell him he needs to lock the door whenever he leaves the cottage. He must check the windows are closed. He mustn't go to the wood on his own. He mustn't go outside when it's dark. That is what I should say. That is what I am wanting to say. Enough to satisfy Martha's demands; enough to give Matty some hope.

I walk outside to my vegetable patch, picking at weeds, inspecting the plants. I cut the end of a ball of string into a series of six-inch lengths. I work my way down the lines of peas, tying their stems to bamboos. I plant out cucumbers from my cold frame at the very edge of the patch. I fill a trug with baby spinach, with lettuce leaves, with a clutch of spring onions. Then I stand at the end of the lawn and wait, looking out over the field.

The sugar beet plants have grown lumpy and large. From the infant seedlings when first I arrived, they have grown to brutal, ugly things with coarse leaves flapping like laboured wings, heavily hung in the breeze. In the partial shade beneath their spread are the scarred white stumps of their roots. I try to imagine how many plants are contained in a field this big; how great the pile of bodies will be when all have been plucked from the ground.

In the heart of the fluttering churning ocean, the farmhouse is a low-lying island waiting to be engulfed by the wave, by the rising tide of inevitable growth. And beyond the sea – on its distant shore – lies the grey outline of the wood.

From here it's no more than a rustle of trees, bright in reflected sun. It is hard to believe there is danger there. From here, it looks safe, it looks harmless. I could walk there now; I could look for Matty; I could talk to him as I must. I could. But I know the closer I come to the trees the more my confidence will erode, the greater my fear will become. By the time I am stood at its very edge, nothing could entice me inside.

Not even my love for Matty.

I make myself a pot of tea and bring it into the orchard. I lie in a hammock between two trees, in the shifting shade, my eyes half-closed, urging my body to calm. I feel the slow decline of the sun, straining a final sweep of heat over the lengthening land. I sense the air is coming alive with a flurry of birds that have come to feed. I watch the ever-transitioning sky, the sheer blue canvas losing its sheen as evening creeps from the east.

I should go inside and make supper.

I look out over the field once more, over towards the line of the wood. Matty should be on his way back home. If he isn't here shortly, I must go and find him. I must swallow my fear and seek him out. As the afternoon wanes the trees become thicker. They are grey and barren of sunlight. I peer at the thorn that girdles them round, binding the wood to itself. At its edge, there's a man who is holding a gun.

I take the empty pot of tea inside and pick up my keys. I lock the front door and walk to the car. I will drive straight there and park by the graveyard; I will take the track that runs past the field. I will call to Matty from the edge of the wood. From inside, I'm sure he will hear.

I climb into the car and reverse from the drive. Down by the church, there's a hazy figure, approaching fast up the road. Matty is running towards me. His face is bright and flushed with excitement. I'm loath to kill the thing he loves most; I'm loath to forge a divide. But Martha is right: the wood is unsafe. He can go there no more on his own.

I get out of the car and stand on the road, waiting until he has reached me.

He interrupts me before I can speak with a torrent of words of his own. He's speaking so fast, so breathlessly, that what he says lacks all meaning. I ask him to slow down, to say it again, but his agitation has brought incoherence. He seems unable to tell me. Instead, he tugs at my arm. There is something he wants me to see. Somehow, in what he is trying to say, I know this is more than excitement. I hold his shoulders and look at his face; I try to gauge what is wrong. There is knowledge buried deep in his eyes, so profound it denies explanation. He has to show it to me. His body tremors with the weight of emotion, with an energy greater than fear.

I seat him in the car beside me, watching him fidget and panting for breath. At the corner he leaps out and races away, urging me follow behind. He leads me away from his usual entrance, round the fringe of the wood to its side, beyond the eyes of the farm.

We come to a belt of short-cropped scrub between the wood and the field. He stops. He points at the grass, at holes in the ground, at openings to tunnels beneath. We walk further on. Now we are right at the edge of the wood, at the foot of the ring of nettle and thorn. He is pointing again at the grass.

There's another small opening into the ground, partially covered by growth. It is dark inside. I can faintly discern the shape of the walls, but I cannot see to the floor. Matty is pointing into the hole. He is willing me closer, to see.

– What is it?
– Can't you see?
– No, I can't.
– Get closer. On your knees.
– I really can't see anything.
– Then get in there. It's not deep.
– No… no I can't.
– Then I'll get it for you. I didn't want to move it. But I'll get it for you, so you can see.

In a single swift movement, Matty slips into the mouth of the hole. He stands chest deep, like a tentative diver about to enter a vacuous sea. He bobs his head out of sight.

For a moment there's nothing but the blackened entrance to a hole which is carved in the carpet of grass at the foot of treacherous thorn.

I can hear the creak of the trees in the wood; the leaves in the soft breeze, quivering with shame.

Matty's head emerges once more. Again, I see a flush of excitement contorting the shape of his face. He is clutching something in both of his hands, though he's still in the hole and I cannot see. Then he lifts up his arms – he lifts them high – his hands raised over his head. And now I can see; I can clearly see.

He is holding a human skull.

~

– Shouldn't we go to the police?

– I think that's a little extreme.

– I don't. I think it's exactly what we should do. We don't know who it is. We don't know how they died.

– It's probably a caveman, Matty. If anything, we should call an archaeologist. Or a gravedigger, to put it back where it belongs.

– But that's just it. We didn't find it in a grave. We found it in a hole. People don't die naturally in holes. They don't just fall in and die.

– It might have happened that way…

– What?! Their head fell off the rest of their body, and it rolled into the hole on its own?! Come on!

– There's probably a perfectly reasonable explanation.

– Like what?

– Like… I don't know. I'm not an expert…

– Which is why you should call the police. People don't just disappear. I mean, where's the body?

– Anything could have happened to it. This is all ancient history. It's dead and buried. He's probably a Neanderthal.

– That's rubbish. It must have happened quite recently.

– I doubt it. How could you know?

– Well, for a start, we found it in a hole by the wood. One of those concrete holes…

– And…?

– And Jack told us they were built during the Second World War. So the head can't be any older than that. It may be much more recent.

– What are you suggesting?

– I'm suggesting that you call the police.

– I think they've got better things to do.

– Better things than to investigate a crime?! This could be murder for all you know.

– O, don't be silly. Of course it's not murder. Murders don't just happen.

– Then how do they happen? Tell me how they usually happen.

– I really don't want to cause a scene. I don't want to stir up trouble.

– You're not stirring up trouble. You're reporting something to the police. That's all.

– But it will be seen as stirring up trouble. We've done so much, we've tried so hard, to be accepted here. I don't want to alienate myself. I don't want to jeopardise all we've achieved.

– You won't. You'll be doing what anyone would do. Everyone will understand that.

– They won't understand. They'll see it as us causing problems. I wish you'd left it where it was.

– So we could pretend that we hadn't seen it? So we could leave someone else to find it?

– Maybe. Just so long as it wasn't us. I told you the wood was dangerous. I told you not to go in there.

– The wood isn't dangerous…

– It is. Can't you see that it is? Why didn't you listen to me?

– That's not the point…

– Of course it's the point. Why did you have to find it, Matty? Why couldn't you leave it alone? It was buried in there. It had been forgotten. We had just begun to move on. And we could have moved on. We could have avoided being reminded.

– Being reminded of what? What are you talking about?

– Why did you have to dig it up?

– I'm sorry?

– Why did you have to bring it back here?

– Are you saying it's all my fault?

– It is your fault. Yes. If you hadn't gone to the wood like I said, if you hadn't rooted around in the ground, then none of this would have happened.

– So, I'm to blame? Ah, of course. How silly of me. Of course, I am. Perhaps I killed him too.

– I forbid you to go to the wood again. Ever.

– You forbid me?

– Yes.

– And you'll make me?

– Yes.

– You, who daren't even call the police?

– Shut up, Matty. Just shut up.

– Is this your new parenting style?

– Just do what I say. You don't understand…

– No, it's you who don't understand. What sort of parent are you? Take some responsibility. All you can do is think of yourself. That's all you've ever wanted to do. It's hardly surprising you walked out on Dad…

– How dare you!

– No one can live up to your expectations. No one is good enough for you. And so now we find ourselves here, stuck in the middle of nowhere, with a skull. Well done, Mum. Congratulations. Thanks for buggering everything up.

Matty turns towards the door and opens it onto the day, walking into the sunlight beyond. He cuts to the right, round the side of the cottage, leaving the door open wide. Nothing will bring him back now.

In the space where he stood is a stretch of lawn, sparkling a luminous green. Beyond it the hedge, alive with birds, with the fickle dance of wind-troubled leaves. I will give him some space now to be on his own. He needs to work this through for himself. It will take him time to see I am right.

There are some things in life that we have to do. And others we can choose to avoid. It's just such a shame it should lead to a fight. I wish he could understand.

I go outside. The garden swoons beneath the eye of the unrelenting midday sun. Leaves idly fan the heat of the breeze which simmers and drifts on the strangled air.

There are sounds from within the bowels of a lean-to at the very end of the lawn. Matty is in there behind a locked door. I can hear the heavy clank of a hammer, the twist and scrape of tightened wire, the stunning shiver of metal. What is he making within his lair? He hides in the dark, from the melt of the sun. No longer allowed to go to the wood. I think he is hiding from me. Too young to understand what is happening; too young to know what is right. It always seems to happen like this – that something prevents us from being together; something prevents me from showing my love. I have to seem cruel to protect him sometimes. It's then I wish he would trust.

He doesn't know what happened between us, or the chain of events that summoned us here. He only knows what he sees. He doesn't know that we chose to part; that we made the decision between us. He doesn't see that living together was tortuous and beyond our endurance. He doesn't understand what was wrong, or how we agreed what had to be done. It was both of us who felt that way; both of us who made the decision. It wasn't just me walking out. I wish he could come to accept that truth; I wish he knew it was so. Then I could break this desperate cycle, where all I create is needless conflict, when all I do is push him away the harder I try to keep hold. Just as I once did with you.

Please let me not lose Matty. Please.

I fill a jug with elderflower wine. I place it down in the shade by the lean-to, calling to Matty to tell him it's there. From inside, I can hear the clatter of metal, the agony of wire being stretched. Such unnatural sounds to tarnish this beauty, this elemental frieze of flush life. What is he doing in there? What would I do if he came out now and said that he wanted to go back home? If he insisted on leaving the cottage, of going to London, of living with you?

I call again.

He's ignoring me; he is punishing me. At least when we fought, we were in the same room. Then, at least, I could see him. I could weave my love through the thick of his hate; I could speak in a language unfettered by words. This avoidance he pays me is so much more painful; it's more hurtful for consciously blocking me out. Somehow, he thinks this is all my fault, though what I am doing is only for him. And in the gap between seeing and knowing I have to be strong for us both.

I return inside. I run the kitchen tap through my fingers until the water is cool. The sensation of coldness shocks me to life. Here, on the table, close to my side, is the skull. I had almost persuaded myself it would leave if only I left it alone. It would get up and go, it would walk away, in search of freedom, of peace. Instead, I find it still here. Sitting here still, on the edge of the table, looking at me with its broken eyes. Has it come to befriend me, or perhaps to torment me? What shall I do with you now? I should take you back to the place where we found you. I should bury you deeper this time. So you no longer fear being re-awoken; so your sleep is no longer disturbed. So you can't blame me for all that has happened; for how it has ended up as it has.

Is that who you are? Are you Dan? Did you come to show me that burying you has failed to let me have closure? That even in death you intrude on my life? To kindle remorse. To drown me in doubt. To fill me with hope. To hint at the answers, deeper and darker than words.

Do you blame me still for what I have done? Don't you see why I did it; why it needed to happen? Surely you do in your heart. You could see all we were, and all we were not; you could see this decision was right. Even though you might regret it was made; even though you knew the pain it would cause. It is better to experience pain than to feel no sensation at all. Surely you knew it was right. It had to be right. It was right at the time. It surely wasn't so wrong.

Though if I had known the impact on Matty, then perhaps I wouldn't have chosen to leave. I could have tried harder to fix what was wrong; I could have bridged the divide. Instead, I was willing to let it happen; I watched it happen; I willed it to happen. Not even for the wanting of it, but because of the change it would bring. Because it would force me out of myself, out of the world I was living. I wasn't unhappy for being with you. I wasn't unhappy for being together. I was unhappy for being myself. That was what needed to change. But instead of facing into that truth, I stole away in the crying night, furtively – all those months ago – half-hoping you'd follow me here.

I could almost believe you are looking at me. I could almost believe that where should be lips there's a motion, a whisper of words. Maybe, if I were to come slightly closer, I would be able to hear. If I put my ear up close to your skull I will know your secrets, your truth. The breath of death is upon my cheeks. It is crawling over my skin.

I recoil. I glance at the clock. Its already twenty past five. That should make no difference to me: time has ceased to exist. Time is told by the rub of the seasons, by the sowing and reaping, by the morning and evening. Time is the fleeting interlude that intrudes between birth and death. And then, when it's done, the vast emptiness, unfolding its weave and embracing us all. It's the time when we rot; the time we are not. When we stare at the void from hollow shells, for there's nothing more to be seen. When time dies too. When everything dies. When all of life fades away.

Except that, somehow, you won't.

I brush back my hair with my hands. I pick up my coat. I round the side of the house to the lean-to and timidly knock at the door. Through the faceless slab of the wood that divides us, I tell Matty I'm off to the pub.

For a moment there's silence. Then the scraping and moulding of metal resumes, shrill from behind the locked door.

My feet feel numb as I walk down the road; my steps are muted and weightless. As if I am gliding over the tarmac which prickles and shimmers with heat. Maybe I'm like you – I am half-dead too – I'm no longer a part of this physical world. I am easing myself beyond its bounds, and not a soul can redeem me. I am walking towards the waiting church, where I can find a grave for myself. Somewhere to sleep, to shake off this toil, to bury myself in oblivion.

As I round the corner I catch sight of Bill, who approaches the pub from the shop. We meet at the door of the Serpent. Bill stretches out to open the latch, but he lets his arm fall when he sees me.

– What's the matter, Sarah? It looks like you've seen a ghost.

– I have, sort of.

– What do you mean? Are you all right?

– Yes. I just need to go in. To sit down.

– O, my poor girl. It must be the sun. You've been out for too long.

– No, it isn't the sun. It's something else. Something Matty's found.

Bill opens the door and lets me enter; he follows me into the cool. All of a sudden, he seems younger, more eager; less of the man and more of the child. He's excited for knowing that something's been found. Something, perhaps, to gossip about.

Inside, the room is cold and dark, as if we have entered a tomb. The door swings closed; it feels like I'm trapped. I should have found the strength not to come. But I need to have a person to talk to. I need to see and have someone to be with. Someone other than you. Bill sits me down in a chair by the hearth. Now Travis is here with our beers.

– How are you doing, Sarah? You're looking awfully pale.

– Yes, I found her outside. She's wobbly. I think she's unwell.

– Would you prefer a cup of tea?

– No, I'm fine. Honestly, I'm fine. Well, maybe. Have you got a brandy?

– Brandy, yes. Now what's the matter? What did Matty find?

– He found... we were walking in the wood, and he found... thank you, Travis.

– He found... what did he find...?

– He found… he found a skull.

– A what?

– You know, a skull. He found a skull. A human skull.

– What? A real skull?

– Yes, a skull skull.

– You're joking?

– No, I'm not joking, Travis. Why do you think I'm joking?

– No, of course you're not joking. I'm so sorry.

– What are you sorry about?

– I don't know. It feels like the right thing to say.

– Yes, yes. But where did he find it?

– In a hole. In a concrete bunker. One of the tunnels they built during the war.

– Do you think it belongs to an airman?

– It could be. It's hard to tell. A skull's a skull really. There isn't a name on it.

– How exciting!

– Is it?

– Well, yes. I think it is. It would be good to find out how it got there.

– I'm not sure how. And I don't know how that would help. The peculiar thing is it was there on its own. There wasn't a body. Only a head.

– Like someone put it in there? Like somebody hid it?

– Maybe. Who knows?

– Who could have put it in there?

– It could have been anyone. Anyone could go into the wood at night without the danger of being seen.

– Not anyone could.

– What do you mean?

– Well, who's always in there? Who watches it all of the time? Who is the person who lives right beside it?

– Uriah?

208

– Uriah, yes. He's there the whole time. He patrols the perimeter; he carries a gun; he lays snares…

– And he warns everyone it's not safe to go there…

– That's right. He doesn't let anyone else do the logging. He chops it himself, so no one goes in.

– What? What are you both saying?

– What we're saying, Sarah, is that in practice the wood belongs to Uriah. He knows everything that goes on within it, but no one knows what he does when he's there.

– Are you suggesting he put the skull there himself?

– Well, he might have done. And if he didn't, he probably knows the person who did.

– It's not just about who buried it there. What I want to know is whose skull it is. And what became of the body.

– Do you think…? Do you think it might be Laura's?

– Now that's an idea, Bill. It could be his first wife. She just disappeared. Nobody's heard of her since.

– That would give him a motive. When Laura died, he inherited the farm, he inherited all of her land.

– Uriah goes and murders his wife, then he buries her body in her own field. That would make a good headline.

– Wait. Wait. What are the two of you saying?

– You remember I told you that Uriah was married to someone called Laura Sheldrake. That she vanished, and since then she hasn't been seen. People thought she eloped with Tom Bayles. Who just happens to be Joyce's brother. What Travis and I are beginning to question is whether she ran off at all. Uriah might have had other plans.

– But that's pure speculation.

– It is, but can't you see that it fits. It makes perfect sense.

– It doesn't make any sense at all.

– Here, Sarah. I'll get you another brandy.

Travis is rooting around at the bar and returns with a glass in his hand. This one is filled to the brim. The first one helped to settle my nerves, but this will go straight to my head. Maybe I've been in the sun for too long. Maybe I should have just stayed at home and worked out what to do on my own.

I watch the others continue to talk. They are spurring each other on with this madness; they lack the will to resist. They are mixing my meagre fragments of truth with a densely embroidered fabrication which is spiralling out of control. I find it hard to absorb their words. I find it hard to sit up. I want to go back home and to sleep; I need to shutter my eyes. I want to sleep and then to wake – to wake in my bed and find you beside me – to find that none of this has been real. It has just been a horrible dream.

Travis is laying cushions around me; he's propping me up in the chair. Bill appears to have left. I try to get up but Travis won't let me. He thinks it is best if I stay here for now. He thinks I'm too weak to go home on my own. He wants me to rest awhile in the pub, until I am able to walk.

I should have known that this would have happened; I shouldn't have tried to confide. I've provided the parts to peddle a poison, to mingle a mixture of truth spun with lies. This is wrong; so wrong. This is none of our business. My heart goes out to Uriah. To see this assault on his tight-lipped pride, his sense of tradition, his dignity. An attack on his honour, which he cannot defend. I must get to the door before Bill returns. I must find the strength to escape.

But it's too late. Bill is coming back into the room; he is walking over towards me. And this time he has brought Margaret with him. There's nothing more I can do.

They sit in a semi-circle before me, like truant pupils mocking their teacher, knowing she's tied to her chair. They fashion theories on how Laura died; on why her head was removed from her torso; on where Tom Bayles might be now. They think if they scratch away at the earth they will find the remains of Laura's body; they will find the body parts of them both. It is clear in their minds that Uriah's the culprit, but they want to go further than this. They wonder how Martha might be involved, and even what Jack might conceal. Their words have lost all sense of the truth; they are cruel and distorted, infused with a stain. A virus has been unleashed in this room, with the virulence to ravage the past, to plague the now and to taint the future, till everyone is infected. They are circling around me like crows to the carrion, feeling a feverish satisfaction at seeing the Pooleys brought low.

– So where is it?
– Yes, Sarah, where is it?
– What?
– Where is it? Where's the skull?
– Did you bring it with you?
– Sorry?
– Did you bring the skull with you?
– No.
– Then where is it?
– It's at home. It's sitting on my kitchen table at home.
– That is, that is so…
– Let's go and see it! Let's go and visit the skull!
– Margaret, I don't think we can ask Sarah to…
– No, you can't.
– Couldn't we just…
– No.

– …touch it.

– So, what are you going to do with it now?

– I'm not sure. What would you do?

– Shouldn't you tell the police?

– I thought of that. But I don't want anyone to get into trouble. Particularly Matty. For moving the evidence, I mean. And now his fingerprints are all over it. Travis, what do you think?

– If you'd left it alone and phoned the police, then I think that would have been good. But now it might appear a bit strange. I mean, why did you take it back home with you? Why did you wait for almost a day before you decided to phone them? You might get asked awkward questions.

– Bill?

– I'd talk it through at the Community Council. The village will know what to do.

– But you can't do that if Martha's involved.

– Margaret, Martha isn't involved.

– How do you know? How can you be so sure? That woman's got secrets. She knows.

– Please, Margaret!

– Well, she does. Bill, you know she does…

I turn to Travis and plead with my eyes. This is wrong; it should end; this is purely destructive. I think he understands my distress. He nods his agreement; he seems sympathetic; but there's nothing he does to deter them. I put the brandy aside and stand up.

The others look on with concern. They want to accompany me back to the cottage. But I doubt their intent is born out of kindness. They would want to come in and inspect the skull. They would poke their fingers at it and abuse it. They would use it to cast their judgement and shame.

I tell them I will go on my own. My voice is firm, and they don't resist. I think they think they've exhausted me now. There is nothing to lose in letting me leave.

The air outside invigorates me. It was stultifying in the pub. As if my life was being sucked from me; as if my body was being bled dry. Already my limbs and my mind feel sharper; my senses feel more acute. I feel the strength of my muscles returning; the certainty of my tread. I want to avoid being caught in their web, though it's spun so tightly around me. I want to avoid this venomous village, though there's nowhere else I can hide.

I walk straight over the lawn to the back. I want to warn Matty; I need to warn him. There is danger here. It is real. It is in the wood; it is in the village; it is in the hedges and fields. This is not just a feeling; it is something alive. It is in the air; it hangs expectant. I must find a way to protect him.

I stand outside the lean-to door, listening for the hideous noise. I call Matty's name. I call again. Then I turn the handle and push.

It is dim in the lean-to. Thin natural light streaks in at the window and is strangled by cobwebs and dust. I search for the switch and turn on the light.

The table beside me is piled with treasure that sparkles in the forced beam. A grotesque hoard of familiar objects amassed as if for display. Loops of wire and sheets of metal, six-inch nails and sharpened sticks. A heap of broken glass. I cannot guess what he's trying to build, nor what it is designed to do. But I sense it can only be cruel.

I turn off the light and close the door; I go back into the sunlight. I call his name out once more.

From the lawn, from the orchard, from the rooms in the cottage, I hear no hint of reply.

I stare out over the field. If he isn't here, he is there in the wood. He's had enough of being imprisoned, and now he can take it no more. He can creep past the watchful eye of Uriah, and he's willing enough to defy me. He has broken away and has gone to the wood, back to the refuge he's built in the trees, where he feels at peace and secure.

I pick up a coat and walk down the road. I must reassert my control. There's no space left for compromise now. I won't allow him outside on his own; I won't allow him to go to the wood. That part of his life has now ended.

As I walk past Six Bells I glance at the field, at the distant island of Rose House Farm that sinks in the murmuring leaf. I can see a silhouette on the track; a person is walking away from the house. I wait as the figure blurs into focus, as the angled sun exposes his face.

It is Matty.

I stand on the road where it meets with the track, waiting for Matty to come. The wind is teasing his unkempt hair; it snatches at the flaps of his collar and ripples the legs of his jeans.

He has seen me, and he sees that I see. I wait till he comes up close; till he stops.

– Where have you been?
– Nowhere.
– Don't take me for a fool.
– All right, then. I've been to Rose House Farm.
– To see Uriah?
– Yes.

– Did you see him?

– Yes.

– What did you talk about? What did you do?

– Not much.

– Were you talking about snares?

– Perhaps.

– Is that what you're making?

–

– I don't like them, Matty. They're dangerous. They're illegal. I don't like you talking to Uriah, either. You don't know anything about him.

– I know more about him than you do.

– You don't know what he does. What he's done.

– What does that mean?

– I don't think it's safe. I don't want you to see him again. Not until I say that you can.

– You can't do that. It's not fair.

– I can and I will. I'm your mother.

– You would never do this if Dad was here.

– He isn't here.

– No, he isn't. He isn't here because of you. Because you ran away from him.

– You don't understand, Matty. It's more complicated.

– It isn't complicated. You just closed him out, like you're closing me out. You can't see shit beyond yourself.

– I can see enough. I'm telling you not to visit Uriah. Not because I want to deny you; not because I want to hurt you. But because I care for you; I love you. I want to protect you. You may not like it, but it's for your own good.

– It's not for my own good. If you thought about what was good for me, we wouldn't be here in the first place. We'd all be in London. All of us. We'd be together with Dad.

– Matty, don't.

– You do what you want, and everyone has to fit in behind you. And if they don't like it, you push them away.

– Don't, Matty. You don't understand…

But already he's walking away; walking away up the road to the cottage; walking so fast that I cannot catch up without breaking into a run. By the time I reach the door, he's upstairs. His boots have been kicked off in the hall. I can hear him moving around in his room. I climb the stairs and knock at his door. He will not answer, nor let me in.

I talk to him softly; I try to speak kindly; I say what I feel in my heart. Not because I want to placate him, but because I love him, I love him so much. He's more than my son: he's my world. He is everything. He's all that I have; he's all that I want. And I am so, so frightened of losing him.

I don't know if he is listening to me, or if he has closed himself off. It doesn't make any difference. Saying these words aloud to us both, I feel the immensity of my love, I feel how fragile it is.

In the silence which spins from his side of the door, I feel his hurt, the weight of that hurt, the weight of all that he bears. I am helpless to help him; I am worse than helpless. I show my love through demands and denial; through a mixture of anger and unkind words. What sort of love is that? What sort of mother am I? It isn't his fault that he is where he is, surrounded by things beyond his control. Beyond his power to comprehend. My purpose should be to shield him from this, to use my love as a staff to guide, to build him a shelter within my heart. But I can't explain what is happening here. And if what I see makes no sense to me, then nothing I do can protect him.

~

A low cloud clings to the land. The hedges stand silent, watchful and wary, shrouded in a shade of despair, dripping a wetness, a gloom. Weeping. Before me, the tarnished sugar beet leaves ripple as waves that fade to oblivion as they merge with the slow-moving mass of the field, becoming an endless and restless sea. The faintest of pink slips over the sky as the blush of the morning seeks to impose itself on this pocketed world.

I stand on the sodden grass in my nightdress, a warm cup of coffee held in my hand. The garden is hung in the spectre of silence. It's another day – a different day – so different to all of the others. The roses which stretch their stems up the walls, the herbs which lay their scent in the bed, the hedges which spy on my vegetable patch, the slip of track where I park the car. They all look so different from yesterday. I sense an invisible Rose House Farm sunk in the field through the blinding mist. I sense the line of the unseen road slipping away towards the church and sliding on to the Serpent. I sense the hidden fields beyond; the thin wet track of clumpy grass; the thicket crouched beside a ditch; the blank white walls of Burnt Tree Farm, with its domes of silos beyond. All different now; all stripped of life. All locked in purgatory. This isn't a village standing as one, protecting itself from the threat of outside. It's a fragmented group of solitary houses harbouring a wretched few people, being consumed from within. The land – the land that is all – has been shamed. The past has been ripped from its womb. Though in time this village may fashion a peace, it can never return to the way that it was. It will never again be the same.

Back in the kitchen I make more coffee; I have breakfast alone at the table. Matty is still asleep in his room, or if not asleep he avoids me. He may not have found a way to forgive me, he may not want to speak to me, but he seems the only person here who sees the truth, who acknowledges it, in all of its imperfection.

As if sensing my thoughts, he is here. Not here to my side, but in the same room. Not speaking, but willing to be seen.

I sit and watch as he eats. His spoon scrapes the bowl, so unnaturally loud in the dampened air of the room. He is wearing the clothes that he wears to school. He has brushed his hair with his fingers. I sense he knows I am watching him; I sense he resents being watched.

Matty has finished; he puts down his bowl. Then he opens the door on the coils of mist which wind their way through the hedge. I follow him out and into the world, into the late-coming day.

Matty walks down the line in the road, and I step behind in his wake. In the absence of words I can hear his shoes, beating a time on the tarmac surface, reassuringly true.

I can see the others are already there. They are in the graveyard; they are on the path; they are walking up to the porch. I see Samantha is there with Travis. Her heels are slipping against the gravel, but she doesn't reach for support. The Pooleys are there, as are Bill and Margaret. The Faradays too, though without their children. All have come to watch and to listen, though it doesn't feel like a coming together born of the strength of being together, a community acting as one. They have come in pairs, and will sit as islands, careful and conscious of those around them.

They will all be inside by the time we arrive; they will all be waiting for me. They will wait until we are all in one place. The accusers and the accused.

Matty starts up the path to the church, with the same measured stride as before. He turns inside, and into its heart. I follow closely behind.

It is as I thought it would be. They are all inside; they have taken their places; they are patiently waiting for the last to arrive. For me and Matty to enter. All are watching, yet no one looks round; all are avoiding the others' eyes. All of us are seated in couples, yet each is blind to the comfort of touch.

The pew is cold; the wooden seat is wet on my thighs. There is no talk, no gentle murmur, though it feels I can hear the accusation which is born and which brews in their minds. I kneel and pray. I pray for the end of today; I pray for a new day, a different day; I pray to evade these bitter people who whisper their treason beneath closed lips.

The thin piping notes of the throaty organ break the film of silence we sit in, tremoring a timid noise through the church which dissipates into the air. We stand and sing in unison, joylessly. Only Martha's voice is sure and firm, her words carved crisp and clean.

The hymn is done. We shuffle and sit. Jack stands alone and approaches the lectern. He spreads a sheet of paper before him, reading the words in a measured tone.

| | |
|---|---|
| Do they know what I've done? Can they see my guilt? Do they know the harm that I've caused? | *See, I have set before thee this day life and good, and death and evil;* |

There was life and good, and I butchered it, bringing death and evil instead. I destroyed what we had when I walked out on you, as surely as if I had killed you. I turned my heart away from the truth; I refused to listen; I was drawn away. I let myself be deceived. Then, in my cowardice, I chose to hide, hoping my conscience would clear. Hoping that here in this quiet village I could find a way to let it erode, to let it all fade away. But it didn't happen like that. Matty has dug up the past that I buried, bearing it forth and holding it witness, to be my measure of shame. Now he has denounced me – truly and fairly – calling heaven and earth in record against me. Life and death have been set before me. And I would choose life – believe me I would – to save myself and to save my seed, if only I knew how to do it.

*In that I command thee this day to love the LORD thy God, to walk in his ways, and to keep his commandments, and his statutes, and his judgments, that thou mayest live and multiply: and the LORD thy God shall bless thee in the land whither thou goest to possess it.*

*But if thine heart turn away, so that thou wilt not hear, but shalt be drawn away, and worship other gods, and serve them;*

*I denounce unto you this day, that ye shall surely perish, and that ye shall not prolong your days upon the land, whither thou passest over Jordan to go to possess it.*

*I call heaven and earth to record this day against you, that I have set before you life and death, blessing and cursing: therefore choose life, that both thou and thy seed may live:*

Jack comes to a close. He folds the paper deliberately, then surveys the people before him. Colin Inchmore attempts to rise, but sits when Jack extends his arm, motioning him to stay still. Jack continues to look at us all, gazing at each one in turn. He searches into our eyes with his own. His body is stiff and formal with pride; his dignity is supreme.

– I am not a man of God, but I am a God-fearing man. I am not better nor worse than you. I am governed by the same morality; I am subject to the same frailty. Something has happened here. We do not know what it is, but we sense it is wrong. And, as such, it threatens us all. It threatens our values and our traditions; our livelihood and the land. It threatens the village, and those in the village, and everything that surrounds us. The village should be our comfort, our strength. Because of its strength, and the strength of its people, we have learnt the ways to survive. But if people do not stand together, then the village itself will fail. If the village fails, then all will fail. Each and every one of us. We will be engulfed by forces beyond us; we will all be swept away and diminished. Something has happened here. We do not know what it is, but we sense it is wrong. We must stand as one, and we must be strong. We must trust to each other and to ourselves till the wrong has been righted and laid to rest. Only then can the village breathe. Only then can we truly find peace. I would ask you all, I would plead with you all – for the sake of our forefathers, for the sake of our children, for the suffering of the past and the hope of tomorrow, for the village itself and for all those within it – do not destroy it now with your doubt. Be resolute, be firm, and be strong. Know yourself, and trust to your neighbour till what is required to be done has been done; till the wrongs have been righted. Be strong.

Jack's voice hangs in the arch of the church long after the words have been spoken. He looks out over the congregation; he looks at us all, without censure or fear, then slowly walks back to his pew. For a moment, there's a hush, a disquieted lull, as the village pauses for breath. Martha reaches out for Jack's hand; she holds that hand in her own. Colin Inchmore resumes the service; he omits his sermon and asks us to pray.

On the opposite side of the aisle to the Pooleys, Uriah is cast like stone in his pew. His thick neck is thrust through the squeeze of his collar; his eyes are unblinking and still. He seems unmoved by what he has heard, or by the shock that surrounds him. He must know that everyone looks at him now, just as they looked at me when we entered. He must know these others have come to this service purely to fuel their own fabrications; purely to witness and relish his shame. He must feel that burden upon him. Their eyes, and the disbelief they express; the suspicion, the fear they convey. They are seeking him out and staring at him, to drawn forth the knowledge they think that he holds, to expose the deeds they believe that he hides.

I have abused you shamelessly, even if you are not without guilt. You may be judged for your manifold sins, but I will be judged for my wickedness. And that is the far greater crime. For instead of acknowledging all my own faults, I imposed them on you to spare myself. I refused to look

*Almighty God, Father of our Lord Jesus Christ, Maker of all things, Judge of all men; We acknowledge and bewail our manifold sins and wickedness, Which we, from time to time, most grievously have committed, By thought, word, and deed, Against thy Divine Majesty, Provoking most*

inside myself, to test my thoughts and words and deeds, to question the things that I did. I was afraid to confront myself. For fear of facing up to the truth; for fear of knowing that I was wrong. I am sorry; I am heartily sorry. For all the pain I have thrust on you, and for what you must be going through now, and for all the pain that has yet to come. For no matter how this journey ends – if you choose to pardon or I to repent – the shame and the memory are sure to remain. They remain beyond all forgiveness.

*justly thy wrath and indignation against us. We do earnestly repent, And are heartily sorry for these our misdoings; The remembrance of them is grievous unto us; The burden of them is intolerable. Have mercy upon us, Have mercy upon us, most merciful Father; For thy Son our Lord Jesus Christ's sake, Forgive us all that is past; And grant that we may ever hereafter Serve and please thee In newness of life, To the honour and glory of thy Name; Through Jesus Christ our Lord. Amen.*

Behind Uriah sit Margaret and Bill. Behind them, Samantha and Travis. They are staring into the back of his skull. None of them daring to move. Travis is looking uncomfortable, his neck constrained by a collar and tie, his square fringe brushed to one side. Neither he nor his wife have followed the service. Neither of them seems to know how to pray. They have come here hoping to witness the pain, to feast their eyes on those who are humbled, to revel in shock and in shame. They have heard Jack's plea on behalf of the village; they have seen Uriah exposed in his pew. Now they watch out this farce to its miserable end, in the hope of witnessing more.

I cannot change the things I have done; I cannot roll back all that is past. But that doesn't mean that I don't regret. The things we do can be so simple – our words and our actions can form without thought, they can enter the world without pity or mercy, they can crush what is good and bring pain. Even if we believe they are right; even if we are true to ourselves. For once they are done the deeds becomes truth, even if, through the passage of time, we learn that that truth is a lie. It is easy to hurt; it is harder to mend. It is harder still to bend back time and right what we know to be wrong.

*… we offer and present unto thee, O Lord, our selves, our souls and bodies, to be a reasonable, holy, and living sacrifice unto thee; humbly beseeching thee, that we, and all others who shall be partakers of this Holy Communion, may worthily receive the most precious Body and Blood of thy Son Jesus Christ, be filled with thy grace and heavenly benediction, and made one body with him, that he may dwell in us, and we in him. And although we are unworthy, through our manifold sins, to offer unto thee any sacrifice; yet we beseech thee to accept this our bounden duty and service…*

Each of us rise in turn for Communion. In turn we kneel near the base of the altar, feeling the pinch of the eyes on our backs. We take bread and wine; we return to our pews; we lower our faces towards the floor. Matty comes and kneels at my side; he is blessed by the hands of the priest.

The service ends. Colin Inchmore walks to the door, followed by Martha and Jack. Uriah waits till his parents are clear, then he sidles into the aisle. Matty gets up, swiftly and suddenly, pushing past Bill. He hurries to hasten away.

Perhaps he's been trapped in this stifling tomb for longer than he can endure. Or maybe he doesn't want to be seen here, close to my side and caught in my prison, though I pleaded with him to stay near. I sit in my pew pretending to pray, purposefully, till the others have gone. I want to avoid the questioning looks, the inevitable chatter to come.

Now the church is unpeopled and noiseless. I am the only one here. The silence squats in the hammer-beam vault and watches me, holding its breath.

I rise. I shuffle towards the door. I walk towards the infant light, and all that is lying beyond. Outside, the congregation fragments, it melts away in lone pairs. No one is left in the graveyard now. No one is left but Uriah.

He is stood by the side of the gravel path, on the grass beside a clutch of headstones, unhurried in taking his leave. He is focusing on the boy before him, locked in earnest debate. There's no condescension from adult to child; no fear of the man from the boy. Instead, from both, there's an urge to share, a desire to hear what the other would say.

I watch them from the twilight porch. They are both engaged and excited. Their hands reinforce their unheard words through the gestures they weave in the air. Their subject seems of mutual interest; it captivates and enthrals them. There's not a hint of guilt in Uriah. Not in his manner, not in his speech. There's nothing threatening about him. Even the sullenness stamped on his face seems to have been grafted away. I have been unfair on this man, I think. I judged him before I got to know him; I feared him before I tried to like. My prejudice has soured my perception, while Matty has merely engaged. He has seen Uriah for who he is, and it seems what he sees is enough.

Then that should be enough for me too. If I trust in Matty I should trust in Uriah; I shouldn't think so badly of him. There is much that Matty could learn from Uriah, much that would strengthen and serve him well. And, in the absence of his father, it is good for Matty to have a man who can stand by his side to teach and to guide. A strength of presence for Matty to draw on; a role that I cannot fulfil. I should have encouraged them both to talk, right from when they first met. Instead of forbidding Matty to see him; instead of learning to fear him myself.

Uriah looks over Matty's shoulder and sees me here in the porch. He glances down and shakes Matty's hand. There's a final hurried exchanging of words, then Uriah turns and is gone.

I want to pick up where Uriah has left off, to talk to Matty plainly and simply, to win back his confidence and his trust. I need to be open with him.

– Hey.
–
– Are you hungry? Do you want an early lunch?
– Not yet. I'm busy. I need to get home.
– O. All right. What are you up to?
–
– I saw you were talking to Uriah…
–
– What were you talking about?
– Not much.
– Did he say anything about what's happened?
– No.
– Shall we go home now?
–

226

Matty's eyes don't meet with mine, though I'm staring into his face. I sense he'd prefer that I wasn't here, that I wasn't standing so close. And he would also prefer to be elsewhere; I can tell he's itching to go to the wood. Until I let him, he won't forgive me, he won't want to trust me or share what he thinks. In that, he is so like Uriah. Both of them caught by the same fixation; both unwilling to yield.

I look up. The congregation have all dispersed; the road is empty and blind. The mist is lifting, revealing a day which is colourless, airless, breathless.

I wish there was something more I could say; some way I could draw Matty into the open. I cannot believe we have come to a point where there isn't a topic of mutual interest, there isn't a pastime in common to share. I want to rebuild our intimacy, to win his respect and his affection. To return it to the way it once was.

Matty doesn't grasp my desire, or, if he perceives it, he doesn't respond. This is a cold, cruel place to start from, here exposed on this rise. All I can feel is a yearning within him to be somewhere else. Almost anywhere else. Anywhere that I'm not.

It is Matty who breaks through our silence.

– What's Jack's problem anyway?
– Sorry?
– Why's Jack giving us a lecture?
– It's because of the skull, Matty. Everyone knows about it now, but nobody knows what's happened. At least, nobody claims to know what happened.
– What does Jack think has happened?
– I don't know.

– Then why's he being so gloomy?

– Because there's a rumour that it's Laura's skull. If it does belong to Uriah's first wife, then naturally Jack would be worried. He's concerned about what will happen.

– That's stupid.

– It's not. He's worried about how the skull may have got there. He's worried about whose it might be.

– It's pretty obvious what happened, isn't it? Somebody must have killed her. Uriah probably.

– Matty! How could you say such a thing?!

– Well, why not? I can easily imagine him murdering someone. Can't you?

– No. You mustn't talk like that. You mustn't, even if you secretly think it.

– Whatever. It doesn't matter.

– Of course it matters.

– It doesn't matter if none of you dare to call the police. It'll all blow over, and that'll be it. Things will go back to how they were.

– How can you think Uriah's a murderer? You've just been talking to him…

– That's different. He doesn't want to murder me. He's got no reason to. But I bet you think he murdered her too. You just don't want to admit it.

– Of course I don't.

– Don't you? Isn't that what everyone thinks? Isn't that what you agreed with the others, when you all went down to the pub? None of you like him, so it's easy to blame him.

– Matty, no! For all we know, Uriah might have thought she was still alive. He might yet love her. He might be in shock. I only sympathise with the man.

– You know, there are times when I don't believe you…

– Matty… Matty…

Matty has started off down the path, through the gate, and onto the road. He is walking so fast that I can't keep up, and there's no point in trying to do so. I watch him walking away. He doesn't look back. He is moving on to something else – to something that no longer involves me.

There's a breeze in the air, and with it a chill. The clumps of bush to the side of the road scatter and dance their silver leaves: a swirl of movement, of shadow and light, winking and blinking at me. I feel exposed on the road on my own. I wish that someone was here. Someone to walk up the road beside me; someone with whom to walk it together. Whether that's Matty or you. But now there is no one. No one around me. I have cut you both away from me. Wilfully and purposefully. Now I have no one left to be with.

Now there is no one left to blame.

It is reassuring to see the cottage, reassuring to cross the lawn. I could almost pretend it's like coming home. This house is the place where I've chosen to live, where I can lock the doors and feel safe. The hedges bristle their indignation, scornful of my foolishness. I linger, listening, before I enter. Round the side of the cottage, borne on the breeze, I can hear the livid scraping of metal, the snap of a switch which is triggered by movement, the tear of a tightening wire.

I place a cold lunch outside on a tray, with an inverted colander sat on the plate to keep the flies off the food. I call to Matty through the door, though I hear no words in reply. There is no respite to his fiendish toil; there is no respite in his feelings for me. I will try, I will keep on trying to reach him. Through my words, through my actions, through what's in my heart. And eventually he may choose to relent.

He may see that I've changed, that I'm trying to change. Now all I want is to broker a peace. A peace that will keep us together.

Inside, in my bedroom, through the thin wattle walls, through the silent space which pervades the cottage, I can hear the regular sound of a hammer skidding over a brash metal surface as Matty manufactures his snares.

I take off my shoes and lie fully clothed on my bed. I stare at the ceiling above me. I examine the labouring arms of the beams, the tired blemished walls with their flaking paint, the broken end of the curtain rail. This cottage has stood for centuries, and in all that time almost nothing has happened, nothing has forced it to change. Families lived here for generations, and these walls protected them all. Three families in three tiny houses under this single roof. If Martha is right, then twenty people were living here at one time. How could so many live so close and still be at peace with themselves? Just you and me was one too many. So much so, that I broke away. But for those that were here there wasn't a choice. They learnt to depend upon each other; they needed each other to harvest the fields, intensively turning the earth by hand. They couldn't survive on their own. For centuries it happened that way. But then they were caught by an unseen occurrence, and all those people, those houses, that life, were irretrievably changed. In a single stroke their world disappeared; a way of living was suddenly ended. The village was brought to the edge of extinction. Something had happened to shock their system: as momentous as what is happening here now. No wonder Jack fights as hard as he does. He knows the past; he is cautious of change; he knows that if he can't halt the slide then this village will cease to exist.

I sense time pass as I stare at the beams. The day has yet to break and to shine, though already it stumbles to closure. A dull ray of light slips in through the window; it illuminates specks of static dust which hang suspended in frictionless air, in this shapeless expanse of grim grey. I can feel the thin mist creeping back in, the moisture dampening the air. Even here, when hidden, safe behind walls, I can feel the day fold in on itself.

I get up and walk through the hall to the bathroom, splashing my face with a cupful of water, wanting to wake myself up. From the bathroom I enter my study. There's a manuscript here, but I don't feel incentive. Three times I read the same paragraph. The words refuse to make sense. My mind is elsewhere. My ears are alive to the noise downstairs, to the coughing and wheezing of beaten metal as Matty hunches over his anvil, creating some ugly device.

In my head I rehearse the words Jack spoke, as he warned of how the village would die if its people failed to come together, to trust each other, to stand as one. I look through the window away to my right, to the field of sugar beet laid in the mist, and within it I see an army of people scratching the earth with their hoes.

The afternoon drifts aimlessly on, seeming unhurried to fade. In the garden I harvest a blackcurrant bush. The fruit is soft and bursting with ripeness, spitting its blood in my mouth. I trim the grass round the side of my patch; I tie back the stems of tomato plants; I fill my trug with carrots and lettuce; I cut a spray of sweet peas.

The mock-heat of the day is drifting away; it is being drawn into the soil. The infinite grey of the sunless sky is washed with a wisp of dark cloud.

I look out over the field of beet. On the track which leads to Rose House Farm I can see two people are standing and talking. It's Uriah and Martha; mother and son. Martha, so small, so seemingly fragile, though her body is sturdy and straight. Uriah, a square shape, broad and heavy, towering over her frame. His shirt-tails flap in the faceless breeze; his big bull neck stands proud of his collar; his face is weathered and raw.

I sit on the bench which faces the field. I wonder how big the beet will grow before it is time to dig up. Already its skin is furrowed and ugly, the root of its body is plump and stout, its coarse green leaves have grown stale.

I follow the range of the field with my eyes, from its farthest edge past the farm at its heart, to its fringe where it meets with the road. There, in the mid-distance, I can see Martha, crossing a curtain of grass. She walks beside the bordering road; she slips from sight as she comes to Six Bells; now she emerges again in the field – cutting along its boundary before being hidden by bushes. I expect she is crossing over the road, and then onto the track that leads to her farm.

The hedge behind me seems to cough. I look up. It is Martha, here, at the edge of my patch. She has followed the fringe of the field all the way, until she has come to my lawn. Her face is thin; her skin is stretched tight; wisps of her hair are caught in the breeze. She stops three paces before me.

– What's that sound coming from the cottage?
– O hello. That's Matty. He's making things.
– Making things? Does he know how to handle tools? You need to be careful. You don't want him to come to harm.

I look at her; I look at her face. At her eyes; at her lips. I wonder if she seeks to provoke me; if she's trying to break through my guard. I wonder if she means to threaten, or to offer me honest advice.

– Would you like a cup of tea?
– No, thank you. I've got things to do. But I thought I might just pop by. I've been wondering how you are.
– I'm fine. How are you and Jack? I was very moved by Jack's speech.
– He did what he had to do. He's the head of the village.
– And how's Uriah? How's Joyce?
–
– I haven't seen her recently. Is she ok?
– She's fine. We're all fine. You needn't worry about us.
– If there's anything…
– No, thank you. This is what life in the country is. You learn how to survive. You improvise. Or you die.
– Yes. But right now, it's all a bit strange.
– Are you finding it strange? Has anything strange happened to you?
– To me? No.
– Apart from finding a skull…
– Well, apart from that of course.
– Have you come across anything else unusual?
– Like what?
– Has anyone else shared anything with you?
– No. No, of course not.
– Why of course?
– Well, they haven't. That's all.
– Good. I came to ask you round for supper.
– That's kind. But you must have a lot on your plate.
– No. I have plenty of time.

– I would like to, but I'm quite busy myself. I've just got a new assignment. A project with deadlines. I'm afraid I'm going to have to work through the evenings…

My voice trails out like my lie, growing feebler the longer I talk. Martha is looking at me. I can feel her eyes as if slicing my flesh, seeking beyond it to seek out my truth. I raise my hands in front of my face, as though they would act as a shield from her gaze. But she persists in her asking.

– I'm sure you can start it tomorrow.
– And there's Matty…
– Matty will come for supper too. Jack likes the chance of speaking to him. And there are things for you and I to discuss.
– That's very kind Martha, but…
– Good. Seven o'clock then. Now I must be on my way.

She nods; she almost smiles. She strains to keep her self-control. Then she turns and follows the edge of the field, past the hedge, across the road, before I am able to speak.

In the bathroom I stand in the pool of my clothes and look at myself in the glass. I should phone her to say that I'm busy tonight, that I need to start on my work. I should phone to say that I'm ill. In my throat, in my stomach, I feel a sickness, as though I'm going to be physically sick. As if it's my first day at school. But she wouldn't believe me, whatever I say. I don't believe she trusts me now. She thinks all I say, all I do is a lie. She can't force me to come, yet I know that I will. It's not fair to say that my life is a lie. That accusation no longer holds good. Now there's purpose; now there's a reason to be. I just need to put it into effect. Somehow, I need to make it happen. I need to do it myself. So as never again to be on my own.

My face stares back at me, distrustful. How do you think you'll accomplish that? You, who were once called pretty. You, with your tired and your blemished skin. You, with your bags and your flaps and your creases. With your swollen knuckles and your broken nails. With your hairy armpits, your nasal hair. With your yellow teeth and your stale breath. You, who so want to be loved.

After my bath I call to Matty. I feel more assured, having something to say. Something to say that is more than myself; that counters his accusations against me. I have a message I need to convey.

I hear Matty put down his tools to listen. I know he will open the door and come out; he will come to Martha's tonight. Though he'll come for Jack, not for me. He'll come because Jack is much like Uriah. Though both are so different in every respect, they share between them a piece of this land; they are part of this earth and this clay.

It's time to go.

We leave the cottage in the last gasp of day, locking the door as we do so. It is windless as we cut between fields, as we stoop through the thicket, towards Burnt Tree Farm. I feel myself vulnerable, watched. I see a dull glow through the lower windows burning more deeply the closer we come, but it doesn't spread warmth nor welcome within me. I am glad Matty's here to my side.

Martha is waiting for us at the door. Her face is passionless, pale. Looking at her, it seems so absurd to think she might welcome my help. I would be the very last person she came to, not that she's wanting for strength.

Martha ushers us into the living room, where Jack sits reading a book. He rises and smiles, he greets us with kindness. It is Matty and I who uncovered the skull, who threatened his village, who forced the divide. That is a crime, no less of a crime than the act that led to the skull itself being wrongfully placed in a concrete grave. A skull divorced from its torso and limbs. A skull with no owner, no name. If Jack is aware of our part in that crime, he disguises it, laying no blame. He doesn't even mention the skull. No gossip will ever darken his home. He invites us to sit and brings us a drink. As the host, he is bent upon humouring us. The topic that fills every house in the village will never be broached in this room.

Instead, Jack tells us about the church. He travels far through the chapters of time, uncovering all that was lost and buried with a sharpness of eye, a sureness of detail, as though it was he who laid its first stones, as though it is he who has guarded it since. The church is over a thousand years old and has been worshipped in since without pause. It began as a humble wooden structure erected in Saxon times. When William first laid foot on this soil the church was reconstructed in stone. It's recorded in the Domesday Book, in chronicles of the bubonic plague. It has defied a fire and countless air raids; its walls are etched with medieval graffiti; its floors have been chipped by axes and swords, they've been buffed by penitent knees. The traffic of worship has worn it down; the devotion of lost souls has raised it up. Its tower stands tall of surrounding trees, as a conduit from Heaven to earth. And now, even though its bells are broken, its steps are tired and its graves are full, it still endures, it will endure. Like the faith which is practised within its walls, it will come into glory again.

After dessert I gather up plates and walk them through to the kitchen. Martha stands with her back to the door, placing the bowls in the sink. She turns around as I enter.

— What I want to know is why you chose to involve Colin Inchmore?

— I'm sorry?

— Why didn't you give the skull to me?

— I thought I was doing the right thing.

— The right thing?

— It needed to be buried.

— You ought to have come and talked to me first. That would have been the right thing to do. To talk to me, as you've done before. I know what is needed. I know what to do.

— I thought I was doing what's best.

— What's best is not upsetting my husband. Can't you see how you're making him suffer?

— I'm very sorry. I didn't mean...

— I'm sure you didn't. But you have. You're reminding him of things in the past. You're opening old and painful wounds.

— I am?

— Yes. And it's hurting him badly. It's another threat you've brought to the village.

— Another...?

— You seem to be bent on hurting him. Although I can't fathom your motive.

— Anything that I might have done I've tried to do for the best.

— That's as may be. But that hasn't been the result. You've brought about hurt. I told you not to explore in the wood. Repeatedly, I told you not to.

– I tried to tell Matty, but he didn't listen.

– You didn't do what I asked. And now we need to put things right before you load more grief on Jack. Before you cause more harm.

– Of course. I'll do anything I can.

– Yes, you will. Perhaps the most helpful thing right now is not to do anything at all. But there's more than that.

– There is?

– Yes. You remember what I said this afternoon.

– I remember.

– Well, have you seen anything else unusual?

– No.

– Has anyone said anything unexpected? Have you received anything out of the ordinary?

– Like what?

– You would know what it was if you saw it. Have you?

– No.

– You would tell me if you had.

– Yes.

– You will tell me if you do.

– If… if you really insist. I don't like secrets.

– I do insist. Yes. I want to know. You will tell me if something unusual happens.

– If you like.

– I would like. Yes. I would like you to come to me first. If you see or you hear anything of concern. Then we can agree the correct course of action. Then we can agree what to show or tell Jack. I worry about him, Sarah, you see. He isn't as strong as he looks. I know him. I know the man that he is. I need to protect him. Do you understand?

– I think so.

– Good.

We make our way through to the living room where the men are waiting for us. Jack is talking about the land — as it was, as it is, as it shall be forever. He unfurls it, here in this room. It brings him no harm; it brings only pleasure. It is Martha who feels all the pain.

Out of my eye I can see her face, I can see her hands pressed tightly together as if she is struggling to maintain her calm. And it is so great an effort for her. I sense she would like to end the evening; she would like to ask us to leave. But she dare not. She suppresses the impulse and holds it in check, as if knowing its rigour might drive me away, eroding the trust that she craves. She sits quite still, subduing her feelings, believing that no one can see.

But I can see; I can see quite distinctly. I can see her fear, her anger, her pain. The only thing that I cannot perceive is its cause, and what gives it rise.

~

Martha is standing in front of the urn, pouring herself a strong cup of tea. She's precise in her movement, almost composed, though her arms are constrained by her plain black suit. We are sitting expectant — Travis, Peter Faraday, Bill and me — here in a half-circle, silent and waiting, hearing the sound of the tea fill her cup, seeing the steam emerge from the tap, feeling the warmth of the mug in her hand, the warmth that steals up her spoon as she stirs.

Martha sits at the head of the circle, briskly commencing our meeting. She is businesslike in all that she does — in her words, her eyes, her demeanour. It is almost as if she is forcing us forward, thrusting us into the current continuum, casting a handful of earth on the past.

I can see the words that she doesn't speak clearly imprinted in all of her actions. All that has gone is ended and buried, and now we need to move on. The land demands that we toil without ceasing; we dare not pause nor tarry awhile. Our focus is now on the mending and reaping. We should never look back to the past. It is dead, it is lost, like it never existed. And we cannot live it again.

Martha reminds us the Community Council is here for the good of the village. Its function is to enhance our welfare: to preserve, to protect, and to nurture. It considers the issues facing the village; it makes decisions on behalf of the same. It works because we care for the village as much as we care for our families; because its members believe in each other; because we know we are stronger together, and apart we are certain to fail.

I look at the faces of those around me. The level of trust is so slim. If the Council was honest and true to itself, it would question how we have come to be here – with all of its members dressed in black – and what has led us to this. It would acknowledge that a skull has been found; it would seek consensus on what to do next. Its members would come together in truth, joined in a shared pursuit of that truth, with only the truth in their minds. Instead, I feel continued suspicion; a doubt, a sense of inevitable guilt – nameless and shameless, and wanting a home – as strong as when Martha took me to task, as when Matty locked himself in the lean-to, as when I made the decision to leave. There is only one person I truly trust, only one person who knows my truth. And, like a fool, I have left him behind; I buried his memory and walked away.

Like a fool.

Peter Faraday leads the discussion; he shares the proposals for building new homes behind the church on Whatling's Land. He explains the planning process to us; he updates us on the stage we are at. He speaks in facts and intricate detail. When at last he comes to a close, Martha thanks him and invites our comments, wanting a shared and collective response to the application to build.

Travis thinks new houses are good. They are good for business, they swell the village, they will help to sustain us and make us prosper. Bill agrees; it would be nice to stem the decline of the village, to welcome new blood, and to grow. He knows how vibrant this village once was; he fears its death by decay. But he is concerned that in building new homes the character of the village will change. The occupants won't be working the land; they'll be people carving a daily commute to towns and cities nearby. They won't know the strength of our traditions, and they may not honour our past. They won't know what the land represents, and they may not respect what it is. He doesn't know the consequence of the older order meeting the new. And because he doesn't know what will happen, his fear fans his caution and warns him against. Bill knows the past, he knows it is safe, though he knows our future is bleak.

Peter reminds us the past was not static. It changed, it moved on, or it would have failed. Hedges were cleared to increase the yield, machines were built to improve the harvest, nutrients have enriched the soil. These were threats when first introduced, but now we benefit from them. He urges us not to reject the proposals. For in protecting an old way of life we may jeopardise our children's future, we may strangle the village and let it die.

Now that all the others have spoken, their eyes are turned towards me. They want to know what I think.

In truth, I don't know what I should say. I tell them I moved here six months ago. I have never lived in the country before; I had no presumption of what it was like. At first, I found it was hard. It is more than a different way of life; it is a different way to live life. Aspects of being here fill me with joy: the taste of the air, the clear bright skies, the abundance that springs from the earth. And aspects of living here fill me with terror: the loneliness, the slow drip of time, the scale, the silence, the emptiness. But it's in our nature to survive and adapt; it's in our gift to develop and learn. All of those who are sitting around me have helped me, have taken me under their wing – teaching me, making me feel at home. Without them, my doubts and fears would remain, my joys would be fleeting and few. I know I am not a part of the land, yet it's growing on me and me within it. When I came, I didn't think to impose, nor expect it to change to accommodate me. Instead, I embraced what was here. I see no reason why others who come shouldn't do and feel much the same. And if that is so, if we care for the village, if we truly want it to prosper and grow, we should seize any chance that may come our way to allow others into its fold.

I have said too much, and what I have said is lacking in credence and truth. Even to me it seems false. I shouldn't have shown them my frailty by inviting them into my mind. I had no need to state an opinion. I should have been factual and stayed objective. I should have weighed my words like Peter. I should have be guided by you. I should have saved what I think and I feel for a different context, in a different village, with a different set of people around me.

I should have saved what goes on in my mind for another day, for another time. For any day but today. Not now, when the room is so full of suspicion, so pregnant with poison and pain. Not now, when people look at each other, wanting and fearful of stealing their secrets. Not now, when fresh from finding a skull that someone brutally struck from its torso. Anytime, but not now.

Martha thanks us all for our views. She inclines towards Bill's opinion. She sees the benefits that new houses will bring, but she is concerned about what is preserved. She acknowledges Peter's need for change and accepts my own experience. Our approach should be proportionate. If the village seeks to grow too fast it may find itself overwhelmed, with no safeguards to our tradition, with nothing to stop it from being erased.

She suggests that we don't object to the planning, but that we watch it develop with care. We should find ways in which to protect what we have, to preserve the integrity of the land.

I look at her as she speaks: her body is rigid; her tight lips are thin. If the choice was hers, she would be more robust, resisting the influx, obstructing the plans. Yet she feels the sheer momentum of change, like an eager tide whipped up on the beach, that has still so far yet to rise. A momentum of change from within the village as much as from the pressure beyond. And she doesn't yet know where to build her defence, nor at what stage to rally and stand.

Martha asks if there's any more business. She is looking at me for fear I will speak, not trusting me to keep silent. She is looking at me, for she thinks me most likely. But it's Peter, not me, who begins.

– The Council considers all the issues facing the village. That's right, isn't it?

– Yes.

– I apologise for raising such a delicate matter, but I think there's an issue we need to acknowledge. A very real issue facing the village that the Council needs to address.

– What might you be referring to?

– At the end of this meeting we're attending a burial. I believe, as it stands, that is wrong. I believe there must be an inquest first to determine the identity of who we are burying. I believe we should find out the cause of the death.

– Are you suggesting there has been foul play?

– Not at all. Quite the contrary. I think that by following correct procedure we may clear the air and restore a level of confidence in the village.

– Is there something you think we are hiding?

– I'm not suggesting we are hiding anything, but we may not all know the truth. And the law requires it. You told us, quite rightly, that we're stronger together; that our loyalty should be to the village. I understand how distressing this is, but I feel that until we resolve this issue the village we know remains in danger, and we are in danger of damaging it further by not insisting on finding the truth. The Council needs to do right by the village, and for me that means closing this matter.

– The matter is closed, Peter. The past is buried, and the dead can't speak. There is nothing more that needs to be said. Like you, I don't want to drag on the pain. I want it to die; I want to move on. An inquest would be inconclusive. There's no more to know. There's no more to find. It is buried too deep in the past. It is gone. An inquest would merely protract all the fear; it would draw out suspicion and fuel the divide. It would feed those dangers you mention.

The Council's job is to bring us together. We can do that now by closing this chapter. By respecting what's dead and returning its soul to the body of earth from whence it once came. There it can rest and find peace.

— I care about two things. I care about the village, and I care about the truth.

— And would you sacrifice one for the other?

— I care about both equally.

— And do you think that both can be satisfied?

— I would hope so.

— Then let me assure you, they will be. You won't have to sacrifice one for the other. But you must learn to trust and believe me.

— I do trust. I just want that certainty.

— That certainty I give to you now. It is over.

— How can you be so sure?

— Because I am.

Martha stands up; the meeting has ended. It is over. I feel an ugliness in the room, an unpleasantness cloying around me. I feel smothered, as though I'm about to be sick. I hurry to the door and push it open, bending over as I lean on its frame, sucking the life from the air.

I sense that others are coming towards me. Bill is the first to arrive. He takes my hands; he looks into my face. He says he will walk with me to the graveyard. Travis and Peter are here with us too, but it's Bill who leads me away.

We walk up the road towards the church; his voice is a constant in my ear though I pay no heed to his words. I drink great gulps of urgent air; I feel the cleansing heat of the sun burning away the ill of the hall and its sickened fingers which clawed me.

I strain my eyes away up the road, wanting and willing to catch sight of Matty on his way from the cottage to join me. To my surprise, he's here already; he has been in the churchyard waiting for me; he comes to me now he has seen me. He is taller and stronger and abler than Bill. He takes his place by my side. He has brushed his hair and polished his shoes. He is even wearing a tie. Now he takes my arm and walks with me through the gate and along the gravel path. He is my son, and I love him for it. He is here for me now, when I need him most. That is all that I want or could hope for.

We walk up the path, round the side of the church, in the raw brutal heat of the startled sun, through shifting pools of light and shade, till we come to the trees at the rear. Here, before us, is a small sunken hole, cut crisply into the fine green turf, with a ruff of matting around it. So deep I cannot see to its floor, though I have no desire to go close.

We congregate in an awkward circle, uncertain of where we should stand; sensing the hole should be at our heart, though so cold, so empty, so bare. Travis, Samantha, Bill and Margaret, Peter Faraday, Matty, and me.

From the tower there's a single knell of a bell. We look up.

At the side of the church stands Uriah. He holds a wooden box in his hands. Square, like a hat box, coated with lacquer. So simple, so soulless, so quite without feature, I wouldn't have guessed what's inside.

Colin Inchmore comes to the front. He leads Uriah along the path – past the harvest of ancient headstones, the marks of the dead which jut from the earth – until they are here to my side.

Martha and Jack are close behind them, walking stiffly, with care. Her arm is leant in the small of his elbow, her hand on the back of his palm. They come towards the hole in the ground, to the matting beside it, and here they stand – dry-eyed, firm-mouthed – to attention.

Colin Inchmore speaks through the silence. His voice is measured and slow. The sound is dissolved in the heat of the day. It wafts through the churchyard; it is caught in the breeze; it is hurried away to the wood.

Peter is right. How could we not have determined the truth before we thought to bury the skull in this resting place, so it can find peace? I think perhaps there is more than one truth. We each hold onto our own. We clutch it close to our hearts. The truth that I have is all that I have; it is all I need to be whole. I walked away, but I didn't quite lose you. I may have found you again. Let others cling to their separate truths, for my own is what I believe. I believe the dead can come back to life. That those we thought buried can be reborn. That is all that matters to me. My only truth and my peace.

*I am the resurrection and the life, saith the Lord;*

*he that believeth in me, though he were dead, yet shall he live;*

*and whosoever liveth and believeth in me shall never die.*

*I know that my Redeemer liveth,*

*and that he shall stand at the latter day upon the earth;*

*and though this body be destroyed, yet shall I see God;*

*whom I shall see for myself and mine eyes shall behold,*

*and not as a stranger.*

The heat of the morning bears down upon us. Colin Inchmore squints at the fury of the bald white page he is reading. I feel the weight of the warmth on my shoulders; the sweat which slides down the ridge of my back.

I look with envy at Margaret's hat, at her face which cannot be seen. The sun is cruel and unrelenting. The leaves on the trees are scarcely in motion. The air around us is absent.

I should share the weight of the box with Uriah, since I bear an equal weight for my crime. My crime of causing the death of a man by stifling love, by withholding my own. All men must die, and each to his own, but not before their course has been run. And surely not by my hand. My hand which is already covered in blood. The time for resurrection has come. Whatever that looks like; whatever that means. I would see you alive, I would help you to live. If it's not too late; if I have the power. If I'm not perceived as the enemy for all the wrong I have thrust upon you. For all I have done to destroy you.

*For since by man came death, by man came also the resurrection of the dead.*

*For as in Adam all die, even so in Christ shall all be made alive.*

*But every man in his own order: Christ the firstfruits; afterward they that are Christ's at his coming.*

*Then cometh the end, when he shall have delivered up the kingdom to God, even the Father; when he shall have put down all rule and all authority and power.*

*For he must reign, till he hath put all enemies under his feet.*

*The last enemy that shall be destroyed is death.*

I look at the matting, at the cords laid across it, and into the mouth of the hole. It is deep; the earth is rich and dark, it is hard-packed and stamped in the ground. I wonder how fertile this graveyard is, and what I would sow – what things I would grow – above the bodies that lie here. The trees are gasping at each gust of wind. I can see perspiration on everyone's face. It's not just the heat, it's the fear, the unknown. I could snatch it out of the air.

All of us stand in an ungainly circle, seeking the faces, avoiding the eyes, of these random strangers around us. Sensing uneasiness, sensing the horror, wondering what others are feeling. Feeling the doubt of who we are, of what it is that we will become. Fearing that this shall be our fate: a faceless box in somebody's hands, a torso lost in the earth. I look at the hands which hold the box. I wonder if they're the same as the ones which placed the skull in the tunnel. Or if those hands were the hands of another – of one of these others around me.

Uriah is asked to come forward. He places the box on the web of cords which is strung on the lips of the bald, blind hole. It sits suspended in time. This box, so unlike a human being. Unbodied, and having no name. Soon to be returned to the earth, to the body from which it so recently came. Was the life that it lived a life well-lived? Could we look upon it and say it was good? How much fuller might that life have been lived if left to run its full course?

That is the shame of what I have done, of the life I have cut from us both. Snapping the thread that held us together; the heartstring

*In the midst of life we are in death;*

*of whom may we seek for succour,*

that made us both whole. And, once cut adrift, we were both adrift – floating through a meaningless life, filling the hours in meaningless ways, lacking in love and displeased. Finding ourselves in the prime of our lives to be walking the earth as though dead. Dead to ourselves, and dead to each other. Shedding the shadow of death on our son. In the midst of life, we are in death; and in death is the secret of life. You know the secret of my heart: you can feel within and see to its core. You who are only still but snared on the fringe, on the cusp of death. Half-dead to the world, and half-alive. Then what is the judgement you pronounce – now, in your final hour? That we both suffer death and fall away, or we claw a way back to life?

*but of thee, O Lord,*

*who for our sins art justly displeased?*

*Yet, O Lord God most holy, O Lord most mighty,*

*O holy and most merciful Saviour,*

*deliver us not into the bitter pains of eternal death.*

*Thou knowest, Lord, the secrets of our hearts;*

*shut not thy merciful ears to our prayer;*

*but spare us, Lord most holy, O God most mighty,*

*O holy and merciful Saviour,*

*thou most worthy Judge eternal.*

*Suffer us not, at our last hour,*

*through any pains of death, to fall from thee.*

I watch as the earth is placed in the hole. I feel the finality of this covering; there's so little room there to breathe. Planted so deep it's unable to grow, unable to stretch to the sun.

The Pooleys turn away from the grave, walking down the gravel path that runs through the graveyard and leads to the gate. The remainder stand and look at the ground, at the spoiled earth which has been disturbed, at the scatter of soil on the mat. Nobody speaks. We all know something is buried beneath. It is real, and yet so unreal.

I put my arm around Matty's shoulders. He doesn't try to prevent me. He has paid his respects, though he seems unaffected. Either he doesn't comprehend, or his is a knowledge so complete he's untroubled by doubt or by fear. I steer him on to the gate. He has done his duty, and now he is free. He looks at me strangely, as if reading my thoughts, not thinking that I would be thinking of him. I tell him he doesn't need to stay near me. He has done everything I have asked him.

For the first time, he hesitates. Then, reassured, he runs away – he runs up the road in a rush of life, pulling his tie from his collar.

The others still stand in the quiet churchyard, somewhere distant behind me. But I don't want to stay here, to see them, to talk. There is nothing more to be said.

I walk away slowly, following Matty up the drag of the road in the ruthless sun, feeling its scrutiny fix on my back, shielding and puckering my eyes. The tarmac shimmers with furious heat, extending before me and into the haze of the low horizon beyond it. Above me, an infinite effortless sky stretches up to the heavens.

Even before I reach the lawn, even while I am still on the road, I can see a brilliance burnt through the hedge: the fierce purple blossom of lilacs. Joyce has been here again.

She has been here while we've been with the skull. She's been in the hedgerow plucking the living while we have been burying the dead. It seems so long since she last left me flowers. I thought she might have forgotten.

Unlike before, they're not left on the wall. They are thrust in the claw of the letterbox. They spill from its jaws and scatter the step which stands at the foot of the door. A long blue ribbon is threaded between them, but it doesn't clasp them in a bouquet. I think, perhaps, she was in a hurry; she was interrupted by Matty. She ran away; she slipped into hiding. She could still be here in the garden.

My eyes are swift to follow my thoughts. I look at the lawn, at the clumps of bush, at the dense rose arch, at the silent hedge, at the fields that are lying beyond. There is nothing besides the brilliant day, unveiled and proud; the wind which shivers these gold-green leaves; the intense, pure blue of the frigid sky; the ache of the sun as it casts a sheen on the majesty of this land. There is no one here but me.

I reach out to pick up the flowers, then stop as I recognise what they are. This isn't lilac, as I thought it to be. Instead, these beautiful deep blue blooms are monkshood. They're poisonous to the touch. Fatal if they're ingested. I wonder if Matty has picked some up; I wonder if it was he who spilt them. I wonder where he is now.

I look around me once more. I call. The saturating heat that swelters around me absorbs the fear in my voice. It deadens the dread on the air. I call again, then shove at the door.

It's dark and cool in the cottage. Again, I call out loudly to Matty. Again, I hear no reply. If not inside, then he's in the garden; he's gone to the back, to the field.

Please let him still be outside.

I take rubber gloves from the kitchen cupboard. Then I gather the stems of trailing monkshood and throw them all in a binbag. I fill a bowl with soapy water and swill it over the doorstep. Then I scrub it hard with an iron brush, scratching its claw-marks into the screed.

I tie up the bag and place it outside. I wash the utensils under the tap. Through the window a stream of sunlight is panting its pitiless heat on the lawn. Arguing birds sound shrill in the bushes, each jostling for a position. The hedge is alive and frets in the breeze; its leaves are winking at me.

Again, I call upstairs to Matty. He might have gone to his room. I stand in the very heart of the house, listening out for a noise. Here, from within, through these living walls, any noise would bring peace. An alien screech from the guts of the lean-to, a soothing scrape of metal on metal above the stultified silence. I listen for something; for sounds of movement; for sounds of breathing or life.

There's only an emptiness.

Matty's not here. Either he's gone to see Uriah, or else he has gone to the wood. Both of which I have sought to deny him. There is nowhere else he would go.

I look through the vacant pane of the window. In the hedge I can see a pair of sparrows pecking each other with furious beaks. Now they are fluttering, startled and frightened; now swooping down to scare and be panicked; both ecstatic with rage. At last, one darts decisively – low and away – and now it has gone. The hedgerow ripples its fragile peace; it dances again to the tune of the wind.

I need to find Matty and bring him home. He's in danger, although he doesn't see it, although he may not ever see it until it's standing before him. I turn on the tap and run it cool, splashing cupped handfuls into my face. I fill a glass and drink deep. Then I open the door to the world outside.

The day doesn't soften as I re-enter. I feel the furnace heat of the air; the scorch of the sun as it burns at my face, still wet from the stain of the tap. There is no one outside, but I feel myself watched – those eyes that are watching me, watching me always – across the lawn, then down the road, then past the side of Six Bells.

I cross the track to Rose House Farm; I walk to the bend in the road where the path breaks off and leads to the wood. First, I will look for Matty in here, and if not here, I will go to the farm.

I pass the pile of bone-dry logs, stacked like a funeral pyre. The grass is crisp beneath my feet, sucked dry of colour, and coarse. The belt of thorn which shields the wood stands firm and scratches the sun. I follow it round till I find a way in. Here, through the nettles, is Matty's entrance. It is freshly trampled and disfigured, stamped into the earth like a shallow grave.

It is cool inside the bowels of the wood. I am blind from the sun and I cannot see. I stand in a pool of feinted shadow, of gradations of liquified grey. I can hear the gradual creaking of trunks, of their brittle limbs, of their splintered bones. I can hear the canopy shiver its leaves; I can sense the brilliant sky beyond, the pockets of light which penetrate deep to enliven this whispering world. I can hear my feet on the living floor; the empty gasp of my breath.

I walk forwards, into the heart of the wood. If Matty is here, he may show himself, he may step out into the open. Or else he may choose to stay where he is, lost and hidden from sight. The trees above me stoop and bend, swaying and falling, then shivering tall. They creak as if they are walking on tiptoe; they groan as if they're alive.

— What are you doing here? Why are you following me?
— Where are you?
— I'm here. In front of you. Here.
— Where?
— Here.
— Are you safe?
—

—

— Why did you come?
— Because I thought you'd be here. I was afraid you'd be here. Even though I forbade you to come.
— You don't like the wood. You're afraid of it. Why did you come if you fear it?
— Because I was more afraid for you.
— You don't need to be worried about me. I'm fine.
— I want you to come home. We need to leave now. I told you never to come here again.
— Look, I want to show you something. It's this way.
— We shouldn't be here.
— But we are.

I want to be angry with him. No, I don't want to be angry. Never again do I want to show anger; never again do I want to force distance. I want to capture him in my arms, to hold him close in a hug. I want my love to percolate through him, spreading its heat, its immediacy, till he cannot doubt what I feel.

Matty stands and awaits my response. I come towards him, stopping just short, and raise my eyes to his face. For a moment, there's silence between us. This silence alone may be enough. Enough for us, for the now. A space that we share, that we live together, filled with no poison, no pain.

Matty turns and leads me further, deeper into the wood, through streams of variegated green and shifting pools of luminous shade. We come to a circle of trees.

Beside a trunk he shows me a wire, wrapped round the limb of a peg. It leads to another peg in the ground, then climbs and loops itself round a branch. At the end of the flex is a heavy bough: one end on the ground, one raised and bound with sticks that are sharpened like fangs. He shows me how the wire can be tripped: the mechanics of cause and effect. Then he points me towards his other machines. He shows me a deadfall beneath a rock; a platform trap with its double noose; a baited hole-noose dug in the ground, with splintered sticks at its mouth; a sprung spear-trap made out of a switch with rusty nails in its end. He's proud of the work he has on display. He's proud of its beauty, its artifice. He's proud to show it to me.

I look at this child I have brought into being as he shares his snares and explains how they work, as he demonstrates what they can do. I hadn't realised – not until now – how far he has come along this journey, how far removed he's become. He's speaking a different language to me; he's programmed into another world. This is inhuman; devoid of pity; devoid of reason or sense. It has spiralled beyond my power to control. I can no longer comprehend.

There was a time when I feared I would lose him. But that time is past – now there's nothing to fear. There is only the truth to recognise now. There is only the fact of what is.

This child, my son, is no longer a boy. He's a creature born of the wood.

– Are you listening to what you are saying?
– What?
– Do you know what your words mean? Do you know what you're doing?
– I'm building stuff.
– What are you building?
– Snares.
– And what do they do?
– They catch pests.
– No, Matty. They don't catch pests, they catch animals. Things that are living; that have made their homes here; that have a right to exist. And they don't just catch them, they mutilate them. They crush their skulls, they spear their bodies, they inflict massive trauma and pain. These things you have made, they are made to kill.
– They only destroy pests.
– Pests? Who told you the victims are pests?
– That's what they are.
– What are?
– Badgers, foxes, rodents, rabbits…
– Matty!
– Well, they are.
– They aren't. How can you say you like the wood if you kill the creatures within it? You've had pets before. You cuddled not killed them. What do you think you are doing?
– I'm doing something I know that I'm good at. Something I know how to do.

– Do you really like making snares?

– If you don't like them, why don't you go? Why don't you leave me alone?

– Because I'm your mother. I care. I want to teach you right from wrong.

– You're not my mother. You're a crazy woman who ran away. Who left my dad. Who spends her life in a vegetable patch feeling sorry for herself and hard done by.

– Matty, that's not true.

– What can you teach me? What do you know about right and wrong?

– I've got more experience.

– You've made more mistakes, that's all.

– I can help you. I am here to support you.

– Maybe you could, but you haven't. Not since we got here. And now it's too late.

– It's never too late to try.

I can feel the anger surge through his body. It blurs his speech; it distorts his movement. Such anger he cannot fully express it. He can neither control nor contain it. It has been suppressed within him too long. An anger borne of what I have done, fanned by all that I am. Poisoning everything around us. Poisoning him and me.

Maybe he's right. It's already too late.

Matty is no longer here. He's ducked and woven into the scrub, and I can see him no more. All I can hear is a hollow groan from the trees at the very heart of the wood, from their tortured boughs which imprison the sky, from their roots which writhe in the earth beneath. A grief so deep it becomes their motion, it becomes their bark and their sap.

I am standing in a small circle of trees surrounded by a network of snares. On every side is a wall of nettles, of broken boughs and hidden ditches, of tangled brambles and thorn. Through it, a fleeting sense of light catches the mottled undergrowth and is snatched away by the shadow.

This is what my life would feel like, being alone without Matty. Now I know how it feels. I no longer feel the fear of loss. It is actual and real; it is happening now. And it doesn't fill me with fear. Instead, it brings a lack of direction, a lack of purpose or reason to be. An incredible sadness; a perfect stagnation. An incapacity; a failure to move. An emptiness; a vacancy. A place beyond yearning, beyond desire.

So much love has been buried inside me. Love that has struggled to find a means to show itself and be shared. Love that has ached to find a way to enter into your heart.

Love that has failed us all.

I walk away from the circle of trees. I step through the sea of bramble and nettle, round the contortion of broken boughs, over deep wounds in the earth.

I steer towards a patch of light. I can hear the creak of aching trees, the crack and snap of brittle branches, the tremor and fright of their leaves. I can hear the smack of sudden wings as a startled bird takes to air.

I come to the barbed ring of thorn. Beyond it lies the stretch of Road Field. I wade through the waist-high barrier, and now I am back on the track. It is warm in the open; it is clean and clear. A thick breeze blows its heat in my face; it drags at my wearying limbs.

The rooms in the cottage are stark and cold, suspended in silence and dumbed by dust. The only sound is the muffled scratch I hear from within the lean-to. I would go in search of the sound and its maker. I would seek them both out for the comfort they bring. But I know in my heart it's too late.

I'm helpless to be with him now.

I fill a bag with Matty's clothes and take it out to the car. I place it under a cover of sacking so it can't be seen from the road. Then I return to the guts of the cottage to make sandwiches for us both.

The kitchen is cool but alive with flies; they are tapping urgently at the panes, filling the air with haphazard music, settling on the bread and the sideboard, catching themselves in my hair. I uncoil a strip of flypaper and pin it onto a beam. By the time the sandwiches are made, five bright black bodies are captured there, twisting their furious legs in the air and spinning their frantic wings, as they strive to escape a sticky death on the unforgiving strip.

I am ready now, but I'm still not ready. I can't quite bring myself to depart. Now is the time, but not yet the time, to go to the lean-to and summon Matty, to winkle him out of his hole. Each moment here is so precious, so prized. Even without him beside me. Just knowing he's here, still here in this house. Here, so nearly together, so close.

I walk through the arch to the fringe of the field. The sugar beet sweats in the breathless heat, shading its precious root beneath a sweltering garb of thick leaves. Rose House Farm is washed away in the haze of the melting sun. The wood is no more than a thin brown strip spread on the lip of the low horizon, shimmering as though it's a mirage.

It is such a beautiful day.

I should busy myself by inspecting my plants, picking my produce, hoeing the earth. Performing all those laborious chores which seem so irrelevant now. All those hours, all that work, so misguided and futile. A foolish diversion from where I should be. From where I should always have been.

I walk to the door of the darkened lean-to, feeling its dampness, the chill of its bones, even before I dare knock. I whisper my words from the warmth of the garden, asking Matty to come. There's one more thing that we need to do, and then I will let him alone. One more time, and that will be it. I won't worry him ever again. I promise. I won't get annoyed, and it won't be for long. But I need him to come out and see me.

I think he understands from my voice that this isn't just another request. This is more than me being me. This is somebody else who is speaking to him. Somebody else, with a genuine need, who is making an honest entreaty. And, in his heart, he is good.

I can hear a movement from inside the lean-to. The scrape of a stool on the concrete floor.

Matty's head appears through a crack, shrouded by darkness inside. He comes out and closes the door behind him; he follows me over the grass to the car.

I open the roof and wind down the windows, allowing the inside to breathe. I back up the track and onto the road. Then we are away, we are driving away from the cottage and all that surrounds it.

We drive through Marshfield in silence. I wait until we have passed through the town, till we reach the main road and are driving at speed, till I know I am past going back. Then I tell him, while keeping my eyes on the road. I say it straight, without pause. I'm taking him to the station at Ipswich; I'm going to put him on the next train. Dad will be waiting for him in London. That's where he needs to go now. Nettlesden isn't a good place to be. What's happening here isn't good. He's going to stay at home with his father. I don't know how long he will be there.

I can feel Matty's anger as he sits beside me absorbing all that I say. Anger at being manipulated; anger at being so crudely used by someone he despises so much, by someone he thinks of as weak. He doesn't want London; he's done with London. Now he's caught by the wood and enslaved. The trees and all that is sheltered within them – all that they hide or choose to reveal, all that dies or is born in their cradle – that is the world to him now. He isn't the person he used to be: the child, the boy I once knew. Yet, despite that, I know he won't argue with me, he won't show any weakness to me. He has closed himself off from all that I am, and he won't let me see how he feels.

Besides, he has one consolation. For all that London represents, for all that is hateful and aimless about it, he knows that I won't be going there with him. Instead of me, he'll be there with you. And that is something he needs.

It's something he needs. To see you again, and to be with you, where he has always felt safe. I'm just surprised he has lived for so long on his own with me and deprived of you. The more I think it, the stranger it is that he has submitted to living with me, he hasn't demanded I let him go home.

For he has missed you – he must have missed you – even more than I miss you myself. He didn't start out by hating you; he didn't start out by running away. He was happy living in London. He was happy being with you. You were playing tennis and catching fish; you were cheering the rugby and jeering the golf; you were sprawled on the sofa eating sweets; you were at the cinema watching a film. You did the things I couldn't or wouldn't. You enjoyed the being of being together. You didn't want it to change. Neither of you wanted or needed to change. I focused so much on what didn't work, on what on the surface appeared to be wrong, that I seem to have missed everything that was good – all those simple things that I took for granted. Maybe for you they weren't taken for granted. Maybe you worked at them hard. You spent a lifetime building a bond, a stable platform, a sure foundation, from which our son could grow strong.

A lifeline that I cut away.

How hard have these last few months been on Matty? How hard have these months been on you? How hard have I focused on either of you, on what you must feel in your hearts? I wish, I wish you would have complained, to trigger reaction in me. But as it is you have both been mute; both of you letting me live out my lie, letting it work its way through my body till I cannot deny what it is.

We drive through the sun-shot suburbs of Ipswich. Matty is silent, unwilling to speak, but he points out the signs to show me the way. I park the car, and we walk to the station. There's a train that leaves in ten minutes.

I buy a ticket and we go to the platform.

Matty stands at a distance from me. I give him the space and let him be, fixed in a pool of arching shade, the sun burning brightness beyond him. He looks incongruous surrounded by buildings, by concrete, by a host of hoardings and strangers. But I know his strength and resilience. I know he's no longer a child.

We wait for the train to arrive. I would smother him in the fold of my arms; I would talk to him in a soothing voice, as once, when I laid him down to sleep, when I smoothed his brow, when I kissed his cheek, when I wiped the fears from his mind. When I felt the warmth and touch of his skin, when I smelt its freshness, when I knew myself loved. When all I felt was that love.

The train is approaching.

I would say kind words; I would ask his forgiveness. I would tell him I love him – that my love is so strong it will never diminish, it will not go away. It's my love, within the heartbreak of living, which has brought about all of this pain. It is painful loving, infinitely painful; but it's better than being alone. I wish that none of us were alone. That none of us find ourselves lonely again. Never again on our own.

If only I could look into his eyes, perhaps he could see what I feel. And then perhaps he would recognise me, he would understand what I cannot say. Instead, he is looking down at his bag, he is looking at the chasing windows which gradually slow to a halt. He is looking at anything but at me.

The train comes to a stop; he approaches the carriage. I take his hand in my own. I don't want him to go. I want to go with him. Please don't let us be parted like this.

He turns to look at me. There is something I see in his eyes; some spark of the child I used to know, of the boy I loved, of the man I love. He may yet know. Who knows what he knows?

He opens the door and climbs into the carriage. I watch him seat himself by the window. I watch as he stares out into the distance.

I watch the train pull away.

~

I have harvested my first potatoes; I have stripped a whole line of peas. Salad, spinach, carrots and beetroot have all surrendered to me. Infant pumpkins and courgettes peep out beneath maternal leaves. The cabbage has begun to swell; the broccoli has sprouted buds; the runner beans lace round bamboos, and curl with bright red flowers. The patch is heaving with new life. Each day I come and take from it; each day I find it yields me more – replenishing its natural store much faster than I eat it. I am an island of my own, marooned but self-sufficient. What's here is all that I require. There's no one who I have to be with; nowhere that I have to be.

In the absence of having a purpose for being, I've established a different routine. I leave my curtains open at night, so it's by the light of the sun that I wake, in the fragile fingering dawn. I wash and dress and go downstairs; I make a pot of herbal tea which I take to drink in my study. I sit there through the morning hours, fresh and busy with work. The air is cool and clear in the room; it hones and cleanses my mind. I look from the vantage point of my desk out through the window and into the world, watching the timid colours of dawn as they strengthen and sharpen the image to life. I feel the heat envelop the day as the sky melts blue and arches its back, as the sun lifts upwards and spreads in a smile. A gentle commotion captures the garden as birds awaken the yawning lawn, as the trespass of wind comes and vexes the trees, as strange sounds intrude from the field. When the air is hot and the breeze has tired, when the plants are weary and the birds seek shade, I go to the kitchen to eat. Then I open the door and enter outside. I tie back my plants, I pluck out the weeds, I pick from the stock of what grows. I lie in the hammock, hid in the orchard, easing and emptying my mind. From the shade I can feel the heat in the field; I can see the disfigured bodies of beet wilting beneath the weight of the sun; I can smell the sweat of sweltering summer, the pungency of the earth. I am part of the garden, I am wrapped within it: fed by the breeze, caressed by the grass, cooled by the whispering shade. Sometimes, I find I have slept. In the early afternoon I go in. I pour a cold drink, and I eat some more. I return to my study and work. I work till the rays of the sun stretch through the welcoming window and tarnish my desk, spreading an amber caress on my arms, inviting me into their warmth. I respond to their gentle insistence. In the lengthening day I can work no more. I walk through the creeping shade of the garden, watering plants, or watching the light on the fringe of the field as it starts to turn – as the sky slips white then blushes pink, as the air shakes off the stagnant heat, as swallows chase through the cooling air snatching at insects to eat. I watch as the day is drained of life, as the dusk bleeds away, as the wood petrifies, as the beet dissolves in a shapeless sea. I return to the cottage and there I eat, under the punishing light of a bulb. Then I climb upstairs and I go to sleep.

I have lived my routine for weeks. For days on end, not a single being has entered this inaccessible world. I have stayed near the cottage; I have not gone out nor looked for anything more. I am building a new normality; a modest and sober reality. One devoid of both pleasure and pain. I've divorced myself from Nettlesden now, from the people who live here, from the lives that they lead. I've removed myself from its core. Nothing more has been left by my door; nothing more has been found in the ground. No one has reason to see me. It's as I had thought the country would be. A paradise, a purgatory. A place to be on my own.

And I am alone. I am all alone. I have never felt so alone. Within the cottage is hollowness: an emptiness so pregnant with nothing it promises only oblivion. There is nothing around me, nothing beside me, nothing which sits on my shoulder and smiles. My life is so shallow it has no breath; my body's surrendered its shadow. When I enter a room, I feel no pulse; when I close its door, I feel it die. I feel the insistence of furious silence like a drum in my ears which is beating a rhythm that I'm no longer able to hear. I know that nothing will enter my world, nothing has power to move within it, unless it is forced to by me. It is only routine that keeps me alive. Routine that reminds me when to arise, that sits me down in my study to work, that ushers me out and into the sun, that prompts me to dress, to wash, and to eat, that tells me when day has drawn to a close, and when it is time that I sleep. Without it, there would be no start and no end, no movement, no reason to move. Beneath it, I have lost all desire. For wanting to live, and for living itself. Instead, I exist in the now. I don't question why it is what it is; I don't question why I do what I do.

The answers are so fearful to me, that I've buried the questions in silence. Life on one's own is not a life, it's not a meaningful role. It's a shadow, a silence, an emptiness; a reflection of nothing; a substitute being. I'm surrounded by brilliance, by birth, by breath; by an earth and a sky of such great splendour that it's sometimes painful to look. I wonder what I am doing within it, but casting a shade, a dullness upon it, a spot that will tarnish its beauty. I sense, at my core, there was life in London. It wasn't the sheer raw life of the country, but something more solid than this. It had a purpose; a reason to be. I sense that London, for all its concrete, for all its noise and people and dirt, offers more life than I'm living. I would go there, I would get in the car, I would find you both, I would live with you. But I fear my stain is certain to follow, casting its blanket of grey upon all, shrouding it, squeezing its lungs of their breath, till once more I find myself here on my own.

Then perhaps we should all live up here. Do you think you would like the living of this? With hours that are told by the height of the sun; with days that lack meaning and fuse into one; with minutes that hang suspended in time and never roll on to the next. Would you like to live this eternity too? Would you walk through the fields with your friend Uriah; would you hide in the creaking wood with your son; would you share its secrets with him? Would we do well here, living together? All of us living beneath the one roof. Erasing the past and starting again, with no expectation and no demands. Perhaps that's all that we needed. A changing of places, a swapping of scene. Perhaps we all should have come here together. Perhaps I overlooked the truth that London was the cause of the rot. Perhaps I needed escape from the city, but instead I projected the problem on you.

Perhaps that is so, but the past is now past. What follows from here is what happens next. And this, the present, which hangs on the weight of an unticking clock, in an infinite pocket in time. This single moment. That till now I have lived on my own. Sure, for a while, I shared this with Matty; I fed off his warmth and his company; I tried to give him the same. But there are some things you can't confide in a child; some things you need to face on your own. And so much of this life has been on my own, so much of this living is being alone. And in that void is my isolation; the immense cold solitude of my heart.

For, in truth, I have been so lonely here. And that truth has appeared more hideous and huge for my foiled attempts to hide it. I didn't know what loneliness meant until these last few months. I didn't realise how it consumed – expanding until it sucks you dry. Here, where no antidote can be found. Here, in the sharpened light of day, so stark and severe, beyond lies. My life has crept so long on a broken wing. I have crawled through the days, not daring to look, not even daring to open my eyes, not even daring to breathe. Frightened of all that there is. Of the noise, of the silence. Of the day, of the night. Of meeting people, of being alone. Of the fields, of the wood. Of the objects around me, of the emptiness that claws at my soul. I have tried to disguise it from everyone. Even, I think, from myself. I have tried to block it all out. I have tried to pretend it doesn't exist. Just like I pretended you didn't exist, because I thought that would spare us the pain. I thought it a kindness on all.

But has it been kind – this cruelty, this shame? I thought that, with time, all things could be mended. Isn't that what we are taught? That time is the healer, the honest forgiver.

It allows the memory to fade. And, as it fades, so too does the need, the tie that exists, the bond and the oath that we took in the past, when we came together as one. How utterly foolish. How absurd. Not a day has passed – not a single hour – without your voice in my ear. Whispering, questioning, soothing, supporting. An unwelcome pleasure, a merciful pain. Exposing my myth as a lie.

You have to believe that what I did was done with the best of intent. I believed we would be better off on our own. We had come to a place, a barren place, stripped bare of all that was good. Where nothing within it seemed right. Our life wasn't working; it didn't make sense. There was no direction, there was only decay. We had built a wall of indifference between us; brick by brick we had fuelled a divide. We encouraged a physical distance to prosper. We removed ourselves from each other's lives. That was how it appeared. That was how I thought it to be. I honestly thought it was so. And since we were separate, it seemed to make sense that we found a purpose apart. Where we could both start again and afresh. Where we could build new worlds of our own – in the promise of something and somewhere else – and in doing so we could be happy. Wasn't that what we agreed?

It's morning. The day is humid and bright. I am on the farther side of the hedge, bending over the rampant trellis to cut a clasp of sweet peas. I forget how quiet it is outside the raucous world of my head. The orchard is ripening; the cherries are ready; the apples and plums and pears have grown large, though their compact bodies are hard. I can smell the scent of the flowers in my hand; I can feel the breeze which frets in the boughs; I can hear the strangled whisper of grass as it's crushed beneath oncoming feet.

Martha is standing beside me.

I straighten my back and turn to face her. I have lost all sense of what she looks like. She is wearing a suit with a wide-brimmed hat. I guess that it must be a Sunday. She is staring at me in a curious way, as if she doesn't know who I am, as if I'm not a person at all. It has been so long since I have spoken, or heard the sound of a voice.

She comes towards the edge of the patch, inspecting the wigwam of beans. Then she turns towards me; she forces a smile. She tells me I should nip the ends when they reach the top of the tied bamboo. It will make them thicken and increase the yield.

She casts her eyes across my patch. I can see in her face a faint surprise that things are growing and being tended; that I've learnt to live on my own.

She asks if all is well with me. She had thought that she might have seen me at church: I haven't been there for a while. I tell her I forgot it was Sunday; I've been occupied and busy with work.

Again, she searches into my face as if to tease out a meaning. She hesitates a while before speaking. Then she asks me to come to lunch with her – to come with her now – to go to her farm. She catches me by surprise. I've forgotten the practice of company; I've forgotten how I should interact; I've forgotten how to deceive.

I find myself falling in line behind her, as we cross the scorched road and the margins of fields, as we duck through the thicket and trace the worn track that follows the ditch towards Burnt Tree Farm, the sweet peas still clutched in my hand.

Jack welcomes me, though I know from his face that he isn't expecting a guest. He walks me through to the chairs in the garden where we sit while Martha makes lunch.

He points to the fields that are sweating with growth beyond the slope of his garden. He talks of the harvest, of the produce, the yield, of the annual rotation of crops. He's already laying his plans for next year. Not just for what grows, but the earth itself – what it needs and how he needs to tend it – so that man and nature can coexist. He thinks of it as a living body, an organic entity that subsists beyond the mortal coil of man, serving and feeding each generation with its bounty, its treasure, its plenty. In return for his nurture, it will provide; it will sustain him through all of his years; and, at the end of his span, it outlasts him. Then, for the balance of all that is time, it will hug him close to its chest.

We sit at the top of the shoulder of earth, looking down from the crest of the slope where once we crouched to roll eggs. The brittle fields are laid out before us, sapped by the searching rays of the sun, the green of their youth sucked out of their stems. We eat lunch outside, beneath an umbrella. There's no talk, no mention, of the things that have happened. The earth is greater and grander than that. Jack speaks of the seasons, the cycle of life; of the past and present and that which will come; of the certainty of renewal and rebirth as the land turns over and breathes.

Martha asks me into the kitchen to help with the clearing away. We leave Jack gazing out at the fields and return to the heart of the house.

I stack the bowls beside the sink and start towards the door for more. Martha is still washing up.

– Why did you send Matty away?

– He hasn't seen his father for a while.

– That hasn't troubled you before.

– It may have been troubling him.

– How so?

– He was getting restless. I thought it was time for a change.

– Why was he restless?

– It's difficult to know with boys. They don't talk much. I think he was missing his father. He was getting bored.

– I don't think he was bored in the least. Quite the contrary. He seemed engrossed in what he was doing.

– Maybe.

– Though you have constrained him, preventing him from doing all that he wants.

– I thought that's what you wanted. You told me to keep him away from the wood.

– Away from the wood, yes, that's true. But not away from everything else. Not from the chance to grow and to learn. Here in the country. Here with you.

– I thought a change of scene might be good.

– It is, but it may not be the cure.

– The cure to what?

– I've been through this all before.

– With Uriah? But that was different, surely?

– It was different, but it was also the same. Uncannily the same.

– How do you mean?

– I mean, I can see what is happening with you. What is happening between you and Matty. The sacrifice you think you are making. The decision you haven't yet made.

– What decision is that?

– You feared he was growing too close to Uriah; he was becoming too much like my son. You feared you were losing control. You feared the danger of losing Matty. That's why you sent him away. Those fears are a part of growing up. Of his growing up, and your own.

– I think there's much Matty could learn from Uriah.

– There is, but that doesn't mean that you like it. You brought him here without thinking through what it might be like for him. You have watched him; you have seen him grow in a way that is different to what you expected. That is different to the way that you want. You would have preferred it if Jack was his mentor.

– I can't say that.

– Can't you? Can't you say how you want him to grow? Don't you know what model you want him to have?

– Not exactly.

– Well, I know what you don't want, Sarah. You don't want him to like the wood; to like building dens and making snares; to like being there on his own. Because you don't like those things yourself. But it's not just your fear of the wood. It's your fear of him growing apart; of finding new interests at odds with your own. Of forging a life that is his.

– No mother would want to lose touch with their son.

– And nor would they want to constrain them. To deny them the chance to be happy. If you knew what they wanted and who they were. And surely you want his happiness, Sarah. Isn't that more important than all?

– Yes. Any mother would want their child to be happy.

– If so, you have already made up your mind. You've decided that your love for Matty – for him as a person, for him as he is – is stronger than the selfish desire to make him something he isn't. Because in that you risk losing your son. And the thought you might lose him appals you.

– But I want what is best for him, too. I want him to know right from wrong.

– He's learning right and wrong for himself. This is a good place to learn it. Though his values may not be the same as your own. And by sending him back to stay with his father you're unlikely to change what he does. Either you live with who he is, and love him for the person he is, or you must sacrifice your love, and accept the danger you'll lose him.

– I don't want that.

– Then maybe you should compromise. You should learn to relax your expectations; to let him feel more of your love. You should use that love to help him develop, even if he isn't the person that you might want him to be.

– I do love him.

– Then why did you send him away, Sarah?

– Because I was scared.

– Of what?

– Of so much. Of nothing.

– Were you scared for you or for him?

– For us both.

– And are you better for being apart? Are you any less scared than before?

– No.

– What stops you from being together in London? What stops you from all being here?

– Who? All of us? Him and his father?

– Yes.

– I don't know. I'm not sure anymore.

Martha has finished rinsing the dishes. She leaves them to dry on the draining board and crosses the room to turn on the kettle. I watch her fetching cups and a tray, grinding the beans as the water boils.

It is airless in the muggy kitchen. I look with envy through the window at Jack surveying his land. He is at peace, at one with his world. Martha asks me to carry the tray, and I take it into the garden.

The breeze comes at me in a welcoming rush. I breathe it in; I feel it inside me; I feel it filling my lungs. I feel alive. We sit on the patio drinking coffee, hearing the gentle hum of the fields, stroked by the soft summer heat.

Martha walks me through to the hall; she sees me out through the door. She asks in an offhand way if I've seen or heard anything she thinks I should tell her. She reminds me of the promise I made.

I walk through her courtyard and over the fields, feeling her watching eyes are upon me – intense, like the sun – till I'm over the road, till I'm lost in the shade of my garden.

I enter the cottage.

In following Martha so hastily, I'd forgotten to lock all the doors. The first thing I see in the silent room is a posy of marigolds choked by blue ribbons, lying on the table before me. They are dead. Their stems are brown and brittle with age; their heads are shrunken and hard. A handful of petals still cling to their seams, while others are scattered about on the floor.

I look behind me, into the kitchen, into the darkened heart of the house. The air is thick with dust and disuse. I know there is nobody here. Yet I know that somebody was. Someone who knows my every movement, someone who knows wherever I go. Someone who sees me without being seen; who tirelessly watches and waits. That person has waited for me all these weeks, watching with patience until

I departed – until they were free to enter the cottage and give me another bouquet. And now, for the first time, they have entered my home, they have trespassed into my world.

They have trespassed within. They have left their stain.

I stand on the step in the giddy sun, squinting into the brilliant air, refreshed by the motion of life. I could go straight back to Martha now. I know she's like you: she would know what to do. Or perhaps I should call the police. I need to find someone in whom to confide. Martha says she can offer me that; she has offered it right from the start. But with that offer comes obligation, unstated but certain in all that she does, in how she engages with me. And as yet, I don't know what she expects, or what she'll demand in return.

I close the door and lock it fast. I walk round the cottage inspecting the windows, ensuring that all are secure. Then I cross the lawn and stand by the car, at the very edge of the road. Burnt Tree Farm is staring at me from its low dark eyebrows, its impenetrable windows, the glaring domes of its silos. Hers is not an open offer; hers is a rigid demand. One which requires a servitude, a bondage greater than I would give.

I glance at my watch. It's two o'clock. In the breathing heat of the afternoon, I walk down the road towards the church. The wind in the graveyard tugs the singed grass, it scatters the uppermost branches of trees, it scintillates the dancing leaves till they shuffle with pleasure, speckled and silver, delighted at being alive. The occasional bush which lines my path sways with a gentler fainter motion, watching me as I round the bend, as I cross the road, as I reach the pub, as I raise the latch and push at the door.

I let my eyes adjust to the light. At the farther end of the room is Travis; he is busily wiping the tables. He is clearing up, preparing to close. He's unaware I am here. Uriah is leaning against the counter, staring into the unseen void of the room that's obscured by the bar. It is only the two of them here.

Travis looks up and comes towards me, reaching out for my hand. I shake my head and ask in a whisper if there's somewhere else we could talk. He looks at me, then he nods. He glances over towards Uriah; he takes my elbow and steers me through the atolls of tables towards the doors which open onto the back.

We stand outside in a shaded corner between the pub and a wooden fence where the empty barrels are stored. He is looking at me like a cocker spaniel, tilting his head to one side. I don't know where I ought to begin, so instead I hold out the flowers.

He looks at what I am holding before him, then looks back up to my eyes. His face expresses uncertainty: a hope, a doubt, a wanting to be. Could he possibly think I am giving him these? That I'm making some sort of advance?

– What are they?
– They're flowers, Travis. But they're dead.
– Yes. I can see that. Why are you showing them to me?
– I found them at home.
– You found them?
– Yes, just now. On my kitchen table.
– On the table? You mean inside?
– Yes. I left the door unlocked by mistake. Someone came into my house.
– To give you flowers?

– Yes. Though not as a gift. Not if they're dead. Someone's walked into my home and just dumped them.

– Bloody hell…

–

– Do you know who it was?

– No, I don't.

– Do you know why they did it?

– No.

– Maybe someone is trying to tell you something.

– Like what? What could they possibly be wanting to tell me? It doesn't make any sense.

– Do you think they were meant as a present?

– It's a weird sort of present. Not one that anyone wants to receive.

– Then perhaps it's a threat. It might have something to do with the skull. Do you think it might be a warning?

– It might be. Someone has left me flowers before. But they've left them outside. And they haven't been dead.

–

– Martha thinks they were left by Joyce.

– You've talked to Martha about this?

– The first time. But not since. I've been receiving bunches of flowers ever since I arrived. So many times, I've got used to it. But they've always been placed on the wall by the door. They've always been freshly picked and alive. They've always been tied with blue ribbon.

– And were these?

– They were tied with a ribbon, yes. But not in a bow. These were almost strangled.

– Do you think they're from the same person?

– They could be. Or they may have come from somebody else. From somebody else who knows.

– Who knows what? How are you feeling right now?

– How do you think I'm feeling?! Someone has just walked into my home. They've left dead flowers on my table.

– So, what are you going to do?

– I don't know. That's why I'm talking to you. What do you think I should do?

– I'm not sure. You could follow it up or forget all about it. If you ignore it, it might go away. But there again, it might not. You might get more visits, more bunches of flowers. Or who knows what they'll do next.

– That's not very helpful. What would you do if it was you?

– I think… I think it's difficult to ignore. It'll stay on your mind. You'll always be left with unanswered questions. What did they mean; who did it; why you. You'll never rid yourself of those questions, so you'll find it hard to forget.

– Then you're saying I should…

Travis squeezes my hands in his own. I sense he is warming to this. Not because he likes what it is, but because of the opportunity: the chance it affords him of being with me. He can sense my doubt – that I'm reaching out – and he thinks I'm in need of him now. He can seize this chance to show he is here, to forge a closeness, an intimacy. He is here for me now that he sees me alone, now he senses I've no one to turn to.

A window is opening somewhere above us, from one of the rooms in the pub. Travis looks up and I break away, wondering what Samantha has heard, wondering if she has looked down and seen.

I walk swiftly round the side of the pub, hugging the contours of the walls till I reach the foot of the road. I walk past the graveyard and turn the corner, without once looking behind.

As I start up the slope towards the cottage, I can sense someone's presence in Steeple Field, cutting across the grass from the pub, intercepting my path. I continue walking, turning my head just a touch to see who is there.

It's Uriah.

Uriah is walking faster than me; he's coming directly towards me. He must have heard the two of us speaking; he must have heard what we said. Now he is striding across to confront me, here in the open, in the broad light of day. He is coming to get me; he is coming for me. Surely someone will see him.

I quicken my pace, half-thinking to run, half-thinking to stop and to scream. I feel the heat of the blunt afternoon, the breathless air which is closing around me, the heavy sky which is leaning its weight on this flat, flat land – which suffocates me – strangling the life from my limbs.

A hundred yards ahead of me there's a scratch of bushes beside the road, between the road and the field. That is the point at which we bisect; that is where we will meet. There, at those bushes, where no one can see us, obscured from all of the houses.

I slow my pace without turning around. Better he catches up with me here, where the world is not blind to his deed.

I can see Uriah approaching the road. Now he is stood at its side. He's standing facing the concrete drive which leads through the field to Rose House Farm. But he doesn't wait for me there. He crosses the road without looking at me. Now he is starting along the track.

Uriah is going back home.

I reach the point where, moments ago, he was standing, at the mouth of his track. I follow him with my eyes. I watch the heaviness of his tread; his thick-set body, his shaven scalp, seared by the scorch of the sun. He doesn't look round. He is going back home. He has no interest in me.

I stand by the clump of sheltering bushes where I thought that he and I would collide. They squat on a lip above the road, their bodies buffeted by the breeze, sparkling and winking at me. I stare at the leaves and through their membrane, into to the very heart of the bush. From deep in the shaded pool of their core, a pair of eyes is staring at me. I can hear a rustle, a crackle, a tread. There's someone inside; they are watching me. There cannot be, but there is. If I scramble up the side of the bank, if I rifle in amongst the scrub, I'll be able to see who it is.

I hear the crack of a branch as it snaps.

I find I am walking fast down the road. Fast and blind down the road, as though drunk. The blur of Six Bells skids close to one side, then the hazy stretch of the field. Now I have almost reached the cottage; now I am crossing the lawn. I'm fumbling in my pockets for something. My fingers fold round my key. My ears are alert to every sound, to all that is hidden behind me. But I hear nothing. Nothing behind me; nothing beside me; nothing from somewhere inside. Only a distant sigh from the hedge as it twitches uneasily in its slumber, as it sweats in the fearsome gaze of the sun.

I unlock the door. I shunt it open. Then I close it and lock it behind me.

~

From my bedroom window I watch the dawn. I see the grey sky twisting white and fringed with palest gold. I see the gradual crest of the sun raising its head from the bed of the field and peeping over the land. I see thin trails of morning mist hanging low on the crowns of the beet; I see the earth as it slowly awakens, yawning and stretching towards the day. I hear staccato sounds of birdsong; the scratch of the creeping rose which steals across the livid-pink walls. I hear the empty call of a crow, the weep of boughs in the nodding orchard, the creak of a lean-to door.

I go downstairs to make coffee and toast. Again, the day is calling to me; it beckons to me through the window. It's alert; it is waiting for me. The sky spins spectres of cloud on the lawn which scurry away behind the hedge; the grass is stroked by pools of sun, glanced by shadows which shape to the wind. I am its slave; I cannot resist.

I unlock the door and stand on the step. I can feel the wind in my face. I can feel it snatch at snags of my hair; I can taste the sharpness of the air; I can feel its clarity. It has been many days since I entered the garden. It has been so long. So long. I feel the life of the earth and the sky washing around me and breathing through me. I feel them breaking the mould of the cottage; I feel them threading their being within me. I cross the lawn and enter my patch.

My courgettes are bloated and large, they have turned into marrows with darkened skins which are coarse and thick to the knife. My runner beans are over-long, they are rough in my hands and their seeds are hard. My tomatoes weigh on the weary truss, or lie on the earth, split vertically, staring at me like demonic eyes. My cabbage is spoiled by the slugs; the bald heads speckled with mud and blanched by the sun.

There's an ugliness to this ripeness. My progeny has transformed itself from supple and green to a tiring crop which stands defamed and awaits the cull. Half of my plot is now naked. The potatoes are torn from the belly of earth, the broad beans and peas, the carrots and salad, stripped from the bounteous soil. The bare patch waits for the creeping growth, the weeds which will seed themselves and take hold, till I rip them from this tainted body and prepare the ground for next year.

If Matty was here he would be in his lean-to, hammering metal against his anvil like a furious dwarf in a darkened palace, building his treacherous snares. He would be on the track that leads to the farm, sneaking out to meet with Uriah. He would be on the road, on the path round the field, sidling up to the watchful wood, creeping through the circling thorn; he would be in the midst of the sorrowful trees.

But, as it is, he is not.

I feel a person's shadow upon me. I look up and see it is Travis. He is standing near the gap in the hedge, watching me as I work. He is watching my fingers scratch at the soil; watching me bending down to the plants; watching me, soaking me up with his eyes.

I stamp the imprinted earth from my boots, wiping my face with the back of my hand, brushing my hair from my eyes. I have lost all sense of the passage of time. We stand in the melt of the morning sun, facing each other, exchanging no words, hid in the closure behind the hedge. He looks at me with timorous eyes – those eyes so big and so wanting. I know there are streaks of mud on my face; I know there are beads of sweat on my forehead; I know that my hair is wild.

I know my clothes are muddied and torn, my face is bare and stripped of make-up, my palms are dirty and scratched. This is as you liked me best. When I was unaffected. And, strangely, it is here that you meet. This is what you both have in common: a single thought that you share. I can see from his look, I can see from his eyes, that it's this that he likes, it is this that he wants. It is this that isn't in reach.

I ask him to sit on the bench while I change, knowing he wants to come in.

I go to the bathroom and turn on the taps, watching the room fill with steam. I take off my clothes and lie in the water, feeling the sting of its heat on my skin, the rub of enamel against my shoulders, against my buttocks and thighs. I stand up and wash myself clean. I scrub at my limbs, I scrape at my nails, I tease the earth from between my toes. I can see my skin in the stare of the mirror, glistening with water and soap. I know that Travis will never see this. This unspecial body is yours alone. It has only ever been yours.

I peer out of the window while crossing the landing. Travis reclines, his legs kicked out, his arms stretched over the back of the bench. He has told me that I cannot retreat; I have no option to walk away. I need to follow, to uncover the truth. Only then can I rest. Only by challenging what is happening can I hope to bring it all to an end. I wonder why he is keen to discover. If for my sake, or his own. To help me end a thing that has started, or to start off something anew. Travis isn't the same as you. He is nothing like you; he cannot be you. He's here to my side, but he's not beside me. I wonder if he already knows the truth he seems so eager I find. I wonder if the flowers are from him.

I wonder if they're a lure to trap me. I wonder what it would feel like beneath him, his soft paunch flattened against my stomach, his square fringe full in my face.

I put on fresh trousers, a new clean blouse. I brush my still-wettened hair. I look in the mirror; I look at my skin; I look at its texture, its pores. I should put on some make-up to hide who I am. But then, maybe, he would think that I care.

I pick up my bag and a linen jacket, locking the door as I leave. I look through the rose arch, down the long lawn, to where Travis still sits on the bench. I try to picture him there in the evenings, or cutting the hedge or mowing the lawn, or stood on a ladder mending the gutter, securing the wandering rose. Each image I conjure is ludicrous. I call over to him and he walks towards me, shielding his eyes from the sun.

It was foolish of me to agree to this, but it cannot do any harm.

It is hot in the car. Travis has wound down all of the windows, and the air comes thick from all sides. We pass Six Bells and the Rectory, the church, the Serpent and Wayside House. I wonder how many eyes can see us; I wonder how much he cares.

Travis is silent as we drive through the village and onto the intimate lanes. I think he would like to talk to me; he wants to talk; there are things he would say. I can't believe that he's lost for words. It's more a question of which words to use, of how he wants to begin.

The landscape distracts me; I look away. We wind round the right-angled corners of fields, passing nameless hamlets and pubs, buoyed on bright oceans of bearded barley which whisper to us in the wind. We hustle through magical clumps of trees, feeling the darkness, the cool of their shade, then finding ourselves spat out into sunshine, the warm air breathing its rage.

We pass a meadow where sheep are grazing; then, on a rise, a stately home. The land is starting to change around us: the thick clay soil is sandy and soft; the grass is grown to a wild savannah; the hedges have dwindled to gorse. Then the earth falls away to an estuary, its waters muddied and mired. We mirror its movement, snaking through marshland, until we come to its mouth with the sea.

Rackham. We drive up its crowded, ancient street, past totter-down shops and teetering houses; the pavements busy with families holding pushchairs and dogs on the pull. How alien this reality seems. We continue through to the end of the town, to a large village green, to the battlements, to a final terrace of small-windowed houses. We park in a hollow to the side of the road, shaded by low-reaching trees.

Travis leads the way through the copse, following a path to its crest. Then, of a sudden, we are standing on sand. A beach spreads before us, open and welcome, cluttered with clutches of laughter and banter, of semi-clothed bodies laid out in the sun. Beyond them, a murky stretch of blind sea.

We climb over the sloping brow of the beach, across the shingle and sand of its face, till we stand in the slip of the tide. I kick off my shoes and enter the water, feeling it bubbling and cleansing my feet. The sea is cool and sandy-brown; its slow waves sweeping across the mute surface, washing diagonally into the shore. It feels as flat as the farmland behind us, as barren as a freshly ploughed field.

I pick up my shoes and we stroll down the beach, wandering alongside the sea. We saunter past colourful patches of people, round towels which are neatly spread out on the stones, past children who dig in the sand.

We come to a walkway that faces the shore. At the foot of the hill there's a long line of beach huts, brightly painted, with small hunched doors, with tiny terraces stood at their fronts, with nameplates nailed on their brows. People sit on chairs in the porches, staring out at the featureless sea, drinking tea and exchanging words, watching the day slide away. The beach is interrupted by groynes. I watch the water heaving its mass against their half-sunken frames. I think of Jack; I think of the land; I think of the stealth of gradual erosion; I think of the changing shape of the coast.

Travis wants to buy an ice-cream. Beneath an umbrella, surrounded by coolers, a man is serving some children. I watch them eagerly grasping their cones; the ecstasy of the first thrilling lick. I look at the mother, who is turning her back, who is searching through her bag with her fingers. By the time she has paid, they have skipped away; she stands on the pavement alone.

Travis hands me a cone.

On the top of the hill there's a white-bodied lighthouse; in front of us there's a peopled pier, its dull limb extending into the sea. A crowd is rippling through low-fronted buildings which mask the face of its deck. Above them, the noise of electronic games blends with the cries of the seagulls. We turn inland, ambling back to the town. At a fish and chip shop we come to a stop. Travis demands that we enter. The fish here, he tells me, is so recently caught you can taste the salt from the sea.

I stand on the pavement watching the traffic, watching the families frisk down the road with buckets and spades, with beach balls, fishing nets, prams. Travis returns; he is grinning at me. The wrapped paper package is oily and soft; its skin is bloated with heat. He hurries me on to the village green which lies at the end of the town. He buys us both a pint from the pub. Then we wander directionless over the grass, finding an unpeopled place where we sit.

The sun declines; the heat of the day seeps into the ground; the rasping grass is lined with shadow; the distant sea is so calm. I sit cross-legged with my chips in my lap, feeling their sinking warmth on my thighs, the pungent vinegar sharp on my tongue. The fish is meaty and succulent; the chips are mouth-hot and crisp.

– So, what do you think of it, Sarah?

– It's tasty. Good. And yours?

– Nice. You know, I think I could live by the sea.

– Have you ever?

– No. But I like the idea of a tavern. Or even a smuggler's inn. What do you think?

– I'm not sure. It's a nice idea. But I don't know about the reality. I don't know that life would be any better than it is where you are at the Serpent. The summers may be busy, but I expect the winters are dead. It would be quite insular.

– Maybe. But next time, next time perhaps, it will be by the sea.

– Why do you say that? Are you thinking of moving on?

– I've stayed in Nettlesden for too long. If I don't move on soon then I never will.

– Why would you want to leave? Isn't the pub sustainable?

– Not really. But it's more than that. It's the thought of staying here till I retire. Of being here till I die.

– That's a bit morbid.

– Yes. But I can picture it. The thought of it terrifies me.

– Is Nettlesden that bad?

– It's not Nettlesden, it's life. It's what you do with it. It's how you spend it. It's who you spend it with. Life needs to have purpose.

– You do have purpose.

– Do I? Managing a pub, wiping tables, serving drinks. What sort of a purpose is that? Why am I doing it?

– You're doing it for a living. For you and Samantha. What more do you think that there is? What more do you want?

– Something that makes it all worthwhile.

– It's your life. If you really think it's lacking in purpose, then you have the power to change it. You know you can.

– That's why I'm thinking of moving elsewhere.

– Moving is fine, if the issue is location. But moving away from Nettlesden won't solve anything else. It will deflect your attention, that's all.

– How did you break from London?

– I got in a car and left. At the time it seemed the only solution. At the time it seemed to have worked. But I'm not sure it has dealt with those deeper issues. It disguised them and delayed them. It hasn't resolved them.

– You don't think it's helped?

– I like to think I've moved on, but I'm not sure how far.

– Would you return to London if you could?

– That's an impossible question to answer.

– I think you've got more purpose than me. At least your options are better defined.

– You have got options too.

– I have and I haven't. I can't break away on my own. I can't. And I don't really want to. I wouldn't want anything more than I've got if I felt I shared it with somebody else.

– And you don't?

– No. That's why it's not enough. That's why it doesn't seem worth it. That's why I'm thinking of moving on. Because I've got no one I feel I can share with. There's no real connection; no incentive to stay.

– Then moving won't change anything. You need to address the real issue.

– What's worse: being unhappy together, or being alone?

– It depends.

– You must know. You have experienced it.

– They are both difficult. Both in their different ways. But if being with someone becomes too painful you have to risk being alone. You have to believe that in going away you won't always be on your own.

– That's the risk, isn't it? I can't do that. I can't move on without knowing there's someone. That someone is waiting; that someone is there. I can't walk away into nothing.

– Not even if there's nothing left where you are? Not even if it's causing both of you pain?

– There's nothing left where I am. There hasn't been for a very long time. I have just closed down; I am ticking over. It's the only way to survive. And I thought that was all that was left for me. But then, for the first time in years, I saw someone. Someone I instinctively felt I could share with. Someone who could make it worthwhile.

– You need to be sure that person is real. Not an illusion; not a trick of your mind.

– Yes, I know.

– And whatever you do involves making a choice. A decision on whether to leave or to stay. No one likes being one of your options. You should make a decision and stick to it. It's getting late, Travis. I think we should go.

I get up swiftly and pick up the glasses, taking them back to the pub. Travis is standing alone on the green, crumpling the papers into a ball, tying them up in a plastic bag. I can see he wants a signal from me, something to help him make his decision, something to lessen the risk. I think of Samantha waiting at home, lying in bed or watching TV; I think of Travis returning alone; I picture them both, in the same empty room, at a loss for something to say.

In the silence of the long afternoon Travis drives us slowly back home. I look out over the lengthening fields, over the rich golden land. It's been good to visit Rackham at last; to find an excuse to get out. This will make a good ending for us. I know this will be our final excursion. There can be no more secretive trips with Travis. No more sneaking away from the village. I don't want Bill to look at me knowingly whenever I enter the pub. I don't want Samantha to sit in her home thinking that Travis has gone out alone. I don't want to feel the guilt that I feel when I know that I've done nothing wrong.

Travis draws up in front of the cottage. He gets out and comes round to the passenger side, insisting on opening the door. I try saying goodbye, but he wants to linger, he wants to see me safely inside. He looks at me as if wanting to speak, as if wanting to say a fraction of all that has occupied his mind in the car.

I turn the key and half-open the door, starting into the room. Travis has reached out, he's taken my hand, forcing me to turn round. I can see he is struggling to find the resolve; he's uncertain of how to begin. He's exploring my eyes to seek out my thoughts; he is trying to guess what I feel.

I withdraw my hand. I thank him for taking me out for the day. I have enjoyed it; it has been good. I say goodbye and take a step back, crossing over the threshold. Still, he is standing here on the step, unwilling to turn, unwilling to leave, unable to ask himself in. There's a sadness, a helplessness set in his eyes. He has lost all he has; he's already alone. And deep in his gut he must know it.

I push the door to a close.

The room is breathless and silent. There's a stillness, yet a fullness of being. I sensed the change when I opened the door, but now, in turning around, I can see. The room is all as it was before, when I left it, locking the door. The room is all as before, save for the table which stands in the centre, strewn with books and half-read papers, with a coffee cup which I meant but forgot to tidy away after lunch. The table is just as I left it, yet its legs are no longer bare. Instead, there's a living growth on its limbs, which climbs from the floor, which clutches and curls up the wooden sides. All four legs are a rash of leaves, a wreath of strands of morning glory, stretching upwards, striving for light, seeking the warmth of a wrongful sun. The posts are thick with leaf and flower: choked by its carnage, clogged by its weight. Strips of blue ribbon weave through its jungle, ensnared in the tangle of stems.

Travis is standing still in the garden, midway between the house and his car, lacking the courage to knock on my door, lacking the willpower to leave. He is lost. I watch him seeking direction. At last, he turns and walks away, slowly over the fading lawn. He opens the door of the sun-hot car; he rests his arm against its lip; he looks towards the cottage once more, though he cannot see me inside.

It is not too late, for him or for me. Either of us could call to the other; either could step out onto the lawn.

That is all it would take.

Travis climbs into the driver's seat. He pulls at the door, and it closes upon him. I watch the car ease onto the road. I watch as it trundles away.

I turn back into the room. The door was locked; the windows were closed. What is here was brought with intent. But what would bring a person to do this; what could they hope to achieve? I picture Joyce in the thick of the hedgerow, stripping the creepers from low-hanging boughs, consciously bundling them into a bag, stealing along the fringe of the field, under the sightless gaze of the village, under the watchful eye of the sun. I can see her testing the locks on the lean-tos; I can see her pressing against the door; I can see her finding a secret entrance somewhere unknown through these living walls. I can see her setting about her task. In my mind I can see it so clearly. I can see her feet, her arms, her hands. Time and again, her curious actions. Yet when I look back up to her face, it is Martha not Joyce who is wreathing the creepers through the silent heart of my home.

And, having entered, she could be here still.

I stand with my back against the door, my fingers clutching the knob. Travis will have reached the pub by now. I could call; I could beg he returns. Knowing that if I did, he would do so. He would come to the cottage for me. I could ask him, knowing there is nobody else. Knowing that someone is better than no one, and that's better than knowing yourself on your own.

That is the wretched truth that I live. That is the person that I have become.

I can hear the scratch of the rose on the wall, I can hear it tapping against the door, as if it wants to come in. Over my shoulder, across the lawn, I can see the hedge is winking at me. I can feel it is watching all that I do.

I will not be drawn. I will not be consumed. I will not see my world destroyed.

I open the door and stand on the step. I feel a freshening breeze on my face; I feel it whispering into my ear. It tells me I am not on my own. I do not have to be on my own. I haven't been; I just haven't known it. Matty has been here, but you've been here too. You have been with me right from the start. You've always been here – here at my side – though I've done my best to deny your existence, to rupture it, to force a divide. Despite that, you have remained. I am drawn to you both, not to all that is here. Not to this that I hold in my hands. Not to this, that tempts me from where I belong, from all that I want and from all that I am.

I walk out onto the grass. The air is still thick, and the sun is heavy in the milk-blue wearying sky. I stoop through the thickening arch to the back; I look out onto the wood. I stare at it in defiance. No good can come from what's there. Its intrigue oozes into the soil, into the soul of Nettlesden, tainting all who trespass within it, poisoning them with its stain. But it won't contaminate me. I won't allow it; I won't let it in. I will not be consumed by its hate.

I can hear a noise from behind the hedge. A rustling, a shuffling. Someone is there. I can see a shape; I can hear their breath. Someone is coming towards me.

Samantha.

She is wearing a skirt which comes to her knee, and heels which sink into the earth. Her make-up is spoilt; her face is swollen. She is standing here in front of me. She is standing, trembling with hatred and fear. And she is screaming at me. She is clawing the air as if she would harm me; as if she has come to scratch out my eyes.

I stand before her, unmoving; letting her vent her raw emotion; watching and waiting until it subsides. I see her fury reduce to cinder, till she is no more than a plaintive whimper, a low lost cry on the wind. I want to go up to her, and to hold her. I want to wipe away all her pain. I want to tell her the truth. That no matter how wretched and lonely life is, our lives are worth living, and living is good. There is so much to life; so much more than this moment.

She has stopped; she has exhausted herself. She stands limp and pale in the restless shadow. I can see she is shivering; her skin white and cold. I want to come close, to hug her with warmth, but she will not let me approach. She recoils from me; she walks away. I watch as she awkwardly crosses the lawn, as she fades through the rose arch, and then past the hedge, till the sound of her heels on the blistered road is all that tells she was here.

I turn away. Across the field, beyond Rose House Farm, the wood is shrinking to nothing. It hugs itself, embracing its pain, burying the secrets that burden its depths. I will not scratch at its putrid sores; nor will I look for anything more. But that doesn't mean I will hide. I have hidden too long from what I am; I have hidden myself from myself. I have let myself be distracted. In watching in on this other world, I've neglected the world of my own.

I look up into the vacant sky. The day is drawing in fast. A faint chill is carried in the evening air. The summer begins to grow stale.

~

The morning mist hangs low on the fields; it blankets the land and stops all sound. I can see the dim yellow orb of the sun, straining to pierce the close-hanging gloom, striving to burn it away. The day is neither cold nor warm. I feel the curling air in my lungs, the condensation moistening my skin, the taste of dampness fresh in my mouth. I hear no noise, no birds in the hedgerow; no more than the sound of my boots on the road, echoing off invisible walls of light and shade, of the nothingness dripping around me.

The field of beet fades into the fog, its body blanching and sinking from sight; the grey of its leaf-world blending within the lifeless mist that absorbs it. I come to the mouth of the track, seeing it trail to ubiquitous cloud. I can only guess at Rose House Farm, standing alone in a pool of silence, lost in an indiscernible sea.

Through the haze I can hear a single sound, dampened and faint, yet steadily building the closer I come to the farm. It cuts through the air from the nearing wood, twisting its noise through the trunks of trees. The ugly wail of a motor.

It stops.

I stand and wait; I wait for the whining complaint to return, to reverberate through the cloud. But it doesn't. Instead, there's a clammy cavernous stillness. Then, through the silence, a yawning, a wrenching. A splitting, a tearing of wood. A moan spat out through the blinded distance.

Friendless and laden with fear. Then the crack of a branch, a crush and a thump as a body comes to the earth. I can hear the flap of panicked wings rising into the sightless skies, but, looking up, I see nothing. The world is drowned in uniform whiteness – measureless, sightless and empty.

Endless.

In the silence which follows, I look all around me. I can no longer see the road or Six Bells, nor the Rectory, nor the roof of my cottage, nor the shape of the church tower lost in low cloud, nor the trees which line the low middle distance. Only the crust of the crumbling track, with broken bricks and chips of stone which stick through the concrete like spears. If I closed my eyes and spun around, I would lose all sense of backwards and forwards, confusing advance with retreat.

I put out a tentative arm before me, steadying myself on the air. I step out into the shrouded haze, waiting for shadows to rise as objects, for the fog to solidify into the farm and the motionless trees which surround it.

The mist darkens; it grows into furrows and patches; it melts from nothing to a spectre of being, shaping itself to a large grey cloud hovering low in the field.

I walk on. The cloud cements to a clump of trees, to a line of roof, to a heavy wall hanging suspended in air. I come closer. I can see the sweeping lines of a willow; the long, thick crimson arms of a beech. I can see the weathered boards of the barn, the shape of the tiles which clutter its roof. I can see the courtyard, the spit of its gravel. The ditch, like a moat, surrounding the farm, severing it from the field.

I am closer now. Trees stand proud of the passive field which squats submissive on every side. Bushes cling to the lip of the ditch and bristle defiance through shivering leaves; they flutter to whiteness like opening eyes, though there is no hint of a breeze. The barren courtyard opens before me, and beyond are the scars of sightless windows scratched in the dreary face of the farm.

I stop.

I can hear the scrunch of feet on the gravel; I follow the sound with my eyes. Uriah is approaching, sweating and raw, a chainsaw held in his hand.

His look is impassive; there is no recognition. His eyes are dead to the world. For a moment, I think he will walk straight past; he will walk away and into the barn. But he doesn't choose to walk by.

He comes forward slowly; he is coming towards me; his eyes are fixed on my own. Now he is standing before me, above me. He's staring into my face. He stares at my hair, at my cheek, at my ear; his gaze moves down to my mouth and my lips. Now it sinks from my breasts to my belly, my crotch; to my hips, to my waist, and back up to my neck. He is staring straight at me, and through me, inside me. He can see who I am, and I cannot hide.

– I've come to see Joyce.
–
– I want to talk to Joyce.
– Joyce isn't here.
– I don't believe you.
– She isn't.
– Where is she then?

– She's out.

– Where?

–

– Where has she been? What have you done with her?

– I haven't done anything to her. She's been here all of the time.

– But not now?

–

– Why doesn't she ever show her face?

– She doesn't want to. She wants to be on her own.

– What have you done to her?

– I haven't done anything. She's not here. I suggest you go away.

– No. Not until I've seen Joyce.

– Leave. Now.

– I won't.

Uriah takes a step closer towards me. He stands so close I could reach out and touch him. The curl of the chainsaw he holds in his hand is almost touching my knee.

His face is huge when framed in the mist; his skin is fissured and red. I can see the shape of his heavy skull through the tight-cropped shave of his hair. A bead of moisture clings to his chin. I can smell his sweat. His eyelids half-close on the balls of his eyes, blanking their daylight from me. But he doesn't blink. He raises a hand in the air before me; holding it high, before letting it fall.

– Another time, perhaps.

His voice has softened, as though he is speaking his thoughts to himself. Already, he is turning away, he is walking back to the heart of the courtyard, his footsteps thick on the air.

He turns again and watches me. I think he might be waiting for me. Waiting for me to follow behind him, or waiting for me to blur with the coils of the creeping mist and be gone.

We stand and stare at each other. There's an emptiness to the shallow courtyard. An emptiness to the soulless house. A deadness. Perhaps he is telling the truth.

– Joyce!

–

– Joyce. I want to speak to you. Please come out so I can see you.

–

– I know that you're here. Don't be afraid of me, please.

–

– Is it you... Is it you who's been watching me? All this time, you've been watching?

–

– Is it you who gives me the flowers?

–

– Why do you give them to me?

–

– Why do you bring them into my home?

–

– Please come out and talk to me.

–

– You needn't be frightened. You can say what you like.

–

– I'm willing to listen to you. But not like this. It can't continue like this.

My voice sounds forced. It bounces off the walls of the house; it's swallowed up by the static mist which wreathes round the field like smoke.

Uriah is unmoved, though he hears my words. He has watched me, and he watches me still, his face devoid of expression.

I look at the ditch, at the breathless leaves, at the crying willow, the barn. I look at the broken tiles on the roof, at the faceless windows, the yard.

I know in my bones that Joyce isn't here. She's no longer here on the farm.

I find I am walking back down the track. The only sound is that of my boots scrunching the loose chips of concrete and stone. I can feel Uriah's eyes are upon me – on my legs, on my head, on the back of my neck – until I'm enveloped by cloud.

I come to the road. I turn up the slope and towards the cottage, passing the silent shape of Six Bells. I follow the line of the infinite field till my hedge rises out from the gloom. I walk diagonally over the lawn, the teetering frontage of the pink house thickening the closer I come.

The key sounds large in its lock. I push open the door. I'm not afraid of what I might find, and there's no surprise in seeing it here. The legs of my table are choked with bindweed, twining and twisting and spilling its body into a writhing sea of green till the wood beneath it is drowned. But more than my table has been engulfed. The chair has become a misshapen mass, densely embroidered with smothering leaf. The bookshelf, the mantelpiece and the boiler are all submerged in its strangle. The curtain-rail, the inner doors, the pipes to the boiler, the standing lights are plagued by the all-devouring creepers that are weaving in and out of their fabric, clasping onto their bones.

I step back onto the porch, turning around and facing the lawn. The mist is washing over the grass, sliding up the face of the cottage, slipping through cracks in the cowering bushes, lacing itself through the herbs in the bed. I can hear the breath of the murmuring leaves, the tremor of life in the hedge.

– Joyce.

–

– Joyce. I know you're here. Come out and speak to me. Please.

–

– I've just been up to Rose House Farm. I came to see you. I wanted to talk.

–

– I know you've been waiting for me to leave. You've been waiting to let yourself in.

–

– But it can't go on like this. You know it can't.

–

– If you want to talk, you have to come out.

–

– We can speak if you want. I promise to listen.

–

– You can tell me whatever you want.

–

– But not like this. This isn't the way. This isn't how you can win my trust. It can't continue like this.

I reach back into the bowels of the cottage and drag an armful of bindweed outside. It shudders as it meets with the day. The fog stands aghast as I tear at the leaves, as I let them fall from my grasp. The bindweed lies on the grass, unloved, seething with anger and bristling with rage.

In the blur of the hedge there is scarcely a rustle, scarcely the sound of a sigh. A silence. As though there is nobody there.

I sit down by the table, the door opened wide, watching inquisitive mist creep inside. There's an emptiness to the half-clothed room; a hollow that needs to be filled. I look out over the windless lawn, expecting to see a strengthening shadow, the stamp of the oncoming spectre of Joyce. Waiting to hear her foot on the step.

A minute passes. Two minutes. More.

I can hear the rasping rose on the wall; I can hear it tap on the windowpane. I wonder when she will come.

I fill the kettle from the tap in the kitchen. My back is facing the door. I wonder if I will hear her enter; or if, when I turn, I will see she is here. I wonder if she will reach out and touch me; if she will grasp my shoulders with both of her hands.

The kettle huffs indignantly, raised from slumber to urgent action, stirring and shaking itself to life, busy and bustling with noise. I watch it boil. I watch the steam which bursts from its spout, which drives back the mist and burns it away.

Maybe it won't be Joyce who comes. It might be Uriah instead.

I sense the day is gradually lightening. I sense a sentient world beyond. Not only beyond, but here in the cottage. Here, in the room where I stand. I can feel the weight of another presence; I can see the press of another body in the chair to the side of the dresser. It is you. You are here; you are here with me now. As you were in London, so too in

Suffolk. You are here, beside me again. A refuge, a harbour, an anchor, a hope. How could I ever have failed to see you? How could I ever have been so blind? There is no one else in my life to care for; there is no one else here who cares. There is only Matty and me and you. If others come, then let them come. But I won't go looking for them.

There is nothing here that I want to find. There is nothing here that I want.

The mist is melting into the hedge; I can see a glow on the farther side. I can see a limpid luminance, a pencil line of blue in the sky. I can see a shadow of stretching sun printed on the face of the cloud. I can feel the whitening glare of its warmth ease through the window and onto my face. I can hear the banter of birds refreshed; the gradual rise of the newborn breeze searching over the lawn.

I go upstairs to change my clothes. By the time I step out into the garden, the summer's day is exquisite.

Bill and Margaret are walking towards me up the slope of the road. I wait for them and greet them warmly. They seem surprised to have met me. Together we follow the twisting path which leads round the fields to Burnt Tree Farm. We walk across the smiling courtyard; we enter the welcoming door.

It's as I remember it was over Easter. The same trestle tables put up in the kitchen, the same cakes and biscuits laid out on the plates, the same linen sheets draped over the tables. A tradition repeated, forever the same. Always exactly the same. First Easter, the birth, the start of the season. Now August Bank Holiday, when we reap what is sown. The dawn and the ending of life.

I walk through the patio doors with Margaret, onto the crest of the sloping lawn. The Faradays are already here; the Merediths too, with their children. The youngsters are chasing each other and laughing; they are running in circles, they are hiding in bushes, they are rolling dead-bodied to the foot of the slope.

I wish that Matty was here.

Uriah and Martha are walking alone at the very end of the lawn. Jack is stationed by an umbrella, greeting those who arrive. Samantha and Robert are stood side by side, talking in whispers, content on their own. Behind them is Travis, standing alone in the shade of a shadowing tree. I can see he is looking at me. He is looking at me; he is starting towards me; I think he is eager to talk.

I walk down the slope towards mother and son: I want to establish a peace.

Martha looks up and sees me closing; she detaches herself and climbs up the slope, calling the children around her. I guess Uriah has mentioned this morning; I guess she knows what I said. She may not know the reasons behind it, but she knows I've broken her trust.

Uriah is standing alone by the fence, his large head thrust through a tight-buttoned shirt, his face like a crimson stone.

– I can't see Joyce here.
– She isn't here.
– I'm sorry. Isn't she well?
– She's well enough.
– I thought I saw her today. Near my garden. Do you know if she was planning to see me?
– She may have been.

– Do you know what she might have wanted to say?

– I'm not her keeper. I wouldn't know.

– No. But I thought you might be able to guess.

–

– I'm sorry if I surprised you earlier today. Coming out of the mist like that.

–

– It has turned out well. The weather, that is.

–

– What did you mean when you said 'another time'? What is that supposed to mean?

–

– Do you think we can ever be friends?

– Who?

– Joyce and me. You and me. The three of us.

–

– I know that you like talking to Matty. And he likes to talk to you, too. I wish that we all could be friends.

– If you know that, why did you send him away?

Uriah raises his eyes to meet mine. There is accusation in what he is saying. It's in his voice and his face. But there's something else too – there's almost a longing – as if he, too, is wanting to share. I could tell him the reasons why Matty has gone; I could talk through my motives for what I have done. But I doubt he'd believe what I say. He feels as betrayed by me as does Martha. Despite my attempts to bridge the gap, despite my desire for harmony. To them, I remain the pariah.

Uriah is no longer facing me. He's looking away, beyond my shoulder. He's looking up to the top of the slope, where Jack is calling the village to him.

Uriah stretches his hand towards me. He takes my elbow and steers me away, up towards the convergence of people stood by the side of the house. It's a curious grasp. It is firm. But his touch is unexpectedly kind. Even gentle. Is this the way that he steers his wife, guiding Joyce through the course of the years? Has she clung in the crook of his arm for support, not because he would hide her away?

– I would like to welcome you all once more. The summer is drawing to a close. It has been another good year. The sun has shone; it has ripened the crop; the harvest is almost complete. We have profited from the land once more, we have reaped the spoils for which we have worked, as our fathers before us have done. We have watched ourselves and our children grow. We have witnessed another seasonal cycle in the life of the village of Nettlesden. Each year that cycle repeats itself, but each year isn't the same. This year, we have taken from the fields something we didn't think to find. That is the power of the land – it holds the past within its grasp. And sometimes it chooses to open its hands so we can glimpse at the treasures within it, or we can witness its shame. We unsettled the past when we dug within it, disturbing what was at peace. And what we saw was unkind. We needed to lay it to rest once more by placing it honestly into earth, into the womb from whence it came. And that is what we all did. That time was a time of doubt for us all, a time which disrupted the life that we know. But I believe that time is now over. And we are better it's done. The village has shown resilience. It has shown we are able to pull together – that nothing can pull us apart. Adversity has made us stronger. I would like to thank you, dearest friends, for coming together again, as one. I would like to give thanks for this year.

Jack spreads his arms wide, like the priest of nature, embracing the village, his flock. I want to go and congratulate him. I am starting towards him when a hand on my arm distracts me and begs me to turn. My timid assailant is Travis.

— Can I have a word?

—

— Maybe we could walk.

—

— I've been thinking about what you said the other day. I've done a lot of thinking. I've decided I'm going to move away. The pub isn't doing that well. To be honest, the pub is losing money. For several years now, it's run at a loss. It's eating into my savings. It can't continue, and I can't see a way to turn its fortunes around. I need to move on.

— I'm sorry to hear it.

— But the pub isn't the main reason for deciding to go. I'm leaving Samantha as well.

— Does she know?

— Not yet. I'm planning on telling her soon. I wanted to talk to you first.

— What about?

— I want to talk to you first. I've got a proposition for you. It's something I hope you'll consider.

—

— I want you to come with me when I leave. I want us to be together. I've never been happier than I have been this summer. I've never been happier than when I'm with you. Thinking about you, being with you. There's so much I think we've both got in common. There's so much I think we could share. So much potential for happiness that we could give to each other. We know who we are, and we fit.

– Travis…

– I want you to think about it. That's all. To think about us. To think about sharing the rest of our lives. Of being together forever. I don't need an answer right now.

– Is your mind made up?

– Yes.

– To leave the village? To leave Samantha? No matter what I might say?

– I think so.

– Have you thought through all that this means?

– Yes. But somehow, now, it seems less of a risk. It seems the only option I have.

– What if I say no?

– I'll still go. I think. I'm afraid to be on my own. Of course I'm afraid. And I want to have you beside me. To be here with me, to share with me, to know that you'll be here forever. But I think on my own – even without you – even then, I still have to leave. Samantha and I are different people. It's only my fear of being alone that has kept us together so long. But that's not a reason for staying together.

– Travis…

– I don't want to pressure you into an answer. I want you to think about what I've said. Promise me that you'll give it some thought.

I look beyond Travis towards the fields, at the broad, flat plain of stubbled earth. The sun spills its warmth; it buries its richness deep in the welcoming land. At the foot of the garden, where the lawn meets the field, I can see Bill and Margaret are looking at us.

I think I could answer him now if he wanted. There is almost no doubt in my mind.

From behind us, I hear there is someone approaching. A confident step, a sure tread on the earth. It is Jack who is coming to join us. I reach out, wanting to take his hand, but he holds his arms to his sides.

– Sarah, would you come with me, please? Travis, would you excuse us?
– Of course. Is anything wrong?
– Come through here. Follow me. I thought we might speak in my study.
– What is it?
– Here. Yes. Would you mind if I close the door?
– What is it, Jack?
– Thank you for coming today. Did you hear what it was that I had to say?
– Yes. I thought it was a lovely speech. I was coming to congratulate you.
– I believe we are over what happened this summer. I believe we are beginning to heal.
– So do I.
– Will you listen to what I have to say please. It has been a dangerous time for the village. I don't wish to have it repeated. I don't wish to make us vulnerable, from those on the outside, or from those from within. I think that people are settling down; they are willing to accept what is past. In time, they may even forget. There is only one aspect I continue to fear.
– What's that?
– It is you, Sarah.
– Me?
– Yes. I fear you won't let it lie. I fear you continue to worry the village. You don't seem to respect what is buried. You want to keep it alive.

311

– Jack, I respect you enormously…

– Then hear me out. I know neither the detail of it, nor the motive. And, in truth, I have little interest in knowing. All I know is what I can see. I see a woman who arrived in our village, secretly, on her own, and at night. We didn't question why you came on your own; we didn't intrude on your past. Instead, we sought to welcome you here, to embrace you into our fold. And, as honest God-fearing people, we felt it our duty, we wanted to help. We hoped you would make this your home. We hoped you would settle down and be happy, but it hasn't happened that way. In the months since then, I have seen you send your son back to London, I have seen you stop attending our church, I have seen you consort with a married man, I have seen you hound my son and his wife, I have seen you disappoint my own wife – a woman who offered you nothing but kindness. I don't know why you have done these things. It's possible each has a reason behind it. But combined, they do nothing to strengthen our village, they do nothing to serve or support it. Instead, they seem wanton and purely destructive. I won't put this village at risk for your pleasure. I would ask you to pay more respect to these people – to those who are living and those who are dead. I would urge you to value all that is here; to consider the village and place its needs above what you want for yourself. Or, if you cannot, if you do not want to, then politely, I would request that you leave.

~

# Autumn

So this is it. It is happening once more. It is happening the way I want it to happen. It is happening the way it must be. It has been so long since I turned towards London, since I faced to the south and to all that is there, since I drove down the A14. When I came up here, all those months ago, I didn't know where the road would lead me; I had no idea what I'd find. Back then, I was angry and blind. But now I know my destination. I know where I'm going and what will be there. And all I want is to hold it tight; and never to lose it again.

The morning sun is growing in strength; its early heat is filling the car. It warms the wind which brushes my face, it glances my elbow which rests on the frame. The fields lie undone, exposed to the air; their severed stalks awaiting the plough which will churn them back into the earth. The trees are weary; their leaves are crisp. This is an aging land. It is wise and mature; it basks in the warmth, knowing that warmth will soon die.

I'm approaching Ipswich. I look for the signs I followed before, trying to remember my way. It feels so long ago, and so different. As if I am living my life in reverse. Now, though, I know my direction is good; I know where I'm going is right. I follow the signs till I reach the station. I park the car and get out.

I buy a paper from one of the kiosks, and take it into the thick morning sunshine, resting against the back of a fence as I flick through its crisp crumpled sheets. I find it hard to concentrate. The words are blurred; they blank all meaning; even the photos fail to make sense.

I can feel an irregular stream of people walking past where I stand. I sense there is such happiness here, and such ineffable pain. These people are caught in a fractional cycle of coming together or taking their leave; clung to each other or torn from each other, with tears which span the spectrum of life. Before me, acted out on this stage, a continual contest of reunion and rupture, a cauldron of charged and changing emotions, a chaos of cameos leading to nothing, melting away in the sun.

There are posters of perfect families who are boarding a train with buckets and spades; of children pointing at landmarks in London; of a businessman wearing a bowler hat with an umbrella hung from his arm. I remember seeing Matty stood here, on this very same platform, half-hid in the shade. I remember a sheer pool of brilliant sunlight spilt on the tarmac behind him. I see the same pool spread out before me, smiling and waiting for him to return.

I can hear the approach of a train, I can see it draw close, sluggishly wheezing its wheels on the track. Two or three people are standing like me, awkward and giddy with hope. The train is slowing; its body slides past me; its windows flicker like frames in a film. I try to capture and freeze just one snippet: to see inside its confusion of colour, and from within it to try and draw sense.

The train has come to a halt. I hear the sharp click of opening doors; the smash as the same doors are closed. People emerge from all points of the train, pulling at bags as their searching eyes latch on this patchwork of shade.

Now I see Matty. I can see he is climbing down from the carriage; I can see he has picked me out from the crowd. He is wandering over unhurriedly, a single bag in his hand.

He's taller than I remember he was. He's less a boy than a man. His hair is tangled; his skin is smooth: it looks unblemished and soft. I want to enfold him in an embrace; to feel the warmth of that hug returned. I want to show him how much I have missed him; how much it means to see him return. I rustle his hair with my hand. I try taking his bag, and I hear him laugh. I see his teeth, the pink of his tongue. My fingers touch against his arm as we stand in a queue at the foot of the stairs.

The seats are hot in the car. I open the roof and wind down the windows. Matty climbs into the passenger side. I had thought to ask him so many questions, but the words don't come to my mind. Where he has been and what he has done doesn't matter now he is here. It's enough just to have him beside me. I feel the same contentment from him: a content to be in the country once more, a content to call it his home. He looks out over the short-cropped fields, over the tapestry of hunched trees, up thin tracks and over gates, across parched plains and gentle hills, at this flat land laid out around us. He's re-engaging, he's breathing it in; he's recalling its texture, its substance, its smell. His face is alive with expectation. This is where he has wanted to be.

We drive through Marshfield. I sense a growing anticipation, a restlessness that he cannot contain. It seems he wants to reach through the windows, to explore this world with his hands. These roads are like old friends to Matty; he knows their pattern so well. But never before has he seen them like this: the fields stripped bare, the trees so ripe, the hedges full, the leaves turned pale, the ditches cracked and dry. There is so much more for him to discover; there is so much more he can find. He watches it all; he asks no questions; he wants to learn it himself.

I turn the car down our stunted track and let it glide to a halt. He opens the door and gets out. I watch him as he drinks in the garden, feeling the rush of its life wash round him, almost frightened to touch. I follow him over the lawn to the house. Inside, he's inquisitive too. I watch his eyes unpacking the room: the approval of seeing familiar things, the attentiveness to what's new. He notices the haphazard detail: where books have been placed, where a jug has been moved, where spoils of petals are strewn.

The baked potatoes are cool in the oven. I place them on two plates from the fridge, alongside slices of ham and some cheese, a handful of pickles and salad. I am carrying them out to put on the table when Matty appears in his boots.

– Matty, not now. Have some lunch first.
– I'm not hungry. I want to go out.
– Let's have some food first, and then I'll come with you. I've found some new places I think that you'll like.
– I want to go to the wood.
– You've only just arrived.
– So?
– So, wouldn't it be nice if we did something together?
– What? Like digging your veg?
– No. Like going for a walk.
– I don't want to. I want to go to the wood.
– I want you to eat first. I don't want you just running off.
– What are you trying to do? When you want me here, you make demands. When you don't, you shove me onto a train. I'm not just a thing to manipulate.
– I'm not manipulating you. I'm thinking of what's good for you. Of what would be best.

– No, you're not. You want me to do what you want when you want it. You don't care about what I want.

– Of course I do.

– No, you don't. You know what I want to do now. You know what I want, and you've told me I can't.

– Because it's lunchtime. Because I haven't seen you for so long. Because…

– Why don't you do what I want for a change? Why don't you let me do what I want? For God's sake, I've only just got here. I didn't want this conversation. I wanted to start off afresh.

– I do want you to do what you want.

– You don't show it. You only appear to think about you.

– Matty, please.

– You never think about how what you do might affect the others around you. You don't think about the hurt that you cause them. You don't think about how they might feel.

– What's wrong, Matty? What have I done wrong?

– As if you care. If you knew me, you would know what is wrong. If you knew me or Dad, then this wouldn't have happened. Then none of it would have had to happen.

– None of what?

– How can you be so blind? It's almost like you don't want to see. Like you're purposely shutting us out. I'm going now. You can come if you like. I'm going off to the wood.

Matty walks into the gleaming garden, leaving the door ajar. I look at the laden plates in my hands; the potatoes are damp and deflated. I can hear Matty's boots on the dry whispering grass as he follows the lawn round the side of the house. Now, I can hear only silence. The room is dull in the constant shadow. I can see Matty's bag on the floor where he left it, in the hall by the foot of the stairs.

I lay down both of the plates on the table. I walk through the door and into the day. A slow breeze ruffles the air. I follow the path that Matty has taken, till I'm looking out over the field. Matty has gone; he's obscured by the hedge; he is lost on the rambling track. I picture him marching close to the road, steadily closing in on the wood.

I stare out before me, but I can see nothing. Nothing besides a mountain beet, its large white roots like rotund corpses heaped in a pile of the dead. Nothing besides the clods of ploughed earth stretching into the endless distance like a vast, brown, desolate sea. Nothing besides the island of trees where Rose House Farm juts out like a mirage, stood in the vacant heart of the field.

I find I am tracing the track by the road, around Six Bells and the Rectory gardens till I reach the edge of the graveyard. I find myself passing the body of logs, skirting the bone-dry girdle of thorn, seeking an entrance into the wood. It is here.

I glance back into the day. At the pastel sky, at the huge dirt field, at the lines that are forged in its broken skin, then I slip within the curl of the wood, bending under its boughs.

I can hear the creak of aching trunks, the scatter of birds, the shiver of leaves. I imagine the deep roots sunk in the soil, feeling blindly into the earth, binding themselves round a headless body, drawing their life from its bones. I feel the give of the living floor, the snap of dead branches, the shake of dry leaves, the velvet touch of obsequious moss.

I scratch my way to the heart of the wood, shuffling down ditches, stooped beneath branches, feeling the spring of sinuous saplings, the snag of bramble and thorn.

Matty emerges before me. He's dragging a broken bough through the leaves, its smaller branches trawling the ground, trailing behind them the strands of a vine. He's heaving one end in the crook of a tree, pulling it firmly into position, testing its strength with his arms.

– Is there anything I can do?
– It's you. I didn't hear you. How did you find me?
– I just did. What can I do?
– What do you mean?
– How can I help?
– What with?
– With that. What are you building?
– This?
– Yes. What's it going to be?
– Why are you here? What are you doing here?
– I'm not doing anything. Not at the moment. Can you give me something to do?
– Like what?
– I don't know. What do you want me to do?

Matty examines my face for a moment, as if he is searching for something within. I wait for him to finish his study; I wait till he's ready to speak. I can hear a murmur amongst the trees; I can see bright patches of blinding light filtering through the canopy. The wood is making its choice.

– All right then. This is a den. It's quite basic. It's going to be a single room, but I might build onto it if it works.
– What do you need?
– More branches.
– What sort of branches?
– Thin, long, straight ones. I'm making the skeleton. I'll cover it once we've made the structure.

I look about me for pieces of wood. The floor is strewn with detritus. I pull at a branch that is closest to me, dragging it out from a strangle of nettle that holds it fast to the ground. I can sense that Matty has stopped and is watching; he is watching me till I come to his side, till I lay the broken limb at his feet. I ask what he wants me to do with it now. He seems confused. Not because of what he is building, but because I am here, right beside him. He points at the shoulder which leads from the spine; he helps me to raise one end of the bough. Together we bring it into position. I lift the upturned end in the air while he stoops and shunts at its base. Then I seek through the scrub for another rib, wrenching its body from under the leaves, dragging it back to the den.

I make more journeys, building the ribcage, bone by bone, down the supple length of its spine. My arms are tingling with the weight and effort; I can feel a gentle warmth in their sockets, a trickle of sweat down my sides.

Matty designs in his mind as we work; he sketches the next stage of build. I search for creepers to thread through the ribcage, binding the torso in place. Then we ground the legs of the den in the earth, using our feet to sink the branches into the mould of soft soil. We seek out a scatter of thin leafy branches, strapping their stems through the chest like its sinews, clothing the body with skin.

And now, it's complete. Matty and I stand back to admire. His breathing is hard; his face is flushed. He leans against me, just for a moment, to remove a twig from his shoe.

We sweep out the floor of the den, using our palms to flatten its surface. Then we enter our newly made world. It is shaded and cool, though the earth beneath us is warm.

The structure seems a part of the wood: it shivers and moans and bends like the trees, though its body is firm and secure. I catch his eye for an instant. I think he can feel the same feeling too: a sense of sanctuary, of refuge, of peace, here, in the heart of the wood. His hair is tangled with leaves and twigs; his face is slightly swollen and scratched; his skin is speckled with earth. I touch at my face and feel the same. He stares at me, then he laughs.

We crawl from the entrance and stand to its side as Matty talks through his creation. I am starting in search of a new crop of branches when he puts out his hand to prevent me. He says we have built enough for one day. It's hot and he's hungry; it's time to go home; the den can wait till tomorrow.

We trace a trail through the pathless wood, leading each other towards the light. The steady sun stares down at us as we reach the encircling thorn. We skirt the furrows beside Road Field till we come to the cottage's lawn. The plates on the table are just as I left them. The ham has curled; the potatoes are cold. We sit on the bench in the eye of the day, picking at food with our hands.

It is late afternoon. I feel the gradual wane of the sun, the stealthy appearance of lengthening shadow casting its shade on the lawn. I ask if he wants to return to the wood; to build on what we have made. Once more, I feel a cautious enquiry from Matty's questioning gaze. He says he would rather stay in the garden; we've done enough in the wood.

I suggest another project to him. Though the grass has scarcely grown in the heat, the surrounding hedges are dense and disordered. Their long leafy twigs are straggling upwards; their stems are scratching the air.

Matty needs little persuasion. He assaults the hedge with a pair of shears, diving amidst the waving branches, cutting them back to an even base, clipping clean lines down the length of the lawn till the chaos is once more contained.

I watch him as he sets to the task. He works with speed, and with care. He plans the line, the shape, the height; he instinctively knows how to keep it straight. He's at peace and happy when here in the garden, no less engaged than when in the wood, when building his dens in its depths.

I walk around the side of his hedge and enter the vegetable patch. I take out my knife and sever a marrow; I pick a clutch of tomatoes. I am taking them back towards the cottage when I hear steps approach from the road.

I lay down the fruit on the low brick wall and turn to see it is Travis. His face is flushed though the day is not hot; he seems bothered and struggling for breath. Patches of sweat melt his shirt to his chest. He has never been here without being asked.

– Travis. How are you? What's wrong?
– It's Samantha. She's gone.
– What do you mean, she's gone?
– She's left me. She's left the pub. She left me a note. She's taken her clothes.
– When?
– At lunchtime. While I was serving behind the bar. She came downstairs without me hearing. And now she's gone.
– I'm so sorry. Maybe it's because of what you told her. Maybe it's a natural reaction.
– What did I tell her?
– About you leaving her. About you leaving the pub.
– But I haven't told her yet. I still haven't told her.

– I thought you said…

– Yes, but I was waiting on you. I was waiting, in the hope you would answer.

I look at Travis. I look at the man with the angular fringe stood on the grass before me. I feel only pity. I pity his weakness, his indecision. I pity him now that his aimless world is slipping beyond his control. It's not hard to find fault with the things that you have, yet when they are gone then you miss them. Perhaps, in his heart, he still loves her.

– Have you thought about what I said?

– Yes, Travis, I have.

– I haven't pressed you for an answer. I haven't wanted to hurry you.

– Yes, I know. I appreciate that. I've been wanting to let you know what I think.

– And…?

– I think you already know my answer. I think you have always known what it was.

– Will you come with me?

– No, I can't. You know that I can't.

– Couldn't you see us together?

– I've enjoyed the time that we've spent together. And like you, I think we have some things in common. But meeting up once or twice a week is different from living together.

– Couldn't we try?

– I don't think that's wise. I like you, but there aren't any stronger feelings. Besides, there is somebody else.

– Matty?

– Someone else besides.

– In London?

– Yes.

– You never really left. You never really left him, did you?

– Perhaps not, no.

– So, do you think you'll go back there?

– I don't know if I can.

– But, if you could, then would you?

– I'm so sorry, Travis. I didn't mean to lead you on. I hope you've never thought that. What are you going to do now?

– I don't know.

– Are you going to do what you said you would do? Are you going to sell the pub and move on?

– I don't know any more. It all… it all seems so pointless suddenly.

– It's not pointless. Remember Rackham. Remember what you told me at Martha's party. You had the resolve; you had the determination then.

– I still had options. I had the comfort of things as they were. Perhaps, if I wait, Samantha will come back.

– And what happens then? Will you be happier then?

– I don't know. I really don't know any more.

Travis seems to have shrunk. His head hangs low. But not so low that I cannot see the helplessness in his eyes. It looks as if he will cry. I step forward and hug him. I feel the fleshiness of his body; I smell the stench of his sweat. His frame is shuddering beyond his control.

I take his hand, walking him down the gradual slope, leading him back to the pub. His shoes are scraping against the road. He's a little boy lost, beyond his own pity. He has no idea what to do.

We enter the pub. The room is crouched and in darkness. It is empty, like so often before, yet it seems more desolate still. There is no one here. There is no one upstairs. No random tremor of muffled feet to stir the silence above.

I seat him in a chair by the hearth and put on the kettle behind the bar. I pour a brandy, a glass of Baileys. I put cups and saucers onto a tray. I fill the room with familiar sounds, with the welcome clatter and shiver of glass. From the bar I steal a glance at Travis. His body is leant towards the hearth, his palms pressed tight to his ears.

I hand a cup of coffee to him, but he waves away the offer of brandy. I ask him what he wants to do now, but he isn't able to comprehend. I try to give him some reassurance; I say, in time, he will reason it out. But the words have no meaning to him or to me. They are hollow, and both of us know it. All purpose has vanished. The little that ever there was has ended; his resolution is draining away. There is only him in this empty room. Him and a stale cup of coffee.

It's approaching opening time. I try speaking to Travis once more. I clasp his hands in the cup of my palms and raise them till he is looking at me. I can put out a notice to say the pub's closed. He can go upstairs and I'll run the bar; I can say that he's feeling unwell. He shakes his head; he insists he will open; this part of his world will go on.

Travis shuffles round to the bar, doing whatever it is he must in anticipation of opening. Right now, his routine is all that he needs. That daily routine he has kept up for years. For its comfort, its surety, its distraction.

I watch him in silence; he's constantly active; there are so many small things to keep him employed. Polishing beer taps, sorting the crisps, placing the cocktail sticks in a cup. For the next six hours he will keep himself busy, washing his mind of all else. I lose myself in his gentle action, in the soothing noises which come from the bar. I will stay with him and watch for a while. I cannot trust him alone.

The door is opening. Uriah enters. He assumes his usual place at the bar, awaiting his tankard to be placed before him. I watch and I fear for Travis. But there isn't a need. There's nothing to show in Travis' face, nothing to show in all that he does, that this evening is not as the others before. It is as it is – as it has to be – always and ever the same. The same ease of motion, almost of grace, as he reaches up for the pewter tankard, as he draws the beer, as he lays it down, as he takes the money and handles the change. The act of being behind the bar erases awareness of what lies beyond. There, enclosed in its sheltering walls, Travis is safe for the while.

Bill and Margaret have entered the pub. They come over to greet me, to sit down beside me. They offer to buy me a drink. I look at Bill as he stands by the bar, wondering if he will notice a difference. Margaret is eagerly talking to me, but she also follows my gaze. I think she thinks I am staring at Travis; she's thinking the intrigue she wants to believe. Travis is chatting with Bill as he serves. There's no hesitation, no fault to his movement; his voice is easy and low. I could almost believe that he has forgotten. He hands Bill his change with the same honest smile. It's a warming, a comfortable smile.

From Margaret I find out the prices of wholesale; the names of people who work in the warehouse; the scale of the stock they have bought. I discover that baked beans sell better than pasta; that sales of wine exceed those of beer.

I let her talk on without thinking to listen; she gives me a reason to stay. I can't believe that Travis is able to keep the pretence through the whole of the evening. The truth must sidle up and confront him, in a thought, a gesture, a word.

I offer to buy the next round of drinks. Travis comes over and takes my order, though he already knows what it is. I watch him carefully drawing the beer; I watch as he uncorks the wine. All the while, he is talking to us; he is talking of trivial things. He comes and gives me my change. I look in his face, ignoring his words. This is no deception, no sham. He has taken another identity; he's a different person entirely. I touch his hand with my own, wanting to see if a simple touch will jog him back to himself. But there isn't pause to his easy movement, no hesitancy in his speech.

I can feel the others are watching me. I remove my hand from the table.

Uriah has left. Peter Faraday comes in for a pint before he hurries back home. There's no sign of Robert Witton tonight. Bill insists on buying more drinks. He says they have spent the whole of the day moving their stock from a warehouse in Ipswich to the close, cramped store at the back of their shop. He says he has built up a thirst.

Travis washes and cleans and dries. At one stage he comes to clear our table. Once more I glance up at the man. He is calmer now. So calm and assured. I know he will see out the evening. Each evening – every time he is here – he can forge a new self and escape. He can find a way to forget. What I don't know is what is likely to happen when he closes the door, when he goes upstairs, when he sheds the barman, becoming the man. When he has to live that again.

It's dark outside. I'm tired of listening to Margaret and Bill. I'm thinking of Matty, of what he is doing, of what he must think of me now. All I want is to be back home and with him. With the people I care for, the people I love. To hole up and stay there forever.

Bill drains his glass and walks to the door. He's going ahead to lock up the shop. I get up to follow him out. But Margaret refuses to leave me alone. She catches my hand and begs me to stay. Her voice is slurred, her eyes slightly blood-shot. She insists on keeping me with her.

– Have you discovered anything else recently, dear?

– Like what?

– O, I don't know. Something random. Maybe another skull?

– No, I haven't.

– How dull.

– Not really. Actually, I find it quite nice.

– You find it nice not being the centre of attention?

– If you want to put it that way, yes, I do.

– I thought you enjoyed the limelight, my dear.

– Well, believe me, I don't.

– But you're always centre-stage.

– If that's true, it's not by design. It's merely coincidence.

– It must be nice being on the Community Council. Discussing all those different issues. Getting to hear things first-hand.

– I suppose so.

– I get to hear about them too, of course, from Bill. But it isn't exactly the same. Martha invited you on, didn't she? Almost as soon as you arrived.

– Yes. You can take my place if you want.

– Ha! What an extraordinary idea! Did you ever find out whose skull it was?

– No, I didn't.

– It was nice of you to confide in Bill. I think you like talking to Bill.

– He was being considerate. That's all.

– You like men, don't you?

– Margaret, I try to like everyone.

– Yes, but you like the company of men in particular. It must be so lonely on your own in the cottage.

– A bit, yes. But I have Matty.

– That's not quite the same as a man. I think we should fix you up with a man.

– I'm married.

– Yes. But not really 'married' married. I think I should find you a man.

– I really don't need one.

– How about that man, over there? The one behind the bar. He's a man.

– He's married, too.

– That shouldn't stop you.

– Margaret, I think you need to know something. I'm not having an affair with Travis. It might look like it to you. You might like to think it. But it's not true. He's a friend…

– Yes, he is.

– I'm being serious. There's nothing between us. I've met up with him on a few occasions, as I would meet up with anyone else – with anyone else who I like. But that doesn't mean we're having an affair. I am married. I am true to my husband. I still love him.

– Do you? Is that true?

– Yes, it is.

– You love your husband? Then why did you leave him?

– There are some things, Margaret, that I don't want to share. Not with anyone. Not with you.

– You love your husband? I didn't think anyone loved their husbands. Not after so many years of marriage. I don't love mine.

– Margaret, I think you should go home.

– Why? Everyone knows it. The whole world knows it. He knows it. Why don't you ask him?

– I'm sure you and Bill are very happy. You're a pair. You're always together.

– We have to be together, stupid. That doesn't mean we like being together. That doesn't mean we've got a life.

– You do. You've got the shop. You've got your neighbours…

– But nothing happens to us. Nothing happens to me. It does to you. You arrive here, and Martha takes you under her wing. Do you know… do you know how many times I've been to supper with Martha? No times. That's how many. You swan around. You find a skull. Without trying, people are flocking around you. That doesn't happen to me.

– I think you're quite lucky it doesn't happen to you.

– Can you imagine what it's like, being on the sideline, watching it happen? Watching the whole world happening around you, and none of it happening directly to you? Can you imagine what it's like, living through other people's lives? Your whole life being the sum of others'?

– Then why don't you focus more on your own?

– Ha…!

Margaret waves a hand in the air, exasperated, seeming lost for the words. I walk round the table and take her arm, helping her out of her seat. She doesn't resist. I guide her over towards the door, calling to Travis to say that we're leaving. Now he is here on his own. To close the pub and to go upstairs. To confront himself once he's there.

Outside, the sky is a deep rich blue, ponderous with purple-grey cloud. The air is thin and chill. The night is settling into its stride, drifting into eternal darkness, as if ready to spin from its natural cycle, to forge a course with no end.

All will become a boundless blackness, and there is nothing beyond. It stretches into the unknown distance. Beyond all sight, beyond all sound, beyond my power to grasp. Unspoilt by any moon or stars, by any hint of life. Just as awaiting death might be, as it closes you round in its folds.

I walk Margaret over to Wayside House, feeling her resting her weight on my arm. I watch her fumbling to fit her key into the heart of the lock. For a moment, I feel detached from myself – as if I'm looking in on myself – at my tired bent body, angry and wretched, unable to find my way home.

The latch snaps back. Margaret mumbles a gruff goodnight. Then she pushes straight past me. She closes the door.

~

We've completed the den and extended its bounds. I have bought some rope from the store in Marshfield and Matty has built an aerial platform in a cup of split branches, hidden by leaves. He reaches his crow's nest by climbing the rope, bending his knees in a vertical breaststroke, squeezing his feet against the knots to give himself purchase and push to the next. When at the top, he's lost in the mantle; he's only betrayed by the quivering leaves.

He has made more snares; we have made them together. Our traps have spring-loaded doors. Creatures that follow our baited trail can nuzzle their way within the wire cage, though they have no means of escape. We've caught rabbits and squirrels and voles in our traps, and all are released to the wild. In building these cages we've had to dismantle all of Matty's old snares.

A new routine is dictating our days. After breakfast we march round the field to the wood. Sometimes I help him with what he's creating: building more dens, or digging a tunnel, or looping a rope between trees. But more often than not, I sit to one side, my laptop laid on my knees. I never thought I would work in the open, being disrupted by leaves on my keyboard, feeling the breeze in my face. It's harder to focus on what I am doing, but I find the distraction a joy.

I look through the crowded trunks of the trees into the shadowy heart of the wood, hearing the strains of its solemn music, the low natural notes which come from no throat. I feel the comforting earth beneath me, the cover of leaves which settles around me. I think of the dismembered body below. It is lucky to be here, at rest.

I watch Matty interact with the wood, his mind so inventive, his motion so quick. When he tires of his tasks, he comes to my side, his face alert and alive. Sometimes we bring a picnic with us; sometimes we stay here all day. His school can wait before he returns. These are sharing times, and here there is peace. It's a beautiful place to be shared.

When the sun begins to lose its strength, when the heat is filtered away through the soil, we creep back into that other existence, beyond the ploughed spread of Road Field. Rose House Farm is a distant land, a deserted island, set in the heart of a furrowed sea. All that is past is buried behind us; all that is past has now gone. The present is only Matty and me. We spend our evenings sat in the garden, watching the birds give way to the bats, staring at stars and the cold-faced moon, close to a fire whose molten core expands and collapses in luminous worlds where all is vibrant and pure.

Some days we stay away from the wood. We busy ourselves in the idle garden; we go for a walk by a curling river; we cycle down secretive tracks between fields, lost in the depths of the ripening country, happy to be on our own.

We are almost complete.

It seems so long since I last went to church; so long since I went to the pub. I have not seen Martha, or Bill, or Travis for so long they are almost forgotten. They feel like a part of a different world, of a different journey, a different life. One which was troubled and incomplete. One which was poorer for being without you, for not having you at its heart.

Sometimes, when I look out on the field, I can see a faint figure that I know is Uriah, pacing the fringe of the wood with his gun. Sometimes, in the bristling wind, I glance at the silver-tipped leaves in the hedge, I feel the glare of its watching eyes. But neither worry me now. We live off the land, off the food that we grow. We are content as we are. At peace with ourselves; at peace with each other. Happy, and almost entire.

Morning. A thick wind blows down the road to the church. The air is not cold, though the sun is lost behind a belt of closely bound cloud, stretching from end to end of the sky, secured on either horizon. Leaves spin across the unlevel fields, finding a refuge in hollows and holes. Crows hang suspended, upwind, in the air, beating their black wings to nowhere.

People are coming out of the church. The vicar stands to the side of the porch, his cassock caught by the wind. Jack and Martha are shaking his hand while leaning into the gale.

They shuffle down the winding path that leads through the churchyard onto the road. Uriah follows behind. I think, for a moment, that Joyce is beside him, caught in the crook of his arm. Now Bill and Margaret have entered the day, huddling close as they weave through the graves. There is no one else in the church. I can see Colin Inchmore return to its body. Soon he will leave for the service at Marshfield; the church will stand vacant all week.

I have reached the corner beside the graveyard. I wonder if fresh flowers have been laid on the mound which hides the face of the skull. I wonder if those flowers have been tied with a loving strand of blue ribbon. I realise I no longer care. I have no interest in knowing.

In the church hall, Martha is laying out cups. Bill is placing the chairs in a circle, while Travis is standing alone. It is only he who looks up at me, and only then for an instant. He turns away, as if he's ashamed, as if he doesn't want to be seen. He helps himself to some tea. I walk up to Martha and say good morning, but she is preoccupied with the urn and she doesn't respond to my greeting. Now Peter Faraday enters the room. Martha motions us to the chairs.

– I've asked Peter to come and introduce the main item on our agenda. And then, if he wouldn't mind, to leave the room. Since he has got a conflict of interest, I think it only right and proper that he isn't here to witness the process by which we reach our decision. Peter has agreed to my terms. So, shall we proceed on that basis?
– Yes, of course. It seems strange addressing you all from this side. As most of you will be aware, the organic food business is doing well. It may not be in the mainstream yet, but then neither is it a fad. I believe it will only get bigger.

I've been fortunate enough to grow my business on the back of increasing demand, and now I have come to the stage where I need to expand. For a long time now, I've had an arrangement to lease from Jack the fields which lie just south of Jennings' Land. I've farmed them for more than twenty years. Now I'm in need of more land. Ideally, I would like to purchase one of the fields adjacent. Or, saving that, to lease it long term, in order to safeguard my business. I'm not betraying confidence when I say I have already spoken to the Pooleys, and that neither is able to accommodate me. I understand and respect their position. Their livelihoods are linked to the land, and their farms are both being worked. The pressure of expansion isn't on them, but the land is theirs, as is the decision. It means, though, that unless I secure more space for myself, I'll be forced to move from the village. The only stretch not owned by the Pooleys is Steeple Field, which – as all of you know – has always been communal. The Local Authority will lease it to me, and terms are already agreed. However, I would like your approval too, because the field belongs to the village, and the Community Council protects its interests – even if, in practice, it has no sway. I believe the expansion will be good for the village, bringing with it more work and more people. These won't be people who come from the city, but country folk who respect our ways. I've been in this village for all of my life, and this is the only place I have farmed. I like the village and I want to support it. I want to give it the chance to grow. It has been my friend, and with your consent I can help to give it a new lease of life. Nettlesden is where I have based my business, but it's also the place I call home. I appeal to your hearts as much as your heads, to approve my lease of Steeple Field. I will respect your decision in this matter.

– Thank you, Peter. That was nicely put. Now, if you wouldn't mind leaving us, the Council will consider your proposal.

– Thank you.

– So, unless there are questions of clarification, I suggest that we proceed to debate. Bill?

– It seems a shame to lose Steeple Field. It will mean an end to the Summer Fair, unless we can find somewhere else. But other than that, his points are good. Both Travis and I will gain more custom, and growing the village based around farming has to be the best way. I guess it just feels a little bit daunting, having more people around us.

– Travis?

– More trade would be a good thing. As would more work. The village is so small. It sometimes feels dead. Peter's proposal should bring it to life.

– That's an interesting perspective. Sarah, do you have any thoughts?

– I'm glad for Peter that his business is booming. I think we ought to support him. Isn't that what the Council is all about – supporting each other as well as the village?

– Yes, it is. Though we need to look at the broader context. It's important that all of us benefit from it, not just a few at the others' expense. Steeple Field is ours for a reason, because, like the church, it is there for us all. If we give it away, then we forfeit a part of the village to which we belong. Something we share would be lost to us all. We would also sacrifice a tradition in no longer hosting a Summer Fair. An occasion which helps to promote our village, which brings rewards of its own. An event we have run every year since the war. If we lose our tradition, we confuse our purpose. We endanger all that we have.

– I understand that. But if we lose Peter's business, we lose the village. He's the only one here who makes any money. He's the only one here who has any children. Without him, the village would die. He's offering to bring in more custom and farming, to build back the village on traditional lines. And he's generously agreed to consult with the Council when he's already got a green light. I don't see the problem.

– The problem, Sarah, is one of tradition. How we use the land. How we choose to farm.

– Surely it's good that his farm is thriving. It's good for us all, not just him. Why does it matter he's an organic farmer?

– It matters completely. We're exposing ourselves to different ways. We're exposing ourselves to things we don't know.

– We know Peter. He's been here all of his life. You can't wrap the village in cotton wool and expect that it will survive. You can't block out what's happening around us.

– You don't understand tradition. How things are done.

– And, with all due respect, I don't think you understand how precarious the future is for the village. If you deny him, then you're denying us all. It feels sad to me your objections seem to be based on the arbitrary fact that Peter's family don't own the land; that they haven't lived here for generations; that he's spotted a trend in our eating habits and has had the sense to embrace it.

– Don't under-estimate tradition. We wouldn't be as we are without it. If we start by sacrificing a part, we may end up losing the whole.

– What are you actually sacrificing? An empty field that's used once a year for a Fair. You could run that Fair on Jack's set-aside. You wouldn't lose anything; you would only gain. The whole village gains. I haven't been here for as long as you. I don't care for the village as much as you.

And frankly, this isn't my world. But I think it would be an enormous mistake if we were to say no to Peter. And I can't believe you can't see that.

— Well, I think we all know Sarah's view, and I hope I have made my position clear. I think it is for the other two to express a stronger opinion.

— I abstain. I think it is right that I should. The pub's on the market; I'm moving away. I no longer have a long-term interest, so I don't think it's proper I vote.

— Thank you, Travis. I believe you are right. I'm afraid, Bill, it comes down to you.

— I could do with more custom. You all know that I could. But, as it is, I survive. I am well into my fifties now. I'm getting close to retirement. This is where I live, and it's where I will die. I know this village. I know what it is. I know it as the place that it is. I don't want to see it wither away. But I don't want to see it radically change. I like Peter immensely. He's a very good man. I see good in what he's proposing. But I also see risk. More unfamiliar faces, more traffic. A future that's maybe less certain.

— Then you're not in favour?

— I don't like risk. I don't like disruption. I like things the way that they are.

— I take that as being you are not in favour.

— Bill, things won't be as they are if Peter leaves. Are you speaking for the village or for...?

— Sarah, I would ask you not to try and influence the vote. We have all had a chance to speak. We have all expressed our opinions. We should let members vote of their own free will.

— Then, if we are done, would you excuse me?

— Of course.

I get up and move away from the circle. Bill and Travis both shift in their seats; I can sense their discomfort, their shame. Travis is feeling he shouldn't have abstained. Bill is sensing he shouldn't have been led by what was expected of him. By what Martha hoped he would say.

It is all too late.

I push the door open and stand by the road. The wind feels thick and heavy around me. On the farther side of the road is the graveyard, on the closer side is Steeple Field. Both are desolate, harbouring death, for being bereft of the promise of life. I shouldn't care. This isn't my village. This isn't my home, nor where I belong. The change, or the lack of it, won't affect me. I may still live here, I may still be here, but in truth I've already moved on.

Bill has come out and is standing beside me; he follows my gaze over Steeple Field. I wonder if he considers the village an entity entire in itself, or merely a fiefdom of Pooleys. I wonder how he will see out his days, and how much change he will witness by then. I wonder what will become of the village, for all that Martha does to protect it, for all that she does to halt its progress. The land is all that there is to the village. It holds the future as much as the past. Both are in need of protection.

We walk back along the road to the pub. Bill wants to buy me a drink. Travis opens the door to the bar; he draws us both a half pint.

We take a seat near the empty fireplace, while Travis eases back to the barman: sorting the glasses, wiping the counter, replacing a barrel of beer. Bill is watching him, too; watching until he has rolled the barrel into the yard outside.

Then, in a low voice, he asks me directly if I know where Samantha has gone. Some say they have seen her in Marshfield, he tells me. Others believe she has gone back to Essex. They say she is seeing another man. She was never really a part of the village. In all the years she was here she knew no one, except Robert Witton of course.

Bill stops and looks up expectantly, hoping his innuendo will lead me to divulge a secret he doesn't yet know. I look away, and don't answer. I wonder how Travis is taking it all. By now he must know she's not coming back. Perhaps she has already told him as much. He's selling the pub; he's moving away. He's facing up to a new way of being. He's been forced into making a choice.

Bill tries again. He wants to know if Travis has told me where he is thinking of going to live. He wants to know what I think about Travis. He wants to know what I feel.

I turn to Bill. I tell him straight there is nothing between us. We're not having an affair, and we never have. I feel sorry for Travis, that's all.

Bill looks away and inspects his glass. He's resistant to hearing the truth. It is so much simpler, and so much duller, than what goes on in his mind.

But I haven't finished. I suggest he should pay more attention to Margaret; to invest more time in the life that they share. That is where his attention should be. He has made an important decision today, and he should reflect on what that might mean. On how his choice will affect his shop; on how it will shape the rest of his life. That is enough to worry about, without needing to busy himself with others. With Samantha and Travis and me.

I excuse myself and go to the toilet. When I return to the room, Bill has gone.

I want to go home and be with Matty. That is what I want right now. That is all that I want. I have almost reached the door of the pub when Travis comes in from the yard.

– I'm sorry I didn't support you today.
– That doesn't matter. We won't be affected by the decision. We won't be the ones who live with it.
– You will, if you decide to stay.
– Yes. But I'm not a part of the village. I'm not a part of the past. I'm part of the change. Part of what they are frightened about.
– They shouldn't be frightened of you. You care more about their village than they do. They only care for themselves.
– Maybe.
– Do you think you will stay?
– I can't see myself growing old here like Bill. But, in the short term, I really don't know.
– What will make you decide?
– I'm not sure. I see you have made your decision.
– Yes, the pub's being sold. In fact, it's already been sold. I just haven't had the guts to tell them.
– To tell them what?
– It's been bought by a couple from London. But not as a pub. They want to convert it into a house. They want it to be a holiday home. The Serpent is going to lose its licence.
– That's a shame.
– It's inevitable. I know it; you know it; Martha knows it. The problem is that she won't accept it. She won't accept that change will happen, whether or not she resists it.
– And you?

– I'm off soon. I'm not sure when. I think I'm going up north.

– Where?

– Are you interested?

– Interested in where you are going?

– Interested in coming with me.

– It's cold up north.

– It can be cold here, too.

– Yes, I know that.

– If ever you change your mind…

– I won't. My mind hasn't changed. It's never changed. I haven't always known it, that's all. Not as I know it now.

– Then I hope that things work out for you. Not just in your mind, but in your life.

– That's kind. And I hope the same is true for you, too.

– Do you want to know where I'm going? Would you like to keep in touch?

– Honestly? I think it's better not. Nothing will come of it.

– Well, goodbye then. And good luck.

– Goodbye, Travis.

I open the door and walk round the pub till I'm standing alone in Steeple Field. The wind gusts at my face, it tears at my hair, it whips my collar against my cheek. Leaves race across the storm-tossed grass, gusting through the fence to the road, swirling into the air. The low clouds locked against the sky close out all sense of a sun. Theirs is a facelessness, a greyness. They hang suspended above the earth. They do not move with the wind.

On the farther side, there's a gap in the hedge, leading into the car park. I picture rows of vintage cars; the roundabout and its giddy music; the engines puffing their steam. Here the children sat on bales, cheering the eager contestants.

Here Matty bounded across the line, clasping a sack to his chest. The white of the track is all washed out; the straw has all blown away. The only noise is the blast of the wind. All the people have gone.

Beyond Steeple Field is the stretch of Black Acre: the plot where Uriah first learned to hoe. It is ploughed and rolled, awaiting the seed, awaiting the oncoming year. Like the rest of the land, it stands ready. The fields themselves will always endure. They are as the seasons, in constant cycle. It is only mankind who moves on. The land takes the seed, it brings it to birth, it nurtures from youth to maturity, until it is ready to yield. It is cropped and made barren, it rests and it breathes, then it gives its succour once more. We tend to the land through our several lifetimes; we change through the years; we grow old. We leave the field, we traverse the road, we enter the churchyard to rest. We are laid at peace in its cradle. Only then do we pause on our journey, becoming a part of the cycle around us, confirmed in the body of earth.

Stood in the centre of Steeple Field, I can see the face of Burnt Tree Farm with the two black silos rising above it. I can see across the fresh ploughed earth to the desolate island of Rose House Farm. This is the dominion of the Pooleys: these two proud farms marooned in the fields. This sweep of land is their birthright. The infertile time is upon them now. The earth is empty, at rest. The wind sweeps over the fallow soil, churned by the blinded plough. Crows and seagulls peck at the entrails.

Winter waits for us all.

~

The air is fine and crisp; the sky pure crystal blue. From within the church there are faint sounds of voices, muffled behind the thick walls. It's been a while since we went to the wood, yet Matty walks straight past the track. He wants to follow the road instead; to explore the fields on the farther side. That is where he would lead me.

We walk past the graveyard and then the Serpent, beyond Wayside House and over a brook. We are through the village and out in the fields – in the vast sweep of all that belongs to the Pooleys.

The wind is pushing against our backs, blown from the north and chivvying us south, urging us up a slight rise. We walk quickly, not from feeling we need to, but from wanting to keep ourselves warm. I can feel the ruddiness of my cheeks, the clammy cold of my hands in my pockets, the wind which straggles into my hair, breathing its chill on my scalp.

I look across towards Matty. His face is scorched by the wind; his eyes are bright and forever alive, absorbing all that he sees. He is marching on, steadfast, determined. And all the while, he is talking to me. He's sharing his mind, his half-formed thoughts. For the first time for months – perhaps for all time – he is letting me into his world.

For the last few weeks, he's been going to school. And now, in the evenings, we stay in the garden, or go for a walk, or hunt for flints that lie buried in one of Jack's fields. Sometimes I drive and meet him in Marshfield, surprising him as he comes out of class. We go to the river and sit on the bank; we eat biscuits and feed the crumbs to the ducks; we find hidden paths, we climb into trees, we lie on our backs and look at the sky, tracing clouds with our fingers.

I watch his hands as they act out his thoughts, shaping the pictures that spring from his mind. I don't need to hear all the words. From watching him, I know he is happy. And I am happy for knowing him happy. We are happy merely to be.

We follow the road to the crest of a hill, then traverse the glide of a plain. There's a flicker of green on the skin of the earth, as fine as an emerald mist. The wind chases past us, catching his words, spinning them giddily over the fields, snatching them, casting them up in the air, almost before they are said.

Matty points to a track to one side, partially shielded by trees. We turn down into its shelter. Beyond the scrub is the scruff of the village – the church tower standing rigidly upright, the squint of pink that I guess is our cottage, the nestled carcase of Burnt Tree Farm.

We have come to an opening carved in the hedge that leads to an untended pasture. We climb through the ditch and onto the grass; we follow the line of the bushes. The growth is thick and tangled around us, entwined with brambles and thorns.

Matty has stopped; he's approaching the hedge. He stretches up and reaches within it, returning his hand to his mouth. Facing him is a ripe patch of blackberries, bursting with colour, flush with the sweet-bodied fruit.

I search in my pocket and pull out a bag; we gather the spoils which spill from the hedge, hungry to hoard and to eat. Matty laughs as he picks. I can see the wind-tears blurring his eyes, the jealous prickles scratching his hands, the line of purple encircling his mouth.

We plunder the hedge and its fertile clumps. Matty dives deep to reach to the largest, glancing the barbs away with his forearms, shunting his body inside. It is sheltered and calm in this pasture. The wind on the farther side of the hedge is a low cold moan, a splutter of gusts, that convulses the trembling leaves. But here, in the still, there's a curious quietness, an unbreathed breathing, a hush.

Matty is plugged in a bite of the bush; he has stretched his hand between the thorn for a brilliant bright black bunch of fruit. The wind has died; the air is charged. The tips of his fingers are almost touching the bulbous bodies of swollen berries. He extends and stands on his toes.

From the farther side, there's the snap of a twig. For an instant, I see the silvering leaves shiver despite the lack of the wind.

– Matty, did you see that?
– Yes, there's somebody there.
– Can you see who it is?
– No. Shall I find out?
– It's not important.
– I'll look, just in case they're in trouble.

Matty backs deeper into the bush, sinking into the cut of the ditch, fading into the tangle of thorn, till all I can see is a snatch of his jacket, torn and scratched by the twigs. Then even that is erased.

I can hear his boots on the hardened mud as he climbs up the farther side of the ditch. I imagine him crouched at the fringe of the hedge, his senses alert, as when in the wood, listening and watching, smelling the air, stalking invisible prey.

I stare at the blinded tangle of thorn. It is quiet; it no longer moves. Inside there is only a solitary bird, insistently piping and flapping its wings. The grass at my feet is knotted and damp; it is long, almost lush, like it was in the spring. The air hangs in folds like a transparent veil, weightlessly laid on my shoulders. The delicate sun spreads over my back, shedding its light but no warmth.

I hear a sound in the grass beside me. It is Matty. He has circled around to re-enter the pasture. He lifts his feet so his tread is noiseless; each footfall is chosen with care. He motions to me with his hand to keep still. He comes up to me, his mouth near my ear. He breathes his words in a whisper.

– On the other side. In the middle.
– Who? Did you see who it was?
– It's Joyce.
– What's she doing?
– I don't know. I don't think she's doing anything much. She's just crouching and watching.
– Watching what?
– Watching us.
– Did she see you?
– No.
– Do you think she's still there?
– I think so. I would have seen if she'd gone. She's been watching us for a while.

A sliver of wind awakens the air, lisping its scourge at the reckless branches, stirring the leaves to a fickle dance. I stare at the hedge, at the twisted twigs, at the sinewy bramble, the clutches of thorn. There is nothing there I can see.

– Joyce.

–

– Joyce. It's me. Sarah. I know you're there.

–

– Matty has seen you. You're on the other side of the hedge. We heard you. We know that it's you.

–

– Why don't you come out?

–

– Come round and talk to me. Don't you think that it's time?

Matty and I stand shoulder to shoulder, staring in front of us, waiting. There's no glimmer of movement, no splutter of sound. My words sink into the wanting bushes; they glance through its leaves and are gone.

Matty looks into my face. There is no understanding within his eyes; just an asking, a wanting to know. His lips come close to my ear once more. He offers to sneak up behind her and catch her; to bring her into the light.

I look at the hedge. I look at the ditch. I look at the jumble of interweaved boughs, at the pockets of berries which dot its dense skin. I turn away, shaking my head.

We walk back onto the track, dragging our feet through the still-wet grass, the sodden earth sucking our boots. From the path I can see where Matty slipped through; I can see the hollow where Joyce was hiding. She isn't there, or, if she still is, then she's backed still further into its web, into the snarl of brambles and nettle, the labyrinth of impenetrable scrub. From there she is watch, capricious and cagey. Her movement unseen and unheard.

We walk on. The track dissolves in the timorous sun; the hedge recoils and withers away; we are out in the open between ploughed fields, the wind ripping into our sides. We skirt the border of a field and stroll along its farther edge, then cut back onto the road. I sense that Matty is curious still, but the farther we walk, the farther his questions fade from our minds and our thoughts and our cares. Now all that we know is what is around us: the gentle pitch of the earth underfoot, the sting of the breeze, the glance of the sun, the sound of birds in the air.

We march on the road to Nettlesden. Matty is talking again. He's describing the trees, the fields, and the earth; he's describing the things he has seen and has heard; he's describing all that he wants us to do, and all that he wants us to be. I picture the words that he hasn't yet said. Of that time in the future, when we are restored. All of us living our lives together – be that in London or elsewhere, or here. I imagine him laying it out before me, breathing his fantasy into a truth. Such simple, magical, beautiful words. Those words which haven't been spoken.

We need more milk. Matty peels off and walks up the road, not wanting to enter the shop. I watch him striding away. His back is straight, his tread is firm, the stick in his hand is thrashing the verge. He's so like you, but he isn't you. He is the best of us both. It is he who would bring us back together. We hardly deserve him; we cannot thank him. But he deserves to be with us both if that is truly his dream.

Matty follows the curve of the bend, starting up the slope to the cottage. I turn in the other direction to him, towards the brick frontage of Wayside House.

I push at shop door and enter. The room is bright with electric light, but it's cold and gloomy inside. Bill is hidden behind the counter, as if afraid to come out. Margaret is only a noise in the stockroom: a scraping of boxes and tins.

Something is different here.

I look towards Bill. His body is almost ethereal in the pool of light where he stands. The window beside him is boarded over. He points at it, but he doesn't speak.

– What happened?
– The window. Last night.
– What happened last night?
– They came through that window last night.
– Who? When?
– I could hear them. I was lying in bed. I could hear them when they came in. But what was I supposed to do?
– Who came in?
– I phoned the police. But the people who came must surely have known it takes fifteen minutes to get here from Marshfield. And who wants to come on their own in the night to confront a posse of thieves?
– You were burgled? What did you do?
– We lay in bed and we listened. What could I do? Margaret wanted me to confront them. She wanted me to come downstairs. She thought I could sabotage their car. But what would have happened then? What would have happened if they came upstairs?
– What did happen?
– They went to the post office counter. They forced the till. They didn't care about the noise. I think they wanted to scare me. I could hear them as they moved round the shop. Everything that they did. I could picture it. I could feel it.

As if they were walking over my bones. Then they left. We heard the car drive off. But I stayed in bed. I stayed in bed till the officers came; till we heard their voices here in the shop. That was half an hour later, I think.

– Bill, I'm so sorry.

– It was bound to happen. We knew it would happen. It was only a matter of time. But the knowing of it doesn't make it all right. It doesn't help how you feel.

– Do the police know who it was? Did they catch them?

– They know that shops like this are a target. Village shops are so easy. They are constantly being broken into. That is all they could say. There isn't much money, but there isn't much risk. The chances of being caught are... are...

– What can I do? What are you going to do now?

Bill turns and stares at the crude slab of chipboard which serves to block both the threat and the light. He looks ancient and weary and worn. Not because of a night without sleep, but because of the lifetime he's lived in this village resisting the threat from beyond. Now someone has come; they have entered his shop. He knows that nowhere is safe.

I put out my hands to take his. They are lifeless and limp. I try to look into his eyes. But he looks away, as if he's ashamed, as if he is somehow at fault. My words of comfort are hollow and crude; they rebound off the chipboard and fall to the floor. They are useless. I would give him my strength, but I haven't enough. I feel my feet retreat to the door, though my eyes are still resting on him. On him as I reach and grasp at the handle; on him as I step out into the open – feeling the fresh wind cleansing my mind, feeling the sun caressing my face – on him as I pull the door closed.

I walk past the Serpent to Steeple Field. There, in the bones of a skeletal tree, Matty is waving at me. I cross the grass, watching his body sway in the wind, watching him clutched to the thin higher branches – fused to the wood as if part of the tree. He's shouting delight; he's smiling at me. I watch him from the foot of the trunk. I watch him as he clambers down – each branch like a stair which opens before him – till he stands beside me, grinning his joy. Together we walk up the road.

I unlock the door.

Inside, on the floor, is a single large arrow, sketched from a heap of dead ivy. It is pointing into the heart of the cottage, and through it, beyond it. It points to the wood. And twisted around the coiling mass is a trail of blue ribbon, woven within it, holding the symbol in place.

Matty is looking at me. I can feel his eyes are seeking my own, asking me questions which cannot form words. The room is stifled; it's choked by the dust. It's tired, abandoned and old. I don't belong here. I've never belonged here. I don't know why I am here.

I step outside and into the light, into the welcoming clear, cool air.

– What is this? What's going on?
– Don't worry, Matty. It's not important.
– Who put it here? What does it mean?
– It's from no one. And it doesn't mean anything.
– Has this got something to do with Joyce?
– It may have, but it doesn't matter. This is all a delusion. A pathetic way to get my attention.
– What does she want?

– I don't know. And I don't really care.

– Then why did she do it?

– Because she refuses to let things rest. Because she's trying to draw me in.

– Into what?

– Into something that's nothing to do with us. Into something locked in the past.

– What are you talking about?

– I'm talking of things that are dead and buried. Of things that can't be brought to life. Of things that have never concerned us.

– Then it's all right?

– Yes, Matty. Everything's good. We've got our own lives to lead. And that is enough. That's more than enough. There's so much living for us to do. There's so much living to come.

Matty is shielding the sun from his eyes as he searches into my face. He understands nothing of what he can see. But from watching me he knows there's no threat; there's no reason for him to feel fear. And that on its own is enough.

We have lunch. In the afternoon I pick the last marrow. I can see in the hearts of the weary plants the infant growth of new fruit. Those delicate bodies will never mature. The heat has gone from the sun; it is stripped from the earth. They will strive to find being, but they will not thrive. The nights have begun to grow cold. The dawns are speckled with frost. The sun limps, distantly, into the sky, bringing a light, but with it no warmth. I look at my vegetable patch. Leeks are marooned in a sea of mud, with a clutch of bald cabbage, a line of dry carrots, a clump of spinach which is going to seed. All year I have taken, I have lived off the earth. Now this is all that remains.

In the lengthening day we stand by the field. The sky is huge and fiercely blue; the sun is mellowing the land with its glaze. I suggest we should have a bonfire. A final barbeque for the year. The nights are closing in. It may not be till the coming summer, till the cycle begins anew and repeats, that we find ourselves here again. We should forage for logs in the wood.

Matty switches his gaze to the field, over the frame of Rose House Farm, to the distant band of the trees. He thinks we have plenty of wood in the garden without needing to scavenge for more. I leave him alone by the firepit. It's hard to imagine that winter will come; that Matty and I will be forced round the stove; that the evenings will lengthen and the garden grow dormant; that the wind will strip the earth in its fury; that the cottage will be the extent of our world. It's harder still to conceive of a time when the days are long, when the sun is hot, when the earth awakens, bringing new birth. It's hard to imagine us here.

Matty has lit the fire by the time I return. I watch him rouse it to life. He enjoys being busy, honing his skills, being close, being touched by the earth. He moves easily, and with infinite energy, snapping branches and stoking the fire, absorbed in the moment, the task. His is an elemental life, sworn to the simple enjoyment of nature, having nothing to hide. He could never lose himself in the wood; nothing could lead him astray. There is too much to life, too much living within him. An innocence wrapped in a truth.

The fire spits out a shallow light against the lingering day. We watch the skies as they darken and fold; we watch the orb of the heavy sun sink slow and low through the dull horizon, casting a deepening blush on the sky till it almost hurts to look. I cook sausages over the grill, sandwiching them in thick slabs of bread. We eat hungrily. The garden is slowly dissolved into darkness; the sky pressed down on the earth. I go in search of winter jackets while Matty tidies the fire with a fork, fuelling the core with the last of the wood.

In the final fury of the flame we sit on the bench, by the life-giving heat, watching the spent logs shiver to cinder. The fire is sinking; it's collapsing into a thin smoking pile of hot coals. We skewer marshmallows on the tips of long twigs, holding them over the shimmering heat, watching them blister and melt. We bite into their crusted skins, tasting the molten flesh of their core. This is all I have ever dreamed of. This is all I have ever wanted. This is more than I hoped it could be. For Matty and me. For us all.

We stare at the pool of invisible night, feeling it weaving and curling around us; closing us tight in its frigid sheath.

– It's nice here. Even in the autumn, it's nice.
– It's lovely. Yes.
– Does it feel like home to you, Mum?
– In some ways, yes. I guess. And you?
– It felt odd going back to London. And it felt odd coming back here. I don't really know where home is any more.
– Home is wherever we are. Home is being together.
– Do you think Dad would like it up here?
– I expect so. He likes the countryside.
– I think he'd like the wood. And doing stuff with his hands.
– After a time, he would get bored, though. He'd like it for a holiday, but I don't think he could live here forever.
– I don't think any of us could stay here forever. I can't imagine living here. Not for the rest of my life.

The flames are dying. There's no more wood except for the logs which Matty has stacked like a wall in the lean-to, that are saved for the winter stove. In the faint amber glow of the fading fire, his face is obscured by the shadow. I can't see his features nor guess at his thoughts.

The cold has begun to creep in. I draw Matty to me. He is tired. He's happy to lay his head on my lap; to let me run my hand through his hair. I am humming a tune with no words. I look through the fire and see darkness within it. Above it, a deeper darkness still. And in that darkness are pin-pricks of light, unmoved, spectral-white, and so cold. I cannot comprehend their distance, their age, their changelessness. Through millennia they have shone as this. They have witnessed all earth's history. They have seen it all: the whole sad story. They have watched it all with patient eyes. All this pettiness, all this confusion of living; this chaos, this hurt we inflict on ourselves; this darkness we draw over our eyes. If only we could see as they – with their clarity, with their boundless wisdom – through to the core, to the essence of life. To know what life is at its heart.

I brush Matty's cheek with the back of my hand, feeling the warmth of his skin. He's asleep; it is time that I took him in. The fire is faint; its breath is failing: sinking into the night.

In the embers of the dying evening, I bend down and touch his brow with my lips.

~

I can hear the buffeting wind; the gasp as it forces under the door. I can hear the stark trees groaning their weight; the boughs attacking the sky with their swords. I can see their shifting shadows in alcoves, the charcoaled bones of their barren branches grating against the stained-glass windows, casting their gloom on the pews. I can see the cross aflame in the sun, then tarnished as the sky is swamped by remorseless folds of grey cloud.

The seat is cold beneath me. I feel its lack of warmth on my thighs; its ice which seems to steal up my spine, squeezing cool fingers around my throat as if it would starve me of air. The church exudes the smell of disuse; it's hung with dust; it is damp and stale. Spiders spin with confidence, and sneak a spindling path between pews. A long settled silence breathes from the walls. This is a house of the dead.

Jack walks to the lectern. He lays a paper out on the Bible, flattening the sheet with his palms. His hands lock onto the neighbouring wood. He leans towards us and reads.

I have come here once more, for a final time. But I haven't come here for God. I have come for the village, to give thanks to the village, for what it has given to me. When first I arrived I was looking for something, unsure of what I would find. I thought I was searching for something new, moving me on from the world that I knew towards a healthier place. But Matty has shown me that what I was seeking was not something new but the

*What profit hath a man of all his labour which he taketh under the sun?*

*One generation passeth away, and another generation cometh: but the earth abideth for ever.*

*The sun also ariseth, and the sun goeth down, and hasteth to his place where he arose.*

*The wind goeth toward the south, and turneth about unto the north; it whirleth about continually, and the wind returneth again*

very same thing I had tried so hard to escape. All that is lost will come round again. We will see it again with new eyes. It's worth the pain of thinking things lost, if through that pain we can find. My pain has found peace; there is hope it will heal. For that I give thanks to you all. To this village, which endures its own pain – a pain which cuts deeper and keener than mine – so deep it's unable to mend. I give thanks to the village for what it has given. I pray it can find its own peace.

*according to his circuits.*

*All the rivers run into the sea; yet the sea is not full: unto the place from whence the rivers come, thither they return again.*

*All things are full of labour; man cannot utter it: the eye is not satisfied with seeing, nor the ear filled with hearing.*

*The thing that hath been, it is that which shall be; and that which is done is that which shall be done: and there is no new thing under the sun.*

Jack closes. He eyes the people who are sitting before him. Uriah and Martha. Margaret and Bill. And, if just for this morning, Matty and me. He looks at us individually, not thinking to move though the lesson is done. I think he would like to talk to us all. He's thinking of giving a speech.

An apology more than a speech.

He wants to know what he has done wrong, when all he has done is what he was taught, is what his ancestors did before him. He's preserved tradition, he's fought for the land, he's humbled himself before God. He's paid his homage with equal devotion. With dignity, nobility, honesty, truth. And his reward for showing such faith is now to steward a dying village into the final throes of death.

A village where thieves have come and plundered, where homes will be built for those who serve Mammon, where seven lost souls are all that remain. The Faradays have been driven away: turned out by their own of their own volition, and with them the hope of a new generation. Travis will follow his absent wife, on a journey which leads from here to nowhere, closing the pub when he goes. Robert Witton has not been seen. Bill and Margaret cower in a shop and shrink from all beyond its grey walls. Matty and I are wandering pilgrims, and nothing could tempt us to stay. He who inherits the fruits of the earth – the land and the two farms that make up the village – is his childless son, Uriah. That is all that remains.

Jack slips the paper back into his pocket. I think he would speak, but there aren't any words. His step is slow; his head is high as he walks with stiffness back to his pew. He sits in his seat and looks before him as Martha presses his hand.

Colin Inchmore commences Communion. I watch as he takes and breaks the bread; I watch as he sips at the wine. I watch as Jack steps into the aisle, ushering Martha up to the transept. I watch as they kneel at the foot of the altar. I witness the pain of contrition. They get to their feet and walk to their seats. Martha's face is blank of expression; her grey hair is lank, her tight lips are thin, the skin on her cheeks stretches white on the bone.

Uriah is the next to his feet. His shoulder almost brushes his mother's, but their eyes are downcast and don't meet. He stands to one side, making way for his father, honouring the man whose steps he will follow in the fullness and sureness of time. Alone he walks to the silent altar to receive the bread and the wine. Alone, he gets to his knees.

His rude neck is thrust through a strangling collar. His skull tips forward as he eats of the body, then nods again as he sips of the blood. He stands and walks heavily back to his pew, though no sound emits from his steps. Now he is sitting and staring before him, sightless and motionless, lost to the world.

Bill and Margaret approach the altar. They are tired and hunched, as though they're oppressed by the weight of the walls that lean in around them, by the squeeze of the roof that presses above them, by the penitence borne on their backs. They kneel with discomfort and rise with pain. They rest on each other – both propping each other – their feet shuffling forwards, their arms stretching out, seeking asylum within their own pew.

Now it is Matty and me. We walk to the altar and kneel. The vicar lays his hands upon Matty; then I take the bread and the wine. We stand and turn. In the church before me are a clutch of old people, and behind them a sea of vacant pews which are ranked like waves to a far horizon, unbroken by feature or light.

Colin Inchmore gives us his blessing. He's a pale spectre hung in an ocean of grey. His voice is absorbed by the empty chamber; his words fall flat on the flagstone floor. We stand and sing a single hymn, the reedy sound of our straining voices reaching up to the roof. Then he leads us through to the back of the church and opens the door on the day. The stifled wind gusts into the chamber, flooding the church with its life.

We walk out into the fierce morning sun. Into the vast cathedral of earth.

The others are walking over the gravel, down the path and into the road. Jack and Martha are leading the way, up the slope and towards the track which breaks between fields and points to their home. Uriah is marching a distance behind them; he splinters off when he reaches his turning, crossing the wilderness of Road Field towards the seclusion of Rose House Farm. Margaret and Bill are locked together, stumbling round the side of the graveyard, shuffling past the doors of the Serpent, till they reach the retreat of their shop.

I turn and look at the empty churchyard, at the broken lines of angled tombstones: their harsh faces worn and speckled with lichen, their inscriptions scratched away by the air. In the corner where we buried the skull, where we laid the unbodied down to rest, I can see the proud mound, still partially brown, cradling a bunch of flowers on its breast. The stems of the flowers are caught in blue ribbon, lovingly tied in a bow.

I look at the trees standing vigil around it, at their branches twisted as twigs in the wind. I look at the startled hedge to its side, at the absence of anything sitting and staring from its hollow sockets of eyes. I pull Matty closer. He doesn't resist. We walk firmly up the wind-polished slope, between the cut of two fields.

There are baked potatoes for lunch. I slice at the skin of their bloated bodies, stirring the pulp of their flesh. There is something magical in knowing these mine, in knowing I've nurtured and grown them. The storeroom is full of boxed potatoes, of platted onions hanging from hooks, of marrows in netting that's strung from the ceiling, of beetroot buried in sand. A hoard of food for the autumn.

After lunch, we go to the orchard. Matty squirms up the trunk of a tree, squatting within it and reaching for apples, throwing the ripest towards me. I pull at my sweater with both of my hands, making a target for Matty to aim at, making my stomach a basket. I empty my belly-loads into a barrow until it is full to the brim. We lay the apples out in long lines on stretches of wood in a lean-to. Then we go outside in the face of the wind – feeling its restless sweep in our faces, hearing its throaty howl in our ears – to dig out the roots of the beans.

I'm pruning the bushes of currants and gooseberries; Matty is sifting the earth to my side. I look up and over the furious wash of the stranded, fresh-furrowed field. In the distance, the trees which fringe the wood are shaking the last of the leaves from their boughs. Before it, the island of Rose House Farm has hunkered down in the wind.

I switch my gaze to the hedge. Through the brittle bones of its fleshless body, I can see the shape of a person approaching along the line of the field. I straighten my back and await them. I can see them slicing their way through the wind; I can see the shadow, the form of their body, so insubstantial, so soundless. I watch as they weave alongside the road, as they cut around the back of the lawn, as they slip past a crack of restless hedge till they are standing before me. Standing directly in front of me.

It is Joyce.

I know it is her, though it's been so long, though I've never properly seen her. Not her as a person, full in the face. I know it is her who is standing before me, materialised into matter. Yet even now, in the full flush of daylight, she seems less a person and more like a shadow; a spectre, a phantom of being. That were I to stretch out, seeking to touch her, the shape would dissolve in my searching hands; it would chase away in the air, and be gone.

Her hair is wild; her skin is coarse. Round her neck she is wearing a thin blue ribbon that is tied in a delicate bow.

– Come with me.
– Where?
– Come with me to the wood.
– Why?
– I want to show you something.
– What?
– Something. You'll see.
– Why me? Why do you want to show it to me?
– It's important.
– Why's it important?
– It is.
– I'm not going to come with you, Joyce.
– You must.
– Why must I? Why should I have to? What has it got to do with me?
– Come now.
– No.
– We need to go now.
– No, Joyce. Whatever it is, it doesn't concern me.
– Come.
– No. I'm not interested. I've got my own life to lead.
– Please.
– If you like, you can come inside for some tea. We can sit down and talk like two normal people.
– Inside? No. I can't go inside. You must come with me.
– I won't.
– Please. Please. Come.

I look at her face; I look within it. I try and read what is there. All I can see are the lines of the face – the shape of a face – that bears within it no form. No features, no substance, no seeming expression. There is only a voice, a repeated lament, that is fading away, that is dying. Till the words become as the hollow wind which strips through the hedge and races away across the stretch of the field.

Behind her, through her, in the sea of Road Field, Uriah and Martha are standing together. Standing together, side by side. Silent and staring at us.

Joyce is reciting her dirge like an echo. But she's no longer looking at me. The words are uttered as if to herself – as if to the elements, to nature around her, to all natural objects but me.

I don't approach, but I cannot retreat. I watch, and in the watching of her I see her fade and depart. I see her melt in the crystal air, I see her dissolve in the crying wind, I see her vanish within the hedge. She wanes like the summer, like smoke.

Matty is questioning me with his eyes. A blend of doubt that is mixed with desire to understand what he's seen. I pull him towards me, my arms round his shoulders. I pull him into my chest. I can feel the strength of the growing man; I can feel his heat and his love. I can feel the return of his arms round my waist, the rise of his ribs as he breathes.

It is done now. It is over for good. I whisper it into his hair.

As the afternoon fades, the wind breathes low and shallow beneath the darkening sky. I look out across the empty field. For the first time, I know that there's nobody there. I suggest we stop for some tea.

We sit at the table and feast on hot toast, our hands and our feet thawing out in the warmth, cocooned in the comfort of home. Matty tells me of places to visit, of things that he wants us to do. There's so much of this land we have yet to explore, so much we have yet to uncover together. He wants to discover and share it with me. His face is electric with life. With a frenzy of energy, urgently charged, expressing his fervent desire. He's so open to living, so eager to start, so guileless and guiltless and sure.

I glance through the window beyond him. The evenings are lengthening; they are drawing in faster; already the darkness is stood at the door. There's a beauty here that I long to capture, that I long to enter with him. Though splendid, I know that beauty is waning. It is tired and weary; it is losing its sheen; it is sinking into the earth. The land returns to its raw, rude state. It is settling itself, preparing to sleep.

I crave the radiant glow of a fire. I send Matty into the lean-to for logs. It's time for our first autumn stove. I watch as he sets a cradle of twigs, as he strikes a match at their base. As he closes the doors and opens the vents.

From within the heart of the cast-iron cage, we can hear the crinkle of burning paper, the wheeze and gasp as the fire takes hold, the rush of the air as it draws up the chimney, the crackle of flame through the glass.

Matty throws open the doors of the stove; he reveals a cauldron of flame. The heat bursts into the darkened room, numbing us, dulling our senses. We kick off our boots and kneel before it, staring into its soul. Matty stokes the fire; he loads it with logs. Then we fall back onto the waiting sofa, admiring the magnificent blaze.

This is my life; this is all that there is. My life is this pleasure of being together; my life is in being here now. There's nothing beside it; there's no need for more. We have what we are, and we know it is good. It is all I have wanted; it is all I have sought. This moment contains all within it. What we do, how we live, or how long we might live – tomorrow, next week, and into the future – means nothing when set beside this. There's no forwards nor backwards. There's only the present. Moving on, we return to what we once were; returning, we find things anew. We are as the land; we live and we grow; we close and we sleep. But it's wrong to think that we die. We are born to a world we have known before. We return to the cycle of life.

We watch the fire as it ages before us; we watch the logs as they shatter to ash. We eat supper, then Matty goes up to his room. I read a book in the fiery light of the spoiling, reddening flame. When I go upstairs and stand by his door, I can see there is darkness within. He's asleep.

Tenderly, I lift at the latch, I push at the wood, I go in. I can smell the freshness of his skin; I can smell the soap on his face. He sleeps on his front, his head to one side, his brow unwrinkled, his eyes at peace. He's dreaming. I stroke the hair from his cheek. I watch him breathing; I hear its sound; I know for sure he is safe. I kiss him goodnight. A single kiss. I leave the door open and go downstairs.

Through the ground floor windows there's only a darkness. So dark, as if nothing is there. I close the curtains and turn to the room; I put more logs on the fire. The bed is a rich red chaos of ember; it scorches the skin of the logs without flame. It emits no more than a line of smoke. I recline on the sofa and urge the fire to breathe itself back into being.

Though warm, it is weary; it won't catch hold; it won't surge back to a blaze. The seat where Matty sat is indented, but the cushions around it are cold. What we have is so much, so much more than before, so much more than I feared I could hope. So much more than I dared to believe.

Yet deep in my heart, at its very core, I know it is still not enough. It is not quite enough to bring harmony. It is not quite enough for us all.

~

— So, they're bringing in the diggers, then?
— Yes. They're starting to clear the plot. The noise will go on all day.
— You'll get used to it. And they'll go up so quickly. You wait.
— I didn't realise how big it was going to be.
— Well, there are six houses, aren't there?
— That's the first phase, yes.
— It'll be good for you, Bill. It'll be good for your shop. It's doubling the size of the village.
— If they come to my shop, it'll be good. But these are people who are used to the city, to supermarkets and buying at discount. I can't compete. It's a village shop.
— You'll be fine. They'll all run out of milk. They'll all want to be a part of the village. They'll actively support you.
— Do you think?
— Of course. I did. Why should they be any different?
— I suppose. The problem is that it will be different. It's going to change the way things are.
— Change can be good. The builders may use the shop too.
— Yes, one came in this morning. But I'm frightened about security.

– The builders won't steal from you. If anything, you'll be more secure for knowing they're just down the road.

– They've got fences and lights. They've got everything.

– Well, that's more than you need, Bill. Have they told you how long it will take?

– One of their people is attending the Council. They'll tell us what's happening then.

– That's good.

– He'll be a bloody salesman. I think we should all meet earlier on to work out what we want to ask him. Do you think that's a good idea?

– Probably, yes. Bill…

– What?

– About the Community Council…

– What?

– I've been giving it some thought. I've decided to resign.

– Resign? Why?

– For all sorts of reasons.

– We need you. We need your support. We need you to challenge Martha.

– You can always challenge her yourself, if you feel strongly enough about something.

– I know I could. But you see things differently.

– I think that's the problem.

– We need you there.

– I don't think so. My views don't resonate with the village. With the whole way of life in the country.

– But you said yourself that this life is changing. And you're right. You're like Peter in wanting to help us to change.

– That's the point. Peter could only change by moving. Because the village resists change. It lives in denial. It buries the truth and is locked in the past.

– That's why we need you.

– No. You need more people like Peter. Those who are truly a part of the village. Those who care about it and live here. Those who want the change to occur because this is where they belong.

– And you belong, too. You're a part of the village.

– I'm not. Not really. I have been staying in it for a while, that's all. But it's not my home. I'm just passing through. I'm not committed long term. That's why I have to resign. The village isn't where I belong. I've been looking in on it; I've been glancing against it. A casual observer, no more.

– I don't agree with you. And I think it's a shame. The village has changed because of you.

– Has it really? Has it changed for the better?

– Of course.

– It's nice of you to say so, Bill. But I really don't believe you. Anyway, my mind's made up. You'll have to find a replacement for Peter. And you'll have to find one for Travis. So you might as well look for one more. And you'll soon have a bunch of new people to choose from. People who want to belong to the village. People who really care.

– But we don't know who they are. We don't know how they might want to change it.

– I wouldn't be too worried. They are choosing to come and live in this village. They are consciously choosing this way of life. Even if they don't quite know what it is. That has to be good for the village.

It has to be good, though Bill cannot see it. For him there's nothing but threat. And to counter that threat he's adopting a stance. Not to resist it, as Martha is doing, but to be suspicious of all. He stands behind the protective counter as if shielding himself within a fortress, his shoulders and head peeping out from behind an army of chocolate bars.

He packs my shopping into a box without speaking or looking at me. His mind is distracted by thoughts of the future. By the thought of new houses, the thought of new people. All of it different, and none of it known.

I look round the shop while he works. The chipboard has been removed from the window, and in its place is a new pane of glass. Yet the room is much darker than I think it once was. Now there are bars on the windows. The sun strives to enter, but all I can see are the lines of their shadows which reach from the floor and stretch up the wall, as if he's entombed in a jail. A prison that he has built for himself, in which he is able to hide. The eye of a camera winks from the ceiling; on the wall is a box which screens an alarm.

Margaret comes out from the stockroom in silence. She shuffles round to the back of the counter to be together with Bill. They stand side by side, these small sad people, lost in their fragile diminishing world.

It's clear outside; the sky is a distant and infinite blue; the air is sparkling and sharp. Each breath is pure, enriching and vital; each breath brings the promise of life. I cross the road into Steeple Field. The last of the golden leaves are hanging by the threads of their stems to the boughs. The grass is deep green and filled with moisture; the earth below it is soft. I know Bill will share my news with Martha, and I would rather tell her myself.

As I am ambling back to the cottage, I remember the dish that Martha gave me – filled with her gift of apple pie – still sits on my dresser inside. I go to retrieve it, then close the door, crossing the road and taking the path that leads towards Burnt Tree Farm.

I follow the ditch which divides the fields, and slip through the arch of the thicket. The wind drifts over the fresh-planted earth. I can see the velvet sheen of new growth, the tiny specks of quivering green sprouting their infancy.

The bald white face and the staring eyes of the windows of Burnt Tree Farm await me, with the huge black beacons of silos behind. I come to the hedge; I cross the courtyard. The door before me is closed.

I knock.

I can feel a shiver of breeze steal round me, as if it comes from the house. I knock again on the wood. I step from the porch and peer through a window. Inside, I can see the living room, and the dim empty world it contains. I can see the sofa where once I sat. I can see Jack's chair stood ready to greet him; the fire prepared but unlit.

I walk backwards into the heart of the courtyard, crunching the gravel beneath my boots. For an instant, I see – I think I can see – the faint orb of Martha's white face. Like a cold dull moon, it hangs in the gloom, in the frost of an upstairs window. Then, like the moon being shrouded in cloud, it slides back into the sheath of the night. It disappears from my view.

I start forward, thinking to knock once more. She could easily not have heard my approach. I wonder if she is coming downstairs, or if she has backed away from the window and looks at me still from the darkened room, waiting until I have gone. I look at the door, at its heavy frame. I imagine it being opened before me. I imagine Martha stood on the step. I have as little desire to speak to her as she may have to heed what I say.

I lay the dish on the mat in her porch, then turn and hurry away. Glad, so glad to be walking away.

I follow the path between the fields, back towards the pink-framed cottage, knowing that no one is looking at me, knowing that now I am free. In a field in the distance, I can see Jack's tractor. I can hear the struggling blast of the engine as it labours over the empty earth, as it scratches deep furrows into the land.

At the cottage, Matty is waiting for me. He wants to show me around the garden. He has made wooden shelves that rest in the branches; he has fashioned wire cages which hang from their sides. Now all that he needs is some feed. From the kitchen, my study, and from both of our bedrooms, we can watch the birds as they come to seek food, as winter settles its cloak on the land. He has plans to build houses – whole towns in high branches – where squirrels and birds can nest without fear. And then, in the grass, at the base of the trunks, he is building retreats for hedgehogs and voles. He wants the garden to come alive, to become a thriving haven for creatures to rest and be warm through the dormant months. And he wants me to build it with him.

He hands me his tools as he levers his body into the frame of a tree. I watch him as he feels through its branches; I watch him as he crafts his inventions, absorbed in his intricate task.

A car horn sounds from the road. Reluctantly, I leave him behind me and walk through the arch to the front. On the verge by my track a car is waiting, its engine running, its windows wound down. Travis is leant on its bonnet.

– Hi there.

– Hello. How are you?

– Good. At least I think so.

– So, this is it?

– Yup. This is it.

– How are you feeling?

– I've been too busy sorting things out to worry about how I'm feeling. But I think, perhaps, when I drive away, then...

– Then you'll need to focus ahead.

– Yes. Look, this is everything. This is me. All of it in the back of my car. Can you believe that?

– I envy you not having much clutter.

– How can my whole life fit in a car? Is this all I've got to show for myself?

– Don't start, Travis. There's much more than is in this car. There's everything that you are; everything that you know. The sum of your experience.

– I don't think that amounts to much. I'm not sure I want to take it all with me.

– It's huge. Use it wisely. Learn from it; profit from it.

– You know, I haven't heard from Samantha. Not a word.

– Then it's a clean slate. An opportunity. I wish you well. I do, honestly.

– Will we meet again?

– I don't think so. Not by design.

– I can't imagine not seeing you again.

– Don't think of it like that.

– Don't you think perhaps we could...?

– No. Not even Christmas cards. I don't mean to be hard on you, Travis, but I know it's better like this.

– It's been good to know you. I enjoyed the time we've spent together. More than enjoyed it. It was good. It felt good.

– Yes, I know.

– Too good to be true.

–

– Goodbye then. I'll miss you.

– Don't miss me. Look ahead.

– Yes. Goodbye.

– Goodbye, Travis.

Travis is standing awkwardly, not quite meeting my eyes. I think he wants this moment to last, though he knows that nothing will come of it. I think he would like to give me a hug, but even now he doesn't quite dare.

I hope he is happy in what he does; I hope he finds some form of contentment. I really do. More than I think it is right to tell him. If only he knew and was true to himself; if he had more faith in the person he is. But that is not for me to disclose. He must find it himself, or find someone else who is able to tease it from him. That is the challenge that lies before him. He can meet it if only he dares. And that is for some time later, not now. Now it is time to move on.

I extend my arm. We shake hands firmly. I watch him into the car. I stand on the road and look through his window. He glances up, and he smiles. It's a timid smile, and so gentle.

I watch the car draw off the verge; I watch it creep away towards Marshfield; I watch as it slips out of view. Now I am looking at an empty road, hearing the engine's hum in the distance till the sound is no more than a thing of fancy, no more than the murmuring wind.

Matty is still up his tree in the orchard. He's demanding I come and inspect his work. He wants to know what I think.

I tell him I like it; how much I admire it. And I do. I love what he's done. But not simply because of the thing he has made. I love what he's made because he has made it; I love him merely for thinking to make it; I love him, the person who made it.

I love him.

Matty slithers down to the ground. I wish I was able to say what I feel. He is flushed and freshened by wind. His hair is tousled; his hands are scratched. His eyes are bright and fierce with living. He looks me full in the face.

There's no need to say the words in my mind. He sees through to my heart, and he knows.

After lunch we return to the patch, uprooting all the growth that remains except for the last line of leeks. Now the earth returns to the earth. It is bare. We spread manure on the naked soil; we begin the deep winter dig. Line by line we cut into the earth, turning the topsoil in on itself, allowing its body to breathe. It is now for the frost to break down the clods, for the goodness we spread to seep through the tilth, for the earth to repose and replenish its stock before the cycle renews.

I pause to straighten my back. Rose House Farm stands silent before me, a blunted shape in a barren field, carved from the calm, bare earth.

Beyond it, over the deeper distance, the wood is unclothed and unmoved. I can see at its fringe the mark of a person, a gun in their cradling arms. It's Uriah, sternly patrolling the land, protecting all that is his.

To every thing there is a season. A time for every purpose.

I have been so afraid of being, and of not being. With you, but also without you. It has been so confused in my mind. But not in my heart. Whenever I look there, I know. I know there is no distance between us. I know there has never been any distance. I know there is only you. You are here for me, and you always will be. You've been here for me all the way. It cannot be other than this. For you are me, and I am you, and we are one. We are. I am with you and in you, and you are in me. Wherever I go, whatever I do, you are here. You are part of my body; you are locked in my core; you are my essence, my soul. You're my heart, you're the thing that beats within me, the thing that keeps me alive. There's no life beyond you; there's no life without. You are who I am; you're my reason for being. You are where I begin and I end.

– Matty, let's stop for some tea. We can finish this later.
–

– It's getting dark.
–

– I think… I think it may be time to go home soon.
– Into the cottage?
– No. I mean home. I think we should go back home.
–

– Don't you think, perhaps, that it's time?

I watch Matty finish his line. I watch as he presses his weight on the spade; I watch as the blade sinks into the earth. This is the beauty of being. I can feel the wind caressing my cheek; I can feel it tug at my hair. I look up and into the broad spread of sky, seeing a greyness approach from the east, seeing it closing upon the land.

~